Friday, October 17

"If Maxwell Howard wins the election, we are going to launch a pre-emptive strike against the Americans," Tchebychev said.

Stanhouse swore and punched the recorder off. He felt sweat rolling down hot against the cold of his face. A pre-emptive nuclear strike. The Pentagon experts had been predicting it, warning of it, and here it was.

And there was no protection.

That's what Project Parasol was all about, but the Deputy Secretary of Defense had just gutted Project Parasol. If Maddock lost, America would die on Election Day.

And Maddock was losing.

Also by Steven Spruill

KEEPERS OF THE GATE
THE PSYCHOPATH PLAGUE
THE JANUS EQUATION
HELLSTONE
THE IMPERATOR PLOT

THE GENESIS SHIELD

Steven Spruill

A TOM DOHERTY ASSOCIATES BOOK

THE GENESIS SHIELD

A Tor Book
Published by Tom Doherty Associates, Inc.
175 Fifth Avenue
New York, N.Y. 10010

Tor® is a registered trademark of Tom Doherty Associates, Inc.

ISBN: 0-812-53508-1

First Tor edition: November 1985

Printed in the United States of America

0 9 8 7 6 5 4 3 2

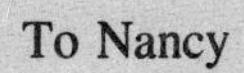

To Nancy

Acknowledgments

I take pleasure in acknowledging the important contributions of the following people to this work: Lt. Colonel John Gaither, U.S.A.; Mr. Harris Eisenhardt; Dr. Richard Setton; and special thanks to Dr. Faye Austin of the National Institutes of Health.

I am most grateful to my wife, Dr. Nancy L. Spruill, for her many hours of editing and her special insights.

I would also like to thank my literary agent, Dr. Al Zuckerman, for his instruction, his patience, and his faith.

Finally, heartfelt thanks to my good friend and fellow novelist, Dr. F. Paul Wilson, for giving my manuscript the parallax view.

August 23, 1968

Prologue

Saigon, South Vietnam
1900 hours:

In twenty-four hours, the killing would be over.

Morrissey savored the words: *the killing, over*.

He tipped back his chair and let the slow, broad sweep of the ceiling fan cool him. Ah, Froggie's, ah, the first beer of the evening—the first beer of the *last* evening. He pressed the icy Kronenbourg to his face, groaning with pleasure. Picking his soaked shirt away from his chest, he concentrated on coolness, the caress of the fan. Another hour before Vandiver got off shift. In the meantime, what was he supposed to do with this fantastic feeling?

He grinned around the room, then sobered, shocked at his breach of manners. It was like giggling at a funeral. He might be going home, but these poor devils were still stuck here. For them, the killing was not over. The misery of it rose from their pores. They hunched motionless over the teakwood bar, slumped around the tables as though gassed by the blue haze of cigarette smoke. He knew most of them—medical corps officers from the Saigon base hospital. He'd seen their eyes too often in his own mirror—moist, peeled negatives of death.

Well, screw it.

He jumped onto the table, swinging his arms and kicking a salt shaker off before he caught his balance. Some men at the bar turned and gave a few derisive claps.

"Thank you, thank you . . ." He waited until everyone was looking at him, the men at the tables too. "As you know," he said, "after twelve months of debauchery here at Mr. Dang's Froggie Bistro, Vandiver and I have run out of steam. We're packing it in."

"Rear echelon mother fuckers!" someone yelled.

Morrissey grinned and waited for the ripple of laughter to die down. "You're half right. West Virginny is about as rear echelon as it gets. But that part about mothers—you'll have to ask Madame Tho." He nodded toward the curtained door at the back of the room.

Tho stepped from the curtains, swept her robes around her, and bowed to the hoots and applause like the noblest of courtesans. Her face beamed under the heavy makeup. "Not in mother business," she said, "but you pay extra, we pretend."

There was more laughter, hearty this time.

Morrissey shouted, "Hooch for everyone, Mr. Dang. Captain Vandiver will pay you when he gets here." The men laughed again and then began to cheer. He jumped down, waving clasped hands over his head until the cheers died down and they began pressing in on Dang.

He restored the shaker to its place and sat down again, listening to the clamor of drink orders. Ah, that was better—noise, life. He craned his neck as Mr. Dang slipped toward him through the crowd. Good—Dang was bringing the usual two bourbons. Morrissey swallowed in anticipation. He hadn't thought he'd *need* a drink tonight, not with his natural high over going home. But he did.

Dang looked nervous, nibbling his lower lip with stained teeth. "Captain . . . you say . . . Vandiver pay?"

Morrissey dug a wad of bills from his pocket and dropped it on the tray. Dang beamed and set the drinks in their customary places. "Sank you, Captain. Good luck in U.S.A."

The weary, wrinkled smile slipped past Morrissey's defenses, paining him. He squeezed Dang's arm. It felt fragile, just fatless skin over bone. The old man looked half eaten away, as if the miseries brought here by his patrons had turned on him. Will I really miss the old hooch-waterer? Morrissey wondered. Palest damn Jack Daniels in Saigon.

But he said, "Thanks for taking such good care of us—*Cám ơn ông Đặng kinh Dang*." He traded bows with Dang, extending the courtesy of lowered eyes and sober expression until he knew the old man was gone. Then he gazed into his shot glass, tapping the rim and admiring the ripple of brown and gold under the light. I've abused you, old friend, he thought. You've been my whore. But I'll treat you right tonight. We'll have one last dance together at Froggie's for old times' sake.

He offered the glass to the room before drinking: To 149 Cliff Street, Ridgetown, West Virginia. To the elm in the backyard, the streaks of cat piss on the basement windows, and the front step that always creaks. *To home*.

He held the first sip, letting it sting his tongue. What would it be like tomorrow? I will get on the plane, he thought. I will fly out of Bien Hoa. The sky will be blue, and there will be no shelling. I will come down in the U.S. of A., America the beautiful. Janet will be there, waiting for me . . .

Suddenly he was almost breathless. He swallowed more bourbon. Janet, Janet. What would she feel like? Soft against his chest, firm along his legs. Her hair would have a faint herbal smell from that shampoo she always used. When they kissed, he would lick her lip gloss and taste cinnamon. Later, she would wrap her legs around his waist and . . . Morrissey realized he was rising under the table and groaned. No, it was too soon, twenty-four hours, still too far away, he'd go ape-shit if he went on thinking about her now.

He sat, grinning. Okay, a month in the sack with my wife. Then Alan and I will set up the medical clinic in that old storefront on Jackson Street. A nice family practice, all clean and easy. No more bossing thirty men. I'll do all the lab work myself. I'll write reports that say women are pregnant or not pregnant. I'll tell Alan whether his fat old patients have too much cholesterol. When a kid drags his ass in from Ridgetown High, I'll see whether its mono or just a bad cold.

Morrissey envisioned the long brick L of Ridgetown High—tan shades behind grimy windows, the flagpole in front blackened by lightning. He and Alan would cruise over there the first Sunday they were back. Sneak in through the boiler room. Find out if the two of them could still pop the lockbar on the football cabinet. Then hit the field, run some patterns. Yeah, the "Deadly Deuce" strikes again, still the best quarterback-end duo in Ridgetown High history. Maybe some kids from the current team would be hanging out. Let them watch him and Alan read each others' minds. Coach could never teach them that. You could practice pass routes all day, but when you and the other guy were closer than brothers, that's when the magic happened.

Morrissey tried to picture the kids on the sideline. Thick necks, coal dust under their nails, watching him and Alan with awe under their adolescent deadpans. The picture would not come clear. Instead he saw the kid at the hospital yesterday, and his stomach plunged down inside him. *Oh, shit.* He pressed his fingers against his eyelids until he saw red splotches. In his fingertips he could feel the heat of the kid's forehead: temp, 107°, high enough to boil the brain. Had to move fast, get a make on the infection. The kid hadn't even noticed when the scalpel cut into his foot. Then, back at the lab, leaning over the microscope . . .

Morrissey twitched the shot glass to his mouth. The bourbon burned all the way down. It only sharpened the memory: the ugly swarm of *E. coli* bacteria straight from the bowels of some Vietcong. Human shit. That's what the sons of bitches had put on the spike before they'd hid it under the leaves for the kid to step on.

Morrissey's throat tightened with pain. The poor, damned kid. Too skinny to be a marine. Dark-frame glasses sliding down his nose. Pimply face. So young. He hadn't lasted the night. Dead like the others, an average of two lost kids every week for twelve fucking months, and not a thing could be done.

The great Dr. Morrissey, he thought bitterly. Number One in his class. Gregor Mendel Award for the best Ph.D. dissertation in genetics. Chief of labs for the biggest army hospital in all of 'Nam. Hot stuff. For a year, countless milliliters of blood and urine, sputum samples, and bone and tissue-mass biopsies from thousands of suffering ex–high school kids had passed under his supervision. He had been the base hospital's ultimate diagnostician.

And a hundred of his kids had died. Not such hot stuff.

Sweat began to pour down Morrissey's face. He spread his fingers; tried to relax his hands. It was pointless to feel so furious. The kids had died and there would be more of them. He had done his best, and there was no one else to blame, nothing *behind* it all to smash back at. Might as well scream at the sky for raining.

Disgusted, he thumped his empty shot glass onto its side, watched it circle to a stop. Damn it, this was Froggie's. No lab thoughts allowed here—his most sacred rule, and he couldn't seem to make it stick anymore.

Yes, it was time to get out.

Morrissey's throat began itching for another drink. He picked up Vandiver's glass and checked his watch as he sipped. 8:10. Come on, old buddy. Let's *party*!

And there Alan was, ducking to get in the door, golden hair sweat-plastered straight back. Morrissey felt his face split in a ridiculous grin. Vandiver grinned back and threw him a comic salute. Chairs scraped as men stood to shout out greetings. A few officers broke away from the bar to intercept Alan at the door. Morrissey shook his head, amused. All this fuss, and the big bastard hadn't even jumped up on a table.

He didn't have to. Look at him: Alan pushed up a bow wave of well-being wherever he went, bowling people over and sweeping them along in his wake—not just tonight, but every night. The truth was, Vietnam had not fazed Alan. He'd waded in a year ago, rolled up his sleeves, and started plunging his giant hands into the wreckage of kids' chests. Spitting in death's eye, and laughing every night afterward. Making the rest of them laugh too.

Morrissey watched with pity the other officers converging around Alan. *They* were losing him tonight. Instinctively they crowded around for a last clap on the back, a final joke. Over their heads, Vandiver gave him a helpless smile. He responded with the O.K. sign, conscious of a relief almost uncomfortable in its intensity: *he* was not losing Alan tonight.

He closed his eyes, walling out the noisy good cheer around Alan that was really grief. With his eyes shut, he immediately noticed a spicy aroma. Delicious, some kind of meat, probably charcoaled *thit heo* from one of the braziers on the street. The smell must have drifted in when the door opened. Morrissey realized his mouth was watering. Had he eaten tonight? No. The aroma grew stronger and he opened his eyes to find Vandiver waving the meat under his nose.

"Brought you some supper. Roast pork."

Morressey accepted the *thit heo* stick, surprised at how good it made him feel, like a kid at Christmas.

"Eat, man, eat. You're as skinny as a 'Cong."

Morrissey took a bite. It was tough and overdone, but Alan was watching him like a worried nanny. He chewed with what he hoped was the proper gusto. Vandiver beamed. "That's it, dig in. Janet's going to bust her easel over my head when she sees how thin I let you get. Better she should ease her bust over my head."

Morrissey laughed and almost choked on the meat.

Alan picked up his bourbon and gave the level a calculating squint. "Am I that late? Almost a centimeter."

"Evaporation," Morrissey said, dropping the remains of the *thit heo* under the table for Dang's dog.

"Evaporation my ass." Vandiver drained the glass and smacked his lips. "Let's dance."

"What would the men say?"

"No, jarhead. Those two over there."

Morrissey followed Vandiver's nod to where two of Madame Tho's joygirls sat at a table. One of them caught him looking and smiled. He felt heat rising up from his collar.

"No thanks. Not my type."

"You only have one type, Peter old boy."

Alan sounded almost wistful. Was he remembering what it had been like to dance with Janet, hold Janet? You could have married her, Morrissey thought. But you didn't—

He cut the thought off. "You go ahead." He watched Vandiver approach the women and bow gracefully. One of the joygirls smiled and stood. Alan pulled the other one up too. Beyond him, Morrissey noticed a young Vietnamese man sitting at the table across from the joygirls, staring at them. Odd, a Vietnamese man his age coming into Froggie's, a notorious hangout of American army officers. The guy looked mad, glaring like he was about to lunge across the table at Alan and the women. Morrissey tensed. Music started—the Rolling Stones. The man buried his head in a newspaper. Then other officers got up to look for dance partners, blocking him from view.

Morrissey relaxed. The guy probably objected to his countrywomen being in a place like this, letting a foreigner—a big yellow-haired *Ngư ơ i dãman*—touch them. A legitimate beef.

Morrissey ordered two more Jack Daniels. When his was gone, he started on Alan's. He noticed that things were beginning to soften around the edges and tilt slightly. He felt a rubbery smile on his lips. Trying to erase it only twisted it into an outright simper.

When he looked up, Vandiver was sitting across from him again, grinning.

"Wha's so funny, apeface?"

"Today they medevaced a guy in from up the pike," Vandiver said. "General's son, as a matter of fact. A Captain Stanhouse. The battalion aid surgeon missed some bleeders. Bastard was gray as wax, just about gone when I zipped him open again. I saved his ass. It made me feel good."

"You dreaming about how you can make his daddy pay off?" Morrissey said. But then he reached across and grabbed Vandiver's wrist, squeezing down hard. "Good going."

"Hey." Vandiver gave him a close look. "Take it easy."

"Right," Morrissey said. "We're almost there. Tomorrow, we're bailing out of this butcher shop."

"Yeah," Alan said without enthusiasm.

Morrissey saw that the two Vietnamese joygirls were back at their table, chattering and batting their eyelashes at Vandiver's back. The angry young Vietnamese man was gone, though. What was that under the table where he'd sat? A black briefcase. Morrissey labored to remember. Had the guy been carrying a briefcase? Better check the thing out. He started to get up, settling back when Vandiver caught his arm.

"Yeah," Alan repeated. "Tomorrow, the killing is over. We're going home, but that doesn't mean we'll forget. We were here. We saw what we saw. We can run, but we can't hide."

Morrissey glanced at the briefcase and back at Alan, torn between the two. "Speak for yourself. I aim to stick my head just as far down into the sand of Ridgetown, West Virginia, as it'll go."

Vandiver smiled. "You do and old Roger Blotz will come along and pick your pocket and then kick your ass."

Morrissey laughed and felt the tension blow out of him. He pictured Blotz, Ridgetown's most dedicated derelict, weaving down Main Street.

Tomorrow.

There was probably nothing in the briefcase but papers. He'd just take it out carefully and set it in the alley next to Froggie's, then call the MPs.

He stood. "I'm going to check something."

Vandiver gave a knowing grunt. "Take the girl on the left. She loves your black hair. Thinks you're an Indian. I told her your father was Geronimo."

Morrissey nodded absently and gave Vandiver's shoulder a squeeze on the way past.

There was a brilliant flash. Pain jammed through his eardrums. The room veered on its side and spun around him. He felt the floor striking him, front, back, front, back. Something crunched into his shin. He screamed at the pain, saw dark things blossoming.

He lay still and listened to the clanging inside his head, loud and meaningless. He watched the shelves behind the bar lean slowly forward. The bottles skittered silently over the bar and broke in noiseless cascades on the floor.

He turned his head the other way and saw a smoking crater in the floor where the briefcase had been sitting.

A bomb. The briefcase *was* a bomb.

Alan!

Morrissey tried to sit up. He gasped as pain exploded in his shin. Shit—broken! He screamed for Alan. His voice seemed to vanish, as though the room had sucked it away. His eardrums must have been ruptured.

He scrabbled across the floor, dragging his broken leg. A shattered half-moon of table blocked his way, and he flung it aside. Beyond it he saw a slim arm with gold and silver bracelets lying in his path. The arm was attached to nothing. The fingers twitched.

He put his head down and choked back the vomit. He crawled over the arm. There! Under the other half of the table, Alan's long legs sticking out. He hurled away the rest of the table and stared at Alan's face. So peaceful, as though he were sleeping. He groped Alan's wrist. No pulse. Alan's chest was still, no rise or fall.

Horror pumped through him. Alan was dead.

He tipped Vandiver's head back and cleared the tongue from blocking the windpipe. Pinching off the nostrils, he forced air into the slack mouth. "Breathe," he groaned.

He bent over Alan's chest and rhythmically pumped the sternum. He counted off fifteen beats, then stopped and fed Alan more air before going back to the heart massage.

Smoke rolled down around his face. Heat seared his back. The place was on fire! He had to get them both out of here, now. He set his heels to drag Alan away, and pain exploded up from his leg. Everything went gray. He clenched his teeth and the room knitted back into focus. His face was drenched with sweat. It was no use; he'd never be able to drag Alan's weight.

They'd *both* die.

Morrissey felt a kick of panic in his chest and legs and

knew he could make it alone, squirm and whip across the floor like a snake if he had to, *now*!

He grabbed Alan's shirt, holding himself in place. He started punching Vandiver's sternum again, then began to choke. He hunched down to get better air and lost leverage, his elbows giving way, the heel of his hand sliding to the side of Vandiver's chest. He forced himself to straighten again. Spasms of coughing tore at his throat. His arms were dead meat, barely jolting his shoulders with each thrust.

Alan drew a shuddering breath.

"Yes!" Morrissey yelled. He grabbed Alan's arms and tried to pull him along the floor. He was too weak. Please, he prayed, I can't lose him now. He doubled over, coughing his lungs out, and collapsed on top of Alan. Everything went gray again, and then he saw Janet's face inches away in the floorboards. He tried to reach for it, but his arm wouldn't move. Good-bye, he thought. I love you.

He felt hands encircling his chest, pulling at him. He fought them, trying to hang onto Alan. They pried his hands loose and dragged him over the buckling floorboards of the bistro into the street. He saw more men, Vietnamese police in white suits carrying Vandiver out behind him. He struggled up, standing on one leg, watching one of the policemen bend over Vandiver and press an ear to his chest. The man smiled and nodded up at him, giving the O.K. sign, and he knew in his mind that Alan was all right.

But he began to shake. The war was over, he thought. I was going. It isn't fair.

He hopped to a lightpole, clutching it hard against him to stop the quaking that seemed to come from his bones. He became aware of hands pulling at his arms again—policemen, gesturing and chattering at him in Vietnamese. Their voices were muffled, but he could make out the words: "Please, sir, we must get you to hospital, examine your leg."

No, he couldnot leave this place yet, leave Alan.

He waved them off, pushed their hands away, pretending not to understand. At last they left, shaking their heads.

He edged from the lightpole to a parked Citroën, leaning

against the hood. He watched them carry Vandiver to the ambulance. He tried not to blink. He would be all right as long as he could see Alan. One of Alan's arms dangled from the stretcher, his fingers dragging on the ground. Then he was out of sight inside. The siren began to blast and the wagon lunged away from the curb. It disappeared around a corner. Morrissey lurched over the hood of the Citroën, reaching after the ambulance, realizing he was losing control, seeing red, feeling pulses of pain from his fists, someone screaming through his throat.

Vision returned in a rush. He was leaning over the hood of the Citroën. The front windshield was punched out. He saw his fists still pounding the dash inside the window. He stopped and stared at the beads of glass all over the front seat and floor. His knuckles were numb and slippery with blood. He took long, deep breaths. After a minute he was able to look back at Froggie's. The bistro was only a burning shell now. He watched a roof timber fall, shooting sparks against the black sky. He strained to see into the glowing cavern, searching, feeling his teeth bare in a snarl. What was he looking for? A prancing goat-thing, with gloating, crimson eyes and the smell of rot in its lungs?

No. That was not death. He'd seen death already. A hundred kids. For a year he'd looked into their blood, their piss, and their tissues, torn, burned, poisoned. He'd watched their faces as the cells ran down and stopped inside them.

And he'd planned to walk away.

There could be no walking away now.

Just a few seconds, but looking down at Alan's dead face, he had learned how death was going to feel when it got really close.

It was no longer a pain he could stand.

He would have to fight. Fighting would be his life.

But how?

There must be ways. He was trained for it—perhaps better than any man alive. He would find the ways.

"I'm coming after you," he said. He spat toward the fire.

28
DAYS

Tuesday, October 14

Chapter 1

Washington, D.C.
2000 hours:

"Uno!" June squealed.

Tsong threw down her single card in disgust. Morrissey looked at his handful and groaned. "Dead last again."

He listened to June and Tsong giggle. The crawl of nerve in his stomach eased.

"Another game, Daddy," Tsong said.

"No, it's bedtime."

"We'll let you win." June tugged at his wrist pleadingly, leaning close to his face. He felt his eyes crossing, blurring her hair into a red torch.

"The sandman's coming," he said. "You have to be in bed so you won't fall down."

Tsong regarded him with sober, dark eyes. He held out his free hand to her. The warmth of her fingers filled him with love. So small and perfect. June let go and ran off to fetch her cushion. She brought it back and held it up to his face: plastic lips, a lush red, inflated to the bursting point.

"Kiss Marilyn," she instructed.

"I'd rather kiss you," he said, and did.

He squeezed both girls to him, nuzzling their soft faces, smelling soap and the fabric softener in their pajamas. He wanted to hold them all night. He could be content just to sit here hugging their warm little bodies and gazing at the Poohbear in the rocker, getting slowly high on the sweet Play-doh vapors that leaked from the toybox. But that could not be.

The L-6 rats were ready.

Why wasn't *he* ready? This time was the hardest yet.

He felt June whopping Tsong with the lip cushion behind his back. "Come on. Off to bed with you. I'll tuck you in."

He followed them up the stairs. When he finished tucking June in, he went across the hall and settled on the edge of Tsong's bed. She still looked somber.

"Daddy, where are you going tonight?"

"Just the lab, honey."

"Are you going to do genetics?"

He smiled, pleased. "Yes."

"What are genetics?"

He folded his hands over one knee and drew a breath. "Let's see. Genetics is what makes you like you are. Everybody's got tiny things inside their body called genes. They decide whether you'll have red hair like June's or black hair like yours. They decide what color your eyes will be, and your skin, and what your face will look like."

"Do the genes vote?"

Morrissey laughed. "Sort of. Together, they make a code. What that code says, that's what you are: a little girl with black hair and pretty brown eyes, or a cat, or an elephant. Everything alive has its own genetic code . . ." He realized he was getting too technical. "Anyway, I work with genes. I study that code and try to change it a little bit so that people won't get cancer." *And other reasons*, he added silently.

"Could you make a sandman so he wouldn't get people?"

Morrissey hesitated, noticing that her lips were pressed tight to keep from trembling. She's scared of the sandman, he realized. And you've been hitting her with it every night. "The sandman won't get you, honey."

"June said he's big and cold and made of sand. She said he's like a zombie and he comes walking after you . . ."

"June was teasing you, honey. The sandman is just a nice man who comes around and sprinkles sand in your eyes to help you be sleepy. That way you can go to bed and have nice dreams and not be tired the next day. But it's only a story. The sandman isn't real."

"You'll keep him away?"

Morrissey sighed, then looked reassuring. "You bet."

She snuggled down and he kissed her and pulled the blanket up to her chin.

In the hall he thought: *Kids*, and smiled. When *you* were a kid, he reminded himself, you were scared of deer because of the big horns.

He checked to make sure June's light was still out, then went past their bedrooms to the attic steps. A bar of golden light fell through the trap and he thought, Beam me up, Scotty. The old fracture site in his leg pained him a little on the steep fold-down ladder. As his head and shoulders cleared the trap, he drew in the heady musk of old linseed oil and turpentine from the paintings stacked around the walls. The varnished oak floorboards stretched away from his eyes, a sheet of glare under the klieg lights.

He rested his arms on the floor at the top of the ladder. Janet was standing in front of a blank canvas, her back to him, head cocked. Her hair swung down to the side, a gorgeous blend of chestnut and deep brown under the blaze of lights. He saw that she was wearing one of his old sweatshirts, the hem falling halfway to her knees. It pleased him—a small, unconscious gesture of intimacy.

He watched her avidly. If only he could peek into her mind right now—see the colors swirl, the ideas take form. Later she'd pull some of them from the blankness of the canvas. But it would be fascinating to see them now, uncensored. How did she choose and shape? He couldn't even draw a decent stick-man.

Ah, well. There was always his woodworking. He thought longingly of the birdhouse that waited unfinished on his worktable.

He began to feel an unpleasant pull at the top of his vision. He looked beyond Janet to the ceiling. There, behind the coronas of the kliegs: the black slits of the skylights. They seemed to focus on Janet like the eyes of a beast.

His neck prickled. *A beast, hungry, waiting for Janet.* He stared at the eyes until they became skylights again.

Janet came over and bent to kiss him. "Time for the biopsy?"

"Yes."

"Good luck. Call me the minute you know."

He pulled her face to him again and closed his eyes, smelling her hair, feeling her eyelashes against his cheek, still conscious of the dark beyond the skylights. It can't have you, he thought. Never.

"I'll call you," he said. If it works, he added silently.

On his way in, Morrisey saw a light in Alan's office and cursed silently. Alan must still be at work in the radiation lab. A rotten stroke of luck. What if Alan dropped by to shoot the breeze when he was in the middle of the biopsy? It would start him wondering. Alan knew Morrissey's latest cancer study was just under way; there'd be no reason to biopsy rats yet.

Christ! He'd have to put the biopsy off a night. No. He couldn't stand that. He was ready now. He had to know.

Then Morrissey recalled the MP guards he'd seen outside the lab for the past few weeks. It would be all right. Alan wouldn't come by. Alan obviously had his own secret to worry about.

As Morrissey hurried through his shower-and-change routine, he dulled the clamor of his nerves by puzzling over Alan. What *was* Alan doing in that radiation lab with the marine guards? Why would Alan keep his research from his best friend?

Morrissey saw the irony of the question and grunted. Irony or not, hiding his research from Alan wasn't the same thing at all. For one thing, *his* secrecy was for Alan's own protection. As head of Army Labs, Colonel Vandiver would be put in a difficult position if he *knew* his star civilian employee was using the army's billion-dollar equipment for unauthorized work.

And if L-6 worked, it would be more dangerous than a thousand 50-megaton bombs. It had to be controlled. The only way to guarantee that was to tell no one—no one at all.

Alan, on the other hand, had no such excuses. He could not possibly be working on anything as earthshaking as L-6. And Alan always told him everything.

Morrissey had to laugh at himself. What conceit! He was like the man with five mistresses who kicked his wife out for a one-night stand. He toweled off and slipped into one of the white zip-suits, with its pajamalike booties. As he tugged the drawstring of the hood around his ears, he smelled the familiar, bleachy tang of disinfectant. Tonight it knifed straight to his gut, twanging his agonized stomach back to full pitch.

Outside his lab door he saw a smashed cricket on the cement floor. He looked away at once, irritated. That lout Harvey Goins again, and his murderous, hungry boots.

He locked the door behind him and pulled the L-6 notebook from the safe. How black it looked on the lab table, with the stainless steel gleaming all around it. Like a Bible on some futuristic altar.

Morrissey's mouth went dry and his heart began to pound. He wanted L-6 to be it; God, how he wanted it.

He tried to imagine it and could not, and realized he wasn't just nervous. He was afraid, damn it—scared stiff. He could see only failure tonight, and that he didn't have to imagine. He could remember it all too well. Five other nights like this one, five other L-genes. Five failures.

He rolled his head around, trying to ease the tension in his neck. He opened the notebook and thumbed quickly past the pages of notes and formulas to the back of the book. On the last page were the 104 names. The leftmost column started with Spec 4 John Ewald and the rightmost ended with Captain Alan Vandiver. He looked down the columns, noting the checkmarks. Only fourteen names remained unchecked. Twelve years since 'Nam and he'd found the families of all but fourteen. Still, it was disappointing. He'd planned to be through long before now. But some of them were hard to find, and, with the passing years, it didn't get any easier.

He remembered his last visit, the small, irrelevant details standing out with unwanted clarity in his mind: walking down the dim hall of the apartment in Denver; the dirty fingerprints all around the doorknob; the black-haired woman in the bathrobe, with the tell-tale spiderwebs of vein on her cheeks and nose. She was rosy with false health—gin on her breath and it wasn't noon yet. Even the black hair had come from a bottle.

Mrs. Specht? I'm Peter Morrissey. I knew your son Jimmy. It was just for a short time. He was in the hospital in Saigon while I was there. I was with him, off and on, those last few days. I tried to help him all I could, but it wasn't enough. He seemed like a very good kid.

Morrissey turned away from the book. He waited until his stomach stopped paining him.

He looked at Alan's name and felt better. The one name he wouldn't have to check off. But it belonged there, at the bottom of the list. Alan had been dead. No heartbeat, no pulse.

Morrissey stared around the lab. "Are you here?" he said softly. "You son of a bitch."

He heard nothing but the whisper of air through the filters.

He smiled grimly. *Poor Doc Morrissey. One of those Vietnam vets, you know. They all came back a little crazy. He likes to pretend death's an actual thing that crawls inside and eats you. Poor bastard. He's all right most of the time. Just humor him—and don't make any loud noises.*

Morrissey slammed the notebook shut and shoved it back in the safe.

He went into the animal room, to the last rolling cart of rat cages. He checked the tape label to make sure the animal-care men hadn't switched the carts during cleanup. CANCER STUDY, CONTROL RATS. Cancer study control rats—right.

Like hell!

Almost reverently, he slid the closest cage drawer out. The rat was curled up, sleeping atop the mix in its feed jar.

He lifted it gently by the nape of the neck and watched it uncurl, smelling the pleasant, malty odor of the feed dust in its hair. He stroked its back, trying to absorb some of its sleepy calm. The rat peered nearsightedly at him. Its rear leg blurred as it tried to scratch its side. He laughed, and some of his tension evaporated.

What the hell. He would just do it now and see.

He shaved a patch of hair away from the rat's pink belly. Then he scraped the skin with the edge of the blade and drew it over the end of a slide, transferring the film of epidermal cells. He eased the rat back into its cage, and inspected the glass pipette to make sure its delicate tip was unbroken. Good thing he'd remembered to draw it last week, before his nerves had started to fray. Last time he'd been unable to stop his hands shaking. He'd ruined four glass rods and burned his fingers before getting the dropper narrow enough.

Morrissey picked up pinpoint droplets of dye with the pipette and tinted the rat cells on the slide. He put the slide under the scope and flipped on the stage light.

Here we go!

He eased the focus knobs around until he saw the cells from the rat jitter into view. If the gene was there, it would appear as a tiny dot of green stain.

He felt cold sweat rolling down his forehead. *Just do it!*

He looked. There was nothing.

He sat back, rubbed the sweat from his eyes, and looked again. He held himself still a moment. Then he let himself go, punching at the black tube of the microscope. He pulled up an inch away. His fist shook with frustration and he slammed it on the table.

He couldn't take it!

He rubbed the aching heel of his fist. For God's sake, what was he doing wrong? The cells in culture had performed perfectly. So why hadn't L-6 taken hold in the living animal? He would go back to the safe, get out the L-6 notes and go through them again.

But he made no move toward the safe. He sat, head down.

After a moment he began sluggishly to fight off the despair. *Misery is chemical.* He grimaced at how familiar the phrase was becoming. He must go through the rest of it anyway. It was important to analyze now, to stop the internal chain reaction of misery. You didn't see the stain, he told himself. You realized that nothing had happened in the L-6 cells. Then you *said* something to yourself—*you failed, you miserable S.O.B.*

Mistake: As soon as you make the harsh judgment against yourself, your brain sent signals to the hypothalamus, the pituitary; other endocrine glands. Adrenaline and other hormones spurted into your bloodstream. The seratonin balance shifted in your brain.

You felt like shit.

Once you'd set the chemicals loose, they were beyond your control. You couldn't regulate your endocrine glands with your conscious mind—not directly. But you *could* control your thoughts.

That was the trick—to catch yourself, keep from thinking *you dumb shit* over and over. Then the balance would gradually shift back. Your cells would convert the corrosive chemicals to harmless sludge that would drain out of the bloodstream. You would feel better.

It took time and vigilance. The more vigilance, the less time.

Okay, he thought, you feel terrible. It will pass. You will try again and do better.

The old fatalistic calm began to settle over Morrissey. He *could* take it.

L-6 was the past now. Time to go home.

Tomorrow he would start planning L-7.

He reached for the microscope switch, his arm as heavy as lead. His finger stopped above the switch, unable to do this final small thing and officially admit defeat.

All right, one last look. He bent over the scope and saw the band.

He stared at it, uncomprehending at first, and then caught up in growing excitement. There *was* something! Not a dot of stain, but a faint pink circle around the cell border. So faint that he had missed it the first time.

Morrissey switched to the intermediate power lens, bringing a group of cells into focus. The back of his eye began to itch and he sat back, closing both eyes. He waited, controlling his impatience. No good straining himself blind. He bent over the scope again.

It was there in every cell—a very faint pink band.

Sweat poured out, soaking his shirt. He rocked on the stool, driven by spurts of energy. He stood, knocking the stool over backward. He started to caper around the lab, and stopped short, wincing at the stab of pain from the old fracture site. He leaned against a table and massaged the leg, squeezing hard in his excitement. *Yeah! Crazy Viet Nam vet who thought he could beat death. Now we would all fucking see!*

Okay. Be calm. *Think.*

Point one: The L-6 gene was *not* a failure. It had already performed an operation in the rat cells. He'd hoped simply to see the gene in place. But this was better—it was already working!

Point two: This band wasn't one of the effects he'd expected. He hadn't seen it in the petri-dish cells. But these cells came directly from a living animal, not from the artificial environment of a petri dish. Some variation could be expected.

Point three—what was point three? Plans: Tomorrow evening, after everyone left, he could see if the pink band was also there in the L-6 dogs. Then, in the next week, he could set up a battery of tests to determine whether the band was actually shielding the cell. Radiation, toxins, the whole spectrum.

Then for the coup de grace: waiting for a cell division and looking for aging errors. If there were none, then he'd done it. L-6—*Life-Six!* A giddy smile transfixed his face.

Janet! She'd said to call her the minute he knew. He reached for the phone. No, he couldn't do this over the phone. What time was it? 10:40. If he hurried, he could get to a 7-Eleven before it closed and pick up some champagne. Probably nothing at a 7-Eleven but André. No matter—André would taste like Dom Perignon tonight!

By the door Morrissey saw a tiny dark movement at his

feet and jumped back. He smiled to himself—it was only a cricket. What a bundle of nerves.

Yeah, a cricket, and if it was still there in the morning, Harvey Goins would stomp it flat.

Morrissey got out his clear plastic cup and crawled after the cricket, cursing himself for a mush-hearted fool and thinking of cold champagne. It took him ten minutes to trap the cricket under the cup. Bye-bye, champagne.

Resisting the urge to give the cup a vindictive shake, he took the cricket down the hall and put it in Dr. Pancek's lab, out of range of Harvey Goins's boots.

27 DAYS

Wednesday, October 15

Chapter 2

0750 hours:

Vandiver waited while the master sergeant swung the safe door shut on him. When he was alone and closed in, he sat.

He looked down the length of the table to the photo above the Chairman's place: Warren Maddock posed at his desk in the Oval Office. Vandiver remembered the day two years ago: Secret Service men smuggling Maddock into the Pentagon basement before dawn. The President sitting there at the other end of the table, under his own photo. Vandiver straightened now, the muscles of his back and legs coming alert with the memory of him standing to attention to accept command of Project Parasol from the President of the United States. He flexed his fingers, enjoying the tingle of blood and nerve, the feeling of strength in his hands. Project Parasol: so secret it was known to only a dozen men, so important that it could save 165 million lives; so dangerous that a single premature leak of its success to Soviet intelligence could lose those same 165 million lives.

And it was *his*.

Vandiver filled his lungs, relishing the damp, basement scent that the air conditioners could not scrub out. The smell of bunkers. It touched him with yearning. If only this could be his day of victory. He imagined himself facing the generals and saying, *Gentlemen, we have the shielding material.* The most important words anyone could ever speak in this room. By the sacred Virgin, he *would* say them. But not today.

Damn it, how much longer?

Vandiver heard the massive door whispering open and stood to attention as General Stanhouse and the two major generals entered. Behind the generals was the Deputy Secretary of Defense and a stranger—a slender man in an elegant European-tailored suit. Vandiver tried not to gape at him in surprise. The only civilians cleared for Project Parasol were the Deputy Secretary and the Secretary of Defense.

Surprise turned to vague suspicion. Who was this guy?

Vandiver sized the man up in discreet glances. First impression—negative. He looked too cocky, wearing a fixed smile of superiority. This man thought he was better than other men—better and *smarter*. He showed it even now, in the select company of this room.

A prick, Vandiver thought.

He looked to Stanhouse for a clue. The old general looked tight-lipped and unhappy. He's been trying to catch my eye, Vandiver realized. He wants to get something across to me; he's almost in pain with it. What is it?

Stanhouse sighed and looked at the other men. "All right, gentlemen. Let's get started. Deputy Secretary Pennylegion, I don't believe Colonel Vandiver has met Dr. Fitch."

Pennylegion scrunched his fat body around in the chair. Disgusting, Vandiver thought, keeping his face carefully neutral. Soft. He can't even master his own body.

And he's the most powerful man in this room.

The Deputy Secretary gestured: "Dr. Vandivah, Dr. Fitch, head of Bah-log Lab'ratories. Dr. Fitch, Dr. Vandivah, head of the Army Radiobah-ology Labs."

Vandiver returned the civilian's nod, running the Deputy Secretary's introduction through again, with the heavy southern drawl filtered out: Bah-log—*Biolog Laboratories. Civilian experts in radiobiology. They'd landed a bunch of fat government contracts since Maddock came to office.*

There'd been something in the Post *about Fitch. Wasn't he an old classmate of Pennylegion's?*

All at once Vandiver realized what was in the Chairman's eyes: pity.

Stanhouse said, "Alan—Colonel, for the benefit of Dr. Fitch, could you please summarize Project Parasol before you proceed with your interim report."

Vandiver stood slowly. Damn it, the president of a competitor lab, here—with no advance word to him. A consultant? Or worse?

Vandiver swallowed, trying to wet his dry throat. "Okay, Dr. Fitch. We've been trying to formulate a new material to block radiation and fallout from a nuclear attack. Of course, lead and a few other heavy, bulky materials will do this already. But we want a material that is lightweight, flexible, and cheap. We need something we can mass-produce for homeowners, landlords, commercial building management, and so on. Something people can tack up in their basements in an hour . . ."

Worse—it was worse. Fitch was not here to consult. Fitch was here to replace him.

Vandiver glared at the Deputy Secretary, furious. You fat bureaucrat. You found another government contract for your old buddy, Dr. Fitch.

Vandiver went on, trying not to bite off the words. "We believe that the Soviets are considering a pre-emptive nuclear strike. Apparently, because of their clear superiority in civil defense, some of the top Soviet generals think they can win a nuclear war with us. It *is* true that more of their people would survive an exchange—especially one that they started with a sneak attack. That's why Project Parasol was initiated. We hope this civil-defense gap will be closed with the new shielding material. If the Russians do decide to hit us, many more people will be killed by radiation than by all the immediate firestorm, blast, and drag effects combined. But if we can shield these potential victims, we could cut the casualties from a possible high of one hundred and sixty-five million to perhaps thirty-five million."

"That's still a staggering figure, Colonel."

Vandiver stared at Fitch. The jerk-off! Fitch had to know what the figures meant. Lord help them all if he didn't understand even that much. "Of course it's staggering," he said. "But the point is, if the Soviets knew we could prevent a hundred and thirty million casualties, they'd know we'd come out of an exchange in much better shape than they. They'd have to throw out any idea of a pre-emptive strike. So we're really talking about going from one hundred and sixty-five million to zero casualties.

"Of course, absolute secrecy is necessary—especially at the moment we succeed in the lab. If the Russians learned we had such a material before we got it in place, they would hit us at once."

Fitch looked down, avoiding his eyes. Vandiver heard Pennylegion shift uncomfortably. Chew on that, Deputy Secretary. Then think about bringing another lab in on the secret.

"Thank you for the summary, Colonel," Stanhouse said. "Proceed with your report."

Yes, Vandiver thought bitterly. Proceed, and give Pennylegion his opening. "We still don't have the final breakthrough we're all looking for, but I'm sure we're getting close. Since the last report, we've tested eight more variants of the new alloy I briefed you on last time. We've reduced the porosity by half again. We've kept it lightweight and cheap to make—"

Pennylegion lifted his hand. "Yes, yes, Colonel. But can it withstand radiation at the four-hundred-and-fifty-roentgen level?"

Vandiver fought to hide his contempt. This lawyer, this born talker. How he could roll the scientific terms off his tongue. But he understood nothing about science, or he could not dream of shifting the contract. "No sir," Vandiver said. "Not yet."

"Then when?"

"I think very soon. Unfortunately, with scientific breakthroughs, there is no way to be sure of the timing."

"Ah seem to remember you sayin' you'd run *nine* variants during the extension period?"

"Yes, sir. The ninth is almost ready for testing, but we had a piece of bad luck. We're temporarily out of lab rats to test the shielding effectiveness. At the moment, our supplier of laboratory rats can't fill our orders for more animals."

"Even if you had the rats now," Pennylegion said, "is there any reason to think your ninth variant would be any less a failure than the other eight?"

Vandiver felt the blood rushing to his face. He saw Stanhouse glaring at Pennylegion. A deliberate insult. The fat bastard wanted him to lose his temper, make it easier. He would *not* lose his temper. "We don't think of the first eight materials as failures, sir. They have been stepping-stones to the present level of progress. The ninth variant may very well be—"

The Deputy Secretary waved again, and Vandiver imagined grabbing the fat wrist, twisting it until the fingers spread into claws.

"I may as well be frank with you right from the top, Colonel. Save us going round and round. Defense is opposed to any further extension of this contract to Army Labs."

Vandiver clenched his hands behind his back.

"We have another worry now," Pennylegion went on. "The coming election may affect the Russians' thinking. The White House is confident that Governor Howard isn't going to win, of course, but even the outside possibility of a hawk being elected is going to sensitize the Russians even more. Gentlemen, we think the pre-emptive strike option is tempting them. Army Labs has clearly failed to produce an adequate shielding material, and the White House thinks it's time for some new blood—a fresh approach, completely different from the one we've been taking. I've been talking to Larry—Dr. Fitch—for several weeks, and I'm convinced that Biolog has devised such an approach—"

"Excuse me, sir."

Pennylegion sighed. "Yes, Colonel?"

"If the committee believes Biolog has a promising approach, why not fund both them and Army Labs?"

Pennylegion rolled his eyes. "Now, the Colonel knows that's not possible. We have to live with the budgetary appropriation we've been given. There's not enough money for both labs to proceed."

Vandiver felt the muscles of his back and neck turning rigid with frustration. How could he make this man understand what he was risking? "Sir, it's unthinkable to stop Army Labs this close to the goal and start over cold. Army Labs brought in the finest minds in our country for this project. Dr. Hisle, Dr. Wintermeier, Dr. Pancek—all the others. America has not assembled so much talent in one place since the Manhattan Project. With all respect to Dr. Fitch and Biolog, no one can possibly be in a better position to succeed than Army Labs. We've got to stand behind my people, sir. I'd stake my professional reputation on them."

"Perhaps you already have, Colonel," Pennylegion said.

Vandiver looked down, humiliated and sick. He heard Stanhouse grunt. One of the other generals started digging in his briefcase, making the papers snap. Vandiver realized that the other men—the military men—were embarrassed too. One of their own was taking a drubbing from a civilian. There was no way he could win. His shoulders turned heavy, trying to drag him down. He resisted the urge to lean forward on the table.

"I think we should hear from Dr. Fitch now," Pennylegion said.

Vandiver saw Stanhouse nod. The old man looked ill. He's taking this as hard as I am, Vandiver thought. Through his pain, he felt a pang of sympathy. Poor old George. He must have wanted desperately to head this off. But Pennylegion had the real power. There would have been nothing the Chairman could do.

Vandiver groped behind him for the back of his chair. His legs felt weak. He concentrated on keeping them from dumping him.

Fitch stood. "I've prepared a slide presentation," he said, "to introduce the new line of research we've been charting at Biolog."

I won't ever sit here again, Vandiver thought numbly.

The lights went dim. He stared at the first slide. It showed a smashed cityscape. The devastation was total except for a building in the middle distance, miraculously still standing. In the foreground was the charred body of a child, legs and arms raised, as if in a doomed effort to hold off the sky.

"Hiroshima," Fitch intoned. "The building you see still standing in the middle caught our attention . . ."

Fitch's voice droned on and on. More slides, more Japanese corpses. Vandiver stared, filled with helpless anger. If the Kremlin listened to the wrong generals, these could become American corpses—American old men and women, American babies—burnt and twisted.

Vandiver watched each slide. When he could think of helpful comments, he made them. When it was over, he wished Fitch luck.

He had a dim impression of wandering the corridors of the Pentagon. Then he was sitting in his car. He looked around the gleaming acreage of the Pentagon's parking lot. How had he gotten here? Christ it was hot. He leaned forward, unsticking his back from the car seat. He realized his fingers were rubbing the white diamond of hair where the back of his head had hit the wall in the Froggie Bistro.

Hope stirred in him. Yes, Froggie's. Every day he lived was borrowed time. He'd known that from the moment he'd come out of the coma. This was his second life, a life that had to make a difference. Project Parasol was that difference.

Determination flowed back into him. Somehow he must find more test rats. The lab could finish the ninth material in the next two days. It would take at least that long for the contract to be officially transferred to Biolog. In those few days he could make one last try. If he succeeded, today's meeting would be undone. Project Parsol would remain on track.

But where could they get laboratory rats? He'd already contacted all the other labs that might have extras.

Vandiver punched the steering wheel with excitement. *Control rats!* Of course! He could take control rats already being used in some other Army Labs study. They would be practically as good as new rats.

It would be expensive. Losing animals in midstream

would mean starting the affected study over again. It would cause a hell of a ruckus. It could stain the rest of his career.

But Pennylegion made it necessary. Switching the contract now was virtually as bad as starting over from scratch—worse, with that smug bastard Fitch in charge.

When the bombs starting falling, 165 million people would die.

So which study should he stop?

Hadn't Peter just started a new study a few weeks ago? Yes. The cost of destroying the project at this early point would be relatively small. The untreated control group of Peter's study was large, forty rats if he remembered right. He could put these together with his own few remaining animals and have enough for statistical significance.

But could he push aside Peter's work for a last chance to save Project Parasol?

Yes, that was the beauty of it: Peter would accept his need without tantrums or questions. What were friends for?

Vandiver squared his shoulders. He started the Porsche and sped away from the Pentagon parking lot.

26
DAYS

Thursday, October 16

Chapter 3

0730 hours:

Morrissey stirred the oatmeal and listened. From upstairs came a volley of squeaks—the girls plunging around, squeegeeing the sides of the tub. It reminded him of sneakers on the wood at a Knicks' game. The familiar sounds seemed very sweet today. He gazed out the kitchen window, beyond his backyard, to where treetops poked up from the great gorge of Rock Creek Park. Mist rose from the park into the pink sunrise like a vast waking yawn. It seemed supernaturally vivid and beautiful.

L-6 was panning out.

Today he'd start running tests on the L-6 dogs. Do some biopsies, culture the L-6 cells, then start throwing radiation and toxins at them. The L-6 cells would withstand the onslaught and divide perfectly, without any aging errors. He could *feel* it: after eleven years of hard work, agony, disappointment, L-6 was the one!

He did a dance in front of the stove, flipping raisins behind his back into the pot. Tsong and June. He would feed them oatmeal, and love them, and protect them always.

And he would never let them die.

He looked up and saw Janet standing in the doorway. She

twitched her fingers above her head, prancing a half-turn and ticking out castanet sounds through her teeth. He realized she'd seen his little dance and threw a raisin at her.

"No thanks," she said. "Just coffee for me today. On second thought, *I'll* get it."

He watched her shuffle to the Mr. Coffee, thinking how beautiful she was, even with his bathrobe hanging to her fingertips and ankles and her hair flaring out, dark and tangled from sleep. He considered tiptoeing up behind her, squeezing her against the counter, and then the girls trudged in, weighted down by the dignity of new school jumpers and knee socks.

Breakfast was wonderful. The girls chattered about school, and Janet smiled across the table at him. He ate his oatmeal, sorting out the raisins in a happy fog, until he heard rapping at the front door. "That's your chariot, kids," he said. "Get your lunches."

He led them to the foyer and turned them over to his father, watching through the window as they descended to the street. June and Tsong held Grandpa's hands on each side, matching their pace to his while he sidled down, peering beneath him to make sure of each step.

"His congestion seemed better today." Janet's voice was bright, just behind his ear.

"Yes," Morrissey said, knowing it had not. Black lung was not something that got better.

Janet hung a hand on his shoulder and he saw her face reflected beside him, smiling out the window. June glanced back at them, patient and serious, and Janet waved to her. "Isn't that a sweet picture?" she said. "I'd like to paint it."

He saw her expression in the glass go intent and knew she was composing the scene in her mind. He was afraid to move, to disturb the mysterious process. A painting of Dad and the girls, the intimate moment preserved. The prospect filled him with pleasure and a little of the awe he always felt for her painting. In her way, she could do so much more than he could ever hope to do: she could freeze June and Tsong forever the way they were this moment.

Grandpa Morrissey's immaculate yellow Corvair pulled

sedately away from the curb. Janet's face relaxed and he knew it was safe to talk. "I thought you didn't paint photographs." He gave the last word her usual snide inflection.

She kicked his ankle with a soft toe. "I'll do it in a way no one could catch with a camera. It's time I did them. Won't be that long before they're in high school, driving their own car to class."

"Six years," Morrissey said indignantly. "Eight for Tsong. At *least* that long before they drive. I'm not so sure we're going to give them a car the minute they're sixteen."

"Knowing you, you'll buy them each a German shepherd trained to attack if a boy tries to kiss them."

He grunted, still thinking about the painting. Yes, Janet could stop time. That's what her paintings hanging in the Cazzeloni gallery did; that's why people paid thousands for each of her works. She and he both saw the girls growing up, his father slipping down the steepening slope of age. She could arrest it and hold the sweet moment out to someone a thousand years from now. In his girls they could see beauty and promise; in his father, much more: a man who had earned every wrinkle and scar, digging coal until his knees were worn out and his lungs had soaked up the color and rigidity of the seams. That man would not age another day beyond her painting, not in a thousand years.

I just want him to keep getting older, Morrissey thought. That's all.

The wish triggered a harsh scrape of anxiety in his stomach. Time to get to the lab, start checking out that pink band in the L-6 animals.

He felt Janet's arm slide around his waist. He hugged her, and she turned, opened his floppy robe and folded him into it, clutching the lapels together against his back. Her body forced its way into his awareness: small, soft breasts, hair brushing his cheek, the pressure of long thighs. Life, regeneration. She held inside her an answer to death more ancient than art or science.

She tipped her face up and whispered into his mouth. "Wanna go in late today?"

He felt himself rise against her. Traitorous body! He

groaned and she smiled eagerly. No, he thought. I have to get to the lab. He kissed her, and kissed her again, and let his hands drop to her buttocks.

Morrissey propped his hands against the shower wall and let the warm water pour over his back. He felt peaceful and a little woozy, as if someone had shot a tranquilizer dart into him. It was a wonder he'd had enough starch left to steer the VW to the lab. Worth it, though. What an hour. Acting like a couple of college kids, right there on the parlor couch. He grinned into the shower stream.

Wake up, Don Juan. There are things to do.

He turned the shower to cold, gasping and gritting his teeth. He cringed away from the stream, pressing his face against the enamel sign on the back wall of the shower: ALL LAB PERSONNEL, SHOWER IN—THREE MINUTES MINIMUM, SHOWER OUT—SIX MINUTES MINIMUM. What was that scrawled underneath? KELLOGG—TEN MINUTES MINIMUM.

Morrissey shook his head in disgust. Why couldn't they give the poor kid a break? Maybe Kellogg hadn't seen it yet. Morrissey tried to rub it out, but it had been scratched through the enamel into the metal.

Well, Kellogg would just have to learn to deal with it. The kid couldn't expect anything else if he went on snubbing the other animal-care workers. Kellogg could get away with talking to the animals—but only if he talked to people too. Being grossly fat and having a dirty neck all the time didn't help either . . .

Morrissey stopped guiltily. Here he was, mentally dumping on Kellogg with the rest of them. He'd get maintenance in and have them repaint the sign before Kellogg went off tonight.

Morrissey stepped through the shower to the inside change room. He pulled on the sterilized white jumpsuit and pushed through into his lab.

And ran into Kellogg.

He reached out to soften the impact and felt the rolls of fat on the kid's arms. He had to steel himself to keep from recoiling. The kid was slimy—he'd sweated right through his labcoat. And his face was pale as dough. Morrissey felt Kellogg's fingers clutch at his elbow.

"Pete, I thought you'd never get here, you gotta come, where were ya anyway?"

"Whoa." Morrissey resisted the urge to pull free. He leaned back from the urgent thrust of Kellogg's face. Kellogg looked just like Private Grosbeck, with that dark hair hanging down over his pimply forehead. *Oh shit. Private Grosbeck. Nicked by a piece of shrapnel. Just a scratch. Then gas gangrene. So fat the anesthetist overloaded him to get him down. Dead on the table. Shit, shit, shit.*

Morrissey felt a pain in his stomach. He patted Kellogg's shoulder. "What's the trouble?"

"Monk is sick. Come on, you gotta do something."

Morrissey hurried after Kellogg into the animal room. Monk! An L-6 dog. If L-6 was working, he should not be sick.

Maybe Kellogg was wrong. Please, God, let him be wrong.

Morrissey edged the kid aside. His heart sank as he examined the Doberman through the bars of its cage. Foam on its mouth. Its eyes stood out, and the rims of the whites looked bloodshot. He watched it sway back and forth, and finally pitch up against the metal wall of its cage.

Distemper.

Morrissey turned away from the cage, sickened. L-6 was up in smoke. If Monk could get a simple disease like distemper, then the pink band didn't offer much protection. There was still some chance for resistance to radiation, but what good was that if the cell could be worn down by any disease that came along?

Morrissey fought the heaviness in his chest. It blocked his lungs up like cement, making it hard to breathe. To have a real hope at last, only to have it dashed.

He'd have to kill the dog. After saving it from the pound, he'd have to kill it. *He'd offered it his protection, and now he must give it to the enemy.* He held very still, trying to contain his anger.

"What's wrong with him?" Kellogg asked impatiently.

"Distemper."

"No!"

"I'm afraid so."

"But he's been vaccinated. We pay for that before we accept 'em."

"It doesn't always take."

"Or some bastard at the pound took the money and gave him saline. I hate those fuckers!"

"Come on, Kellogg, Monk didn't even—" Morrissey bit off the rest of the sentence. *Monk didn't even like you.* But you liked Monk, didn't you? You always kept trying, no matter how many times he snapped at you. And you probably don't even know why he hated you. Lord, I hope you don't.

Morrissey put his arm across the round, meaty shoulders. "I'm sorry."

"It wasn't his fault he couldn't like me," Kellogg said. "I bet some fat son of a bitch used to beat him—before the pound. Some guy who . . . looked like me. So Monk was just confused."

Morrissey felt helpless anger. Kellogg was probably right, and he had known the truth all along. What a miserable world this must be for him. He was fat, not stupid. What must it be like to lug around 300 pounds, to know you were ugly and repulsive all the time—to see it written on the shower wall? Only animals didn't care, accepting your appearance, sensing not ugliness but love. And then one of them turned on you, too, just because you were *fat*.

"Will you be able to hold him for me?" Morrissey asked.

"I can hold him."

Tears began to roll down Kellogg's round cheeks. Morrissey walked out quietly. He took as long as he could getting the needle ready.

". . . and it now appears that, with a little under a month left until the election, Governor Maxwell Howard has pulled ahead of President Maddock in the polls—"

Kellogg snapped the radio off. Who cares? he thought. He poked at the graham cracker crust of his Morton's banana cream pie. He could feel the weight of the filling already in his stomach, a cold, half-thawed ball. Disgusting. Shit, why did he have to wolf it down like that? But what else was there? Eat when you're happy, eat when you're sad, eat when they carry off your dad . . .

He looked out the balcony window to check the time. It was beginning to get dark. He ought to turn on the lights, but he didn't want to move. The hell with it.

Tonto was shuffling around behind the packing-crate desk. He whistled and the raccoon poked its head from behind the crate and gazed at him.

"Hi, hairbag," he said. "Want some crust?"

He watched fondly as the coon waddled over and hopped from folding chair to card table. The damned thing was pretty agile despite its roll of fat. Yeah, fat is beautiful, bet your ass. He watched the coon use its dainty paws to select pieces of crust from the foil pan. Uh-oh, here comes the rest of the gang, Dolly and Dingo crawling from under the sagging bed and hurrying up to share the spoils. That's it, guys. Enjoy. He heard the whisper of paws across the parquet, and saw Fellatio stalking over behind the coons, tail held high.

"What is this?" Kellogg complained. "You'd think I never fed any of you. Shall I get Oscar too?" Glancing at the terrarium, he picked out the snake's brown-and-black camouflage among the leaves. He reached down and scratched Fellatio's ears. A mangy cat, three fat coons, and a lazy snake. God, he loved them. They would never end up like Monk. He wouldn't let anything happen to them, ever.

He thought about Monk. It had been awful. The dog thrashing and trying gamely to bite him right up to the last, as Pete had slipped the needle into the foreleg vein. The red cylinder of sernylan had looked so ugly and final, slipping down the shaft of the syringe. He'd never forget the feel of the life going out of Monk. The cursed memory would stay in his arm muscles the rest of his life.

He remembered the pain on Pete's face. Hard to feel sorry for yourself when you saw that look on Pete. Pain—and *anger*. Who had Pete been mad at? The distemper? I wish I could have touched him, Kellogg thought. I wish I could have patted his arm or maybe squeezed his shoulder. Told him somehow that it was all right.

But it was not all right, even if Monk was only a mean,

ugly dog. Pete was the first man he'd ever met who knew that—who understood that animals were important, too, that they could hurt and suffer just like people, that you had a duty to love and care for them.

Kellogg let the cat jump up on his lap. He sighed and scratched it. He just had to forget it, that's all—the feel of Monk's limp, boneless body as he'd lugged it out to—

Damn! Kellogg sat forward, and Fellatio sprang off his lap with a vengeful dig of hind claws. Pete had said to put Monk in the *cooler*. He wanted to do a necropsy the next day, he'd said. Jesus, he'd heard Pete say it, clear as day, but he'd only remembered it just now. It didn't make sense, that's why. Why would Pete want to necropsy a *control* dog that had distemper? It couldn't be to see if the experiment—whatever it was—had made the dog sick. Control animals on scientific studies never got any treatment. That was the whole point. If a disease or something else not related to an experimental treatment went through the labs, you'd see it hit the control animals too. That way you wouldn't assume that your test animals were dropping over, or wheezing, or whatever because of the experiment. So why cut Monk open, when he wasn't even a test animal?

Kellogg groaned. Whether it made sense to necropsy Monk wasn't the point. He was just a lab assistant. Peter Morrissey might let him call him Pete instead of Doctor this and Doctor that, like all the other high and mighties around the lab, but he was still a director. Pete had told him to save the body. Instead, like a dumb fuckface, he had put it in a plastic bag and laid it out back for the disposal guys to take to the big furnace in Building 20.

Well, he'd better get his ass in gear and take care of it—if it wasn't too late.

Kellogg drove his pickup hard, pushing it over the speed limit the whole way. He pulled right up to the ramp at the back of the lab and got out. He labored, wincing, down the cement ramp toward the pool of light at the bottom, his knees pressing out pain with every step. He stopped at the bottom of the ramp. Yech, look at those bugs circling around the light over the loading doors. Just stay up there and keep away from me. He saw Monk still lying by the garbage cans, in the black polyethylene bag. Good, the night men hadn't gotten around yet.

Kellogg sat on one of the garbage cans and rested, looking down at the plastic bag. A pitiful sight. He'd sealed it up pretty good, and it had been late afternoon. The back of the building had been in shade then, so maybe the decay hadn't started enough to spoil the necropsy yet. If he could just get it inside . . .

What was that? He stared at the bag, feeling the hairs stand up on his neck. No. It hadn't moved, couldn't have moved. It was just that as he'd turned his head, the light had slid over the folds in the black bag. He was . . . there! Again! It moved again.

Kellogg stood up fast, hearing the garbage can bang over behind him. The bag was definitely moving now—shifting and oozing like something was underneath it. He gave a shaky laugh. Of course. That was it. It was only rats nosing around underneath, sniffing out a meal. Rats.

"All right, guys," he said. "That ain't nice, scaring me like that."

He saw the bag thrust up, as though electrified by the sound of his voice. The whole thing lurched away from the wall of the ramp. In the weak light from the bulb, he could just make out points standing up on the tight surface of the bag. Jesus, it was the claws! He watched, paralyzed, as the brown forelegs ripped through.

Monk was alive! He had not died when Pete put the needle in! But that was impossible!

The dog thrashed and tore free of the plastic. Kellogg watched dumbly as it rose smoothly to its feet and darted a few steps up the ramp. It's blocking me, he thought. That's the only way out, up the ramp. He felt fear sliding through him, slick as an eel. *No, no, stay calm*. He looked at the dog and saw light glinting off the insides of its eyes, red-orange. It didn't move. It didn't move at all. The light was steady on its ribbed flanks. He saw that its muzzle was closed—thank God for that, at least. He stared at it and it stared back, as cold and still as a statue.

Maybe he should try talking to it. "Okay, boy—"

The Doberman leapt. He saw its muscles bunch, heard the tick of its claws leaving the pavement, and then its dark shape filled his vision. He flung his arms halfway up, deflecting it just a little, and it barely hurt, the fang puncturing his throat cleanly then slipping out as he pushed it on past. He filled his lungs to scream, but no sound came, just a cold whistle of air through the hole in his windpipe. *Run!* he thought. He pushed forward, feeling the anchoring weight of meat around his legs. The Doberman rebounded from the wall and darted around in front of him, blocking his way again.

He lumbered toward the dog, the air burning in his throat. The Doberman sidestepped easily, and he felt a blow and a sharp pain above his heel, as though someone had chopped him with an ax. He struggled a bit farther, hopping on the one leg before the dog hit him behind the knee, bringing him down. The dog was unreal, it was a fucking demon! Kellogg's lungs pumped, trying to get the scream out.

The dog attacked again. He felt it hit his back, tear at his spine, and he rolled trying to get his hands on the thing's throat—there, got it! He squeezed the throat with all his strength. The dog waited, its eyes on him. It pressed in patiently against his arms. He saw its face closing to within a foot of his, then inches. His arms felt heavy as lead.

The mouth of the Doberman opened slowly, as though it was deliberately drawing out the moment. *No, no, no, no.* The dog's head disappeared from view, and he felt the awful teeth begin to chew his neck.

Everything blurred. The pavement softened against his spine. Pain flared at his throat, and he flopped around until he was on his stomach and the pain stopped. He felt one paw, then two, standing on his back. He heard crickets chirping, very loud above him, a vivid peaceful sound. Before his eye slipped shut, he saw the pavement stretching down. Liquid ribbons gleamed darkly as they unrolled from under his chin toward the halo of light at the bottom.

It was beautiful, a nice end to the dream.

25
DAYS

Friday, October 17

Chapter 4

0830 hours:

Colonel Hagan recognized Tchebychev the moment the Russian walked into the Dulles customs area. Hagan's right hand, buried in his pocket, tightened uneasily around the cigarette lighter. He gave a wry grunt at the tiny spasm of nerve. That's what years of sitting behind a desk did to you. Truth was, he wasn't worried about the lighter.

No, the problem was going to be the exchange.

Hagan eased back from the velvet rope and let the crowd waiting to greet the passengers close around him. Between their heads he watched Tchebychev join the line leading to the centermost of the five customs tables. No doubt the Russian felt safest there, surrounded by the incoming passengers who milled and stretched with post-flight relief, spewing visual noise all around him.

Hagan smiled and waved at an imaginary passenger. In the old days, he thought, we'd have gone through channels and I'd be stepping out of that office over there with a customs uniform on. I'd relieve the official in Tchebychev's line and that would be that. Hagan rubbed a palm along the smooth, hard back of his head, dropping his hand in distaste when it encountered the roll of wrinkles at the base of his skull. These were not the old days. He was no longer a young buck in his fifties working with the general in Defense Intelligence. As for the general, he'd been kicked upstairs to Chairman. They had no standing to do this, none at all.

But he was damned well going to do it anyway.

Tchebychev had moved closer now. Hagan studied him. The Russian looked just as Smith had described him, right down to the rumpled gray suit. If Tchebychev hadn't left his airline tickets in the pocket of that very suit while taking his pleasure with a certain whore, he could now be entering the States unnoticed. His cover of factory official would excite no interest among the customs people. Tchebychev had the proper pallor to be the mid-level apparatchik his visa proclaimed. His few gray hairs were combed without spirit up over his skull. His neck was canted forward like a man who'd spent the last thirty years in his tiny office across from the Kremlin poring over a desk full of factory production reports.

Could this little weasel really be the top man in *Voyevoda*, Russia's most secret intelligence agency?

If there is a God, Hagan thought, let Tchebychev be nobody.

He considered the grim alternative. If Tchebychev *was* head of *Voyevoda*, the general would have to pass him on to the Defense Intelligence Agency and the CIA, and he couldn't do that without revealing that he'd been running his own private mole in Moscow for years. The criticism could be very harsh. Chairman's duties were limited to refereeing the Joint Chiefs, passing on resolutions watered away to nothing by service in-fighting, and playing golf every Sunday.

Hagan growled softly deep in his throat. What bullshit. He was aide to a *general*—the best damned general in a hundred years—not some figurehead chairman of the board. Stanhouse had been *right* to run the mole, right to do all the other things he'd tried when he first made Chairman—steamrolling the bickering services into closer cooperation, a true fighting machine, telling that perfumed senator from the Armed Services Committee to stick his pork-barrel contract up his ass, all the other hard, idealistic things Stanhouse had done.

But that was over now, no matter how the Tchebychev matter turned out. Since Elaine's death, the general was a different man—tired, going through the motions, waiting for retirement. If Tchebychev *was* head of *Voyevoda*, it might finish Stanhouse before he could reach retirement.

Hagan realized that his fist was again clenching the silver cigarette lighter in his pocket. He let up at once. Tchebychev was halfway along. Time to get moving.

Hagan slipped out the side of the waiting crowd and went to the door marked CUSTOMS—SUPERVISOR. He paused a bit. No good giving the supervisor too much time to think.

All right . . . now.

He scanned the room going in: small and cluttered, two-way mirror fronting on the customs lanes, a man about forty sitting at a desk. The man swung around and said, "Authorized personnel only."

Hagan flashed his expired DIA card at the man. "I want you to do something for me," he said, "and do it very quickly."

The customs man frowned and started to say something.

"Listen first. You see that man fifth back in the middle line?"

The customs man looked through the two-way mirror and nodded.

Hagan took the cigarette lighter from his pocket. "I want you to go out right now and relieve the officer at that table. When the man I showed you gets to the desk, open his briefcase. Keep the lid between you and him so that he cannot see your hands inside. You will see a lighter exactly like this one. Palm it and put this in its place."

The customs man looked at the lighter with distaste, as though it were a packet of hashish. "This is U.S. Customs, Colonel. We don't put things in people's bags."

"There's no time to argue," Hagan said. "I'm in hot pursuit of this man. It's urgent. National security."

"I don't give a shit if it's the second coming. I don't put

things in people's bags. I don't even know what the procedure would be for something like this. I've been a customs officer for twelve years, and I've never heard of any such thing."

"You're hearing of it now."

"Absolutely not. My chief would have to have a prior written order from somebody a lot higher up than you."

Hagan sighed. Of course it would come to this. He glanced out the hidden window. Tchebychev was third in line. It had to be now, before the Russian reached second. Hagan plucked the customs officer from his chair by the collar, pulling it tight to stifle the croak of surprise. He rammed the man's back against the wall and raised him until his feet dangled. The man stared at him with bug eyes and made choking noises.

"You will do what I ask now or I will break your neck, put on your uniform, and do it myself. Do you agree?"

The man nodded as much as his position would permit.

Hagan eased him down and waited until he finished coughing. "You are thinking that you can go out there, get your friends, and come right back here. You could do that. Then your boss *would* end up talking to my boss, and you would end up doing U.S. Customs out on one of those cold little islands in the Aleutians. Then I would come after you and break your neck there instead of here because you made me miss my man. Everyone would think you slipped on the ice."

The man nodded jerkily.

"Unless you do exactly what I said, you will never be safe again."

The man gazed at him, pop-eyed and solemn, and Hagan felt a bleak disgust for himself. He made his voice warmer.

"Calm down. It's all right. But you must act normal out there."

The man nodded again. He looked pale and a little sweaty, like a man with a touch of the flu. It would have to do. Hagan handed him the lighter and watched him out the door, feeling a paradoxical regret that the man had not been able to stand up to him. Now the poor bastard would never feel quite like a man again.

But if he *had* resisted, Hagan thought glumly, I would have had to hurt him, and that is not a good thing to wish.

Hagan watched the customs man through the two-way mirror. When Tchebychev reached the table, Hagan was aware of a light sweat on his own upper lip. The customs man leaned on the counter with Tchebychev's lighter doubled in one of his fists until the Russian was past. Hagan nodded, impressed. Most men would have let their arms hang awkwardly, with the one hand half-closed. The customs officer had been very smooth, and Tchebychev had noticed nothing.

Fear might not be the best teacher, but it was the fastest.

Outside the air terminal, Tchebychev got into a waiting van with District plates. Hagan noted the impenetrable windows, silvered over with a forest scene. His heart began to pound.

He walked without hurrying to his car and caught up with the van at the parking exit gate. He flipped on the machine beside him on the seat. There was a steady crackle of static, as impervious as the van's windows.

They were jamming!

That settled one thing. Tchebychev was not a minor bureaucrat on vacation.

Who was he with now in the back of that van?

Hagan paid off his parking stub and pulled out behind the van, staying well back on the long, straight Dulles access road. He watched the Virginia farmland roll by and prayed that the tiny recorder inside Tchebychev's lighter was rolling too.

General George Stanhouse gazed over the emerald-green lawns sloping down away from his office window to the lush wall of trees. He imagined the brown coil of the Potomac beyond, lazy and soothing. It did not soothe him.

Too many things were going haywire all at once.

The worst was Alan Vandiver.

Stanhouse rubbed at his arms, feeling the light ache of

weariness in his bones. He'd let Alan down terribly. But what could he have done? The Deputy Secretary had sprung his nasty little coup too close to the meeting for him to even warn Alan. Alan had saved his son's life on that operating table in 'Nam, and now this was his reward—ruin.

Even worse, there was this damned Tchebychev thing to weigh him down.

Suddenly Stanhouse wanted a cigar. He thought of the half-filled humidor of Punch Coronas in his bottom desk drawer. It had been so long—three years since Elaine had persuaded him to quit smoking. He remembered the way her jaw would set when he'd light up. She wouldn't yell, or even argue about it. For years he'd tried to provoke a good honest fight on the subject. Then he'd given up the damned things and the hacking and spitting that went with them, and she'd been so pleased that she'd gone out and bought him a brand new set of golf clubs.

Stanhouse pulled the drawer half-open. Elaine wouldn't know now.

He eased it shut again and sat very still until the dull ache in his throat went away.

He forced his mind back to Tchebychev. Why had he sent Hagan out today? he wondered. He did not want to hear from Smith and Moscow. All those years when I cared, I never heard from Smith, Stanhouse thought. And now he pops up from his burrow with something like this.

If Tchebychev *was* who Smith said he was, it could only be bad. What mission could be so vital as to force the head of Soviet military intelligence into the field?

Stanhouse felt a trickle of interest. It passed quickly.

He gazed out the window. He would turn whatever he learned over to the DIA and take the flack. In fact, he'd do it even if he learned nothing. Just call Smith in from Moscow, take all the blame for running the unorthodox little spy game, and sit quietly through the tongue-lashings.

It didn't matter.

Stanhouse heard the door to his study open and turned. Hagan strode straight through to the safe-room door and held it open for him.

Just like that—the safe room. No small talk.

Stanhouse was suddenly afraid. He wanted a cigar again, badly. He could almost taste the rich smoke, feel the pacifying meat of the butt between his jaws. Instead of giving in, he followed Hagan into the tiny, windowless room. He sat across from his aide and watched him take the tape from his briefcase and put it in the machine on the table. There was something different about Hagan today. The fierce physical presence was there, as always. His bald, bullet-shaped head glowed under the ceiling lights with the vitality of well-kept leather. His shoulders bulged beneath the uniform, mountaintops for the silver eagles. But the scar beside his mouth was inflamed. No, his face had gone pale around it.

Hagan was scared!

Stanhouse's throat went dry. Hagan, scared? Never, in thirty-five years.

"Tchebychev left his briefcase in his hotel room when he went to lunch," Hagan said. "I switched the lighters back and dumped the tape onto a cassette so we could play it on this machine, and—"

Now Hagan was chatting! "For God's sake, man! What is it?"

"Tchebychev *is* head of *Voyevoda.*"

"And?"

"It's best you just listen."

Stanhouse started to lean forward on the table, then saw it was covered with dust. He held back from touching it, not wanting to disturb the slumbering archaeology of the room. Three years as Chairman, he thought. And I've never had to step into this room. Why on *my* watch? Whatever this is, why couldn't it have waited until after the election?

Because you ran Avery Smith, fool.

The tape began to roll. It was voice-activated, with those odd compressions between sentences. Stanhouse concentrated on translating from the Russian:

". . . not necessary to X-ray that," said a soft, weary voice. "It was a gift from a friend."

"Tchebychev," Hagan said. "He's talking about the lighter."

"And besides, I had it X-rayed in Moscow the day I got it."

In spite of himself, Stanhouse felt pity for Tchebychev. An old man, carrying a lighter from one of Smith's prostitutes and calling her his friend. It made him feel dirty, like a voyeur. He had set this up, from his nice clean Pentagon office. Tchebychev was his age. Was the Russian lonely too? Yes. So lonely he'd had the lighter fluoroscoped and X-rayed and electronically sanctified and then kept it, because even a shadow of love was a powerful thing.

"Excuse these precautions, Comrade Tchebychev." Another voice, dry and grave. Stanhouse found it startlingly familiar. He saw Hagan looking expectantly at him.

"Dobrynin?" he asked, incredulous.

"None other. The Ambassador himself, hidden away in the back of a sport van with enough screening, jamming, and de-lousing gear to clean out an embassy."

"No need to apologize," Tchebychev said. "You are quite right to be careful."

"Finished, Excellency," said a third voice. "You are clean. It is impossible for anyone to eavesdrop either—"

"Fine, fine," Dobrynin cut in. "You may go back up front now."

"The technician," Hagan explained.

"Now then, Comrade," Dobrynin said. "To what do I owe this honor?"

"Listen carefully. We must get this over quickly. At this point, Comrade Charnov, Comrade Ravanchev, Marshall Petrochevsk, and I are the only ones who know what I am about to tell you. The Americans have no idea who I really am, which is why I was able to come. But I must get away from you quickly, and we will not be seen together again. I'm going to attend that factory exhibition in Baltimore just in case anyone does pick up on me, and then I am going home."

"I understand, Comrade."

"If Maxwell Howard wins the election, we are going to launch a pre-emptive strike against the Americans," Tchebychev said.

Stanhouse swore and punched the recorder off. His hand seemed to act on its own. He was suddenly very cold. He tried to push away from the table but the wall stopped his back. He forced himself to turn the recorder on again. He heard Dobrynin gasp. "Comrade, you are joking!"

"Be silent and listen. I am telling you this now for two reasons. First, we plan to strike because we are determined not to see the madman hawk Maxwell Howard become President. Our statisticians yesterday confirmed that Howard is almost sure to beat Maddock in November. Therefore, you must be informed so that you can be ready to play your part."

"But if—"

"Second, I'm telling you now so that you'll have time to secretly destroy all classified material in the embassy and prepare your wife and niece to go with you on a visit home to begin November first."

"What about the other embassy personnel?" Dobrynin's voice was shaking.

"We can speak of that later, Comrade."

They'll be lost, Stanhouse thought distractedly. In spite of himself he was sad for Dobrynin. The Deputy Ambassador, the Charge d'Affaires—all the others he'd spent so much time with—blown up by their own missiles, just so the Americans would suspect nothing right up to the last. And this madman Tchebychev wanted Dobrynin to destroy embassy documents. The documents would be vaporized. The whole city would be vaporized.

Stanhouse thought of Elaine's grave in Arlington Cemetery, the stone shattered into dust, the grass burnt away. Perhaps the graves would burst open . . . He moaned and bent over the desk. He felt Hagan's hand on his wrist.

"This is madness," Dobrynin was saying. "I must go home at once and talk to Charnov."

"Durak!" Tchebychev hissed. "You will *not* go home—not until November first. Bad enough that we have to revise that from your usual vacation time in December. Why do you think I came all the way here instead of recalling you to Moscow? You are the Americans' window on us. You will

do nothing, absolutely nothing out of the ordinary. You will be your usual urbane and soothing self. You will go to all embassy functions, perform all your duties in the usual way."

"But—"

"Comrade Dobrynin." Tchebychev's voice had a deadly flatness. "It would have been easiest and safest to say nothing about this to you. I am here now, at a certain risk, because of your long and devoted service to the state. But you must not overestimate yourself. I said that only Marshal Petrochevsk, Comrades Charnov, Ravanchev, and I know of the pre-emptive strike. There was one other—General Rasnoi."

"Rasnoi! But he just died in that automobile crash . . ."

There was a gap on the tape, and Stanhouse realized that Dobrynin must have uttered some small sounds of distress—just enough to activate the mike without registering on the tape.

"General Rasnoi protested to Secretary Charnov as you wish to do," Tchebychev said. "He protested too strongly. This is done, Comrade. Accept it. Do your duty."

Hagan punched off the recorder. "That's all of any consequence," he said.

Stanhouse stared at the recorder. He felt sweat rolling down hot against the cold of his face. A pre-emptive nuclear strike. The Pentagon experts had been predicting it, warning of it, and here it was.

And there was no protection.

That's what Project Parasol was all about, but the Deputy Secretary of Defense had just gutted Project Parasol. If Maddock lost, America would die on Election Day.

And Maddock was losing.

"You bastards," he choked. "You dirty filthy bastards." He felt Hagan's hand on his shoulder.

"Are you all right, General?"

Stanhouse didn't answer at once. He tried to make his brain work. Thank God Tchebychev's trip had come to their attention through a single mole, unknown to the Soviets. He and Hagan were the only Americans who knew the Russians' secret at this moment. The information on the tape was deadly. A single leak, a single sign that the Americans knew the plan, and the Kremlin would not dare wait for the election. They would strike at once.

Stanhouse pressed his hands against his face. He must tell the President, right away. But the burden would remain squarely on his own shoulders. This is nuclear war, he thought. My field. I'll be in it to the end.

"I'm all right," he said to Hagan.

He clasped his hands together to stop them from trembling.

Chapter 5

0900 hours:

This is it, Vandiver thought.

He faced the wall of the radiation chamber, trying to thumb away the sweat on his fingertips. His shoulders were so tense they sent shooting pains to the back of his skull. He felt as if a bomb were ticking in his chest, ready at the slightest nudge to blow him into a hundred pieces. He was acutely aware of old Hisle, behind him there in the dark, watching him. Bad form, letting Hisle see how shaky he was.

But by the Virgin, so much rode on the outcome: his career, the future of Project Parasol, possibly the lives of millions of Americans.

Vandiver drew a slow, deep breath and smelled the lingering odor of the rats now sealed away inside the chamber's lead walls. He held the air in, feeling it boil together with the blood in his lungs. Then he eased it out, feeling calmer. Good. One last check of the equipment and then it was on.

He looked at the TV screens. Both showed sharp pictures of the inside of the chamber. On the left screen were the last of his own rats, the test group, their cage draped with the new shielding material. It was beautiful, a smooth, iridescent gray, gleaming under the chamber lights like the sleek skin of a shark. It was the strongest yet, and the lightest—plenty light enough to tack up in basement ceilings. Just looking at it made him proud. They'd busted their butts to get it ready.

Now all it had to do was *work*!

Vandiver looked at Peter's rats on the other TV monitor. With nothing on top of their cage to shield them from the radiation gun or camera, they were easier to see. He watched them nose around, bumping casually into each other like wind-up toys. Poor dumb little bastards. Safe and secure an hour ago in Peter's lab, and now here, about to die.

It couldn't be helped. There had to be a control group. Their deaths were necessary to prove that the gun at the top of the chamber was, indeed, blasting both cages with radiation.

Still, he couldn't help but feel guilty looking at them. After all, he could have put them in the test cage and given *them* the chance to survive. But then he would be dooming his own rats to certain death. Strange, feeling loyal to his rats. But Peter's animals had had it good while his own had watched two hundred of their cellmates go out and never come back. It wouldn't be fair to deny these last ones a chance at living after so long a stay on death row.

Besides, why kid himself? If Peter became pissed at all, it would be because he'd taken the rats without asking.

But what else could he have done? The experiment was ready, and he had to run it at once, before the contract was officially switched to Biolog at noon. Where the devil *was* Peter, anyway? Not in his lab, not at home. It was ridiculous. Probably the first morning in eleven years that Peter hadn't been hard at work in his lab by 8:30.

The hell with it. Peter would find the note and there would be time for explanations later. There was no point worrying about it now.

Vandiver nodded a last salute to Peter's rats. He turned from the monitors and motioned to Hisle. "Let her rip, Jack."

He heard a click as Hisle closed the contact, and then silence. It seemed there should be some other sound, a deep, bone-itching thunder, as the gamma rays blasted down inside the chamber. But it was a quiet death, more silent than drowning.

He suppressed a shudder and watched the shielded cage on the monitor. The rats were still walking normally. He felt the tension building up in his neck again, the muscles squeezing down on the bone. He massaged the base of his skull. It was too soon to hope. Even if the gamma rays tore through the shield as if it were tissue paper, it would still take at least five minutes for the rats to show toxic signs and half an hour more for the first deaths.

Come on, shield—*hold*!

He checked the digital time read-out on the screen to make sure it was counting down. Yes: three minutes, twenty-nine seconds.

He looked at Peter's rats. No toxic signs yet, but it was still a little early, even for them.

He tried to make his mind blank and turn his eyes into uncaring recorders.

"Slowing down," Hisle said. Vandiver saw that he was looking at the shielded cage.

No!

Vandiver checked the time read-out: ten minutes, forty-seven seconds. Hisle was right. The test animals had stopped their exploring and were starting to stumble around. One lost its balance and leaned against the mesh. Its sides were heaving. It was trying to vomit.

Maybe it was just the one.

Vandiver looked away. When he looked back another rat was leaning on the mesh. They were all beginning to hunch with nausea, the first toxic sign, as their sensitive gut tissue hemorrhaged under the onslaught of radiation.

The ninth material was no good.

Damn it to hell!

Vandiver turned from the screen, sickened. There was no use in watching anymore. He had failed again.

He looked around the lab, desperate for a distraction. The

images came anyway: Peter and Janet herding the kids to that gloomy basement of their brownstone. Sirens howling. June and Tsong convulsed in the cellar, dying, stabbed through by something that left the steps neatly in place over their heads.

My little cherubs, he thought, agonized. A hundred million others, the same.

Those bastards, Pennylegion and Fitch. The goddamned bloodthirsty Russians. Vandiver realized his hands were clenched. He wanted to hit and smash, destroy. He crossed his arms, hiding the fists from Hisle.

Look at the old man, taking it so calmly, writing in his notebook with clinical detachment. How could he do it—go on watching every movement and twitch? He'd probably write studiously in that fornicating notebook of his until the last rat was dead . . .

Vandiver caught himself. He had no right to be angry at Hisle. He should be more like him. Hisle had never let himself hope too much, care too much. Hisle was a proper scientist.

Vandiver walked away filled with despair. He had failed utterly. He leaned on his desktop, and let his head hang.

"Grosser Gott!"

Vandiver looked up, startled. Hisle never swore, never even raised his voice! He hurried to the old man and looked with him at the control monitor—the image of the unshielded cage. His breath left him. What the devil? The control rats were alive! They were ambling around in the mesh enclosure beneath the gun as if nothing had happened.

The control rats were alive, and the *test* rats were dying!

Suddenly dizzy, Vandiver groped for Hisle's arm. Impossible! The gun was clearly working or the test rats would be all right too. But it was all backwards! By now the control rats should be prostrate, a fourth of them dead. Instead, they were acting completely normal. They continued to walk around easily, the same as when he'd first looked at them.

"Lieber Gott!"

Hisle's face was now white. His eyes had an unhealthy glaze. Vandiver took the old man's arm at last, half holding him up. "Okay, Jack take it easy." *Take it easy? Hisle was right to go into shock!*

"Colonel, what is happening here?"

"There has to be some explanation," Vandiver said. "You know as well as I do, Jack, there's no way those unshielded rats could take five thousand roetgens and live, let alone be walking around with nothing wrong with them."

Vandiver stared at the rats on the monitor screen. *A videotape, that was it.*

He felt a hot rush of anger. It was a trick. Somehow, one of the other men in the research group had recorded a tape ahead of time. It would be quite simple—the VCR equipment was already in the room, there at the base of the wall, supposedly recording the experiment now. All you'd have to do was connect it to the live monitors, put in the prerecorded tape, and switch the "record" and "play" keys. Monstrous. How could anyone call such a thing a joke?

He groped the back of the monitor. There was no VCR line wired into the set.

Vandiver's heart began to hammer. He grabbed the joysticks and panned the control camera away from its cage toward the shielded cage. The picture moved between the cages in perfect synch with his hand. It settled on the image of the shielded rats, now prostrate and twitching under the honeycomb blanket.

The scene on the monitor had to be real.

"We've done it," Hisle cackled. "We've found the perfect shielding material for Project Parasol. And it's *nothing*."

Vandiver paced up and down between the black-topped lab tables, trying to think. His mind kept slipping and sliding around the one fact: The control rats were *alive*.

And it just couldn't be.

A powerful electromagnetic force—5,000 roentgens of gamma rays—had shot through a much weaker one, the electron bonds of the rats' cells. As the rays passed through, they should have broken apart the electron bonds in their paths, slicing up the molecules of the cells, changing them, making them unable to work properly.

Vandiver suppressed a shudder. It was an obscenely subtle way to die. For a while after a lethal dose of gamma rays, a man would look the same to the naked eye. But he would be good as dead, torn across his atoms with a billion invisible, bloodless cuts. His cells, starting with the soft gut and bone-marrow tissue, would no longer work properly. He would quickly lose the ability to absorb water, digest food, make new blood cells. Tumors would rise, skin would slough, sores would break out. Infection would rage unchecked . . .

Vandiver shook his head, throwing off the appalling images. The point was, none of these things had happened to the unshielded control rats. The gamma rays had somehow passed through them without disturbing the much weaker electron bonds of the cells. That could only mean one thing. The electron bonds of those control rats were *not* weaker than the gamma rays. They had been greatly strengthened. It was a stunning idea. The most basic force of life was electricity—the attraction of electrons, filling the body, bonding its atoms together.

The very life force of those rats had been changed . . .

By Peter!

Vandiver began to pace again, struggling with this new hurdle. Peter hadn't done *anything* to those rats. They had been controls on Peter's study too—he'd made damned sure of the markings on the cart before taking it. He'd never have taken actual test rats from Peter's animal room, for fear that something already done to them would throw off the results of his own test.

And something *had* thrown off the results—thrown them straight into heaven.

Maybe Peter had made a mistake in labeling the rats.

Or maybe he had mislabeled them on purpose. Maybe he was hiding something.

Vandiver bumped into a file and stopped, looking down at it blindly. Peter *had* been putting in long hours at the lab lately—nights, evenings, far more time than his new cancer study would require. I've been so busy with Parasol, Vandiver thought, that I let it go.

He went back to the control monitor. Staring at the beautiful, fat rats ambling around, he felt another wave of jubilation. He wanted to jump up and shout and hug Hisle. There was no need to go on wracking his brain. Project Parasol was a success! The Russians were fucked!

All he had to do now was find Peter and ask him how.

Chapter 6

0930 hours:

Morrissey stared down at Kellogg's sleeping face, at the bloodstained bandage on his neck. Under the sheets Kellogg's body made a huge, still mound that almost overflowed the narrow hospital bed. His mouth sagged open with a heavy breath, releasing the smell of vomit.

Morrissey lowered his head and listened to the jagged hum of the fluorescent light above him. Sweat dripped from his face and crawled down his back through the hollow between his shoulder blades and shirt. *Fucking hospitals*, he thought, then shook his head, disappointed in himself. Twelve years had passed since Saigon. Why couldn't he get over his hatred of sick wards? It was irrational—hospitals saved lives—but there it was.

Kellogg's eyes opened. Morrissey patted him on the shoulder and forced a smile. Kellogg tried to grin back, then winced, as the muscles pulled at his throat. He mouthed some words: *Who's feeding our rats and dogs?*

"Tell me who did this," Morrissey said. He was startled by the hoarseness of his voice.

Kellogg clutched his wrist and mouthed more words.

"I don't understand."

Kellogg picked up a pad and pencil from his bed table and printed, bearing down hard: MONK.

Morrissey gazed down at the pad. *Monk.* The kid was obviously confused. "The nurse told me the police thought a mugger had attacked you with an ice pick," Morrissey corrected gently.

Kellogg pointed firmly to the pad.

Morrissey shook his head. "Monk is dead. I killed him yesterday. Remember the distemper? You—"

Kellogg thumped his arm impatiently and jabbed at the word on the tablet. *Monk. Monk. Monk.* He pointed to his neck and pantomimed strangling motions, then let his hands be pushed back toward his face by an invisible force.

Morrissey imagined the Doberman bearing down on Kellogg's throat. The hairs on his neck stood up. He rubbed them down again. This was ridiculous. The dog was dead. As soon as he got to the lab, he was going to necropsy it and see whether it had the pink band in its cells . . .

The pink band!

Morrissey groped for the folding chair by the bed and sank into it. The room slid out of focus. *L-6. Monk was an L-6 animal.* But I *did* kill him, Morrissey thought. I know when an animal is dead. Could I have made a mistake? His mind reeled. There were too many unknowns here. He must remember one thing. He hadn't seen what he'd expected at the rat cell biopsy. He'd made some assumptions about the pink band, but he didn't *know* anything.

Except that a dog that should be dead *might* be alive.

Morrissey suppressed the urge to lean forward, grab Kellogg's arm. *Just keep it casual.* "Kellogg, if Monk attacked you, where is he now?"

Kellogg started to answer, then looked past him toward the door and frowned. Morrissey looked over his shoulder. A man stood in the doorway. Short; skin very black; powerful-looking. His coat didn't fit quite right. The man reached into his jacket and produced a badge. "Detective Ambrose Cummings," he said. "D.C. police."

Morrissey had a sudden, irrational urge to run from the room. *For God's sake, relax. You haven't done anything.*

Cummings said, "Who are you?"

"Peter Morrissey. I'm a friend of Kellogg's."

Cummings's mouth quirked sardonically. "His friend, huh? Folks over at the Army Labs tell me you're his *massah*."

Kellogg made an angry noise and tried to sit up. Morrissey restrained him with a hand on the chest. "Look, Cummings . . ."

"No, I'm sorry." The detective passed a hand over his eyes. "An hour ago, I ran into some stonewalling at you gentlemen's place of employ, and I'm still a little aggravated. Tried to see the head man, name of Vandiver. He's holed up in some kind of maximum security lab. Man's posted an MP outside, a fucking gorilla, got in my face with his M-16 . . . Well, forget that, forget that. Now maybe I can get some straight answers."

Morrissey suppressed a groan. Straight answers? *Well, Officer, there's this dog Pete killed, and then it attacked me . . .*

"Your doctor says your throat is too sore for talking," Cummings said to Kellogg. "Just write on your pad, there. For the yes-no questions, use your fist just like it was your head—nod it or shake it. Okay?"

Kellogg nodded his fist.

"Okay. Did you see who attacked you?"

Kellogg wrote on the pad and handed it to the detective. Cummings read it and stared at him. "A dog did this to you?"

No! Morrissey thought.

Kellogg nodded the fist.

"A big German shepherd?"

Kellogg nodded again.

Morrissey didn't know whether to sigh with relief or curse. Kellogg had covered for him, and it could only be because he'd guessed the truth about Monk. Kellogg knew that Monk should be dead. He couldn't know about L-6 specifically, but he must have guessed that the dog had survived the injection because of something that was done to it in the lab.

"She-e-it," Cummings said. "The Perp is a pup. Okay. Doggy Draculas aren't my line. The dogcatcher'll be around to see you." Cummings took a business card from his badge case and stuffed it into Morrissey's coat pocket. "Doc, you think of anything, you give me a call." Cummings waved at Kellogg. "Stay cool, baby. No yodeling, hear?"

Kellogg gave him a grudging smile.

Morrissey watched Cummings out the door. He turned back to Kellogg and said: "Take it easy, friend. I'm going to check this out." He stood, trapped by Kellogg's expectant face, by the obvious question in his eyes.

Pete, how come Monk is alive after you killed him?

Sorry, kid. The dog might have chewed you up, and you might have covered for me, but that's still classified.

Morrissey suppressed a sigh. He had to say *something*. "Thanks for what you did with Cummings just now," he said. "You did the right thing."

Kellogg gestured for the pad. Where was it? Cummings must have taken it out with him. Morrissey handed his checkbook over and watched Kellogg write on the back. Kellogg pointed to his neck, smiling triumphantly. Morrissey read the words: "Without all those Tastykakes I'd be dead." He stared at the note, not trusting himself to look up. All that fat and blubber on Kellogg's neck. It probably *had* saved him. And now the guy could joke about it—300 pounds, not of blubber, but of heart.

Morrissey squeezed the soft, meaty shoulder. "You're a good man, Kellogg," he said. He walked out, feeling the kid's proud smile on his back like a burden.

Morrissey went straight through his lab to the cooler where he'd told Kellogg to put the dog. It was empty. He phoned the disposal room in Building 12. There was no record on their logs of any dog being collected for burning.

A flood of energy pumped through Morrissey. He paced around the room, punching his fist lightly into his palm. Kellogg's story must be true! He would have to find the dog, and fast. The city pound would be searching for a German shepherd not a Doberman. But they'd probably make a sweep—pick up any stray, including the Doberman. So he'd have to check the pound every day. If the city did find Monk, they'd keep him the usual six days and then put him to sleep . . .

With an anesthetic overdose.

Morrissey began to sweat. I've got to get there first, he thought. Or find Monk on my own. He stared at the refrigerator where the dog's corpse should have been. He blew out a pent-up breath. *L-6!*

But could there be any other explanation for this?

Damn it, yes, there could.

It could have been the anesthetic.

The sernylan he'd used to put Monk to sleep might have been too weak. Drugs lost potency after too long on the shelf. Sometimes they were no good to start with. He had to be sure it wasn't weak anesthetic that had saved Monk before he went off half-cocked chasing the dog around the city.

He could check it right now. He could overdose one L-6 rat and one normal rat. If both rats lived, he would know that the anesthetic had gone bad and lost its potency. But if the normal rat died and the L-6 rat lived . . .

Morrissey took the syringe and the bottle of sernylan from the drug cabinet and went to the animal quarters. As he came through the door, the dogs barked raucously in welcome. Poor devils. They missed Kellogg. With their good buddy Chuck in the hospital and no one there to pet them . . .

Morrissey stopped and stared at the wall where the cart of L-6 rat cages should have been. He scanned the room over and over, trying to conjure it up. It was not there.

The L-6 rats were gone!

Morrissey's eyes began to sting from the pure, filtered air of the room. The bottle of sernylan slipped from his fingers. Dimly he heard it pop on the cement floor.

There was a note on the wall. Morrissey hurried over.

Dear Peter, Sorry but I had to rip off your controls. Waited for you as long as I could. I know it screws the cancer study, but no choice. Back in my office by four. You can chew my head off then. Alan.

Morrissey stared at the note, trying to comprehend. Alan had the L-6 rats. He was using them right now. And he was holed up in Building C, where the radiation chamber was. Nothing good ever happened to an animal in that lab. What if the rats were like the dog? What if Alan was doing something deadly to them, and they didn't die?

Alan, you *fool*!

Morrissey ran out of his lab and headed for Building C.

Chapter 7

1200 hours:

What if Peter didn't want to tell him?

Vandiver stopped at the door and looked back across the radiation lab at the control monitor. Peter must have been working on those rats in secret for a reason.

Vandiver walked slowly back to his desk and sat. Before he went chasing after Peter, he'd better think this through.

Obviously Peter would be upset. Losing untreated control rats was one thing. Having your secret—and therefore illicit—research study stumbled over and wrecked by your boss was quite another.

Vandiver gave a wry grunt. Since when was he Peter's boss in anything but name? Peter was a genius—an Einstein of cellular biology. You did not boss such a man.

Peter would not be cowed or sheepish or ashamed. He'd be mad. He'd come pounding on the door any minute now, fully on the offensive.

Unless I take the high ground first, Vandiver thought. Yes, that would be the way to play it: *Why didn't you trust me, Peter?*

Vandiver frowned in surprise. By God, that's right—Peter actually *hadn't* trusted him! He shouldn't have to fake feeling hurt. And yet, he would have to fake it. The rats were alive! Project Parasol was saved. You're beautiful, Peter, Vandiver thought. You're brilliant! I don't care whether you told me or not.

As long as you tell me now.

Vandiver nodded to himself. That was the best strategy—playing to Peter's guilt. But it might take more than that. He might have to break security and talk about Project Parasol. Vandiver laughed at himself. Break security, hell. From this day on, Peter *was* Project Parasol.

Vandiver clasped his hands behind his head and gave a huge sigh, savoring his sense of release. What a long fight it had been. He'd rather have won on his own, but if he had to have help, who better than his closest friend? What if that slimy grafter Fitch had taken over the project and found the solution?

Vandiver stood. Time to go and find Peter. Hopefully he was in his lab by now. It was after noon, and he had never been this late before. The minute he discovered that his rats were gone . . .

The lab door banged open and Peter charged through.

Vandiver almost smiled—Peter looked like a crazed linebacker—and then he saw the gun. *Damn, an M-16!* Peter was holding it by the barrel like a club. The guard came barging through behind him—Corporal Carrera.

Vandiver groaned. Rick Carrera, the number-one macho guard on the base, and Peter had to take his gun. Peter was lucky Carrera hadn't busted caps all over him.

"Rick," Vandiver snapped.

The MP wheeled from Peter. "No cocksucker is going to come pushing at me—"

"Corporal Carrera!"

Carrera stiffened and dropped his arms to his sides. "Sorry, *sir*. This man demanded to see you, *sir*. I explained that this lab was off limits. One second we was talking and the next he grabbed my gun and—"

"It's all right," Vandiver said. "You can leave us now."

Carrera hesitated.

"Peter, give the gun back."

Morrissey looked down with surprise at the M-16. He gave it gingerly back to the guard. Vandiver caught the look Carrera gave Peter as he left. Pure venom.

"Where are my rats, Alan?"

Vandiver was startled by the strange expression on Peter's face. He didn't just look mad. He looked spooked. The skin around his eyes was white, and his mouth was a tight, lipless line. He practically radiated anxiety. Vandiver felt a paternal impulse to reassure him. He put an arm around Peter's shoulder, but Peter pushed it away.

Baffled, Vandiver stood back. "Easy, old buddy," he soothed. "Your rats are here, safe and sound. Come on."

He showed Peter the rats on the monitors and told him about the 5,000 roentgens. He watched from the side as Peter stared at the rats ambling around their cage. "Dear God in heaven," Peter whispered.

He's as surprised as I am, Vandiver thought wonderingly. Peter hadn't realized his rats could survive radiaticn. "What did you do to the rats, old son?"

"I can't tell you," Peter said.

Damn. Time for strategy. Vandiver tried to look hurt. "Peter, this is *us*."

Morrissey stared at the monitor. "I've got to tell you *something*, don't I?"

Vandiver shook his head slowly, as though he couldn't believe what he was hearing. Peter began to look guilty. It was working. I know him so well I could make him jump through a flaming hoop, Vandiver thought. He felt a little guilty himself but quickly suppressed it.

"You don't understand," Morrissey said. "I didn't want to put you in a tough spot. If you didn't know what I was doing, no one could blame you."

Vandiver remained silent.

"Will you promise that everything stays between us?"

Say yes, you fool! Say any damned thing that will get him talking! Vandiver groaned inwardly. If only it was that easy to fuck over your friend. "I don't know if I can promise that," he said.

"Then there's nothing I can tell you."

Vandiver thought: Time to play card two. "Peter, Peter," he said like someone reasoning with a child. "You saw the shielding material draped over those dead test rats. You don't have to guess what I'm doing here. If the Russians ever decide to hit the buttons and the missiles start falling, three-fourths of the casualties probably won't even have a singed eyelash from the explosion. It's going to be the radiation that kills them. Those rats of yours just took a huge lethal dose, and they're in there filing their tiny little nails. This is too big to be our little secret. You may have just saved about a hundred million people."

Peter gave an exasperated grunt. "Damn it, Alan, I *want* to tell you."

Vandiver felt like a jeweler steadying his hand before tapping the mallet home. Careful, he thought. Almost there. He gave Peter an encouraging nod.

"Okay," Morrissey said. "Obviously, I did do something to those rats."

"Genetic engineering?" Vandiver prompted gently.

"Yes. The idea was . . . longevity."

Vandiver waited, trying to look patient.

"This isn't easy."

"I understand."

"How much do you know about the basic theories of aging?"

"Enough not to take a girl under sixteen to bed."

Morrissey gave him a wan smile. "I think that's *eighteen*, old buddy. But to get back to my question, people age because of tiny errors that occur during each cell division. One of the main causes of these errors is radiation."

Vandiver's mind began to focus. "Radiation."

Morrissey glanced past him at the monitors. "Yeah. The background stuff that we're exposed to all the time. Sunlight, normal emissions from decay of atoms, and so on. Too low-powered to screw up the cells directly, but it causes errors during cell division. Very small errors, but they pile up over time. It would be like using a Xerox machine to make copies of copies. Each copy would look almost as good as the one before, but the fiftieth would be almost unreadable compared to the first."

"What's this got to do with those rats?"

"I'm getting to that. There's something missing in the theory. Turns out when you look at actual cell division errors in people, they're *not* exactly like a Xerox machine—not at first. The Xerox errors occur each time, starting with the very first copy. But in babies and young kids *there are no errors*, even after the fourth or fifth division."

Vandiver gave a tolerant sigh. "Babies are too young to have aged. That's obvious."

"It's *circular*. Kids haven't aged, because they're kids, because they haven't aged. Okay, kids don't *look* like they're aging. They aren't wrinkled and stoop-shouldered. But we still should find the first traces of division errors in their cells. Kids are exposed to low-level radiation from the moment they're born—and even before birth. If the errors aren't there, it has to mean something. I think it means a master gene that protects against radiation."

Vandiver looked at the monitors, intrigued. Now they were getting somewhere. The only problem was, those rats on the monitor were *adult* animals.

And Peter had changed them.

"You mean kids have this protection, then lose it?" Vandiver said.

"Yes, when the gene that controls it gets turned off."

"What would turn the gene off?" Vandiver asked.

"Puberty," Peter said triumphantly. "One day you've got your nice, tranquil, graceful child, and the next the poor kid goes fugazi with hormones. Precisely at that point, we *do* begin to see external signs of cell breakdown. Almost overnight the body looks different. Kids have crazy growth spurts, turn awkward and gangly. They have trouble controlling their muscles. The sebaceous cells break down and they get acne. Their feet and breath start to smell. We've known for a long time that hormones affect cell function. The pituitary triggers growth, the thyroid affects metabolism, and so on. But here's the best part. *Puberty is when sexual maturity comes.*'' Peter paused and looked expectantly at him.

Vandiver found the prompting look irritating. Was he supposed to guess what that last remark meant?

''If a species is going to survive by reproduction,'' Peter said, ''the parent has got to die to make room for the young. Isn't it interesting that, as soon as the kid turns sexual, we begin to see signs of aging?''

Vandiver stared at him in dawning comprehension. Could that be it? Did man really die because a gene clicked off when he reached the age of reproduction? Like salmon, Vandiver thought wonderingly. We swim upriver to spawn and then we die.

But wait: ''What about harem eunuchs—or those little boys that used to be castrated before puberty to sing in choirs. They didn't live forever.''

''It's not that simple. *Castrates* have lost their testes, true, but the pituitary and other glands are still there. The pituitary gives the first push to puberty, whether the testes are there to follow up or not. The pituitary is probably the gland that flips the gene switch.''

''I surrender,'' Vandiver said. He was wasting time asking Peter dumb questions. Peter would *not* have forgotten anything. And the theory was irrelevant anyway. Later perhaps, over a glass of Virginia Gentleman, hell, a bottle—one for each of them. They could sit and philosophize until they slid off their chairs.

Right now he had to get Peter past theory and into the hard facts. He had to find out what Peter had *done* to those rats—the nitty-gritty details—so he could do it too, to people. So he could finish Project Parasol and tell the Russians to stick their missiles up their descending colons!

''So for your experiment,'' he prompted, ''you took a genetic sample from a pre-adolescent kid.''

Peter nodded. ''And from an adult, too. I knew I had to look at pairs of the same gene—one from a child in the 'on' condition and the same gene from an adult in the 'off' condition. I used myself and Tsong so I wouldn't waste time on genes that might run in my family but not be found in all humans. Clearly, any true 'X-gene' would have to be universal to humans—and probably to all higher life forms too. Since Tsong's adopted and Vietnamese, any identical genes from the two of us would have to be universal genes. Each time I found a candidate for the X-gene, the next step was to leap-frog it over the barrier of adolescence—ease a child version into adult cells in the 'on' condition."

Vandiver stared at him, amazed. So many possible pairs to plod through. Humans had 30,000 genes. That meant an immense number of false trails. "How long have you been working on this?"

Morrissey gave him a sheepish look. "Twelve years, ever since I came to the Labs. I used the Labs computer and covered up with my cancer grants."

Vandiver groaned. "I'm going to fire you. Then I'm gonna hire you back at double your salary."

Morrissey gave him a troubled smile. "Better hold off on that. There's a big problem: I don't understand those rats. My theory dealt only with normal, low-level radiation. Prepubescent kids would die under five thousand roentgens as surely as adults."

Vandiver nodded, not listening. It doesn't matter, he thought. Obviously, something about jumping the gene over the barrier of adolescence must change it. It isn't important why. Only the effect is important. Thirty thousand genes, twelve years of searching.

And all Peter has to tell me now is which gene.

"Have you got your notes and gene charts handy?"

Morrissey looked away. "I haven't told you all of it."

"What—the gene makes your balls fall off?"

Peter gave him a bleak smile. "I wish it did. I wasn't just trying for a couple of extra years in the old folks' home, old buddy. I was trying for immortality."

Vandiver looked at him in silence. Peter's face was flushed, almost feverish. His eyes seemed to burn. Vandiver got up and walked to the monitors, looked at the L-6 rats. "I see. What did you plan to do if you made it?"

"Chemically bond the gene to a sterilizing agent."

Vandiver blew his breath out. "Holy shit."

"Yeah."

"So people could live forever or have kids, but not both."

"That's the way it would have to be."

"What about you? You have two kids. Are *you* going to take L-6?"

Morrissey groaned. "Don't ask me that. In the first place, we don't know that L-6 will cause immortality or even longevity. This radiation thing is far beyond what I expected. God knows what other side effects might crop up, good or bad."

"I need to know the gene, Peter."

"I know. I know you do. You mentioned a hundred million lives. But I'm going to see your hundred million and raise you three billion."

"Come on now, Peter, it can't be that bad."

"I hope you're right. If I didn't, I never would have started this. But this minute, and for at least the next year or two, L-6 is possibly the most dangerous thing that has ever existed. Already two things have happened—incredible side-effects that I can't explain."

"Two things?"

"I gave one of my test dogs a lethal overdose of sernalyn and it lived."

"Peter, that's fantastic!"

"Afterward, it almost killed my lab assistant."

Vandiver stared at him, struggling to catch up. "But you can't know that had anything to do with the L-6."

"No. The dog already hated him."

"Well there you are."

"There I am nothing! I don't know either way, and I won't have a hope of knowing until I find the dog."

Vandiver sat down again, feeling numb. First the rats, and now an Army Labs dog running around loose, impervious to a nervous-system poison—a *savage* dog . . .

No, it still didn't matter. The point was the Russians, the mad dog Russians and their missiles.

"Peter, even if L-6 has some side effects, it would be better than a hundred million people dying from radiation."

"For crying out loud, listen, will you? It's not just the side effects. Think what would happen if L-6 does make people immortal and it hit the papers tomorrow. There's this very simple rule in human society today: People are born and people die. But survival is the strongest urge we have. People will kill, steal, even eat one another to stay alive. If your theoretical nuclear attack happened, a lot of people would die. If L-6 works and gets out too soon—if nobody dies and people keep on being born—we're *all* fucked. Where are we going to find room to stand? If we don't kill each other for food, what's going to stop us all from starving?"

"You should have fucking thought of that to start with."

"I did think of it," Peter snapped. "It's you taking my rats I didn't think of. Alan, there can be tremendous good in this—or terrible harm. When I started, I swore I'd never let my work screw up even one person. To keep that promise, I have to keep control of L-6. Why do you think I didn't just go out and hustle up an NIH contract to do this research? There are plenty of people doing that right now, whole teams of researchers out there studying longevity under government grants, looking over each others' shoulders and reporting regularly to the people who pay the bills. If they have a breakthrough, who's going to own it? Who's going to decide what to do with it? The same guys who gave us a perfect atom bomb for World War Two and a set of fucked-up nuclear power plants thirty-five years later. I get cold chills when I think about those longevity researchers out there—especially now, with L-6. Until I'm sure, I've got to be the only one who knows that gene."

"You don't trust me." Vandiver made his voice cold.

"I *do* trust you. You're a soldier, and a damned good one. You'll do your duty as you see it. Nothing could stop you."

"What's that supposed to mean?"

Morrissey sighed. "If I show you my notes and gene charts, will you give me your word not to make any use of L-6 without my consent?"

Vandiver hesitated, agonized. Lie! He should lie like

hell. But he couldn't—not to Peter. It was damned frustrating. Peter was scared of the horizon, of theories, dire scenarios, and futuristic bogeymen. He didn't understand the real danger—the one just around the corner: the Russians and their missiles. And—not understanding—he was asking to take over command of Project Parasol.

"You know I can't promise that," Vandiver said.

"Exactly. You have to do what you think is right. Like now—refusing to give your word. If you were any other way, I wouldn't let you be my hero."

Vandiver looked away. I've got to have that gene, he thought.

"Don't look so glum," Peter said. "At this point, L-6 looks fantastic for what you want it for—radiation protection. As far as longevity is concerned, we have no proof that it does that—or anything else. If it doesn't, and if I verify that it has no bad side effects, you're in business."

Vandiver roused himself. Peter was trying. He had to make a show of faith in return—keep up appearances. "All right. I'll give you all the staff you need."

"No. The fewer people who know about this, the better."

"If you insist," Vandiver said stiffly. "I'll officially clear you under my project. When you're ready, bring the gene to me. But for God's sake, start today, now, this minute."

"You have to realize, Alan. It *will* take time. And when it's all through, I may not be able to give L-6 to you." Suddenly Peter was avoiding his eyes.

"I understand," Vandiver said.

Peter stood. "Still friends?"

Vandiver took a handful of shirt over Peter's stomach and gave it a stern tug. "You're coming to the Labs clinic with me tomorrow. I want to find out how a guy who never exercises stays so skinny."

Morrissey gave him a tired smile. "Pet tape worm," he said and walked out.

Vandiver made sure the door had locked itself. He lifted his stereo cassette player from the file drawer, inserted the

Glen Gould tape—the two-part inventions—and listened intently. The music was so intricate and yet so clean. He tried to follow both melodies at once, pressing his forehead in concentration. No, he couldn't do it. For some reason, the little failure irritated him more than usual. He slid his fingers to his temples, massaging, contenting himself with just listening to the blend, the fitted whole that the two independent melodies made together. If only he and Peter could mesh so neatly in Project Parasol.

But no. They were trapped in a song with no harmony.

Vandiver watched the bluish light from the monitors behind him flicker faintly across the papers on his desk. What was he going to do? It took Peter twelve years to find the right gene. You could autopsy Peter's L-6 rats, tear them down to their component cells, and still not know which gene was doing the work. To get L-6, you'd have to start over from scratch—twelve more years, if you were lucky.

That was unacceptable. Completely unacceptable.

Which gene was it? The computer would not have that information. Peter would never be that careless.

That made Peter's L-6 notes the key. They would reveal the procedures and identify the L-6 gene.

Where would Peter keep the notes? Possibly in his office safe, or perhaps at home. Wherever they had been before, they would be locked up now. Yes, he'd seen that in Peter's eyes just before he'd left: a sudden *purposeful* urgency to get back to his own lab.

Vandiver turned off the music and reached for the phone.

He pulled his hand back. He shut his eyes and pressed his knuckles against the lids, showering his brain with sparks. Somewhere in Kamchatka, a Russian colonel sat in a missile silo right now, his fingers poised over the buttons. If he touched those buttons, Americans would die slowly, bleeding from the nose and mouth, skins sloughing. Fever, convulsions.

Vandiver picked up the phone again and dialed an unlisted number in the Pentagon. Surprising, how it had stayed so firmly in his memory. When they'd given it to him at the start of Project Parasol, he'd never thought he'd need it, and now here he was, about to use it to betray his best friend. God damn, God bloody damn.

He heard one ring and then the phone was picked up.

"Charlie's Pizza, may I help you?" A man's voice.

"This is Colonel Vandiver."

"Just a minute, Colonel."

Vandiver waited, rubbing at the patch of hair on the back of his head, feeling its whiteness as though he had eyes in his fingertips. He began to knead the tight muscles of his neck with punishing force.

No, he couldn't go through with this.

But he *had* to.

He thought about the layout of Peter's brownstone, the room where they'd sat so many nights playing chess. The room with Peter's safe.

"All right, Colonel," the same voice said. "Your line checks. Go ahead."

"I'll need a man," Vandiver said. "Someone good with safes." He hung up the phone. He sat for a long time with his face in his hands.

24
DAYS

Saturday, October 18

Chapter 8

0730 hours:

General Stanhouse stood in Elaine's closet. Walking in, he'd stirred the air, and now he could smell her: sweet Lily of the Valley perfume from her dresses; cedarwood; hair spray. There under the naked bulb her wig perched on the Styrofoam head. He touched the silver-blue strands, carefully coiffed for the next trip to the Fort Myer Officers' Club. His throat ached and he swallowed.

Get out, he thought.

Instead he ran a hand over the satiny shoulder of the sarong he'd gotten her in Singapore, suppressing a shudder at the thin bone of hanger beneath. A vivid image came: her sitting in the peacock chair on the hotel veranda. Yes, it had been this dress. How regal she'd looked.

"I started smoking again," he said softly. "If I could tell you why, I know you'd understand."

He turned abruptly and walked through the silent house to the helicopter that waited on his lawn.

Twenty minutes later he sat with Hagan in the safe room behind his office wall. He fingered a tight circle on the tabletop, around and around. He felt dull, almost witless.

He had to start, but what was there to say?

There would be a searing flash on the horizon. If George or little Todd looked at it, it would blind them. Then the burst of gamma rays, silent, painless at first, ripping their skin, throats, and stomachs to slowly dissolving mush. Then the shock wave, smashing down trees and houses. Thousands of people would be killed by flying glass alone. Perhaps Linda would die that way, the big bow windows in her kitchen slashing inward. Then would come the firestorm. If they survived the first hour, they would be unlucky, so unlucky.

Damn you, Charnov.

Stanhouse looked with envy across the table at Hagan. Hagan seemed to have pulled himself together nicely. He seemed composed, almost bored, as though they were here to discuss the latest promotion list.

"How did your meeting with the President go?" Hagan asked.

Stanhouse pulled one of the Punch Coronas from his pocket and clamped the tip between his jaws, thinking about Warren Maddock's face, the pain at that instant of understanding. *Mr. President, if you lose, we all die.*

"Did you have any trouble convincing him?" Hagan persisted.

"No. His shorts were already riding up over some new CIA reports. Soviet military 'maneuvers' on NATO borders. Civil-defense drills in Moscow and other Russian cities. Stuff like that. The Tchebychev tape hit him very hard."

"Did he have any ideas?"

Stanhouse lit the cigar and drew a sweet wad of smoke into his lungs. He snorted it out again. "Ideas? Yeah. He wanted to publicly warn the Russians that we knew their plan. I had to talk him out of it."

Hagan cursed softly. "Politicians. Might as well ask the Reds to hit us today."

"Maddock will be no help," Stanhouse agreed. "But I don't think he'll be a hindrance. He agreed to restrict knowledge of this to the three of us, at least for now, which is vital. He's ordered me to think of options for his immediate consideration.''

Hagan grunted. ''He ordered you to think about it. Good thing. Wouldn't want it slipping your mind.''

Stanhouse didn't smile. ''I see only three options, and none of them is worth a damn. One: We could hit the Russians first. We'd have more survivors that way, but a lot of innocent Russians would be dead. The body count in civilians would be at least twice as high. And we'd still be blotto ourselves.''

''Maddock would never go for it,'' Hagan agreed.

''No. Option two: Project Parasol—a total snafu. Army Labs is out and those three-martini types over at Biolog haven't even started up yet. We're talking twenty-four days now, then the election. Even if Biolog delivered a good shielding material the first week, we couldn't mass-produce it in time.

''So that leaves us with option three: Maddock might win the election.''

''You think so?''

''Hell no.'' Stanhouse tipped his chair back and rested his head against the wall. He watched the smoke from his cigar roil at the ceiling like a wraith trying to flee the dark, pressurized room. The effort to suppress a yawn pulled his face into a grimace. So tired. And so goddamned helpless.

''We're on the prisoner truck, General, but we're not dead yet.''

Stanhouse looked at his aide, startled. Hagan had never mentioned that, not in thirty-five years. *The prisoner truck!* He thought: Hagan, old friend, if only you could get us out of this one too. ''Have I missed something?'' he said.

Hagan gave him a measuring look. ''I see two additional options. One: You persuade Governor Howard to withdraw his candidacy.''

''I considered that. But do you realize what kind of capital Howard might try to make out of something like this? 'Maxwell Howard, the man the Russians don't want for President.' If he refused to be persuaded, and then tried to use it politically, we could all be dead an hour later.''

"Yes."

Stanhouse grunted. "I can't wait for two."

"Two: Assassinate Howard."

The hairs stood up along Stanhouse's arm and neck. Hagan couldn't be serious!

But he was.

Stanhouse closed his eyes, unnerved by the cold-blooded look on Hagan's face. They were on the brink of a precipice now. He could lose control of Hagan in an instant. He'd wanted his old friend to get him out of this one, too, and Hagan was ready—with the same solution he'd used thirty-five years ago.

His eyes still closed, Stanhouse remembered: December 1944. The Ardennes. They'd slung sandbags around some farmer's granary and used it as a bunker. The early morning had been bitterly cold—too cold to sleep. He could feel it all again, smell it: straw dust clogging his sinuses, air smoky from the fire they kept going in the oil drum. All night long, cold and miserable, trying to doze coiled down inside his sleeping bag. Early morning, the pressure in his bladder too great to ignore any longer. Going out from the bunker into a world that was white all around. There was no horizon; trees only a few yards away undulated on the eye like tall ghosts. He almost tripped over Hagan, who squatted still as a rock, leaning forward on his M-1 butt like it was an extra leg.

"What are you doing out here?"

Hagan did not answer. Stanhouse saw that he was well powdered with snow. He must have been out there quite a while. He grunted with irritation. Any ordinary man would be shivering. But look at Hagan, sitting there like a statue. "I asked you a question, Sergeant."

"Listening," Hagan replied without turning.

Stanhouse stared at his back. What could you say to that? Listening? To what could Hagan be listening? The whisper of the falling snow. "I almost pissed on you."

"It wouldn't be the first time, Lieutenant."

"Well, get your smart ass back inside before you freeze."

Hagan didn't move. Stanhouse walked a few more steps and fumbled himself into the cold, let out a golden arc that steamed as it hit the snow. He shivered at the lost warmth. "You hear me, Hagan?"

"I hear you, Lieutenant. And I hear the Germans, too."

Stanhouse held back his retort, listening. Absurd. He heard nothing. "Okay. You listen to the Germans, then you come back inside and tell us what they said."

"Tanks," Hagan said. "A lot of them. The snow is damping most of it, and they've lubed the treads, but it's too cold to stop all the squeaks."

"You're crazy, Sergeant."

"And you're a shitbrain, sir—off the record."

Stanhouse felt his face redden. Insubordinate bastard! "Is that right, *Corporal* Hagan? And that's *on* the record."

The German forces spearheading the Battle of the Bulge swept them up half an hour later.

They were herded into the backs of trucks, and a German officer who spoke fluent English explained that they would all be taken to stalags where, with any luck, they would sit out the rest of the war in perfect safety. Stanhouse found himself pushed up next to Hagan in the crowded prisoner truck. "Why aren't you ten miles from here and still running?" he asked.

Hagan looked at him. "I wanted to see your face."

Stanhouse laughed before he could stop himself. Who was this guy? Errol Flynn? "You'll be seeing a lot of my face—up close. Those German stalags are going to be crowded after today."

"No they aren't," Hagan said.

"You think they're going to *kill* us?"

Hagan didn't answer. Stanhouse stared at him. His teeth began to chatter and he bit down hard, trying to stop it. He felt his stomach shrink back against his spine. Shameful. Hagan would see how scared he was and feel contempt for him.

What did it matter?

Dead. In a few hours, that is what they would all be. The thought was strangely numbing. For a while it actually insulated him. He felt only the jouncing of the truck while time slipped away. We've got to escape, he thought at last. But he still felt numb, almost paralyzed. He was safe this second, and the next and the next, as long as he huddled against the other men and didn't move.

But what would happen at the end of those seconds? The Germans would empty the truck and set up the machine gun. He would stand there, unable to move or speak. He shuddered, seeing himself sinking down in the snow and taking the bullets on his hands and knees like a whipped dog.

He must do something. He would rush the two German guards at the tailgate. He would lead a desperate charge. He felt the nerves twitching in his legs, but his muscles wouldn't follow. They hung like dead meat on his bones.

The truck slowed. God help them, now it was coming. He saw a blur beside him—Hagan drawing a knife from his combat boot, slicing a hole in the canvas. With a shock he felt Hagan's arm around his neck, and then they were both flying back-first through the hole. The snowy bank slammed into his spine and he tumbled, arms and legs out of control. He heard firing start up in the truck. Horrible screams faded into the muffling curtains of snow.

He felt a pain in his arm, Hagan jerking him up, and then they were running headlong into the trees. The firing went on behind them until there were no more screams. Stanhouse put all of his will into his legs, churning through the snow, seeing only the green blot of Hagan's back. Finally Hagan stopped and signaled quiet. Stanhouse held his breath and listened. There was no one behind them. The Germans hadn't even chased them. Two men stumbling through a snowstorm in the forest weren't worth the delay. Anyway, they would soon freeze or starve.

But this minute they were alive, and all because of Hagan!

Meek and grateful, Stanhouse let Hagan lead. They groped through the forest, hour after hour, long into the night. They drank snow and ate nothing. Stanhouse could not stop his teeth chattering. He was hungry and exhausted, and he couldn't feel his toes anymore. It was so dark. Where were they? Lost, hopelessly lost.

Then they came up on the German tents.

For a few minutes, they lay flat in the snow, watching the encampment. There were two sentries, one of them only twenty yards away. Thank God for the snow, the sweet, blessed snow. Without it, the guard would have heard them stumbling toward him in the dark, and they would now be dead.

Stanhouse watched the German's breath streaming up in slow plumes that glittered through a shaft of moonlight. "We'll go around them," he whispered.

"We need their food," Hagan said.

"I'm in command and I . . ." Stanhouse peered around him, dumbfounded. Where was Hagan? He could not have vanished so quickly, so soundlessly. Stanhouse looked back at the camp, and went still with terror. There Hagan was, gliding among the tents! He would get them both killed for sure.

Stanhouse watched, horrified, as Hagan cut the two sentries' throats. The sergeant slipped into the tents, one by one. He came out of the last tent and motioned. Stanhouse got up and stumbled toward him. What was that on his chin? Blood, coursing down his throat into his shirt! Hagan looked like a vampire. Dear God, had he actually torn the German throats with his teeth? Stanhouse swallowed hard to keep from vomiting.

Then he saw that it was a wound, a bayonet slash. Some instinct must have wakened the last sleeper almost in time, and he'd stabbed up with his bayonet, slicing Hagan from the lower chin through the cheek. Hagan's molars had stopped the point.

Hagan seemed oblivious of the wound. He wolfed the rations from the packs of the dead men, ignoring the blood that poured along his chin. Stanhouse was too shaken and sick to join him, but he finally let the sergeant force some tinned salt herring down him. Hagan insisted that they leave the jeep and continue on through the forest on foot. Stanhouse followed him, trusting his certainty, the uncanny inner reckoning he seemed to have.

Late the next day Hagan joined them up with other regrouping Americans.

Hagan had saved them both. Hagan was a hero. There were medals, a battlefield commission to lieutenant, articles in the *Stars and Stripes*. But the one thing Stanhouse knew he would never forget was the way Hagan had looked flowing among the gray tents of the Germans, never a sound, like the dark Israelite angel of death . . .

Stanhouse looked across the conference table at Hagan. So many years ago. To save them, to feed them and give them the strength to go on, Hagan had killed in cold blood. Now he was readying himself to do it again. *Murder Maxwell Howard.*

Stanhouse realized his face and shirt were wet with a guilty sweat. You thought of it, too, he reminded himself. Last night. You know you did. And is it really so different from what you let Hagan do in that forest?

"General?"

The colonel was giving him a worried look. Those eyes, so hard and sharp. If only he could see through them to the brain. In there, wrapped in the layers of years, was a young soldier who had ignored his command in order to save their lives. And now there was this bull-necked old man who might sit in the shadows of some deserted office, well back from the window, his eye against the scope of a high-powered rifle. Centered in that scope would be the head of a presidential candidate.

Stanhouse blotted the sweat from his face. He must be very firm with Hagan now. He must leave no doubt. This was *not* the same. The Germans had been the enemy, out there in that forest to kill them. Howard was a countryman. He would probably be the next President of the United States, if only for a few hours. The people would choose him. Even if it meant they were choosing their own annihilation, they must not be robbed of that choice, or there *was* no United States.

"I forbid you," Stanhouse said.

"Yes, General."

With relief Stanhouse watched Hagan settle back in his chair.

But was the idea really dead? Or would it linger in

Hagan's mind and gather force? What would happen if they could do nothing and the days ticked down and the only alternative to killing Maxwell Howard was the deaths of more than 100 million Americans?

Stanhouse put the thought from his mind. Now, this minute, he could do nothing about it. He would just have to watch Hagan.

What was next? Hagan's first option. Persuade Howard to withdraw. Stanhouse said, "Find out where Governor Howard is going to be campaigning today."

"Michigan."

"All right. It looks like our only chance. I'll get up there and talk to him. Hopefully, he'll have the sense to keep quiet, one way or the other."

The measuring look was back on Hagan's face. "If you're seen, it will look bad. Hadn't you better clear it first with the President?"

"No. The President can't do this, and he could never let himself order me to do it. But it's got to be—" Stanhouse stopped, stared at his aide. Was this what it had been like for Hagan that night, thirty-five years ago? Knowing what had to be done, knowing that the man he was sworn to obey would forbid it?

No, it had been worse, much worse for Hagan. Hagan had had to cut sleeping men's throats.

"You were saying, sir?"

"I was saying I can't leave this to Maddock. It's my turn, old friend. My turn to be the sergeant."

Hagan stood. "I'm sorry it had to happen, General."

"So am I."

Clapping and cheering filtered through the walls of the caboose. Stanhouse sat up straighter, bracing himself. The governor's speech was over, and the people of Battle Creek liked Maxwell Howard. He would sit down there, across the table, in just a few seconds, flushed with the sound of their adoration. Miserable goddamned timing.

The door opened and the governor slipped in, shook his hand, and sat. Stanhouse felt Howard's firm grip lingering on his palm. Surprising how uncallused the skin was for a man who claimed to split wood for exercise.

The candidate's face was creased with its familiar lopsided grin. "Well, General, this is a happy surprise."

"Thank you, Governor, but I'm afraid it's not so happy."

"Oh?"

Stanhouse watched Howard's face remold itself, the smile receding and the eyes turning watchful. "Governor, I'm going to come straight out with this. It's going to take time to absorb. Hell, if someone told me what I'm about to tell you, I don't know if I could get it to sink in."

"I think you'll find I'm a fairly fast study," Howard said dryly.

Stanhouse said: "I've come to ask you to step down from the race."

"Whoa, General." Howard stared across the table at him. Stanhouse felt the train jerk and begin to roll, picking up speed.

"I came to you entirely on my own," Stanhouse said. "President Maddock does not know I'm here. He *does* know what I'm about to tell you. He and three other men in this country know. Stanhouse paused. He was putting it melodramatically. But maybe that was the best way to reach this man.

He told Howard the rest of it. When he finished, he became aware of his knees trembling under the table. If Howard misused the information, they would all die.

Howard's face was rigid with chill resistance. "You can't seriously believe this, General."

Terrific, Stanhouse thought grimly. "Governor, I can't do anything else."

"What you're telling me is outrageous—almost as outrageous as what you're asking me. Even if I accept that this Tchebychev said it, have you considered that the Russians could be conning you? That they might have fabricated and then leaked this whole thing, knowing someone would come to me with this proposition?"

Stanhouse struggled for patience. "Yes, Governor Howard. It's one of the first things I considered. But think what a risk it would be for them, leaking something like that to us in advance. They'd never do it. They'd be too afraid Maddock would strike them first instead. They'd be wrong, but that's the way they think."

Howard shook his head. "General, I'm going to give you the benefit of the doubt. You seem sincerely to believe this. But I don't. And even if I did, I don't see how I could step down. You're suggesting that we let the Russians dictate who our next President will be. In which case we might as well declare ourselves another puppet state of Russia, like Poland or Czechoslovakia. I can't be a party to that, and you shouldn't either. Frankly, I'm surprised that you, a military man, would let yourself react in this way."

With an effort, Stanhouse held himself straight. It was no use. But he must try once more. "Governor, they have us militarily. You've been saying so yourself. And you've been promising to regain weapons *superiority*."

"And, by heaven, I *will*—if I win this election. And you should be the gladdest man anywhere to know it, especially after what you've told me."

Stanhouse felt despair. I've said all I can say, he thought. I've said more than I had any right to say. In a way I agree with him. Except for the bottom line.

The train slowed beneath him as the steady hum of the wheels broke into distinct measured clacks. "Will you think about it?" he said. "Consider the alternatives if you're wrong?"

"I'm not wrong, General. And let me just caution you about letting this leak in order to damage me, associate me with nuclear destruction—"

Stanhouse held up a hand. *Thank God for that at least.* "No one will do that, Governor. Not us or you."

Howard nodded firmly. "Agreed. I'm going to run, General, and run hard. If I'm elected, I'll deal with any Russian threat. And I'll make sure that our military leadership feels the same way." The candidate stood. "My aide told me you wanted to slip out the back way. I imagine he has it clear for you."

Stanhouse let the candidate take his arm and usher him

into the corridor. "If they tread on us, General, we'll give 'em hell right back."

Stanhouse stared at him. Did the man comprehend what he had just said? *No, he couldn't.*

Howard closed the door in his face.

Chapter 9

2200 hours:

Morrissey ran his fingertips critically along the joint of wood. There—a slight irregularity in the dovetail; invisible, perhaps the thickness of a piece of paper. A few light passes with the fine sandpaper and *voilà*—perfection. He began to whistle softly. Coming down to the workbench had been a good idea. He hadn't thought of Monk once since he picked up his tools. *Damn!*

He grunted and went to work with the sandpaper, fleeing back into the refuge of the wood. It was a perfect piece of Kokradua, golden brown and slightly oily. As he sanded, it released a faint musk of leather. He imagined the forest in West Africa from which it had come, a place of heat and humidity, exotic and vivid. Great trunks sunk in shadowy twilight, the crowns bright with equatorial sun.

A lavish wood for a birdhouse. Most woodworkers would scoff at him for using it this way. But maybe the sparrows who lived in it would share his pleasure in the Kokradura. Who could say?

He'd give this one to Mrs. Steiner. The mad birdhouse man strikes again. Who could he hit next? Mr. Albright, in the end brownstone—he could use a birdhouse. Wait, he was the one who refused to bell his cat. Well, maybe a birdhouse would rehabilitate him.

Morrissey shut his eyes and tested the joint again. When he opened his eyes he found himself in total darkness.

He smiled—Janet and the Mr. Coffee again.

The door at the top of the basement steps popped open. "Sorry!"

"That's all right. Did you unplug it?"

"Yes."

He groped his way from the workbench, past the old cellar door under the steps to the fusebox. He finger-walked down to the fifth switch and flipped the lights back on.

"Do you want to come up?" she asked. "The coffee will start getting cold pretty soon." Her voice sounded wistful, pricking him with guilt. He'd stayed down here longer than he planned—over an hour. He dropped a cloth over the birdhouse and put his sandpaper away.

Janet had the fireplace in the parlor going. He accepted his mug and sat with her on the Victorian loveseat.

"We really ought to have an electrician in," she said. "This old house is ridiculous. Why did they put so many things on that one circuit and hardly anything on some of the others?"

"They knew you'd live here someday and they wanted to get you," Morrissey said.

She pinched his leg, up high, and he almost spilled his coffee. "By the way," she said, "what was that you were squirreling away in the safe after the girls went to bed?"

He glanced uncomfortably at the phone table in the corner, checking to see if he'd left the tablecloth crooked over the safe. No. How did she know?

She laughed. "Don't look so stricken. I heard you all the way in the kitchen. You sounded like a family of mice running under the floorboards. Sneaking rule number one: Never, ever tiptoe. You put down much more weight per square inch."

"Thank you, Miz Wizard."

"What was it?"

"The L-6 notes."

She gave him a perplexed look. "I thought you decided your lab safe was more secure."

Morrissey stared into the fire, vaguely ashamed. How to tell her that he didn't quite trust Alan?

"I just wanted to review the notes this weekend."

"You're worried about that lost dog."

"A little," he admitted.

"Why?"

He hesitated. "Because I was sure I'd . . . put it to sleep."

A log slipped in the fireplace, sending dark monkey shadows pouncing at the edge of his vision. Janet edged against him. "Couldn't it have just been . . . suspended animation or something?"

He gave her shoulder a reassuring pat. "Or something. In very special circumstances, certain mammals can appear to be dead when they're really alive. People have been hauled up after half an hour at the bottom of a lake. They look dead—no vital signs—but they can sometimes be revived if the water was the right coldness."

"L-6 is a very special circumstance."

"Apparently." Morrissey wished they could drop it.

"You'll find the dog," Janet assured him. "It'll turn up at the pound any day now. Just keep checking."

"Right."

"You should be happy about L-6."

"Right."

"Remember last Tuesday night, after the biopsy. All those wine spritzers you drank because the Seven-Eleven was closed?"

Morrissey grimaced, then smiled lecherously. "I remember afterward." He put his arms around her and she slid against him eagerly. He ran his fingers gently along her back, enjoying the fine texture of muscle and smooth skin under her satiny blouse. She tensed as if his touch had shocked her. Then her hands played down from his chest to his stomach, light butterfly touches.

He bunched his hands on her buttocks and stood, drawing her up with him. She wrapped her legs around his waist, grabbed the hair behind his ears, and fastened her mouth to his neck. He pulled her up straight, arching back—ah, that was good, her softness against his growing hardness. He could feel her even through their clothes.

She clung to him as he started toward the stairway. A hot wire of pain ran up his shin along the old fracture line and he staggered. Damned leg! He shouldn't be trying this. He eased her feet down, glad it was too dark for her to see the sudden sweat on his face. He jostled her eagerly from behind, hurrying her up the stairs, laughing in the dark stairwell.

"Maniac," she whispered. "Sex fiend. You'll wake the kids."

He undressed quickly so he could watch as she peeled off her blouse and stepped out of her skirt. She was so beautiful, her slim body smooth as cream in the moonlight from the window.

He fell with her onto the bed. Her skin was warm and damp with a light sheen of sweat. He watched her face let go of reason and control, smoothing out in an expressionless, animal beauty. He marveled at the small perfection of her breasts, the round nipples rising under his fingers. When she was breathing roughly and he couldn't wait any longer, he entered her, closing in, in, *in!* IN!

Oh God yes-s-s-s-s!

He breathed deeply, waiting for his mind to focus. He slid his hand slowly between her legs.

"Oh," she said. "There!"

He stayed with her as she twisted, loving her soft cries, wanting this one to be the best. *Fly, baby, fly. Soar up and let the sun warm you.*

She rolled on top and he held her across the small of her back as she arched wildly and came.

She slumped down on him. He held her, almost in pain with joy, savoring each small movement of their bodies across each other as they breathed. If he could stay like this forever with her against him, he could let go of everything else.

She peeled herself up from him with a shaky laugh. He

watched her take her robe from the closet. She sat back down on the bed and reached for his hand and a cold shock went through him.

He sat up, staring at her, dimly aware of her baffled expression as he tried to concentrate. *What was it?*

Someone was in the room with them!

He scanned the room, his heart pounding. Nothing here. No, of course not.

"Peter?"

"Don't you feel it?" he said.

"Yes," she whispered. "It's outside."

He rolled to the side of the bed, planted his feet and hesitated, staring at the window. He didn't want to look. But they had to.

He heard Janet behind him, felt her pressing against his back. He saw it at once, a dark shadow at the border of the backyard and the park below. The skin prickled tight across his arms and neck.

"Just a dog," Janet said.

"Monk," he said wonderingly.

At his voice, the dog glided backward into the shadows of the park. The movement was so sly, so smooth, that he blinked to make sure he'd seen it. He stared hard at the spot, but Monk had vanished.

"Your dog from the lab? Here?" Janet said doubtfully.

He felt her fingers close on his arm. He hugged her to him. This was fantastic! Monk, in his own backyard!

Now get down there, before he gets too far off.

He picked his clothes off the floor and began to dress.

"Peter, don't! That thing looked . . . weird"

"It's probably just hungry. I've got to get it back. I'll take out some food from the kitchen and it'll come skipping up to me like a puppy."

Janet shivered again and pulled the shade down. She gave him a sheepish smile. "I feel better with that closed. The way it looked at us . . ."

He kissed her. Her cheek was chilled. "You'll catch cold," he said. "Better crawl under the covers. I'll be back in a few minutes."

"Be careful."

His excitement grew as he went down the stairs. What luck! He's been wracking his brain over how to find Monk and instead Monk had found him.

But why?

He rubbed at his neck and found the goosebumps still there. Weird, Janet had said. And she was right. It was out there all the time, he thought. Standing still. It listened when we made love. It could hear us, hear our breathing. It was waiting for me to come to the window. It wants me to come out now. It wants to fix me the way it fixed Kellogg. It wants revenge . . .

He stopped abruptly on the stairway, astonished at himself. He was being absurd. The dog had always hated Kellogg and so it attacked him. It was just a dog that L-6 had somehow saved from death.

He had to have it back.

He loped down the last few steps and stopped short, staring down the hall. A faint reddish square of light fell through from the parlor fireplace, outlining a dark shape crouched against the archway.

A man!

Morrissey opened his mouth to yell. Air fanned his face as a hand clamped down on his mouth from behind. *Two* men! He tried to twist away, but an arm went round his chest.

Janet and the girls, upstairs!

He twisted furiously. The man in front rushed him. He lashed out, but the man caught his leg. He kicked with the other foot. The man caught that, too, and held his legs off the floor. They carried him through the foyer and kitchen and down the basement steps. The hand ground his lips against his teeth and mashed his nose over, sending sparks of pain through his head. The bastards, breaking into his house! If he could just get loose. He twisted and jerked, enraged, unable to make a sound.

"Peter!" A bare whisper in his ear, the voice familiar, just outside recognition. He stopped struggling. His feet were lowered to the floor.

"Peter, will you keep quiet?"

He nodded against the hand and it dropped away. He filled his lungs. Light flooded the basement. He squinted at the man holding the pull-string.

Alan!

Morrissey stared, too shocked to speak. Alan. Wearing his dress uniform, eagles gleaming under the light. A few steps away was the other man. His face was narrow and deeply tanned. He looked unreal, a time-traveler from the sixties in a sharkskin suit and dark turtleneck. What was that in his hand?

The L-6 notebook.

Alan was stealing the L-6 notes.

"Peter, I—" Vandiver began.

Morrissey lunged toward the man in the sharkskin suit. *Get the bastard, tear the book away.* He saw his hands clawing. The man grunted in surprise. Morrissey ripped the notebook free and scuttled back. *The fireplace, upstairs, burn it!*

Vandiver jumped between him and the stairs.

All right then, the backyard. *Get away and outrun them.*

Sharkskin cut him off from the rear door, pulling a stiletto from his suit coat. Morrissey crouched and held the book in front, two-handed, like a shield. Sharkskin's suit rippled blue-green like a coiling snake as the light bulb swung gently on its cord above him.

Alan glared at Sharkskin. "Put that away!"

Sharkskin ignored him.

Alan's face was white. "For God's sake, Peter, give him the notebook. Janet—the kids."

Morrissey straightened and let the book fall to his side. The strength drained out of him. Alan was right. Janet and the girls mustn't see this. He let Sharkskin tug the notebook gently from his hand. The man made a grimace of apology and put the knife away.

"I am sorry, Peter," Alan said softly.

"You're sorry?" Morrissey stared at him, outraged. "You broke into my house."

"Just insurance, Peter. We were going to Xerox the book

and get it back here tonight. Of all the rotten luck, why did you have to get up again?''

Morrissey shook his head, disbelieving. ''Insurance.''

Alan held his eyes closed a second. ''I *had* to do this. You took something from Army Labs, and the taxpayers. We have to have it back.''

Blood rushed to Morrissey's face. ''You goddamned . . . you, you miserable thieving bastard . . .'' Spit flecked his chin and he stopped, unnerved by the raw force of his rage. The taxpayers? Incredible! He wanted to leap on Alan, wrestle him down.

But he had to get hold of himself. His only hope now was persuasion. *They must not take the notes.*

''You have to understand,'' Alan pleaded. ''I had absolutely no choice in this. What you did at Army Labs belongs to Army Labs, and the people of this country, legally and morally. You've worked on L-6 since you came to the Labs. You took the job in order to do it. You never told me. You used the computer, the equipment, the animals. You used our friendship, and took money for it. All right, so I forgive you. And now you are going to forgive me, because it's either fuck you, or fuck my country.''

Morrissey stared at him. ''Bullshit, Alan! Bullshit, bullshit—'' Abruptly the rage drained out of him. He walked to his worktable and leaned on it. No, *not* bullshit. He *had* used the Labs and Alan. It was wrong and he'd always known that. But there'd been no other way.

And he still had to have the notebook back.

He braced his arms on the workbench and stared at the half-finished birdhouse, trying to clear his mind, form a plan.

Vandiver's hand squeezed his shoulder. ''Peter?''

He turned back to Vandiver. ''Give the book to me, and then we'll talk.''

''That high-protein diet I prescribed—have you started it yet?''

''Forget the fucking diet!''

Morrissey stared at the notebook in the safecracker's hands. It began to burn and skitter on his eyes like a live thing. To be rid of it, to put the responsibility off on Alan—would that really be so bad?

But if L-6 went wrong, *he* would be responsible, not Alan.

There was one last thing he could try. "Alan, I saved your life. You owe me, and I'm calling it in. Give me back the notebook."

Vandiver looked sick. "Peter. I . . . *can't*." He walked to the back door and turned. "You are still in charge of L-6 development. You'll stay in charge unless you give me no other choice. That's your decision, Peter, not mine."

Sharkskin touched Alan's arm and nodded toward the door. Vandiver brushed his hand away. "We'll talk at the lab tomorrow. Nothing will happen to this book before then. And start that diet supplement or you'll goddamned well blow away in the next big wind."

Morrissey had the insane urge to laugh. He watched Alan go out into the dark. Sharkskin closed the door softly behind them. There's still a chance, Morrissey thought. Take them from behind.

He hurried into the backyard. There—those bushes moving, right where the Doberman had stood. He glimpsed a patch of Alan's uniform, disappearing out of sight into the vast maw of Rock Creek Park. He ran to the spot and started down, pushing through the thicket. The hill plunged steeply into darkness. Where were they? He strained to see through the dark tangle of undergrowth. A bush moved in the moonlight. He lunged forward and slipped. A branch caught him under one armpit. He winced and hung on, swaying up and down until his feet found a grip in the weeds.

This was useless. He hadn't stopped them before, and he couldn't stop them now . . .

That smell, what was it? Like fish—or damp dog hair.

Monk!

He tore his way out of the bush and scrambled back up the slope. When he reached the yard, he stopped and looked over his shoulder. What was he afraid of? He *wanted* to find Monk. And anyway, there was nothing back there. The dog must be long gone.

He'd lost the L-6 notebook and the dog too.

He gazed at his house, feeling empty and defeated.

After a minute, he realized he was gazing up at the yellow square of the master-bedroom shade. Janet! She must be waiting up for him. Of course she would—she'd want to know about the dog. By now she must be worried. How long had he been gone? He checked his watch, disoriented. Only fifteen minutes? It might be all right then. Thank God she'd pulled the shade. If she'd seen Alan and the safecracker in the backyard she'd . . .

She'd what? Wasn't he going to tell her?

Morrissey closed his eyes and memory images flared on his retinas, vivid as slides in a darkened room: Alan talking Coach into giving that skinny Morrissey kid a tryout at end; Alan slamming his fist down on top of the fullback's head for sneering about the team's new "white-trash bookworm"; Alan dragging Peter along on double dates, teaching him to dress "cool," forcing him to fight his shyness. And later, in college, when the double-dating thing had turned on Alan, and Janet had slipped over from the big, blond quarterback to his puny buddy: Alan squeezing them both in a bear hug that night on the riverbank, joking and pretending it didn't hurt like hell. And oh, yes, Vietnam: Alan prodding him from his dingy barracks room to Froggie's, making him do the drinking in public, distracting him, joking, putting on a show so that the drinks would be fewer and farther between.

Too many other gifts to count.

So I saved his life, once, Morrissey thought—and tried to make him pay for it tonight.

He stared up at the yellow square of the bedroom shade, stabbed through suddenly with contempt for himself. What did Alan see in *you* all that time? he wondered bitterly.

The answer came at once: *brains*. Alan thought he was brilliant, admired him for it the way other people worshipped sports heros or frigging rock stars, for Christ's sake. Alan, with his earnest plodding attempts to appreciate Bach, his ceaseless excruciating efforts to win just one game of chess from him. And he unable to throw that one game, knowing Alan would sense it and be hurt.

Tonight, Alan had finally wanted something back besides his pride in being the friend of a smart man—a piece of that man's brainwork—and the man had fought him and cursed him because the price was too high.

No, he wasn't going to tell Janet about Alan.

Morrissey trudged to the house and leaned against the back door. His heart beat heavily. The dog's smell was still sharp in his nostrils. He groaned. Anything else, Alan, he thought, *anything*. Because no matter how shabby it makes me feel, I'm right. You must *not* use that notebook—not until I prove it safe.

Dear God, for twelve years I controlled the L-project. In fifteen minutes, I've lost it.

Morrissey straightened from the door. Time to pull himself together. It wasn't over. Alan had said he was still in charge of L-6 development. He would hold Alan to it. Tomorrow he'd demand the notebook back. He couldn't stop Alan from keeping a copy, but he *could* insist that Alan stay away from the L-6 animals.

As for Monk, the dog was somewhere down in the park. He'd have to go back down and find it . . .

Tomorrow. He had nothing left for tonight.

23
DAYS

Sunday, October 19

Chapter 10

0900 hours:

What was he going to tell the President?

General Stanhouse gave a hopeless grunt. There was nothing he could tell the President. The only hope had been that Howard would agree to withdraw, and that had been dashed.

Stanhouse paced back to the center window of his office, trying to draw on his Punch Corona. The damned thing had gone out again. He champed the butt and stared morosely out at the clouds. A brigade of clouds, leaping from horizon to horizon, dark and agitated. A gray-clad army in panicky retreat.

He wheeled angrily from the window and stalked along his office wall, ten steps up, ten back. As he passed his desk, he checked the clock: 0915. Less than three hours till the meeting with Maddock. *Sorry, Mr. President. Stumped, ha-ha. I was a whiz at committee meetings, though.*

He heard his door open and turned eagerly, glad for an interruption. Maybe it was the Idea Fairy. No, it was Cathcart, sticking his head in, looking like a scared goose. What a hopeless plebe, that Cathcart. "What is it, Major?" Stanhouse snapped.

"I'm sorry, sir. I know you said that you were absolutely not to be disturbed—"

"Damn it to hell, get on with it, Major."

"Colonel Vandiver is here," Cathcart said in a rush. "He *insists* on seeing you. He says it's fully urgent."

Stanhouse groaned. Alan. This would be painful, excruciating. Vandiver could only be here for one reason: to plead for one last chance on the radiation study. The man who had saved his son, and whom he had failed to save, forced to come in now and beg.

"I'll send him away, General."

"The hell you will. Show him in."

As soon as Cathcart was out, Vandiver strode in and braced to attention. Stanhouse nodded, fiddling miserably with the papers on his desk. Against his will, he felt his eyes drawn up. Alan looked excited, not like a man about to beg. What was that in his hand? A plastic videotape case. Probably a tape on some new line of research, like that grisly slide show Dr. Fitch had put them through. Better just get this over with. Stanhouse motioned to a chair. "Sorry, Alan, but I can only give you five minutes."

Vandiver nodded. "I apologize for forcing my way in."

"About the decision to change the contract to Biolog: if there was any way I could have warned you . . ."

"I understand, sir. What I have to say does concern Project Parasol."

"I can't do anything about the committee's decision. Another extension is out of the question."

"I don't need another extension, sir."

Stanhouse stared at him for a second. Then he felt his legs pushing him up. He was giddy for a second, as if he'd just gulped a stiff martini. "Come with me," he snapped.

Vandiver ducked ahead of him into the safe room. "Video system, sir?"

Stanhouse pulled the door shut and pointed. "Just slide that cabinet door aside. Damn it, Alan, it's safe to talk now. Do you have a shielding material?"

"Better than that, sir."

"Well, confound it, man, let's go!"

Stanhouse watched the videotape and listened to Vandiver.

The tape ended, leaving the screen in static, like a soft snowstorm driving into his eyes. He stared at it, mesmerized. *Rats immune to radiation. A gene called L-6. Holy Mother of God*!

Wait. Even if this was possible, was it in time? There would be a host of problems. He must root them out and decide on solutions. Better get a handle on that before he started celebrating—and before he told Vandiver just how important his find really was. He had to be sure before he could risk telling another man about the Tchebychev tape. Even the man who would be responsible for L-6 production.

Stanhouse closed his eyes, shutting out the monitor screen. His mind was jittering worse than the screen. He must calm himself and think! "The tape proves rats can be protected by this L-6 gene," he said. "What about people?"

"That's the next step, sir. We haven't done it yet, but I see no problems. L-6 is actually a human gene to begin with—one so basic that it's also found in higher animals."

Stanhouse leaned forward, concentrating. It felt good to focus his mind, to tackle a problem with boundaries, options, solutions. Now how had Vandiver said L-6 was administered?

By injection . . . That would kill it right there.

Stanhouse took out his dead cigar and ground the tip fiercely into the ashtray. They'd never get away with an innoculation program. If this stuff worked, and could be gotten to the American public, it would mean the end of Russia as a world power. The minute the U.S. government went public and called for civilians to line up for their anti-radiation shots, the Kremlin would hear the TV and radio announcements too. Within half an hour, they'd have the situation analyzed, and then they'd strike, before the L-6 innoculation of 200 million people could even get started.

"Let's assume it works in people too," Stanhouse said. "Does it *have* to be delivered by injection?"

"Possibly not. I'm working on that now. The problem is

getting the gene into place in the body cells. There's a new technique—an experimental molecule that gets absorbed very fast by stomach tissue. We may be able to attach the L-6 gene to this new molecule. Then we could simply put it into the water supply."

He's ahead of me, Stanhouse thought. Good man. "All right, could we make enough of it for everyone?"

Vandiver grinned. "No problem, sir."

Stanhouse felt dazzled by Alan's smile. Alan looks like Adonis, he thought. A young god, delivering us! When this is over, there'll be nothing Alan Vandiver can't have: the chairmanship—hell, the presidency! I'll manage his campaign myself . . . Stanhouse realized that the hope was flooding him with euphoria. He tried to rein himself in.

Vandiver said, "I made it clear, didn't I, sir, that I didn't develop L-6 myself? It was my best researcher, a brilliant man named—"

"Stop!" Stanhouse held up a hand. "I don't want to know his name. From this point on, until the thing is done and our people are safe, we are going to operate on a strict 'need-to-know' basis. If I start sleep-talking into some damned Russian microphone in my bedboard, I don't want to be able to say your brilliant man's name."

Vandiver gave him a curious look but nodded.

All right, what else? Good Lord, the most important thing. He should have thought of it first. "What about safety? We've got to be sure about that before we proceed. Does L-6 have any adverse side effects?"

"Compared to getting nuked by the Russians?"

"I'm serious," Stanhouse snapped.

"So am I, sir. But to answer your question, there have been absolutely no bad side effects of any kind. My man has been working on this for twelve years. Those rats you saw on the tape are, as far as we can tell, completely normal. It's now been forty-eight hours. They got a dose that should have turned their cells to sludge in a hundredth of that time."

"Good." Stanhouse leaned back, satisfied. The excitement surged up again. Obviously Alan had already thought this out thoroughly. By God, they might make it after all!

It was time to bring Alan in on the Tchebychev tape.

"You said you can make enough L-6 for everyone. Can you do it in less than a month?"

Vandiver gave him a sharp look. "Why, General?"

Stanhouse told him.

Vandiver stood. He turned to his chair and smashed it savagely with his fist. The wood splintered, a large piece striking the door. Cathcart stuck his head in and Stanhouse snapped, "Get out!"

Alan picked up the shattered chair and stared at it with unseeing eyes. "The animals," he growled. "The fucking *Cossacks*."

"All right," Stanhouse said. "Take it easy. Can we *do* it?"

Vandiver's eyes focused on him. After a moment he said, "It will be close, General. Very close. But it will be done." He set the chair down gently and paced to the window and back.

Stanhouse watched him, distracted. Where was the nearest large-scale base for biological experimentation? Fort Detrick, only a few miles north in the Maryland countryside. "All right. Your orders: Go back to the labs and put your second-in-command in charge. Give him some cover story that won't raise interest. Then you and your researchers proceed to Fort Detrick, to the maximum-security research facility back in the woods there."

Vandiver looked surprised. "Detrick is still maintaining that camp?"

"It hasn't been used since 'Nam wound down. Detrick has kept up the grounds and equipment, though. We'll have them reactivate the camp. I'll detail military police to guard it under your command. First you will get production of L-6 started in that big genetic lab on the main base. They've got those huge vats, and all the other equipment you should need to make massive batches of the stuff. Don't tell any of your workers what L-6 really is, of course. Once you've got production going, *then* go back to the camp on the back acres and set up a crash program in human testing. Be sure you proceed in that order. If the human tests turn out badly, we can destroy the L-6, but it's vital we start production at once."

"Agreed. Where should I get the human subjects?"

"The nearest military stockades. Ask for volunteers for medical tests. We're bound by law to give full disclosure. Don't do it. For security reasons, we don't dare tell them what L-6 is. But do inform them as fully as possible of the risks. Offer them reduction or termination of sentence, as you see fit. Keep them locked away from *everyone* until we've seen this through. Be sure they understand and agree to this; we don't want any of them claiming the right to visits from their girl friends or parents, or their lawyers either, God forbid."

"I understand, sir."

"You will report your progress directly to me, using the code name . . ." Stanhouse considered. *L for life, L for Luther. Yes, Elaine would have liked that. By God, if this all worked out, he'd go to her church and put a month's pay in the offering plate.* "Code name Luther," he finished. "Any calls to or from Detrick should be funneled through that name."

Stanhouse leaned back in his chair and reviewed what he'd said. It seemed sufficient. He and Hagan would monitor the project as it went along. The details, of course, would be filled in by Vandiver.

The chairman drew a deep breath. The air was sweet in his lungs. He could feel the energy of hope surging through him. By God, now they had a chance! He stood.

Vandiver rose, too, and looked down at him. "General, we are going to grab the Russians by the balls."

"Let's get L-6 made and tested first, Colonel."

"Yes sir." Vandiver looked a little chastened.

Stanhouse thought of what he had just said—how easy it had been to condescend a little. That would never do. "One more thing. You're going to need more clout than you've got right now to bring all this off quickly. I will ask the President to promote you at once to brigadier general. We won't advertise it—don't want to attract attention. But you can begin wearing the star immediately.'' Stanhouse was seized by an impulse. He pulled one of the stars off each of his shoulders and handed them to Vandiver.

Vandiver gazed down at the stars. He opened his mouth and a gruff noise came out. His eyes looked damp. ''Thank you, sir. I'll never forget where these came from. I'll do my best to hold them up.''

Stanhouse flushed, pleased and a little embarrassed. He might have four stars, but he wasn't worthy to lace Vandiver's boots. Vandiver was the one who had taken the most vital project in history to success, persisting even though he'd been drummed off. Vandiver was the one who would save them all—if they were to be saved. Stanhouse gave him a quick rough handshake and clapped him on the shoulder. He ushered Alan into the hall, saying nothing, afraid his voice might betray him.

He wandered back to his window. The clouds had stopped in the sky. They were white now instead of gray. An omen? Good luck, General Vandiver, he thought. *And don't thank me yet for that star. Thank me in twenty-four days.*

20 DAYS

Wednesday, October 22

Chapter 11

2200 hours:

Morrissey unslung the tranquilizer rifle from his shoulder. He leaned it against a tombstone and looked around the weed-choked hillocks of the cemetery. He saw only dark oaks, and the ancient rounded grave markers, pale in the moonlight.

No moving shadow, no dog shape.

He checked behind him down the long, central valley of Rock Creek Park. He could make out no details in the dark tangle of trees and undergrowth.

He looked up to the rim, searching for the reassurance of the city lights. His own house was too far back, screened out by trees. He could see a few lights farther down toward the national zoo—probably one of the exclusive Connecticut Avenue apartments. The lights glimmered weakly, a million miles away. Morrissey shivered with a pulse of primitive fear. This wasn't a city park, it was an alien planet. He was mired at the bottom of an eerie cobalt sea, looking up through black, treelike tangles of weed. The silvery rounded tips of the tombstones drifted in formation, watching him with the cold patience of barracuda. Far above floated the curving, dead fish-belly of the moon.

Morrissey shivered again, then grunted in irritation. He was spooking himself. Another minute and his imagination would be gibbering out of control. "Rock Creek Park," he said firmly. "Picnics. Joggers. Couples necking." He tilted his watch close to his eyes to catch the moonlight. 10:00. Almost time to get out of the park, climb back up to the house. He was relieved and frustrated at the same time. How could he hope to get the dog this way? If only he could hunt it during the day. But then one of those good joggers or fall picnickers would spot his rifle and turn him in to the park police.

He squared his shoulders. He still had half an hour.

He took one step and his leg buckled under him. He sat, and leaned back against a grave marker, wincing at the shooting slivers of pain. He held the old fracture site tightly, trying to numb the nerve. Four nights stumbling over dark, uneven ground. A bit much for his trick leg.

He gave the shin a final hard squeeze and swore softly. Why wouldn't Monk come in? The damned dog was out there, all right. It had managed, as if by calculation, to show itself at least once every night so far—hanging back and then running off as soon as it knew he'd seen it. If only it would come in close enough for a shot. But it was too smart. It must have been around a rifle before. It's former owner had probably been a hunter. Morrissey was finding it easier and easier to dislike that faceless man.

Except that Monk's strange behavior might not be a faceless man's fault. It might be his.

Morrissey let his back sink against the gravestone. There was a small valley of tombs below his feet. He watched the limestone markers dim then brighten. Must be clouds, passing over the moon. The stones almost seemed to pulse. Eerie. He listened to the crickets chirp sleepily in the grass around him. A soothing sound . . .

He jerked his head up. What? Incredibly, he had dozed off. There was a dream—a weird piece of dream: Alan and he in the holler behind the old house in Ridgetown. The trees were bare, like in winter, with an ominous sky, gray as pewter. Alan was calling the dog in a soft whisper. *Monk,*

Monk. Morrissey rubbed at his eyes. What time was it? 10:20. He'd better get moving back toward the house.

He started to get up, then stopped, listening. The crickets—they'd stopped chirping.

The skin crawled along his neck. He looked around among the stones for a dark, dog shape, but he saw nothing. The wind picked up, whispering around the tree trunks, agitating the leaves into a skeletal chatter. He hugged his bent legs tight, glad to feel their warmth against his stomach. Suddenly, goosebumps rippled along his arm. He pushed forward to a crouch.

The dog, he thought. It's near!

A second later he heard it slashing through the fallen leaves. He scrambled up, looking around. Where was it? There! Coming straight at him, attacking!

He turned back and forth in a panic. *The rifle, leaning on the tombstone—get it!* He grabbed for it and knocked it over into the grass. He fell to hands and knees, groping. *Hurry!* He swung the rifle up. Sweat poured into his eyes, stinging, blinding him.

There it was—*close!*

He fired. The dog kept coming. He threw himself to the side. The Doberman's muzzle snapped toward him. He felt its teeth brush the sleeve of his jacket, saw the tranquilizer dart buried in its chest. The dog wheeled sharply.

It could still get him!

Morrissey jumped behind the gravestone. The Doberman stalked toward him. He pointed the rifle at it. If he could just stop his arms from shaking. "Nice dog," he croaked. "Come on, boy. That's a good dog. Let's go home."

The Doberman froze and stared at him. It showed its teeth, but didn't growl. Morrissey saw a glint of moonlight at its neck—the collar with the metal nameplate. Kellogg must have forgotten to take it off when he put Monk in the disposal bag.

Morrissey stared at the dog. Something was wrong. Its teeth were bared, but still it made no sound. A normal dog would be growling. It had attacked him, and now it just stood there.

A gust of wind dried Morrissey's face, leaving it cold. You're doing all right, he told himself. Keep it away from you until it drops. Then carry it to the car, get it to the lab.

Just don't turn your back on it.

He began to back away from the dog in the direction of his house. Monk followed, matching him step for step. Good. If it followed him, he wouldn't have to carry it so far. As long as it didn't attack . . .

His heel caught on something. He was falling! He fought for his balance as the dog took two quick steps. He planted his feet and got the gun centered and the dog stopped. His heart pounded, spinning blood around dizzily in his head. Damn, that was too close! He remembered Kellogg in the hospital bed, the chalky face, the neck wrapped in bandages. That is how he would look if he made a single mistake. That, or worse. The dog had sought him out from that first night outside his window. It had stalked him through the park, all the time he'd thought he was stalking it. It had been waiting for him to get careless, to put down the rifle.

It had got Kellogg, and now it meant to get him too.

But why?

Morrissey started walking backward again. The dog kept pace. There was nothing left of its distemper symptoms—no drooling, no twitching or staggering. Impossible, unless L-6 had protected the cells after all. Wonderful, except that there was no sign of the anesthetic from the tranquilizer dart either.

And that couldn't be.

A week ago at the lab, the anesthetic overdose had knocked it down. It hadn't killed it as he'd thought, but it had sure as hell knocked the dog out. Therefore, so should the dart tonight. He'd filled it with a double load, and there had been plenty of time now for the anesthetic to do its work.

Come on, he urged silently. Drop, damn you.

As he continued backing up, he felt the ground begin to rise behind him. That would be the hill below his house. His yard should be up there behind him. So close—but a steep climb. Could he make it backwards?

Why didn't the damn dog drop over?

The dog lowered its rump. It was getting ready to spring! Morrissey thrust the rifle out threateningly. Instead of springing, the dog reared up on its hind legs. Morrissey stared at it, repelled. It was a grotesque, leering parody of a man. Its forelegs hung low, like arms at its sides. It was so still, so perfectly balanced. It didn't seem to need to move and prance to stay up, like those dogs you see at the circus.

What had he *done* to it?

The dog arched its neck and lowered its muzzle against its chest. It stared at him. Its mouth grinned in a fixed, coy expression.

Morrissey heard his breath, ragged and shallow. His heart hammered. He was paralyzed with fear. The dog's eyes held him. Look away, quickly! . . . So hard just turning his head . . . There!

Run!

He whirled and bolted up the hill. He ran with all his strength. Branches and vines slashed his hands, but he felt no pain. He churned against the loose dirt of the hillside. Was it behind him? He couldn't hear—too much noise from his own feet. He scrambled through the last clump of bushes and into his backyard. He turned, and there it was, right at his heels.

He flung the gun up, dry-firing the trigger. The dog's chest rammed into the barrel, staggering him back. He reversed the rifle and clubbed frantically at it with the stock, backing up to his basement door. There it went again, rearing up on its hind legs. It pranced in front of him like a boxer looking for an opening.

Where was the damned door handle? He fumbled at it, but it wouldn't budge. Locked! He jammed his rump against the door and it gave way. He fell backwards onto the basement floor. He heard the dog's claws tick on the cement just beyond his feet. It soared above him, back-lit by the open door. He jabbed up at it with the barrel. He felt a jolt through the gun, and then an extra weight, bearing the stock down against his chest. Monk's paws landed, scrabbling on his sweatshirt, but the awful, narrow head did not come down. Monk's collar had caught on the barrel sight. Saved!

Morrissey lay holding the gun up, trying to catch his breath. Janet, he thought. The kids. Upstairs. Dear God, don't let it make any noise.

But it wasn't trying to make noise. The dog writhed above him, still silent, no whining or snarling. Holding the dog away, he got up and backed across the floor, dragging Monk along to the light. He jerked the cord. Ah, light—beautiful!

The dog stopped struggling at once. Its eyes went half shut against the light. Its sides were still. It was not even out of breath. And it had never made a sound, not a bark or a growl.

The door at the top of the stairs opened. "Peter, is that you?"

Janet! What if she started to come down?

"I'll be up in a minute."

"Did you find your dog?"

"No." He listened fearfully for her feet on the stairs. *Please stay up there!* He tried to think. If she came down, he would drag the dog back to the yard, let it loose if he had to. No way would he let it near her. He heard no footsteps, but the door did not close either. He kept his feet planted, staring at the dog. *Stay quiet,* he thought fervently.

"What are you doing?"

"Just getting some dirt off my shoes."

"Lord, help me, I've died and gone to heaven."

He laughed, then put a hand over his mouth, shocked at how shrill he sounded. Luckily, Janet had already closed the door.

What should he do now? The anesthetic wasn't going to work, not after this long. There was no hope of getting the dog to his car and keeping it away from him while he drove it to the lab. He'd have to keep it here until he could think of something better.

But only if he could lock it away. The cellar—that would do.

He dragged Monk over to the door under the steps. He slipped the hook loose and jerked the door open. He turned the rifle so that the end sight would slip out of the collar when he was ready. He forced the dog around and swung its head and shoulders through the door, then shoved it the rest of the way in with a foot on its haunch. As soon as the gun sight slipped loose, the dog whirled under the steps and planted its feet to spring. He slammed the barrel into its head, tearing up a dark flap of skin. As the dog staggered back, he slammed the door shut.

"Peter?" Her voice came down through the door.

"Dropped a piece of wood," he shouted. "Up in a minute. We'll have a fire."

"Good."

Yes, good idea, a nice quiet evening by the fireside. Morrissey stifled the urge to laugh. He felt himself edging toward hysteria. He leaned against the door and fumbled at the hook until it slipped into place. There, got you!

He stood by the door, listening. Would Monk set up a howl now that he was trapped? A minute passed, and the dog stayed quiet. Morrissey went to the utility sink, emptied a pie tin he'd used to store screws, and filled it with water. He saw his hands shaking as he carried it back and slid it through the gap under the cellar door. He stood a minute longer, listening. Good. It was quiet.

Almost too quiet.

What was it doing? He got the feeling it was staring at his eyes through the wood of the door—that it knew exactly where he was.

He covered his eyes and tried to think. All right, he had the dog locked up. It seemed unwilling or unable to bark. He could probably keep it locked up here all night without Janet or the kids being affected. That was very important. He could not let it have anything to do with Janet or the girls. It would terrify them. They must never see it or know it existed.

What a twist of fate. The first living thing to receive immortality turned out to be a vicious brute.

Morrissey's fists clenched. *Immortality*. Could it really be?

He realized he was grinning savagely at the cellar door.

Startled, he backed away. He must get hold of himself. In the morning he would think up some premise to get Janet out of the house, and then he would somehow get the dog to the lab. He would examine it. Then he would see.

Morrissey straightened his clothes and blotted the sweat from his face. He went to the woodpile and got two logs for the fire.

19
DAYS

Thursday, October 23

Chapter 12

0730 hours:

Monk had been quiet all night, thank God.

Morrissey glanced at the basement door, then quickly back to the breakfast table, irritated that he couldn't seem to stop looking at that damned door. He wasn't out of the woods yet. He must keep up his pose of casualness a little longer. He'd done all right while the girls had finished breakfast and got off to school. But there was still Janet. It was just the sort of thing she'd pick up on—him glancing at the door over and over. He listened to her puttering around the sink behind him, and kept his gaze riveted on his coffee mug. The coffee looked unappetizing—brown sludge with a greasy film of oil on top. He could feel the missing half eating away at his stomach, giving him a touch of nausea.

Or was it the thought of facing the dog again?

Suddenly he longed to slip over to the liquor cabinet and top off the coffee with a good slug of brandy. The impulse shocked him. He hadn't wanted hard booze in the morning since 'Nam. Pull yourself together, he thought. Just get Janet out of here so you can get it done.

He heard her stacking the dishes. "Leave those," he

said. "If I'm going to be home all day, I might as well take care of them."

"I'm going to be home all day, too."

Here goes, Morrissey thought. "Why don't you call your mom. I bet she'd love to see you."

"Today?"

"Why not? I'll be here when the girls get in from school. You could drive over and stay the day. I'll cook up some spaghetti sauce and serve you dinner when you get back."

She gave him a curious look. *Don't overdo it*, he thought.

"If you're taking the day off," she said, "I'd rather be with you."

"Don't worry about me. You haven't seen your folks in weeks. Go. Enjoy yourself."

She sat back down at her breakfast seat and looked at him. "Why are you trying to get me out of the house?"

He flushed. "I need some time alone."

She shook her head slowly. "Peter, something's wrong. You're strung tighter than high C on a banjo."

A knot of frustration rose in his throat. Why did she have to make it so hard? *Get out of here*, he thought. *Please*. "Does it have to be a big deal?"

"What would *you* call it? I'm to just leave my own house, my studio, two weeks before the Corcoran showing, because you say you need some time to yourself. Damn it, Peter, tell me. I'd like to help."

"You can't help."

Her eyes rimmed in red. He groaned inwardly. He was making a shambles of this. "I'm sorry. I didn't mean that the way it sounded." He pulled his chair over to her side. She didn't look up. He saw that she was trying to hold the tears back. He moved to cover her hand and she yanked it away.

"Every night you're out chasing that damned dog. Finally I think you're setting things up for a day together, just the two of us, and you want to be *alone*." She carried her coffee to the sink and dashed it down the drain, then spun back to him. "Maybe I want to be 'alone' too. You just make yourself comfy here all day. I won't stick around to bother you."

He was miserable and relieved at the same time. He'd been a bastard. And she was going.

He followed her upstairs, trying to think of something to say. He gazed wretchedly at her reflection in the vanity mirror as she put on her makeup with crisp motions, refusing to look at him. As she dabbed in the jars and smoothed the flesh tones on with her fingers, her face went blank with concentration. Something in the expression frightened him. Makeup: lips turning rich with false blood, cheeks flushed like a child's. The small wrinkles around her eyes and mouth filling, smoothing over. His Janet, unconsciously playing undertaker to her own dying face. Suddenly he was stung by the cruelty of it. One day she would see too many wrinkles, or feel her cheek slide too loosely over the bone. She would realize what she was doing. Even then, she would have to go on doing it, with more and more desperation. He closed his eyes, feeling the old, trapped anger wake and push in his chest. He wanted so much to save her.

Perhaps he could. Perhaps he already had.

The hope helped him to harden himself. This was difficult but necessary. As soon as the thing in the basement was gone and the house was safe, he would bring Janet back, explain, make it all up.

She was finished. Her cheeks were too rouged, as though she'd deliberately made herself up to look angry. He watched her dress in slacks and a light sweater. She held her purse under one arm while she jerked her driving gloves on.

He followed her back downstairs to the kitchen, wanting to touch her, but holding back. "Where are you going?"

"Don't worry about it."

"The summer house?"

"Just enjoy your day, Peter."

"Please, I need to know, in case I've got to reach you."

She looked in appeal at the ceiling. "He's worried about *reaching* me." She strode from the kitchen. He heard her clogs clopping an angry staccato on the parquet of the foyer, then down the front steps outside.

He leaned low over the table with a groan. The room seemed gray and oppressive without her—dirty dishes, the clotty smell of drying oatmeal, silence, pressing him down.

Do it now, he thought, in case she changes her mind and comes storming back.

He went to the closet and got out his old high school jacket with the suede body and white leather sleeves. It still fit almost perfectly after twenty years, a little short in the sleeves was all. With his leather gloves, the sleeves would cover enough to protect him from Monk's teeth.

All right, next the old canvas duffel bag. Where had he put that? Down in the basement, with the footlocker and other stuff from 'Nam. If he could wrestle the dog into it, the rest would be easy.

Right, just wrestle the dog. *Other than that, Mrs. Lincoln, how did you like the play?*

He got his flashlight and descended the basement steps. He shined the light through a crack in the cellar door. The dog was standing exactly as it had when he'd slammed the door on it. He frowned in disbelief. Hadn't it moved all night? He played the flashlight up and down along the crack. The beam fell in a thin line across one eye. It slowly winked shut. Above the eye, he saw a gray flap of torn skin where he'd hit the dog with the gun sight.

There was no blood.

His stomach squirmed as he stared at the wound. He backed away from the door. This was one too many impossibilities: an anesthetic dart having no effect, the dog never seeming out of breath, the way it stood on hind legs, its uncanny silence—and now a wound that didn't bleed. Too much.

He couldn't do it. There was no way he could face the dog again. Not with leather sleeves, a club, or anything else. L-6 had done more than keep Monk alive. It had *changed* Monk. He couldn't hope to control an animal like this. And even if he got it to the lab in the duffel bag, he wouldn't be able to examine it properly. It was too dangerous to try to restrain it—the dog had mauled Kellogg and tried to kill him. And it could not be put under anesthetic—it was immune.

But it was not immune to a bullet in the heart.

Morrissey was filled with relief, so strong it startled him. He *hated* killing. And yet now he could not wait to put a bullet into Monk. It was the only way left. Most of what he could hope to learn would come at the necropsy anyway. He really had no choice.

Morrissey unlocked the horizontal cabinet above his workbench and removed the .22 his father had browbeat him into keeping around "to protect your family, Petey." Exactly, he thought grimly. He chambered a long shell into the rifle. Putting the gun down, he got his electric chainsaw and cut a small square window out of the door. The saw whined easily through the old wood, releasing a ripe odor of sawdust.

He pushed the rifle through up to the trigger guard. His head blocked off the light from the basement. He couldn't see to shoot.

Sweat trickled down his nose. This heavy jacket—too hot. He stripped it off. He strapped his flashlight onto the barrel with thick rubber bands and thrust it through the opening in the door. That was better, now he could see the dog's chest clearly.

Monk stared up at him, and Morrissey was suddenly cold. Shoot! He thought, but his finger seemed petrified. He saw the dog bare its teeth. Its sides swelled, dark hide stretching over ribs as it inhaled. It growled, a low bloodless sound.

Morrissey ground his teeth and focused all his will on the trigger. Squeeze, *squeeze!* The gun fired, a flat, boxed-in clap, and he flinched. He opened his eyes.

The dog had not moved.

The flashlight beam was still centered on its chest. There was a black pucker of flesh just below the tranquilizer dart. The bullet had gone into the center of Monk's chest.

The dog growled again.

Morrissey jerked the .22 from the hole and dropped it. Scurrying back, he tripped over the gun and sat down hard on the cement. He heard a strange high humming in his ears.

Dead.

He got up, stumbled to the woodbox and pulled pieces

out. Yes, this scrap would do. He searched for a long time for the hammer on his tool rack. There it was, long handle, heavy steel head. He spilled the box of nails, scooped a handful from the floor.

He was back at the cellar door, panting and swinging the hammer in a frenzy. *Hammer it, yes, hammer it in good, hammer all around it, that's it.* His arm began to feel tired. What was he doing? Pounding a nail into the door a foot away from the patch. He stopped and stared at his thumb. It throbbed distantly. Must have hit it with the hammer. Clumsy.

Backing away, he stared at the crazy pattern of nails around the edges of the patch. Several of the nails were half sunk and bent over. But it should do. The hole was closed. No one could see the ugly thing ever again.

He heard a loud clank and jumped, startled. It was only the hammer, slipped from his hand, banging on the floor. *Got to sit down a minute.* His knees started caving under him as he headed for the workbench. Made it! He lowered his head between his knees.

Going to pass out, he thought. He lay back on the bench, swung his legs up, and breathed deeply.

His head cleared with a rush. He was filled with revulsion. *He* had done this to the dog—he and his L-6. Monk was dead. The dog had been dead before he shot it, dead for a week, ever since he'd killed it that day in the lab. The L-6 had *not* saved Monk. It had done something else entirely.

Morrissey groaned. When he'd shot Monk in the heart, nothing had happened because the heart was already dead. That was why the dog didn't bleed. That was why the anesthetic dart hadn't worked last night. The dog's blood was cold and motionless in its veins, unable to circulate the sernylan to the brain to do its work. The dog hadn't panted from its exertions last night because it didn't breathe at all—unless it wanted to growl. It didn't eat, drink, sleep, or defecate, either; there was no stink of urine or feces in the cellar even though the dog had been locked up all night. For a week there had been no one to feed Monk regularly, but the dog was no thinner than the day Kellogg had held it for the fatal overdose of sernylan.

Morrissey pressed his fingers against his forehead. The fingertips felt cold. How could he think with that dead thing so close to him? He cocked an ear toward the cellar and listened fearfully. There was no sound.

He picked up his high school jacket and stared at it. A vivid image came, of a day back in high school in the biology lab:

The usual sharp stink of formaldehyde filled the room, making his eyes water. He was applying a weak current to a severed frog's leg, and the leg was jumping, and he was wondering how it could be. How could a dead—a completely severed—piece of muscle move like that? The teacher explained: the current was like the force which moved the leg when the frog was alive.

Chilled, Morrissey bent forward, hugging his chest for warmth. It's not impossible, he thought. A dead thing *can* move.

But what is moving the dog?

Morrissey considered the question. There could be only one answer: some form of electrical force. The dead nerves could conduct nothing else. But the dog was not merely jerking spasmodically like the severed leg in high school bio lab. It had tried to kill him. It was moving with will and purpose—the same will and purpose Monk had displayed alive, now made more horrible, more unstoppable, by L-6.

Morrissey forced his mind further along the inevitable steps of reasoning. He had known already that L-6 acted to strengthen the electron bonds of the cells. That is what he had hoped for, so that the bonds would be strong enough to withstand the weak background radiation that might cause aging errors during cell division. Alan's experiment proved that L-6 worked better than he'd planned: the electron bonds of L-6 cells could hold the molecular structure of the cell together through a lethal storm of gamma rays.

Monk proved they could hold the body together even afer death.

Monk's body clearly *was* preserved. It was fixed in a perfect state that formaldehyde could never achieve: the very atoms of the cells were bound together with an abnormal, ferocious strength.

Just as clearly, Monk's body was dead. Blood no longer flowed; the juices of heart, stomach, and glands were stopped.

But the dog's consciousness persisted. Why?

Because consciousness was electric in nature, not biological.

Morrissey heard himself cackling and clapped a hand over his mouth. Dear God help him, it was the oldest question in the book: Did man have a soul apart from his body? Did the neuroelectric currents of thought, memory, and consciousness arise from the biology of the brain or merely inhabit it, fitting neatly into the intricate structure of the brain and using it to command? It had never been so much a question of biology as of theology.

In the cellar, standing on dead legs, was the answer.

Death had come to Monk without the release of decay. The neuroelectric force of Monk's consciousness was still inside the brain. It still sent commands along the undecaying nerves to move the preserved muscles. That consciousness might not be a "soul," whatever that was. But it had survived death.

What must it have been like for the dog to feel the cold sernylan flowing into its veins, to drop down into blackness as the central nervous system absorbed the lethal blow? To feel its lungs deflating, its heart stopping? Perhaps to lie for a time in the darkness of death, then to gather the threads of consciousness and come to awareness in its own dead body?

And Alan wanted him to develop L-6 for people.

Morrissey jumped up from the bench. He had to tell Alan, now. Make him come here to the house. As soon as Alan saw the dog, he would give up his plans for human subjects. That was the first thing, the most important. L-6 development had to be shut down at once. Then the two of them could decide how to destroy the existing L-6 animals, starting with Monk.

Morrissey ran up the steps two at a time. He tried to dial Vandiver's office, botching it twice before he could get his shaking fingers under control. Snap out of it, he ordered himself. You can't fall apart now.

Vandiver's secretary answered. In a surprised voice she told him that Alan had been on leave since last Monday. Alan was consulting with other military bases, moving from base to base on an unpredictable schedule. Alan couldn't be reached.

Morrissey hung up, numbed. Consulting duties? Impossible. Vandiver wouldn't take on anything else, let alone something out of town, when L-6 was so important to him.

Morrissey stared at the phone, thinking furiously. Alan might be at home. He *must* be. What was Vandiver's unlisted number. Damn! He knew it like the back of his hand . . .Yes. He dialed.

It began to ring.

The secretary's words began percolating into Morrissey's brain. She had said Alan was on leave since last Monday. That was the day after Alan had handed the L-6 notes back. *The notes of which he surely had a copy.*

Seven rings . . . eight.

Morrissey clenched the phone with savage force as he realized the implications. He was a fool. He'd let Alan assure him that he was in full control, the only one working on L-6. Then Alan had gone straight out with the copied notebook and set up a separate testing program. More "insurance."

Would Alan really do that? Morrissey wondered.

Would he break into your house and steal the notes?

Ten rings.

What if Alan had already started human testing? Morrissey felt a grimace of fear forming on his face.

Twelve rings. Morrissey started to slam the receiver down, and then he heard someone pick up on the other end.

"Hello?" Morrissey said. "Hello, Alan, is that you? Answer me."

There was silence for a few seconds, and then Morrissey heard the receiver click gently into its cradle at the other end of the line. Alan? No, they had been friends too long—Alan would surely have answered him.

But who else would be at Alan's house?

"You *bastard*!" Morrissey said. "Stay right there. I'm coming."

Chapter 13

1030 hours:

Janet stared at the canvas. Blobs of brown and cadmium yellow and red. How had the brandy looked over the fire the other night? She held her arm up, imagining that it held the brandy glass, trying to envision the fire behind it. She looked at the canvas again with dismay. Too much brown, muddying up the transparency, ruining the effect.

She chewed her lip anxiously. An actual breakdown between her eye and hand. That hadn't happened since she was a little girl first learning to paint. What was wrong? She could see the colors, the exact effect, in her mind. The brandy glass so, the fire behind it, the overlay of the crystal facets and how it should all be interpreted. But she couldn't get it on canvas.

Peter, you rat! This is all your fault. What on earth are you up to?

She had an ugly thought. Might Peter actually be seeing another woman? She paced to the sun deck and stared out over the pines, swallowing at a sudden lump in her throat. Why not? Peter was attractive. He didn't realize it, but that wouldn't stop a woman on the prowl from moving in on him. Some of the women at the Labs were pretty, and liberated—and smart, like Peter, with their Ph.D.s and M.D.s and their damned 36-Ds.

She went around the living room and up to the loft, picking up the rugs. Out on the sun deck, she shook them savagely, one after the other, watching the dust float out over the slope of pines behind the house. As she finished each one, she draped it over the rail: the bright Mexican one from the loft bathroom; the brown shag from the deck doorway; the oval, yellow one from the kitchen. Peter always got this one tangled under his feet when he chopped vegetables for their summer shish kebabs.

She laid the rug gently over the rail and smoothed it with her hand, feeling better. She was being dumb. There were no other women in Peter's life. And if there ever were, he'd not be so clumsy—booting her out of the house so he could have another woman in.

She walked into the living room and sat in the canvas sling-chair next to the phone, wanting suddenly to talk to him—no, to be there with him. She could swallow her pride and go straight back home. It was only an hour's drive. Or should she call first? He was probably sitting by the phone right now, hoping she would. He'd say he was sorry and ask her to come back home.

She reached for the phone. It rang and she jerked her hand back, startled. She blew out her breath, and smiled. She put a hand on the receiver—no, not so fast, let it ring a few more times. All right—now. She made her voice cool. "Hello."

"Hello, Janet? This is Alan."

She blinked in surprise. How did Alan know she was here? "Hi," she said.

"Hi. I tried calling you at your city place and then took a chance you'd be out here. Glad I caught you. I've been on a trip the past few days, to do some consulting. Maybe Peter's told you?"

"No."

"Ah."

That's odd, she thought. He sounds relieved.

"Well, it's all taking longer than anyone planned, and I've just come back to the house to pack some extra things. I have to head out again this afternoon. I was wondering if you'd like to drop over for a peanut butter and jelly sandwich on Wonder bread."

How tense he sounded, rushing the words out. Almost like this was college and he was asking her for that first date again. The thought made her uncomfortable, and then she smiled. Peter seeing other women? Alan wanting a *date* with her? This was her day for being dumb. "Gee, Alan, that sounds nice, but I'm about to head for home . . ."

"How about if I make it tuna on rye?"

She realized that he was more than tense; he was upset—almost desperate. "Alan, what's wrong?"

There was a strained silence. "You drive a hard bargain. All right then, *crèpes aux rognons* with grilled bacon rolls."

She rewarded him with a chuckle. "I'll be right there. But please, no kidney pancakes."

She drove fast, keeping the M.G. at just under seventy. Strange—Peter and Alan, both in a jam at the same time. The same jam? Possibly. Interesting—Peter throws me out, and Alan invites me over. Another thought struck her: Was Peter just enlisting Alan to make sure she stayed away from the house?

Now she was getting paranoid. The hell with it.

She let her mind float, enjoying the Virginia countryside. That mellow, smoky smell—someone must be burning leaves. It was vaguely exciting, the scent of going back to school, dressing up in soft sweaters and plaid skirts, *dating*. She leaned back in the seat, straightening her arms, enjoying the smooth hum of the M.G., the press of October-crisp air, a million tiny, cool points on her face.

She pulled into Alan's circle drive, slowing down so she could take in the house. What a grand place. The two spacious wings and that imposing center with its tall columns of gleaming white. It looked like something out of *Gone With the Wind*.

Such a big house for a man living alone.

She parked under the portico and walked up to the double doors. He opened them before she could knock. Flattering—he must have been waiting for her, perhaps moving again and again to those little windows beside the door.

He took her hand and drew her inside. The central hall was cool and dim after the sunlight. She soaked him up in a quick rush of detail. He did look splendid in uniform: collar open; trousers fresh, the crease unbroken. Solid, strong, and gentlemanly. His chin looked very smooth, just shaved. He was slow to let go of her hand. She drew it away, flustered.

"Come on in." Vandiver led the way past the curving central staircase into the front sitting room. Through the windows she could see two columns of the portico. Beyond them, the grass made a green ocean with red and brown islands of leaves. He pointed her to an armchair and sat across from her on a dainty-looking loveseat. The soft leather of the chair embraced her. She fitted her hands over the arms, feeling the larger furrows his fingers had worn there over the years. She smelled the chair's faint scents—leather, cologne, and a musky tang of sweat.

"I was about to get something to drink," he said. "How about you?"

"Whatever you're having."

She watched him disappear into the kitchen. As soon as he was gone, she became aware of the emptiness, the huge silence of the place enfolding her. She could never be here without going back to her favorite mystery about Alan: Why did he choose to stay in this big old house? He could live comfortably in the center section alone, without ever going upstairs. For all she knew, he did. In all the times she and Peter had been out here, he'd never asked them upstairs. She'd never even set foot on that grand staircase. Intriguing. To know Alan so well and not know the answer to this.

Alan returned with a tall glass of something clear and bubbly. There was a freshly squeezed lime in the bottom. She took a gulp—gack! Gin and tonic! She coughed. "Alan, this is a *drink* drink. I thought it was Perrier."

He colored. "I'm sorry. Would you like something else? There's no Perrier, I'm afraid, but I do have some soda water."

Why was she being so prim? It wouldn't hurt her to have a

drink. It was almost noon, after all. And that first swallow had been good, spreading heat into her throat and giving her, already, that first nice half-turn of relaxation. "No," she said. "This is fine."

He raised his glass to her and took a swallow. He gazed raptly at her. "It's good to see you."

She looked into her glass. "So. Consulting duties, huh? You say you just came back to pack?"

"Right. Damned nuisance. I expected Peter might have told you by now."

That again. Why was he so interested in whether Peter had told her? She set her glass down. "You sounded blue on the phone, Alan."

There was a brittle edge to his laugh. "*Blue*. I haven't heard that word for a while."

"Come on, I'm not *that* old."

He looked embarrassed and serious. "No, no, of course not. It's a good word—an artist's word."

The phone on the table beside Alan rang.

Alan didn't move.

She counted off twelve rings and then Alan lifted the receiver and set it back in its cradle. He looked at her and said nothing. She felt a fierce tension reaching from him, pulling on her. It was partly sexual, but much more. What am I doing here? she wondered. Where's the peanut butter and jelly on Wonder bread? *Be careful.* She sat very still, putting all her will into it.

"Janet, am I . . ." He put his face in his hands, and she felt a formless rush of sympathy for him.

"What, Alan?"

"We've known each other a long time. This is going to sound strange. Am I a decent man?"

Alarmed, she went to him and put a hand on his shoulder. "Alan, what is this?"

He kept his head down. "I mean, would I do anything badly wrong? Anything . . . monstrous?"

She felt a tremor in his shoulder. "As far as I'm concerned, you're one of the two most decent and honorable men alive," she said firmly.

He looked up at her, his eyes measuring, almost suspicious, as though he thought she might be trying to trick him. "I want to show you something," he said.

He stood abruptly and headed for the staircase. She followed, hurrying to keep up. He sprang up the steps, not eagerly but with bullish resolution, as though afraid he'd change his mind if he didn't hurry. At the top he turned and blocked her for a second. Then he led her down the hall. Only one door along the way was shut. He stopped in front of it, staring at the doorknob. Finally he opened the door.

She hesitated, suddenly full of dread. What in God's name had he done? Murdered someone? Was he about to show her the body? She edged past him and stopped, surprised. It was a boy's room—a young boy! On the wall above an unmade bed was a Redskins pennant and a black-and-gold poster of the Spock character from *Star Trek*. Three model airplanes hung by threads hooked to the ceiling. She saw spots of glue glistening on them. There was an old suitcase-model stereo beside the bed. And over there, on the floor—a catcher's mitt and a rumpled pair of sweat socks, as if a kid had just breezed in and out after Little League practice.

Did Alan have a nephew? No, he had no brothers or sisters . . .

"I once wanted very much to marry a certain woman," Alan said in a soft voice. "I spent a lot of time daydreaming about the house, the kids we'd have. It was a very beautiful time in my life. I keep this room to help me remember. If we had a son, this woman and I, he'd be fourteen by now."

She turned and stared at him, slowly comprehending. Fourteen. And it was fourteen years ago, in college, that she and Alan had stopped dating. Fourteen years since their fun threesome had changed from her and Alan, plus Peter, to the way it had ended up.

But in his mind, Alan had married her. He'd had a son. An imaginary son. By an imaginary wife. By *me*, she thought numbly. She opened her mouth, but no words would come out. *Alan, still carrying the torch for her.* She'd never had any idea—even in the first months. He'd seemed to take it so well. She and he and Peter had simply drifted into a different pattern. Fourteen years ago. Fourteen years, during which he had never stopped . . . had never . . .

"I never used to worry about this room," he said softly. "I knew it was a little eccentric to do something like this, but I . . . care for you so very much. Does it scare you now?"

"Alan, I could never be frightened of you."

He moved to her slowly, took her hands and pulled them up between their bodies. She was acutely conscious of his fingers curling over against her breasts. He pulled her into his arms, held her to him. She felt them swaying together, and then he tipped her head back and kissed her. Her body seemed to float beneath her. She opened her mouth a little under his lips. *No!*

She put her hands against his chest and pushed, gently, then insistently. For a second he held her tighter, then let her go and stepped back.

"I'm sorry," she said. "I . . . just *can't*. Peter . . ."

He held up a hand, stilling her.

She gave a small, hollow laugh. "I should go. Right now." Alan turned and indicated the door with a sad, courtly gesture. She went before him down the steps. Downstairs she returned to the leather chair and picked up her purse. "The room," she said gently. "You've kept it for all this time. Why does it bother you now?"

"There's a thing I have to do," he said. "A very difficult decision, involving people's lives. I can't tell you what it is."

"Part of your work at the Labs?"

"Part of my work as a soldier. That's what I am, Janet. A soldier."

He's trying to justify himself, she thought. "You want to know if you can trust yourself," she said. "You question your judgment now because of that room."

"Yes."

"I don't know about soldiering," she said. "I paint suffering, elation, boredom, anger, love—straight up and turned on their ears. Never ask an artist what's crazy and what isn't. But I *can* tell you this: That room upstairs is a work of art."

Alan nodded slowly. He bent over the pad by the phone and wrote a number and two extensions. Then he wrote something else, quickly, and tore off the sheet. He took her arm and walked her to the front door. "When you reach the second extension," he said, "ask for Luther."

"I don't understand."

"It's a code name. Don't forget."

"Alan . . ."

He put a finger on her lips and handed her the slip of paper. Underneath the phone numbers he had written, "I never stopped loving you. I never will." She folded the paper, put it in her purse, afraid to look up and let him see her tears. *Poor Alan. Poor, dear Alan.*

She felt his hands on her shoulders, and then his arms went around her again.

Chapter 14

1230 hours:

Morrissey sat in his VW staring at Janet's M.G. It sat under the portico, inches from Alan's Porsche. The grills seemed to grin lasciviously at each other.

Morrissey labored to understand. Everything looked so bright and clear, but none of it seemed connected. He heard heat ticking from his engine block. Some grackles that had lifted when he'd turned in, settled again and pecked through open patches of grass, chattering noisily. The front of Alan's house blazed in the noon sun.

Morrissey remembered the day a month after their return from Vietnam: Alan taking him to dinner at Dominique's. Frosted, cut-glass windows, satiny paneling, the discreet murmur of well-bred voices. Alan leaning across the table, gripping his wrist, saying, "Come to the Army Labs, Peter. I'll pay you top dollar, old buddy. I need you. I want you here in Washington with me."

The snippet of memory twisted into a new and ugly shape. Vandiver was leering now. *I want your wife, Peter, your wife, your wife, your wife. She was mine first.*

Morrissey blew out an explosive breath. Christ, that hurt! Why did he want to hurt himself like that? Alan is Janet's friend, too, he reminded himself. You threw her out of the house, and she went visiting. That's all.

He heard his feet crunching on the gravel of the drive. He didn't remember getting out of the car. *Too much noise.* He moved to the grass. Don't do this, he thought, but he stayed on the grass, walking softly, remembering the phone *picked up and silently replaced.* Alan had been here and he hadn't even bothered to put the phone to his ear, or Janet would be out of here by now. Alan was here, and Janet with him, and no interruptions allowed.

Morrissey stopped as his hand closed on the doorknob. Knock, he thought. But he turned the knob and pushed the door open, and there they were.

They were in each others' arms.

They turned, and the blood drained from Janet's face. She pushed away from Alan. Morrissey was suddenly dizzy. I'm done, he thought. Now I'll have to be someone else.

"Peter . . ."

He waited, staring at her, but she said nothing else.

"Come in, Peter," Alan said. "And for God's sake, don't go jumping to—"

"Shut your face."

"Old buddy, don't."

Morrissey felt something snap inside him. Old buddy! The bastard! He felt his fist raise as his legs pushed him at Alan. Janet jumped between and hit his chest with both hands. He stopped, stunned.

"Don't you dare," she hissed.

Gin on her breath! That ripped it.

She pushed past him out the door.

He stared at Alan. Vandiver rubbed his forehead wearily, as though he had tried to reason with a stubborn child and failed. Morrissey heard Janet's M.G. start up behind him. *No, got to stop her.* He started down the steps. He turned back to Vandiver. "You stay here. You *wait.*"

He ran after Janet's car, but she was picking up speed, rear tires spewing gravel. A piece hit him on the shin. He stopped. No good, she was getting away. He ran to his VW, watching her careen down the drive and onto the road. He flicked the key over and pumped the gas. *Watch it, don't flood the engine!* The Volkswagen shuddered to life under him. Good. *Now go!* He backed out and killed the engine shifting and tromping the gas. He swore and got it started again, but now the M.G. was a distant smear, shimmering through sun and tree shadows far down the road. He jammed the accelerator to the floor, feeling the VW vibrate around him. The car crept up in speed until he could see the back of Janet's head through her rear window.

She swerved into a side road. He eased up enough to make the turn, then floored it again. Her car disappeared in a cyclone of grit. He swore at the dirt road. The dust billowed back around him and streamed through the one-inch crack of his window. He coughed and started to choke on the dust. He slowed and took a hand off the wheel to wind his window tight, cursing at the lost seconds.

He was almost breathless with fear. She'll kill herself, he thought. I've got to let her go. No—if she cracks up, there'll be no one to help her. Dear Lord, keep her safe.

The dust cloud thinned as the M.G. pulled away. Morrissey heard himself groaning. He tried to stop the sound and couldn't. Alan. Stealing from him, lying to him about command of L-6, and now standing there with his arms around Janet. How could he have been so blind? Had they been in bed? Alan's hands on her, his mouth and hands, and—*Watch it, she's turning off again!*

Morrissey stamped down on the brake, almost overrunning the side road. God, help—she wasn't going to make it! Horrified, he saw the M.G. slew off the road and plough between two oak trees at the edge of a cornfield.

Dear Jesus thank you she missed the trees!

He pulled up on the shoulder beside her and sat, too shaky to move. After a minute he got out and walked to her car, propping his hands on the sill of her door. He stared out over the roof of the M.G., feeling his heart pound. The field looked desolate. Brown stubble, shocks of corn, spread apart like grim searchers combing the field. Was his marriage lying dead out there?

He felt the glass wind down against his knuckles and stepped back. "Are you all right?" he asked.

She didn't look up. "I'm driving back to the summer place," she said. "Follow if you want. Then we'll talk."

"For God's sake, will you drive slow?"

She looked up then and gave him a wan smile. "Peter, it's not what you think. That's all I'll say now."

Morrissey's mind began to tick over again. He'd left Alan. He'd found him, and then he'd left him without telling him about the L-6 dog.

"Are you coming?" she asked.

"I'll come . . . later."

"Later." Her voice sounded flat.

"I have to go back to Alan's for a minute," he explained, desperate. How could he get her to understand? "I came out here for a reason. I wasn't trying to . . . to spy on you. I still have to talk to him."

She stared out the front windshield at the cornfield.

"If he'd answered his damned phone . . ." Morrissey began. He saw her jaw clench and he stopped. "Don't worry. I won't start anything up with him. But I *have* to see him right away. It's very important."

"I won't worry, Peter," she said coldly. She started the engine and backed onto the road. He watched her drive off. So slow, like a funeral car. I've got to follow her, he thought. Now. We've got to talk. Our marriage . . .

Damn—goddamn!

He could not follow her now, not even to save their marriage. Somewhere, Alan and his friends—his *friends*—were developing L-6 for use on humans. If he let Alan slip away now, it would continue, and soon there would be men who could resist lethal radiation.

But when those men died, they would be like the dog in his basement.

Morrissey got back into the VW and swung sharply around onto the road. He hurried back over the route, rehearsing what he must say. He must be calm and logical:

We have to put aside what just happened, Alan. We'll deal with it later. The most important thing now is L-6. We have a problem. The rats look normal. If you give L-6 to men, they will look normal too. But if they die . . .

Morrissey nodded. That sounded right. And he'd better show Alan the dog too. It wouldn't be enough simply to tell him. Alan would have too many reasons not to believe him—especially after what had just happened.

Morrissey fought the sob forming in his throat.

Just take Alan to the brownstone and make him look at the dog.

Then punch his fucking lights out!

The thought shocked him, cooling his anger like a dash of cold water. Right. And while he was at it, he could punch his own lights out. The problem wasn't Alan. It wasn't Janet. It was *him*. He'd thrown her out of the house. If ever she needed someone to hold her and comfort her, it was today. And who would he rather it be than Alan?

Janet, hugging her friend. What a crime!

Morrissey began to feel ashamed. What had gotten into him? He should have been glad Alan was there to help her. Instead he'd acted like a jealous fool.

And, damn it, he *still* felt jealous. The hell with it. L-6 was what mattered now. He'd get it stopped. Then he'd worry about putting things right between the three of them.

Morrissey pulled into Vandiver's driveway and cursed. Empty! He drove all the way to the front portico anyway and got out, slow with despair. Where Alan's Porsche had been, there was a tiny spot of oil on the gravel, nothing more.

Chapter 15

1830 hours:

The harvest now is over
The summer days are gone
And yet no power cometh to help us

Vandiver turned the volume up on the Porsche's tape deck. The great opening chorus of the Elijah Oratorio pounded through him, sending a tingle up his spine. God, he loved this piece! It had such incredible power.

If only it had the power to drive out the ugly scene with Peter . . . and the terrible thing he must tell Stanhouse tonight.

The harvest now is over
The summer days are gone
And yet no power cometh to help us

I am coming, Vandiver thought. But to help you, I'll have to kill some of you. No, not some—*thousands*. Tears filled his eyes. He blinked them away.

For a while he sang along with the tape. Then he raised a hand and conducted the music, imagining that he was at the podium of the Kennedy Center. If he'd not been a soldier, he'd have led a symphony. He grunted sardonically. Nothing to it. Just go to the Kennedy Center, show them how well he could wave his arms, and they'd hand him the baton at once.

Ah, here came the difficult passage. Pay attention.

Vandiver concentrated on directing each nuance: *Behind him the plush red seats of the concert hall were full. Every eye was on the sweeps of his hands. He pulled bolts of music from the orchestra and flung them like lightning and thunder into the crowd. The men were awed and a little envious. The women gazed at him raptly. They wanted him. He could have any of them, have them all if he chose.*

But the only one that mattered he could never have.

Janet sat in the special seat, up close, that he had provided. Overcome by the music, she was full of love and admiration for him. Peter sat beside her—

Damn it, Peter, how did we come to this?

No—stop it!

Peter sat beside Janet, watching him conduct. Peter wasn't envious like the other men. He was proud, thinking: I grew up with Vandiver, but I never realized he could do something this great. He's as brilliant as I am!

Vandiver grimaced. He'd strained the daydream too far. He could not be as brilliant as Peter, not even in fantasy. And Peter could not admire him now. Peter must despise him.

Everything was screwed up.

Vandiver could not suppress an image of Peter's face at the door; shock, pain, and then the anger. He became aware of the tape again. It was droning on woodenly, its soothing power spent. He punched the "stop" button and turned his attention to the countryside he was driving through. Where was he? Pasture on both sides of the road—there was the gray barn with the faded ad for Mail Pouch Tobacco. Almost to the Ft. Detrick turnoff. He glanced anxiously at his watch: 1845. He'd be there in plenty of time for his meeting with Stanhouse and Hagan.

He stomped the gas anyway, kicking the Porsche up to 75. *Take it easy. He's not behind you.*

He wheeled sharply into the Ft. Detrick turnoff, then slowed, easing the Porsche up to the main gate. The guard glanced at him, then waved him on. He took the curving road through the maze of barracks, labs, and administration buildings, past the hospital, straight on to the tall cyclone fence at the rear of the base. He pulled up to the fence and gazed through it. Just a field and some woods. Hard to believe anything else was back there. Harder still to believe the last hope of America was back there.

He watched two of the MPs quick-stepping out of the gatehouse toward him. Better pay attention now. In an hour or so, General Stanhouse would be following him through. The security procedures had to come off perfectly.

One MP went to either side of the Porsche. He saw that their holster flaps were unsnapped—good. The guard at his window inspected his pass critically, taking a long, careful look at his face and matching it to the one on the card. He saluted and motioned to the other man to open the pedestrian gate. Vandiver nodded. Everything correct.

Vandiver got out of the Porsche, gave his keys to the MP, and walked through the gate. A corporal pulled up almost immediately in a jeep. The third man in the gatehouse must have made the call as soon as he'd seen the Porsche. Very good. Now let them do as well for General Stanhouse.

"Best get in quickly, General," the corporal advised. "The dogs won't bother you once you're in the jeep."

Vandiver hopped into the back, feeling a small thrill. The soldier had called him *General*. And that's what he was!

As the jeep bounced along the dirt trail, he looked around. Where *were* the dogs? Getting too dark. It would be hard to see them now. But they were out there somewhere, and Stanhouse would not expect to see them at night anyway.

Vandiver held on as the jeep headed into the woods. The driver flicked on the lights. A deer froze in the beams and then bolted from the road into the wall of trees and brush. The corporal pointed a finger after it, said, "Bang!" and laughed. Vandiver thought of reprimanding him. No, it was too small a thing.

The jeep rolled into the clearing, giving him his first night glimpse of the research compound, surrounded by its wide moat of grass. Vandiver sat forward, catching his breath. The place looked different at night, beautiful. The spotlights along the fence shone across the grass, making it sparkle like a field of emeralds. He smelled a dewy sweetness—they must have mowed the perimeter while he was gone. The camp looked dark behind the blinding fence lights, the trees inside looming in a single, merged silhouette, like a black castle keep.

Vandiver's confidence surged back. He almost felt good! Instead of groaning under the weight of what he must do, he should thank God he was alive and in this place, charged with this duty. For twelve years, his life had been aimed at these next nineteen days. This was why he had not died on the floor of Froggie's.

He motioned to the gate. "Okay, driver, I'll walk through. Leave your next passengers off here too." The gate guard came outside and locked up behind himself before checking his papers. Good man, Vandiver thought. Forget the locking, and I'll put you in with the prisoners.

Inside the gate, Vandiver noticed the corpse of a crow that had brushed the wire and dropped dead beside a cedar tree. Apparently the fence generator was doing its job. It looked old, though. Better have it checked tomorrow.

He walked around the camp, critically eyeing the main lab, the walk-in cooler, and the windowless detention barracks. The camp was quiet and dark except for the yellow squares of window along the MP barracks.

He unlocked his cabin and stood inside the door, inhaling the pleasant smells of fireplace ash and varnished pine. Feeling his way through the dark to the window, he gazed out at the main lab. How innocuous it looked—a log lodgehouse, making you envision huge stone fireplaces and mounted antlers inside. How different, the truth. Vandiver grunted in distaste, thinking of the things that had been done in that place, in the gleaming, modern lab behind the rustic logs. In the dark he could almost see an aura around the building, a ghostly blue electricity of pain and death.

Thank the Virgin his own test subjects were doing so well.

A rap on the door made him jump. Damn, they were early. Stanhouse and Hagan must have slipped through as soon as it was dark, practically on his heels. No matter; he was ready—as ready as he could be. He flipped on the cabin lights before opening up. Stanhouse and Hagan stood outside dressed in mufti. Hagan wore a battered Homburg, shielding the beacon of his bald head from anyone who might have been keeping a covert watch along the way in. He looked ridiculous, but Vandiver felt no amusement. The hat was a grim, if garish, reminder of how vital security was. He motioned them in to seats on the sofa.

"Drink, General, Colonel?"

"Scotch," Stanhouse said. "Neat."

Hagan gave a slight shake of his head.

Vandiver poured two glasses and handed one to the Chairman, getting a closer look at Stanhouse's face. He didn't look good—tired, haggard. The general was letting this get to him too. And he didn't even *know* yet.

Vandiver settled in the cane rocker across from the two men. "The radiation tests are going well, General. They couldn't be going any better."

"Wait, Vandiver," Hagan said.

The Chairman restrained Hagan with a sharp glance. "We may as well hear about the tests first, Julius."

Why is Hagan so brusque? Vandiver wondered. Refusing a drink. Calling me by my last name—not General, not Alan, but the surname. A subtle signal of animosity. I hardly know the man. What could be eating him? *Tag it and move on.*

"It's been four days now," Vandiver said, "since we injected the ten volunteers from the brig at Fort Belvoir. The gene gets into place in the body cells fast, but to be sure I waited two days for the first tests. During that time we watched the subjects for any problems from the injection. There weren't any. We've now gone through low- and intermediate-level irradiation. There are no bad effects. It's just like with the rats."

Stanhouse nodded distractedly. "Excellent, Alan."

Hagan said, "You told the General that L-6 could be given in the water supply. Can it?"

Here we go, Vandiver thought. "That's not quite accurate, Colonel. I told him I *hoped*—"

"Yes, and in the four days since, you've evaded the question every time."

Stanhouse shot Hagan a reproving look, but he said, "We *do* need to know for sure, Alan, before we go any further."

Vandiver braced himself. "The water won't do, sir."

Stanhouse pounded the sofa. "Damn! Damn it to hell."

Vandiver looked at Hagan. Better set the old fart straight right now. "I've not been evading . . . *Colonel*. I've been *working* on it. Unfortunately, L-6 has to be balanced with the body's other biochemicals. Too much would be harmful or fatal; too little, ineffective. L-6 has to go by injection—a micromilligram per kilo of body weight."

Stanhouse looked at the floor. "Then it's hopeless."

Vandiver braced himself. This was it—the critical moment. "No, sir, it's not hopeless. There's a way to do it. Exactly *one* way."

"How? Damn it, Alan, how do we get people in for injections without alerting the Soviets? And the minute they know, they'll jump for their missiles."

"It's going to take time to set up," Vandiver said. "Just about all the time we've got left. And, General, it's going to take all the guts we've got."

Stanhouse set his scotch down. "Let's hear it, Alan."

"Remember the swine-flu epidemic during Ford's term?"

"The one that never quite materialized?" Stanhouse said.

"Right. Hundreds of thousands of good citizens went out to schools and clinics to get their shots. Millions didn't. That's why *our* epidemic has to be scarier than the flu. This time it has to happen. And it has to *kill*."

From the corner of his eye, Vandiver saw Hagan lean back on the sofa and raise a hand to cover his eyes, as though the light in the room had suddenly grown too harsh for him. Stanhouse gaped at Hagan, as if more surprised by his reaction than by what he had just heard. Vandiver felt a brief bond of sympathy. Hagan's face showed that he understood—all the ugly details, right down to the bottom line. Give the old geezer credit.

"We have to start the epidemic ourselves," Vandiver said. "It has to be deadly enough to kill a certain percentage of people infected, and it has to be something we already have the antidote for. I think we could find something suitable right here on this base. When we start the epidemic, we have to be ready to set up army innoculation centers at once across the country. Probably public school gyms would be best, just like for swine flu.

"It will go like this: The epidemic hits in one or two cities. People watch the news and realize they could die. That, unfortunately, is essential. The flu is *occasionally* fatal, and that wasn't enought for Ford's innoculation program. People have to be scared badly enough to come rushing in for their shots, the minute centers are set up.

"Meanwhile in Russia, Charnov and Tchebychev are not alarmed. A plague on the Americans? They sit back and smile at the irony—if they give it any thought at all. They know they're going to end our epidemic permanently the day Maxwell Howard wins the election. They *don't* know that mixed in with the epidemic antidote is something called L-6, pegged to the same mg/kg delivery rate as the antidote.

"When enough of the public has come in and gotten the shots, we hotline the Kremlin. We give them a demonstration—walk a few people into a radiation chamber for them. They see that they can't hit us after all. They fold."

Stanhouse's face was white. "Vandiver, do you know what you're saying? That we should murder our own people!"

"Only a relative few."

"Damn it, how many is a relative few? A thousand? Fifty thousand?" Stanhouse fumbled a cigar out of his coat. He tore the cellophane off, then dropped the cigar on the floor. Vandiver reached to pick it up, but Hagan beat him to it, pushing his arm away. Vandiver held out a light, but Stanhouse ignored it, holding the cigar in his hand. Vandiver became aware that Hagan was glaring at him, eyes cold and black, full of disgust. Vandiver stared back, angry and bitter. How holy you are, Hagan, he thought. You have the luxury. The curse of thinking up the plan didn't fall on your back. If it had, you'd be sitting in the hot seat now, squirming under Stanhouse's horror and disgust. Because you would be laying the same plan on the table if you'd thought of it. There's no other way, and you know it, too.

"The General asked you a question," Hagan said. "How many of our own people shall we murder?"

Vandiver sighed. "As many as it takes to save the rest."

Chapter 16

1900 hours:

Kellogg was getting his clothes out of the tiny hospital closet when he heard the footstep behind him. He whirled, clenching the backside of his hospital gown together. Stupid thing was made to show the nurses your moons. *Crud, it was Detective Cummings!*

"Hey, do you mind knocking?" He gulped, surprised at himself. Cummings was a cop—and black. He'd probably love to bust a fat, white honkie for lipping off.

Cummings went back and rapped on the doorpost. He had the goodness not even to smile. Kellogg relaxed a little.

"I see they're springing you."

"Yeah. I was just going to get dressed."

"Don't let me stop you."

Kellogg looked down, embarrassed. He couldn't let this guy think he was afraid to show himself. Wasn't that like admitting you were a homo? But he really didn't want to reveal his blubber. How had he handled this in gym back at Kenmore Intermediate?

Cummings solved the problem by pulling one of the room dividers across between them. Relieved, Kellogg began at once to change. He tried not to rush. He'd once caught his foot in his pants that way in gym and sprawled across the floor in front of half the soccer team. Remembering, he blushed. They'd squealed with laughter. A bunch of piglets.

"Throat feeling better?"

"I haven't done any yodeling."

Cummings chuckled. "We didn't get much chance to rap last time."

Kellogg was struck by a dark thought. Cummings had to be back to talk about the dog. And he'd been in such a sweat over dressing he hadn't started to think what to say.

"I thought you turned all that over to the dogcatcher."

"Oh, I did, I did. But I like to follow up on things, you know. It's funny, but the pound hasn't found any vicious German shepherds running around loose."

Kellogg couldn't think of anything to say. He pulled his shirt on and realized his chest and belly were sticky with sweat. Rat-butts, he had to get his head in gear if he was going to keep this guy off Pete's case.

"You did say it was a German shepherd, didn't you?"

"Yup."

"You know how things nag at you sometimes?"

Kellogg looked at the white cloth, stretched over the metal frame of the divider. Through the folds of the gathers he could see Cumming's silhouette, weirdly rippled and still. "Uh, sure."

"Something's been nagging at me, Mr. Kellogg."

"Just Kellogg." Nice of the man to call him Mister. *Careful. He's probably just softening you up.*

"Right, Kellogg. What nags me is how a strong, experienced animal-care man like you could go and get his neck all chewed up by a dog."

"Just careless, I guess."

"Uh-huh. The other thing that nags me is, I dropped around the Labs and looked at some animal manifests. They haven't ever bought a German shepherd for lab work."

Kellogg was glad Cummings couldn't see his face. "Well, sometimes we just get 'em from the pound, like this dog, and the paperwork gets lost, you know?"

"I can dig it. Your friend, Doc Morrissey, went right

along with you, so I guess it must have been a shepherd all right."

Kellogg was starting not to like Cummings's tone.

"The Doc looked kind of nervous that day in your room, don't you think?"

Kellogg pushed the barrier aside and glared at Cummings. "Dr. Morrissey doesn't get nervous. He was in Vietnam, and he saw stuff that you couldn't even imagine, and if he says something, you can bet your coons it's true." Oh no, Kellogg thought. I said *coons*. He had the wild urge to explain to Cummings about Dolly and Dingo.

Cummings gave no sign of being offended. "Okay, Kellogg, okay. I guess you and Morrissey really are friends, aren't you?"

"You bet. I'd do anything for him—" He stopped, realizing how Cummings had trapped him.

"When are you going to stop bullshitting me, my man?" the detective said quietly.

"What do you care? There's no crime. It wasn't your neck that got chewed."

"Oh, there aren't going to be any charges," Cummings said quickly. "Hey, I love a mystery . . . but this one's really getting me waxed."

"It was all just like I said." Kellogg finished buttoning his shirt. "I gotta go."

Cummings stepped in front of him. "Tell me about Monk."

Kellogg went cold. *Monk. He'd never said the dog's name, never once. He'd been very careful about that. So how did Cummings know?*

"That's one of those guys that lives in a monastary and makes bread, right?"

Cummings shook his head sadly. He took a card from his pocket and handed it over. "I gave one of these to Doc Morrissey too. If you or he decides to lighten up, give me a call—or diddlybop over."

Kellogg almost pitied Cummings. This really bugs him, he thought. If *I'm* confused about Monk, think what it's like for him.

The detective stopped at the door. "By the way," he said, "you're right about 'Nam. I can't imagine it. But I do remember it."

Kellogg flushed. "I didn't mean to put you down," he said, but Cummings was gone.

On the road in his pickup, Kellogg gnawed at his lower lip. That was some job he'd done on the detective. *You can throw me in jail, you can torture me, but I'll never tell.* A real hero, the way he'd protected Pete, when the fact was, he didn't know anything *to* tell. Just that it was a Doberman, not a German shepherd, and it was supposed to have been dead—which would make Cummings laugh. But it was no laughing matter. Pete had done something to that dog.

And he had to find out what.

No, that was wrong. He had to *help* Pete, in whatever way he could. Because Cummings had been right: Pete *was* nervous; and if a guy like Pete got nervous, it had to be a bad jam, a real bad jam.

So what should he do? He'd want to head over to the Labs tonight to check up on his rats and dogs. But first he'd better go home and make sure good old Cousin Archie had kept the coons and the cat fed right. Then he'd call Pete and let him know he'd be coming back to work. Then, real casual, he could ask about Monk—just whether Pete had found him yet.

If Pete wanted to tell him, fine; if not, fine. Either way, Pete needed his help, and he'd give it with no strings. That's what friends were for.

Chapter 17

1930 hours:

The second-in-command's office was locked. There was no light under the door and the secretary wasn't at her desk.

Without much hope, Morrissey went next door to Alan's office. It was locked too; no secretary. Morrissey checked his watch. 7:35? He stared at it in disbelief. Brilliant. He'd driven all the way back to the Labs after closing time. He wasn't going to find out a damned thing about Alan.

He leaned against the secretary's desk, weighed down with disgust and fatigue. Clearly he couldn't trust himself to think straight right now. Lying awake half last night worrying about the dog was catching up with him—that and everything since. He listened to his stomach growl—right, and he hadn't eaten since breakfast.

He shuffled back into the main hallway, too tired and depressed to lift his feet. Then he noticed the bar of light falling from a door at the far end of the hall. One of the labs.

Alan's necropsy lab!

Morrissey hurried down the hall. He burst into the lab and stopped in disappointment. Not Alan. Lisa Pancek, the new biophysicist Alan had dated a few times. She was working at one of the necropsy tables. She turned in surprise, then smiled. "Hi, Peter."

He nodded, looking at the table. Rats, ten of them, pinned to the butcher block and sliced open, entrails pulled out. He smelled the sickly sweet odor of congealing blood mingled with the stench of a nicked bowel. He looked away, feeling a queasy movement in his empty stomach.

Pancek peeled off her rubber gloves. The everted fingers of the gloves clung to her fingertips before snapping back. She must have been at it awhile—long enough to work up a sweat on her hands. He watched her shrug out of her labcoat, admiring her despite himself. She moved with the loose-jointed flourishes of a model. She was good-looking, bright, and single. And tall—almost six feet. She'd look good beside Alan. Maybe Alan would become really interested in her, and they'd get married. Then if Alan wanted to hug Janet it wouldn't seem so . . .

Morrissey brushed the thought away, angry with himself. "Would you happen to know where Alan is?"

She eyed him with concern. What was she staring at? He became aware of the tightness of his forehead, the web of wrinkles gripping his skull through the skin. He willed the tiny muscles to relax.

"I did get a call from Alan today," Pancek said, "but I don't know where he is. I wish I did. He said he'd take me to dinner if I did a quick cut-down on some of his rats. Those poor bastards on the table there."

Morrissey looked at the corpses. "*His* rats?"

"Right. The ones he's been keeping in your lab—you know, from that study he's been doing with Hisle."

Morrissey's mouth went dry. The rats in his lab. Those were the L-6 rats. *Alan, you fool!*

"Everybody's been wondering what Alan was doing in Building C," Pancek went on, "with that MP guard and all, and here it's just some cancer study. Do you have any idea why he'd want me to necropsy control rats?"

He stared at the rats, barely hearing her. A perfectly normal scene for this room. Just some dead rats, disemboweled, chunks of liver cut out, kidneys sliced, lung and heart cross-sectioned. A standard gross necropsy. The only question was: Would the rats get up and walk?

How long had Monk lain in the necropsy bag behind the lab before he'd risen up dead?

Morrissey said, "What number did Alan give you to call in the results?"

"He didn't. Hisle called about half an hour ago, after I'd done eight of the rats. I told him there was nothing so far. I offered to call him back after I'd done the last two, but he said that was good enough for now; maybe he'd call me again later. You don't look so good, Peter. You're kind of pale and waxy."

"Sorry," Morrissey mumbled. He walked out of the lab and wandered down the hall. If only Alan had left a phone number to track him. But he hadn't. So what next? Morrissey saw that he was passing the employees' canteen. He stopped and gazed at the vending machines. His stomach growled again, painfully, and a spasm of weakness passed through his legs. Alan had said he should eat more. Maybe if he got something in his stomach now, it would help him think.

He stood at the machines, pushing in quarters until he had a sandwich and a fruit pie. He chewed mechanically, tasting nothing. He felt the calories rushing almost at once into his bloodstream. He still couldn't seem to think, though. Now he felt sluggish instead of weak. He needed rest, just a few hours rest.

But he had to find Alan . . .

No, first he had to do something about those rats. In fact, he should have done it already. He'd better go back to the necropsy lab and get the rats away from Pancek. How?

Just ask her for them.

That was going to seem damned strange to her. No matter. If necessary, he'd just grab the corpses and run out.

Morrissey went into the hall and stopped. The light at the end was gone; the door to the necropsy lab was closed. He ran down and tried the door. Locked!

He swore in frustration. Stupid! He should have hustled the rats out when he'd had the chance.

What could he do now? There were no outside windows on this lab. The door was solid, impassable. Would one of the MPs have a key? Probably not, and even if they did, they wouldn't let him in. This wasn't his building. He needed authorization even to be here after working hours.

All right, just calm down and think. What would happen to the rats? Pancek would have dropped them into a plastic deadbag. There was no pick-up ramp behind this building, so she'd leave the rats just inside the door. Later, the night man with the lab keys would come around and collect the dead L-6 rats and take them to the furnace to be burned.

Morrissey felt better. Maybe that would take care of it. The night man would burn the rats and that would be the end of it.

Unless they rose up first.

What would happen if the night man discovered dead, disembowled rats moving in the bag? Morrissey labored through the scene in his mind, past the man's disbelief and horror, past the incredulous people he would call to see with their own eyes, to the headlines: RATS COME BACK FROM DEATH. Then: POSSIBLE IMMORTALITY SERUM DISCOVERED.

And the worst part would be that, even when the real, macabre truth came out, there would still be those who'd want to go on fooling with L-6.

Suddenly Morrissey was almost feverish with alarm. He had to make sure it didn't happen. The night man came on around nine. He'd have to be here then, hide, watch the man and be ready if necessary to get the rats away.

He put the last of the sandwich down and checked his watch. 7:00. He had a few hours before he would be able to do anything about the rats. Should he go home or—

Home!

There was no one at home to meet his father and the girls. Janet had driven back to the country place. This was Thursday evening. The girls would have finished their after-school basketball hours ago. Dad would use his key to let himself and the girls in. They'd be worried. They'd search the house for him or Janet.

They'd go to the basement!

Morrissey spilled his change on the floor trying to dig it out of his pocket. He scooped up a quarter and jammed it into the pay phone by the vending machines.

He listened while his home phone rang on endlessly.

His hand shook as he hung up. Dad and the girls should have been there by now. Why didn't they answer?

Maybe they'd gone on to Dad's place.

Morrissey dialed his father's number. The phone was picked up after two rings. "Petey?"

Thank God! "Yeah, Dad. Do you have the girls?"

"Of course I've got 'em. Janet called me way back, two o'clock. Listen, boy, what's goin' on?"

"Janet called?"

"Your wife. My daughter-in-law. Asked me to take June and Tsong for the night. Didn't you know?"

"Thanks, Dad. That's good of you." Suddenly he knew talking wasn't enough. He had to go there, be with his daughters. "I'm coming over," he said and hung up.

He drove as fast as he could.

June was playing in the backyard and Tsong was taking a nap, curled up on her grandfather's bed, scrunched up against the cherrywood headboard. Her face was serene and secure. Morrissey looked down at her for a long time, feeling warmed.

As he went back to the living room, he checked out the back window. June was romping in the twilight with Ahab. The dog was bounding around her on its three legs, the stump of the left foreleg moving just as if there were a whole limb below it. Morrissey saw a vivid image of Monk, fangs bared, sneering at him from the darkness of the cellar. His jaws clenched with revulsion. He fumbled with the window latch, cursing. *Get the damned thing open! Call her inside, get her away from the dog . . .*

"Hey, Petey. Petey!"

He felt his father's hands holding his arms. What was he doing? Ahab was old and harmless.

And alive.

He let his father lead him to the overstuffed armchair and set him in it. The old man scurried to the kitchen and returned, pressing an Iron City into his hand. The cold, sweating bottle felt good in the heat of his palm. He smelled the familiar father smells of cooking greens and old musty newspapers, and his nerves began to settle. He gave a sheepish smile. His father shook his head worriedly and sat down in his old wooden rocker.

Morrissey tipped the bottle back, letting the beer slide down his throat. He listened to the slow, soothing creaks of the rocker. He felt his father's questioning gaze on him.

"The lab," he said.

"Figured."

The rocker creaked and creaked. Morrissey gazed fondly at the old face, the strong, beautiful lines around his father's eyes, his mouth, under his chin.

"How're you doing, Dad?" he asked softly.

"How'm *I* doing?" The old man hesitated, rocking, rocking. "I mined coal for thirty-seven years, Petey. You know what coal is?"

Morrissey slid down deeper in the chair. Wonderful, he thought affectionately. One of Dad's lectures.

"It's partly old dinosaurs," his father said.

Morrissey tried to concentrate on the words. The beer. Making him sleepy. *Old dinosaurs.* "Yup," he said.

His father looked toward the window. "I think there's some men mixed in with those dinosaurs. Parts of men, maybe dreaming down there in them seams. Other parts are somewheres else. Nothing's ever lost. Things don't end; they change. I'd like to be a fire sometime. Dance over that coal, hot and yeller."

Morrissey was wide awake again. He took a slow, calming breath and said nothing. Why did it make him so anxious—almost angry? Dad just needed to hope.

But it was The Lie: *Thou shalt not surely die.* If you thought you might come back as an angel, or another man, or . . . a fire, why should you fight? You weren't *really* going to die—not you. So you struggled with other things, you worked your whole life to build yourself up. You filled yourself industriously with memories and skills, learning and recording even at your play. You felt your powers grow.

You were gaining *control*. You loved and hated, and made commitments and laid plans—new ones every year—just as if you could go on.

And then it all started to unravel. Your muscles shrank and your skin wrinkled. Your leg began to hurt more until you couldn't walk on it. Your daughters came around often, but never often enough, because it hurt them too much to see you. They were still trying to believe The Lie—for themselves if not for you. Your wife was still with you, and you loved her more than ever. But you talked less. Sometimes when you looked at her you were torn with pain and desperation. You saw her dying. For all you had done, all you had made of yourself, you were powerless to stop it. And then she was gone.

But she mustn't die first, please, Janet . . .

Morrissey's stomach plunged down in him. He clenched the beer bottle in near panic.

"I ain't asking to die, Petey, but I didn't ask to be born either."

Stop, Morrissey thought. Please.

And then he was angry again, as angry as he'd been outside the bombed shell of Froggie's that night twelve years ago in Vietnam. He welcomed the old, cleansing hatred of death, letting it push the fear down as it always did.

"I was probably scared of bein' born," his father went on. "Thought it would be the end of everything. And you—hooo, boy. The way you screamed and hollered, if it'd been up to you, you'd still be in the pod."

Morrissey set the beer on the floor and got to his feet. He pulled his father up and hugged him. The old man resisted a little, then gave him a quick return squeeze and pried him off.

"You're just trying to shut me up," he groused. "Git that beer bottle up before it makes a ring."

Morrissey plucked the bottle up by the neck. "Too late," he observed.

Tsong came in, rubbing her eyes sleepily. Morrissey swept her into his arms gratefully. He held her until she shook off sleep.

"Daddy," she said. "I'm not afraid of the sandman anymore."

Morrissey felt a chill. The sandman. *Big and cold, and made of sand. He comes walking after you like a zombie.* "Good, he said. "Let's go out and play."

They went out back and joined June and Ahab, rolling around in the grass, tickling and giggling. Morrissey heard his father somewhere off to the side in the near dark, chuckling contentedly.

Then it was time to go.

Morrissey lingered on the front porch. His knees were wet with grass stains and his shirt was untucked. June clung to one leg and Tsong hung on his pocket. He looked down at them and knew he could do whatever he had to do.

Morrissey walked across the wide lawn toward the utility building. Utility was half-lit for night, like all the other buildings. The doors were slightly ajar. He hesitated. Someone inside was singing, a faint voice filtering through the crack between the doors. He chanced a quick look through the window. The night man was walking away from him down the hall, a black plastic bag slung over each shoulder. The bags swayed ponderously from side to side as he punctuated his singing with thrusts of his hips. Neither of those could be the deadbag from Pancek's lab—too big and too full. The night man was obviously in a jolly mood, so nothing had happened yet.

Most likely he'd already dumped the rats into the furnace and they were destroyed, burned up.

Morrissey watched him open the door to the furnace room and sling the bags in. He ducked back out of sight as the man turned to come back down the hall. Damn! He hadn't put the bags in the furnace. He was just collecting now. The rats were either still back at the lab or lying there in the furnace room. He'd have to check, and if the rats were there, he'd have to burn them himself before the night man got back with more. Morrissey's stomach gave a rebellious jolt.

Move it, before he gets here!

Morrissey hurried around the corner of the building and

watched the night man exit and stroll across the lawn between buildings. A second movement caught his eye. Another man, angling across the grass to meet the night man. An MP! Morrissey pressed himself against the wall and watched anxiously. He had no business here at night. Army Labs was a high-security military installation. If the guard saw him, it would be all over.

The guard intercepted the night man, and snatches of their talk drifted across to Morrissey. His shirt started to stick against his back with sweat. He projected a thought at the two men: *Go, damn you. Go somewhere else!*

The men turned and moved off toward the main complex.

Morrissey pushed through the double doors. He ran down the hall. At the door to the furnace room, he took a deep breath. He went in.

He tried to breathe shallowly, but the stink seeped through anyway—the stench of spoiling meat. Where was the light switch? He could barely see. No time to look. The red glow leaking around the cast-iron door of the furnace would have to do. His eyes began to adjust, and he made out a pile of black bags to his left. The polyethylene gleamed softly along its folds.

He felt a sharp pain in his ankle. He gasped and kicked out. Something was biting him! The teeth pulled loose as he kicked, and he heard a thud against the bags. *Christ, God!* He flung himself at the door, scrabbling for the handle, looking fearfully around his feet. More rats, closing in on him.

Hold it! he commanded himself.

He found the door handle and leaned on it, using his weight to freeze himself in place. He stared at the rats. They crawled slowly, brokenly, across the floor at him. The fur around their mouths was matted with blood. Their dragging entrails marked the floor behind them with dark smears. Their eyes glittered in the furnace light, a deep red.

He heard something rattling against the door and realized it was his elbows—his whole body was quaking. The nearest rat was almost at his feet. He kicked it back. It squirmed over onto its ripped belly and started its patient stalking of him over again. He kicked two others back and looked wildly around the room.

There, by the furnace, the gloves. Animal-care gloves—rawhide! He snatched them up. They were small and the rawhide was so stiff he could barely bend his fingers. He pulled open the furnace door. Heat seared his face and then his back, face, back, as he turned and scooped up the rats, flung them into the flames.

Finally all the rats were gone.

He was drenched with sweat. He pulled off the gloves and put them back in their place. He pawed among the deadbags until he found the one the rats had been brought in. It was chewed and tattered. He threw it into the fire and watched it crumple in the shimmering heat.

He felt nauseated and bent over but nothing came up.

Then he was sitting behind the row of shrubs that skirted Building C. How had he gotten here? He remembered running right across the lawn, not caring who saw him. Must be no one had. Thank God for small favors. But he'd better be sure he wasn't seen here. This was the tightest security zone on the whole base—the lab where Alan had been doing his radiation study.

He huddled back against the brick, feeling the roughness dig into his back. He wanted to hide, melt into the wall and just stay there. His hands itched. They felt unclean. His ankle throbbed where the rat had bitten it. An aftershock of fear prickled through him. A bite. Could L-6 get into him that way? No, of course not.

He wiped the sweat from his face. All right. He'd got rid of the rats. There was nothing more he could do tonight. He'd come back tomorrow, first thing, and start shaking people down. Someone at the Labs had to know where Alan was.

But right now the best thing he could do was go home and get some sleep. Home he thought with yearning. Bed.

He pushed up from the bushes and saw the man, heard the click of the rifle bolt. His heart leapt and started to pound. *No, it couldn't be.*

"Freeze, buddy. Military Police!"

Morrissey raised his hands. "Perfect," he said.

Chapter 18

2000 hours:

Janet stood on the deck and looked out across the valley. The pines below were already blurred in twilight. On the far ridge, the treetops looked like dark lace against the red bands of sunset. It's beautifui, she thought, then turned away. Beautiful—and totally out of synch with her mood.

She sniffed hard, angry at the tears that kept trying to spill. She had never been so miserable. How could this have happened? All she'd wanted to do was help Peter. So Peter practically throws her out of the house. Then she tries to comfort Alan, and he puts the clench on her just as Peter bursts in. It was diabolical.

She thought of Alan's note and shook her head, distressed. *I never stopped loving you. I never will.*

Such a fantastic man; smart, witty, and gorgeous. Why couldn't he find a woman—any woman but her? With that lordly face, his archangel's body, huge and powerful, he could have any woman he wanted.

Almost.

There was a light, betraying tingle in her nipples. She smiled ruefully. Oh, yes, he turned her on; he always had.

And she even loved him, in a way. But not *the* way. That was only for Peter.

She thought of Alan's upstairs bedroom and a chill went through her. The ball glove, the model airplanes, clumsily glued and strung with thread from the ceiling. Alan, with his precise, surgeon's hands, deliberately making the job look childish. She'd called it art, and it was—a fantasy sculpture.

It was also creepy.

The sun was down now and it was quickly getting cold. She went inside and locked the sliding glass doors, suddenly anxious. Where was Peter? He'd said he'd come later. But maybe he'd changed his mind. He'd looked so crushed leaning on her car, gazing at her through the window. He was miserable too. She could no longer hold that knowledge away. It diluted her anger at once, and she began to see things from Peter's perspective. The little scene at Alan's front door *had* looked bad. And he couldn't know how innocent it was until she told him.

She had been wrong and selfish to demand that he come running after her.

The thought that she might be to blame for all this filled her with relief. She came to a quick decision. She would go to Peter.

She locked up the summer house quickly. In the car she tried to think how it would go when she got home. By now Peter would have learned that his father was keeping the kids tonight. He might be sitting in the kitchen, as he sometimes did late at night when he couldn't sleep. She would come in and join him in the dark. They would sit awhile in silence, and then she would tell him: *Peter, you are all I want from life. You and my girls and my art. Don't ever think anything else.*

She pulled up in front of the brownstone, turned off the engine, and hurried up the front steps, desperate to be inside, in her own home, with Peter. She fumbled the door key in her eagerness. As soon as she was inside, she called Peter's name. She listened. It was so silent and dark. She felt the silence pouncing in on her, sucking away her eagerness in a second. There was something different about the house. She could feel it at the nape of her neck, the backs of her eyes—the whisper of another presence.

"Hello, is anybody here?"

The house swallowed up her voice so completely that a second later she wasn't sure she'd spoken. She forced a smile. "No one but us burglars," she singsonged. Again the house seemed to smother her words. Weird. Better not to say anything else.

Where was Peter?

Could he be out somewhere drinking? Her mind seized on the explanation. He *had* been going back to see Alan. It would be just like the two of them to go down to the Alibi and get wasted on Virginia Gentleman. Patch things up between themselves first and worry about her later. Peter would come staggering in any minute now. Maybe they'd both come staggering in. I'll *brain* them, she thought. No, I'll kiss them, *then* I'll brain them.

It was so *dark* in here. She'd never seen the house like this, *felt* it like this.

Get some lights on. Get them *all* on.

She hurried from one lamp to the next until the downstairs gleamed reassuringly. There, that was all of them.

No—that brass one by the parlor couch. Smiling at her silliness, she walked to it and flipped the switch. The whole house went dark.

Damn! She'd blown that damned fuse again. Or tripped the circuit, or whatever it was. This stupid old house. It was like that big party back in May, when she'd turned on the mixer for the whipped cream. But then the house had been full of people—people laughing, cracking jokes about the dark.

And Peter had been here to grope down to the basement and reset the circuit.

Janet groaned. She *hated* the basement. It was full of jumpy-bugs—what did Peter call them? Camel crickets. Insane monster bugs that would jump toward you when you startled them. And it was gloomy, moldy, old. That cellar under the steps, as dark and cramped as a dungeon . . .

Never mind.

Where was the flashlight? All the way upstairs in the bedroom. And Peter had another somewhere, probably in the basement. Big help.

She followed the rail upstairs. The steps creaked loudly under her feet. Her eyelids strained wide. It was pitch black, suffocating. She sighed with relief as her hand closed around the flashlight, right where it belonged on her bed table, thank goodness. She followed the beam downstairs, waving it back and forth. Shadows feinted and slipped around her. Everything looked different, sly and menacing.

She stood peering at the basement door a minute. The yellow paint looked wet under the beam. "I'm coming down," she said through the closed door.

She pulled the door open and shined the light down the steps. She could just make out the pull-string floating in the dark at the bottom of the steps, insubstantial as a spiderweb.

"Okay, here I come."

Her heels seemed very loud, clumping down the steps. She yanked the pull-string and nothing happened. Terrific! This light must be on the same circuit.

What was that smell? There was the usual mustiness, of course, the mushroom smell from the dirt under the steps. But this was something else—a thin, biting odor like gunpowder.

She blew out her breath and headed for the fusebox. Something jumped through the light and she yelped. A jumpy-bug. The creepy little bastard!

She began to smell sawdust. Must be from Peter's work on the birdhouse.

She opened the fusebox and shone the light along the circuit breakers. There, that fifth switch down. She flipped it over and the basement light came on, filling the room with blessed white radiance.

Good, she thought. Now get out of here!

She turned from the fusebox and saw the cellar door. She faltered back, confused. Someone had nailed a board to the door. Right about at eye level. And there was fresh sawdust at the base of the door.

Peter must have done that today, while she was gone.

Why?

The back of her neck pimpled into goosebumps. There was something in there. Something that had made Peter throw her out this morning. No need to be afraid, because it was not a prowler, or anything like that. It was just a thing of some sort. But it had made Peter act strangely.

She had to know what it was.

She really ought to have something in her hand, a weapon, just in case . . . In case what?

She went to Peter's workbench. Strange—Peter's electric chain-saw was lying out on the bench. He hadn't even hung it back up after using it. That wasn't like him. She put her flashlight on the bench and ran a hand over the tool rack. The hammer. Yes, a good heavy hammer. The handle had a slight oily feel from years of him gripping it. She hefted it, letting the solid feel of its weight travel up her arm. She put her finger under the door hook and flipped it up.

The door swung open and she saw the shape: *a dog, big, springing at her!* She screamed and brought the hammer around. A shock traveled up her arm. Got it! She heard bone snap as the hammer rebounded from the dog's shoulder, pushing it off course. The open jaws barely missed her. It went down and stayed.

She screamed again, just to get rid of the huge overload of fright. She stumbled back against the wall, still holding the hammer out front. Lord, it had scared her! Good thing she'd had the hammer. She'd broken its shoulder. It was laid out good. It wouldn't be able—

She sucked in her breath as the dog rose with a fluid motion. How could it be up again? She could see the lumps at its shoulder where fragments of bone pushed at the dark skin. It should be writhing and whining in agony. But it hadn't made a sound.

It took a step toward her.

"Go away," she screamed. She pressed against the wall and held the hammer out front, two-handed. The dog bared its teeth. Its eyes squinted maliciously at her.

What was this awful creature doing in her basement?

With a shock, she recognized the breed: a Doberman!

This was the dog Peter had been after, the same one they'd seen from their bedroom that night. Peter had caught it and brought it inside. *Why?*

The dog took another step, the broken shoulder wobbling a little.

"Back!" she shouted. She stomped a foot at it. It hesitated. Then it reared up smoothly on its hind legs and bared its teeth at her again.

She froze with terror. There was a spurting pressure in her bladder. If it jumped on her now, she wouldn't even be able to move. Oh, dear Jesus, look at it. What *was* it?

Its tongue lolled out of its mouth, long and ropy and too white, like a slick eel. It gave a low chuckling growl. She felt her teeth chattering.

She heard a pop beside her and the lights went out.

The blackness seemed to press into her nose and throat, suffocating her. The circuit breaker, she thought, agonized. I forgot to turn the lights off upstairs. The dog is going to kill me!

She grabbed blindly for the flashlight on the workbench. *Got it.* The beam stabbed out front, catching the Doberman. It was still standing on hind legs. It had moved up on her in the dark. It was only a step away! As the light hit its eyes, it edged back. The white, dangling tongue withdrew inside the muzzle with a dry, rasping sound that made her shudder. The dog's eyes narrowed to resentful slits. Good, she thought—the light bothers it. Keep it right on the eyes.

Her hand shook violently, making the beam waver around the dog's face. Oh, please, hold it still, *hold it still*! The circle of light steadied a bit. The eyes reflected a rusty red, the color of dried blood.

She felt faint. Her legs went weak—they were going to dump her. She had to do something, get the dog somehow, get away, or it was going to be too late.

The saw! If she could just get the saw before the dog could jump her.

She felt the tendons of her neck straining. Her head stayed locked in place. She was afraid to look away. The moment she did, the dog might spring. The red eyes burned into her brain. Dark spots danced before her eyes. She couldn't even see her arm holding the light out. Her left arm ached. She felt the weight of the hammer pulling her fingers open. If she dropped the hammer, she'd have nothing. Hang on, hang on! She grunted with the effort, felt the oily handle slipping loose. The hammerhead struck the floor a ringing blow. The dog looked down and she whirled, grabbed the saw, thrust it out, holding the flashlight alongside the blade.

The dog backed up as though it knew exactly what the saw was. "Ha!" Her voice came out high and squeaky. "You don't like that, do you. Good! Just get away now."

The dog stayed where it was.

Keeping the light on its face, she fumbled for the trigger of the saw. She pulled it and nothing happened. She heard a little rabbit cry and realized it was her. Sweat poured down her face. Oh God, the circuit was still tripped. The plug at the workbench must be on the same line. She was finished.

Wait, was the saw plugged in? She waved it up high and felt the loose cord brush her ankle. No, it wasn't! There was still a chance. But how was she going to get away with bending over and plugging it in? The dog would tear her throat open in the first second. She could almost feel its cold, slimy teeth there now, ripping, chewing. That's what it meant to do. It meant to kill her.

She felt her finger clutching convulsively at the trigger: click-click, click-click. The dog bared its teeth in that horrid mockery of a smile again and started moving in on her with small, mincing steps of its hind legs. The foreleg on the broken side dangled low.

She was cold with panic. She could hardly breathe.

It had to be now.

She stooped, setting the light on the floor, fingers scrabbling for the plug, jamming it at the box, missing—*there, got it!* She heard the dog's claws ticking over the floor at her. Turn, raise the saw, oh, Jesus, there it was above her, lunging down, please God!

She clenched the trigger. The saw kicked in with a ratcheting whine. She pushed up on rubbery knees and swung the saw. Not enough light. There, its head, a foot away! She homed in on the neck and felt the whirling blade connect, chewing through gristle and bone. She screamed as cold flecks of skin spattered her. In the dim wash from the flashlight she saw the head fly loose, the body dropping away.

She gagged and sat down hard on the floor.

Silence.

Oh God oh God oh God. She'd killed it. She was safe! She sobbed wildly. Gradually she got herself under control, and the sobs became snuffles. Get up, she thought. Flip the circuit breaker again. Maybe the lights will last long enough for you to get out of here.

She tried to stand, but her legs felt weak. They wouldn't hold her up yet.

So quiet. What about the chainsaw? She picked up the flashlight, shined it along the wall, and saw that the plug had pulled out as she whipped the saw through the dog's neck. She shuddered. If it had pulled loose a second earlier, she'd have given the dog a harmless swat instead of cutting its head off. And now she'd be dead.

Where was the body? Better take a look.

The flashlight beam sought it out, lying limp and still by the cellar door. And there was the head, lying three feet from her. It faced her, the stump of the neck down against the floor. Gross! The eyes were still open, seeming to glare into hers. She shined the light at the cement around the stump. Where was the blood? There had to be blood, she could almost see it, knowing it must be there.

But it wasn't.

She moaned. Impossible. This was a nightmare.

Peter, what have you done?

The muzzle of the dog's head pulled back in a snarl. She couldn't find her breath to scream. It was . . . glaring at her . . . and the muzzle was wrinkling . . . No, don't black out . . . hang on, *hang on* . . .

Everything went gray and slid away.

Chapter 19

2100 hours:

"Dr. Morrissey! *Superbo!*"

The voice was sneering, and sharp with delight. It seemed oddly familiar. Morrissey squinted into the glare of the flashlight, but he couldn't make out the face.

Frantically he pressed for something to say. *Lost my watch in these bushes, soldier. I'm collecting fireflies for my daughter's show and tell. I wanted to take a leak and the heads were closed.*

"You don't remember me, do you, Doc? Corporal Rick Carrera, at your service." The man shone the light on himself for a second. The image burned itself into Morrissey's brain: black helmet band with the white MP letters, a lean Aztec face, black eyes with a feline tilt.

Carrera! The MP from outside Alan's lab.

Morrissey groaned.

"Yeah, you remember. You grabbed my gun away. Maybe you'd like to try it again now?"

An alarm went off in Morrissey's brain. All right, Carrera had caught him skulking around a restricted area. He had some creative explaining to do. But why was Carrera baiting him? The whole mess was going to end up in Alan's office.

Restricted area or not, if Carrera kept mouthing off to a senior project director, he could get in trouble, and he should know it.

Unless he didn't plan for it to end up in Alan's office.

"You 'Nammers think you're such hot shit. Think you're the only ones with *cajones*. Everyone else is pussy.

"Look, Corporal—"

"How many slant babies did you grease in 'Nam, big shot?"

Slant babies. Morrissey thought of Tsong and flushed with anger. Wait, that must be what Carrera wanted—for him to get mad and make a stupid move. He kept his hands up.

"You were sneaking around a top-secret military installation, Doctor."

"I can explain."

"Shove it up your ass."

Morrissey's throat was suddenly dry. He tried to swallow. How could this be happening? He barely remembered this guy . . . Morrissey blinked as he saw a movement behind Carrera. There it was again—a dark shape gliding across the lawn behind Carrera! As the shape moved into line with the MP it was wiped from view by the sunspot of the flashlight.

"I could have shot you already."

The tight, high sound of Carrera's voice jerked Morrissey's attention back.

"You attacked me once," the MP went on. "Everyone on the base knows it."

"Everyone knows you have a grudge, you mean." Morrissey's heart pounded. His arms ached from holding them up. *Just keep him talking.*

"Maybe they'd think *you* had the grudge. Didn't like Latinos or something."

Morrissey saw the barrel of the M-16 line up with the beam from the light. He looked behind Carrera again. There was nothing—no further movement. Had he imagined the dark shape? He saw the MP's finger tightening around the trigger. Coldness rushed through him. An image flared in his mind: himself lying on the grass in front of Carrera, his life leaking red out of a dozen holes. *No, please. Senseless . . .*

A dark mound welled up behind Carrera. Morrissey heard a dull thump, like a melon splitting. The MP's head jerked up. The flashlight tilted, and the cat-eyes rolled together. Morrissey dropped to his knees as Carrera flopped toward him onto the grass. Morrissey doubled over, clutching his stomach in reflex where the bullets would have hit. The handful of shirt was drenched with sweat.

"Hi, Pete."

Morrissey stayed doubled over.

"Uh . . . hi, Pete?" The voice hitched in an adolescent croak.

He looked up slowly. Kellogg. A rumpled yellowish bandage at his throat. Morrissey stared at him, weak and stupid with relief.

Then he looked at the MP sprawled in the grass.

"What's new?" Kellogg added.

"Holy *shit*! Do you know what you just did?"

"I saved your arse," Kellogg said happily. He bent an arm up, flexing it tightly. It rolled with fat and muscle. "I'd like to see some *skinny* guy pot an MP with just his elbow. Probably break it."

Morrissey looked at Carrera again, and laughter boiled up in his throat. Kellogg laughed too—genially, as though they were frat brothers, sharing a joke: the silly pratfall by the man in the grass. "I float like a butterfly, Pete, and I sting like a rhino."

Morrissey grabbed the fallen guard's M-16 and threw it into the bushes. "Kellogg, what the hell are you *doing* here?"

"Looking for you. What'd you do to that guy—yank on his nose hairs?"

"Come on, Kellogg."

"Okay, okay. They just let me out of the hospital. I've been trying to call you to ask you about my animals. Then I figured you might be working late, so I came on out. I checked my rats and dogs, then went looking for you. Kojak, there, beat me to it."

Morrissey bent over Carrera and checked his pulse. Slow and regular. His helmet liner was pinned low in front by his forehead, exposing the back of his neck, where an angry bruise was forming. Carrera started snoring.

Morrissey grunted. This was insane. Kellogg had to play the hero. Had Carrera really been going to shoot? It seemed incredible now. Why couldn't Kellogg have just come over and said, "A-a-a-hhh what's up, Doc?" to the MP? If Carrera had seen that someone else was around, surely he'd have got hold of himself.

"That is a military policeman," Morrissey said. "He already doesn't like me too much. When he wakes up . . ."

"We'll be gone, poof, like smoke," Kellogg said. "Let's go. You can crash at my place."

Morrissey tried to sort things out. Shouldn't he call the police? No—*hell no*! At best, the police would stick him on some waiting-room bench and paper him over. At worst, they'd arrest him for assault, or spying, or some damned thing.

He couldn't let that happen. Not until he'd found Alan and stopped L-6.

As soon as he ran out of here, he would be a hunted felon.

On the other hand, he wasn't dead.

"Okay," he said. "Let's go."

He let Kellogg lead him across the lawn to the parking lot. It was surprising how fast the kid could trot, considering his bulk. Morrissey's eyes strained. It was so dark, hard to see. There was no moon. The blacktop was as bottomless as the sky under his feet. He felt his legs clumping under him like wooden posts. Only fifty yards, and he was winded. He'd shot too much adrenaline in too few hours.

Kellogg stopped in front of a battered pickup truck and motioned to the passenger side.

"I've got my own car here."

Kellogg snorted. "Pete, they don't just have your address, they've got your license number, the whole nine yards. And Gooney-gun is gonna wake up pretty soon."

Morrissey climbed into the pickup. He sank back gratefully into the sprung cushions as Kellogg pulled out of the parking lot. I'll just rest a minute, he thought, and then get my head in gear.

He sat for a while in a near stupor. The pickup rocked rhythmically on tortured shocks as Kellogg warped it through a maze of dark residential streets. Vaguely, Morrissey saw that they were heading for the northeast part of Washington.

Kellogg said, "That detective—Cummings—came back to the hospital. But I didn't tell him about Monk. I just gave him my German shepherd story again."

Morrissey nodded. He realized Kellogg was glancing at him, over and over.

"You don't have to tell me nothing, Pete. You don't have to tell me nothing at all."

Morrissey closed his eyes and tried almost giddily to sort through the double negatives. He did *not* have to tell Kellogg *nothing*. Did that mean he did have to tell Kellogg something? Yes. But what? Not about Monk, that was for sure. But thank you might be nice. Whether Carrera had really meant to shoot him or not, it was the thought that counted.

"You *did* save my arse, Kellogg. Thanks."

Kellogg smirked with embarrassment. In the cycles of light and dark from the streetlights, Morrissey watched him chew at his lower lip and twist the wheel back and forth. Who is this kid? he wondered. He's a lot like the ones in Vietnam you thought you could save. Tonight Kellogg *did* save you. So who is he? Where are his parents? Why is he so fat and sloppy? Why does he love animals so much? Why did he stick his neck out for you?

A lot of questions. The kind of stuff he'd wished he'd known about the kids who had died. Here Kellogg was, alive. He'd been around Kellogg for two years, and knew less about him than some of those kids on his precious list.

Morrissey tipped his head back and let the monotonous motion of the pickup lull him. He began to slide down toward sleep. He tried to hold his mind afloat, sorting through a frictionless glide of thoughts and images. He saw the risen L-6 animals attacking him, the rats and the dog, relentlessly coming after him. *What was it like to have the electricity of consciousness without the warmth, the blood, the juice of flesh?*

Morrissey could not hold the question. It slid away into the dark.

18
DAYS

Friday, October 24

Chapter 20

1100 hours:

Morrissey came awake slowly. He realized that his spine was crimped over like a tight-strung bow. His back ached, and the unfamiliar sag of the mattress gave him a wallowing sense of disorientation. Could this be his bed? He lay still. Maybe if he didn't open his eyes or move, everything would drift away again.

The room impressed itself on him despite his sealed eyelids. What was that smell? Like a zoo. No, not a zoo. The place took shape in his mind, the foggy memory of last night. Kellogg's dingy efficiency: a cat, a bird, and—had that been a snake? Yes, and raccoons. Three of them. That weight curled on the covers between his feet—that must be one of the animals.

God, the snake?

Morrissey jerked his head up and stared down the bed. The coon raised its head too, lazily, and peered at him with its bandit eyes. Morrissey sagged back down with a tortured squeak of bedsprings.

From somewhere across the room Kellogg began to snore and smack his lips. There would be no drifting off again with that racket. Morrissey considered shifting to his side, any position to get his back uncrimped, but he was afraid that the bedsprings would wake Kellogg. Before that happened, he needed time to collect his wits. He gazed up at the ceiling. It was a greasy white, flaked with peeling paint which looked like it might shower down into his eyes at any second. He blinked in reflex. I have a firm, king-sized bed, he thought, in a bedroom that doesn't smell. I have a beautiful wife. I have two nice kids. What am I doing here?

Kellogg stopped snoring and sat up, peering at him over the sofa back. Uncanny, Morrissey thought sourly. He must've heard me blinking. He watched the kid's face metamorphose from the dullness of sleep to excitement. Oh my yes, what an adventure.

Kellogg smiled and rubbed his hands together. "Morning, Pete. How about some breakfast?" Without waiting for an answer, he got up, pulled on his robe, and plodded over to his kitchenette. Morrissey nudged the coon off the bed, gathered his clothes, and went into the apartment's bathroom. He grimaced in distaste. The room was rank, the sink almost black and the tub full of grit and hair.

Morrissey straightened his back, then bent and dangled his fingers toward his toes a few times, trying to work out the stiffness. He washed up in the sink, combed his hair, and dressed. He touched his toes again, with more dedication, trying to get the blood into his head.

Better—much easier to think now. He'd want to get out of here as soon as possible, of course. The necropsied rats were taken care of, and he was free to go after Alan. He'd have to stay away from the Labs, though, after what had happened last night.

Or would he?

Carrera *should* report him, of course, but it wasn't obvious that he would. What must Carrera feel like now that he'd let the same man who'd snatched his gun get the best of him again? He'd be furious—and even more embarrassed. He could lose a stripe over it. Maybe he wouldn't report it at all.

Still, it would be best to avoid the Labs if possible for a few days, just to be safe. He could use the phone . . .

Kellogg rapped on the door. "Breakfast is served."

Morrissey joined Kellogg at the card table in the dining alcove. He tried to ignore the noxious smells: burned bacon and eggs swamped in grease. Amazing that his stomach wasn't flopping over. He looked warily for the animals. The coons were nowhere in sight, but the black tomcat sat at Kellogg's feet, front paws tucked primly together, ears and eyes pointed at his owner with perfect concentration. "Okay, okay," Kellogg grumbled. He dropped a bit of bacon and the cat pounced on it, batting it around before scissoring it up with yellowed fangs.

"Use your phone?" Morrissey asked.

"Sometimes," Kellogg said, then flushed as he understood. "Oh! Sure!" He pointed to the kitchen counter and muttered "*Stupid,*" at himself. It was a decorator phone, smeared with fat fingerprints. Morrissey dialed the lab. He talked to the second-in-command, Vandiver's secretary, Lisa Pancek, and Hisle's office. No one knew where Alan was. Pancek had had no further calls from Hisle.

At least no one acted surprised to hear from him. Did that mean Carrera had kept his mouth shut?

Morrissey tried Alan's house. No answer. He tried calling Janet, first at the brownstone and then at the country house. His ear buzzed with the monotonous ringing at the other end. He hung up, frustrated and worried. He had not tried to reach Janet yesterday, and now he couldn't. He needed to talk to her. She might know where Alan was.

A lump formed in his throat. Did he really hope that? Yes, he had to hope it, no matter what else it meant. *Shut up, shut up, SHUT UP.*

He dialed his father. Dad hadn't heard from Janet. He'd taken the girls to school. He'd be happy to keep them until he heard otherwise. Would their mother or father by any chance have a moment to come by and see them today? Morrissey said he'd try and rung off before his father could make him feel worse.

"Breakfast's getting cold," Kellogg observed.

"I need to borrow your truck."

"Sure. I'm still on sick leave until Monday. C'mon, sit

down." Kellogg wiped off a fork with a paper towel and held it out.

"Thanks, but I'm not hungry," Morrissey said. "And I'd better be off."

"How long since you've eaten?"

"Damn it, I've already got a father," Morrissey snapped.

Kellogg looked at him, wide-eyed. "Sure, Pete. Sorry. 'Scuse me a minute." He got up and disappeared into the bathroom. Morrissey heard the water running behind the closed door. *Damn!* he thought. His father had needled him and he'd made poor Kellogg pay. He shook his head, remembering something from Kellogg's hiring interview two years ago: *My mom and dad were killed in a car crash when I was sixteen.* He could recall it precisely: the flat tone of Kellogg's voice, the averted eyes—so vivid now, after he'd shot his mouth off. Morrissey sagged down into the chair Kellogg had pulled up for him, stared at the greasy eggs.

Right, Peter, *you've* already got a father.

After a few minutes Kellogg came out. "Forgot to wash up," he said lamely. His eyes were rimmed in red. Morrissey pretended not to see.

"You want the truck right now, then?" Kellogg said.

"Maybe I *should* have some breakfast."

"Good. Otherwise I'd eat it all."

"You'll never get fat on bacon and eggs," Morrissey said as he sat down. "It's all those Tastykakes."

"Tastykakes saved my life," Kellogg pronounced. "And they saved yours too. That MP was a ten-thousand-calorie job. So just shut up about my Tastykakes."

"Right," Morrissey said meekly.

Janet had been at the country house last, so he drove there. Maybe she'd just refused to answer the phone, to punish him. He couldn't even blame her. Just be there, he thought fervently. Let me talk to you. That's all I ask.

As he got close, he began to worry about the police. He couldn't be sure Carrera had kept his mouth shut. By this morning the D.C. police could have done enough digging to find out about his second house. What if they were there waiting for him?

He pulled down the dirt lane to the house, clenching the wheel and peering through the windshield, ready to throw the pickup into reverse. He made the last curve and sagged in relief. No cop cars.

Janet's car wasn't there either.

He cursed and parked the pickup.

As soon as he walked through the front door, he smelled her paints and the familiar fragrance of linseed oil. It couldn't have been long since she'd been painting here. He called her name hopefully. No answer.

He dropped into one of the canvas sling-chairs, despairing. What was left? Go to the brownstone? It seemed futile. Where was Janet?

No, where was Alan?

He bent over and rested his face in his hands. With his eyes covered, he began to smell the painting again. The back of the easel was toward him, the painting facing the deck. He yearned suddenly for Janet. A piece of her was over there. He got up and looked at the painting. It was unfinished, and he could tell that it wasn't going well. It showed little of her usual command of form. The murky colors panged him—an unintentional painting of her distress.

He longed to hold her, hear her voice. And he couldn't even find her.

Morrissey saw a crumpled piece of paper under one leg of the easel. He picked up the scrap and spread it open. It was a handwritten note: *I never stopped loving you. I never will.*

Alan's handwriting.

He tried to focus on the rest of it, beneath the words, two phone numbers . . .

I never stopped loving you.

He sat down on the floor and stared out the sun deck. Tears filled his eyes.

After a long time, he went back to the phone. He dialed the first number on Alan's note. The phone rang twice before it was picked up.

"Science, may I help you?" It was a woman's voice.

"Oh, excuse me," Morrissey said. "What number have I reached?" His voice sounded soft and hoarse, like he'd been weeping. He cursed himself silently.

"This is the switchboard, sir. May I connect you with a specific lab?"

A lab. Good. "I'm sorry. A friend of mine wanted me to call him and he left me this number, but he didn't tell me where he was. You're the switchboard for . . . ?"

"Fort Detrick. If you can give me your friend's name, I can look in my directory."

Ft. Detrick! "He left an extension. Maybe you can connect me. Four-seven-one-oh?"

"Yes, sir. I'll ring you through." The receptionist sounded abruptly different, cooler and slightly perplexed.

The extension was picked up immediately. This time it was a male voice. "Biop Four."

"May I speak with Colonel Vandiver, please."

"Who is calling, sir?"

"I'd rather not say. It's very important that I talk to Colonel Vandiver."

There was a pause, and then the voice came back on the line. "I'm sorry, sir, but I've checked my listings and there is no Colonel Vandiver at this extension."

They were trying to stonewall him. He mustn't allow it. "But you know him?"

Pause. "No, sir."

"What is Biop Four?"

"I must ask who you are, sir. It's just regulations."

Morrissey considered it. Vandiver had given the numbers to Janet, so he must have left instructions for her to be put through. But if he said he was Morrissey, it wouldn't get *him* through. And if Alan was told about a male caller named Morrissey it would tip him off.

The hell with it. There was no choice. And surely Alan didn't intend to go on avoiding him indefinitely. Morrissey gave his name.

"Thank you." Another pause. Morrissey began to hope. The man must be checking a sheet of people cleared through the extension. That meant Alan was definitely at the other end. Come on, come *on*!

"I'm sorry, sir, but you have reached a classified number. As I said, there is no Colonel Vandiver here."

Damn!

"There could have been a mix-up," the voice on the line said. "Maybe this Colonel Vandiver is to be assigned here, and we just haven't seen him yet. If you'll leave your number, I'll have him call you if he does show up."

"No. That's all right. I'll call back later." As soon as he hung up, Morrissey got Kellogg's number from the phone book and dialed.

"Yeah?"

"This is Peter."

"Hi, Pete. I've been listening to the news, and you aren't on it."

"That's nice. But I don't think I would be. Army Labs isn't the kind of place that likes a lot of publicity."

"True. I never thought of that."

"I want to keep your truck awhile longer."

"No sweat. Do you think I should know where you're going?"

Morrissey hesitated. It might be good for someone to know where he was, in case things went badly wrong in the next few hours. "Fort Detrick," he said. "I think Colonel Vandiver is there. I'm going to see him."

"The C.O.? That's right—you guys are buddies."

"Thanks for the truck," Morrissey said and hung up.

Chapter 21

2330 hours:

Vandiver came awake holding the man's throat.

Adrenaline kicked into his muscles. He saw a dozen details before he could quite comprehend them: a dim light from somewhere below his bed, a sound like water in a drainpipe, a dark silhouette above him, something hard bouncing off his shins before it clattered to the floor.

Not fighting back. Just trying to pry open his fingers. He was strangling the man!

Vandiver let go, catching at the man and easing him to his knees. The man made harsh gasping noises. Thank God he hadn't crushed the fool's windpipe. Vandiver felt the fighting heat inside him cool to mere anger. Who the hell was it, sneaking in on him in the dead of night?

He found the flashlight beside his bed and flicked it on. There on the floor was the thing that had hit his shins—an M-16. Fortunately, the safety was on, or the cabin and everything in it might have turned into Swiss cheese. Vandiver played the beam up over the gasping man. It was one of the camp guards, Sergeant Bruck. Bruck's face was red, but the gasping sounded healthy. He'd get enough air in a minute.

Vandiver shut the cabin door and turned on the light. The bunched muscles in his shoulders began to unwind. He tried to swallow the tinny aftertaste that came from being shocked awake. He began to feel a twinge of pity. Poor Bruck. He should have warned the damned idiot the day he came on base.

But then, Bruck had been there too. He should have known, shouldn't he?

"Sorry, sir," Bruck rasped. "I didn't realize you'd been combat."

"Battalion Aid Station," Vandiver said. "First Infantry, north of Saigon. I did three months out there. They used to sneak in past the wire at night."

Bruck's eyes lost a little focus. "Yes, sir. They were quieter than the rats. Had one drop into my foxhole one night during Tet. You being a doctor and all, I guess I just—"

Vandiver motioned. "It's all right. Just be glad I wasn't sleeping with my forty-five under the pillow."

Bruck picked up his M-16. "I thought you medical guys weren't supposed to carry weapons."

"You also believe in the tooth fairy?"

"Sorry, General." Bruck didn't smile and Vandiver realized it was bad, whatever had brought the sergeant blundering in here in the middle of the night. The tinny taste on his tongue grew stronger.

"There's a problem, sir. Three men are dead."

Vandiver stared at him. "What?"

"Three of the volunteers," Bruck said in a rush. "The test subjects."

Vandiver went cold in an instant. "God damn us all! How?"

"They—I don't know—they were trying to escape, I guess. Or maybe they were just out walking. I don't know how they got past the sentry at their barracks. Anyway, one of the dog handlers was in camp with two of his German shepherds. The things went after them and they ran straight into the wire. I guess they panicked."

Vandiver realized with a prick of shame that he was relieved. They had *not* died from L-6. For a terrible second, he'd been sure Bruck had found them dead at the medical bedcheck. That would have ended Project Parasol.

And it would have meant millions *more* deaths.

What had actually happened was a tragedy, but one that could be endured. "Which three men?" he said.

"Hufnagel, Gilliam, and Warlow, sir."

Vandiver tried to put faces with the names. He could do it only for Warlow. The surly kid from New York. Tall and pale. That horsey, British rock star face, clashing with his brig-shaved head. Confined at Ft. Belvoir for repeated insubordination and for punching a navy lieutenant in a bar fight. Warlow was what passed for a leader among such types. Breaking out would have been his idea.

"Where are the bodies?"

"Still out by the fence, General."

"Wait outside. I'll be right with you."

Vandiver dressed, picked up his flashlight, and joined Bruck outside the cabin. A cold raindrop spattered on his forehead. Must've been a light shower while he'd slept. The air was cool, and he could hear a steady patter of water dripping off the cavernlike roof of maples and pines. A soft, lulling night, and three people were dead. He suppressed a shudder.

Two more guards were waiting with the bodies. The German shepherds stood back from the fence. Their tongues lolled pinkly in an irreverent parody of laughter. The two guards stood stiffly to attention and saluted. Great, Vandiver thought sourly. You screw up and three men die, and now you're all spit and polish.

But I screwed up too. I'm in command here.

Vandiver's fists clenched with anger—at the men, himself, this whole fornicating mess. He looked down at Warlow and the others, sprawled at the base of the fence. Poor, sorry geeks. The other two men were smaller than Warlow. Hufnagel was plump, with wispy hair growing in around his bald spot. He'd come from the brig at Ft. Myer, where they weren't so savage with the razor. Gilliam was just a thin, wiry kid with pimples. His dead eyes stared with fascination at the earth under his cheek as if the dirt and wet leaves held a great mystery.

It was 'Nam, all over again.

Vandiver checked them over quickly, feeling for a pulse at the neck. None. He saw that the hands of all three bore red welts across the palms. Apparently they'd all hit the fence at about the same time and hung there, and then the old generator had blown out under the strain, releasing the bodies before the hands could char.

Reluctantly he sniffed the air. Odd that there was no stink of urine or feces. The electric current tearing along the nerves must have cinched every muscle in the body, including the sphincters, into temporary tetany. The bowels and bladders would probably empty later, unless the bodies could be stored head down.

"Is the current back on yet?"

"No sir. That generator was pretty old. It may be tough to get it going again."

"I don't care how tough it is, get it fixed. Assign extra men to patrol inside the fence. Form a detail, and get these bodies put away. Use the cooler."

"Where the food is, General?" Bruck made an offended face.

Vandiver forced himself to patience. "Take the food out first, Sergeant. I'll get some smaller refrigerators sent out from the main base in the morning. Let's go, move it."

When Bruck had mustered six men, Vandiver let them stand around a minute, getting the sight of the fallen bodies into their heads. "This camp is operating on a war footing," he said quietly. "Maybe some of you jerk-offs don't realize what that means. Get this clear in your minds: If any of the *remaining* prisoners set foot near that wire again, I'll have a stripe from every man here. If any of the prisoners escape, you will be court-martailed on capital charges."

The six faces peered at him, pale and strained in the backwash from the fence's perimeter lights.

"What's done is done," Vandiver finished. "The less said about this the better." He looked at each of them. That one on the end, Corporal Trickett, averting his eyes. A bad sign. Better keep an eye on him.

"Now take these bodies to the cooler. That's it—no, no, keep the feet and hips up. That's right."

Vandiver martialed them along through the compound. No one spoke. He listened glumly to their feet squishing through the damp leaves.

After the food was taken out and the three bodies laid on the floor of the cooler, he dismissed the detail. He squatted on his heels, looking at the dead men. The shock of their deadness had already worn off. Was he still that hardened to the sight of death this long after Vietnam? Well, perhaps it was best. The deaths were a terrible thing, but nothing could be gained by wailing over them or wallowing in witless shock. Poor General Stanhouse. The last thing he needed was a near calamity in security—especially considering how much it had shaken him to approve the epidemic plan.

Vandiver shook his head. He must think about now—the immediate moment. Had he covered everything? The cooler would hide the bodies and slow their decay. When the time came, the corpses could be removed from refrigeration. Next of kin would receive them in preserved condition and the deaths could be post-dated, minimizing any snooping by bereaved or angry relatives.

God help them all, he only hoped there *would* be relatives around to snoop a couple of months from now. If so, he would gladly take the brunt of any unpleasantness over this.

Okay, that was it.

Vandiver started to stand. As he turned away from the bodies, he saw a tiny movement and turned back. There—again! Above the face of one of the men, a flutter of movement. Were there flies in here? Impossible—too cold. But one could have flown in when they'd brought in the corpses. It must have circled, there, over Warlow's eyes to give that illusion of the lids having moved.

Vandiver hesitated, watching the dead man's face, not quite satisfied. He shivered. With the door shut, the walk-in was regaining its chill. He buttoned the collar of his shirt and shoved his hands into his pockets.

The face did not move.

Of course it didn't. What was he thinking of? Time to get back to bed. But first he'd better stop by the power shed and find a good padlock. Then he could lock—

Warlow's eyes!

Vandiver hurried over and knelt beside the body. The eyelids were twitching! Now they were opening! He watched the langorous movement of the lids in disbelief. Warlow's eyes parted to slits, then slipped wider to a sleepy gaze, and finally widened grotesquely. Vandiver began to tremble. He hugged his arms to his chest and stared at Warlow in dread fascination. The dead man looked almost humanly shocked, as though he'd wakened and realized he was dead. *And they woke up in the morning and they were all dead corpses.* A crazy Bible text. He and Peter had sat in those little chairs at the back of old Mr. Babcock's Sunday school class and giggled over it.

Vandiver bent close, studied Warlow's pupils: expanded and uneven. There seemed to be no other movement in the body. He pressed his ear against the dead man's chest. It was still—no heartbeat or respiration.

Vandiver rocked back on his heels and blew out a breath. Spooky. But just a final twitch, that was all, a random discharge of the body's fading neuroelectricity.

He reached over to close the lids. They seemed to resist fractionally, then rolled down to cover the dead eyes.

He stood and strode from the cooler, pushing the door firmly shut behind him. He hurried away. Ah, it was good to get out in the warm air.

The power shed—don't forget the padlock.

Vandiver stopped and looked at his cabin window. He'd turned the light off as he'd left, hadn't he? Why was it on now?

He hurried over and pulled opened the door.

Hagan stood up behind his desk and faced him. Vandiver stayed still, too shocked to move. He stared at the leathery, tanned skull gleaming under the lights. A spasm of near panic passed through him.

"I'd like your report, Vandiver."

"Report?" Vandiver said numbly.

"On the three dead men."

Vandiver shook his head. How could Hagan know about the dead men? Vandiver remembered Trickett, the soldier on the cooler detail who wouldn't meet his eyes. That had to be it. Trickett was Hagan's informer. He must have called Hagan from the gate guardpost, Vandiver thought. Right after the deaths, before Sergeant Bruck woke me up.

No, *still* impossible. It was over an hour's drive up here from Hagan's place in Virginia.

Unless Hagan wasn't staying at his house.

Hagan must be staying right on the main base. Vandiver flushed with humiliation. *Stanhouse didn't trust him. Stanhouse had set Hagan to keep watch on him.*

"Come on, Vandiver, come on."

"Back off, Hagan. I report to General Stanhouse, not you."

"Like hell."

"What's that supposed to mean?"

"Let's don't bullshit around," Hagan said. "You have no intention of telling the general. If I hadn't known that about you already, I wouldn't have put a man in your camp."

"Okay," Vandiver said. "Let's *don't* bullshit. Your man is going out tonight. This is my operation. I won't have spies in here, and I sure as hell don't have to account to you."

Hagan gave him a contemptious look. "First, you don't know who my man is . . ."

"Corporal Trickett."

Hagan paused, eyeing him, and Vandiver savored a moment of satisfaction.

"And second," Hagan said, "he stays. Everyone but you stays here until it's finished. You ought to realize that. It's one of your own security rules. At least you got that much right."

"That's enough, Colonel."

"Third, you'll report to me because it's better than reporting to the general."

Vandiver hesitated, calculating. "Does that mean you don't intend to tell him either?"

"Not unless I have to."

"Then you understand why I wasn't going to."

"The general's a better man than you think. A better man than you'll ever be, Vandiver. He could handle this, but he sure as hell doesn't need it right now. In a couple of days he's going to deal out death to a few thousand of his own people, and, God forgive us, we've got to help him all we can."

Vandiver nodded, filled with relief. "Exactly. And there's no reason for you to worry about this. I've got it under control."

"Tell me about it."

"Go fuck yourself, Colonel."

Hagan stood. Vandiver held his ground as the old man walked up to him, but he felt his eyes preparing to flinch, his hands ready to come up and ward off a blow. He was revolted by his fear. Hagan was nothing but a—

Vandiver jerked his head, feeling the borehole of the .45 push cold and steady against the cartilage of his nose. Where had the gun come from? He hadn't even seen Hagan pull it out. The pressure was light, but it followed him back until his head met the doorframe.

"Okay, *Shtarker*, I'll go fuck myself. But first I have a little speech for you. I've been watching you, and I'm going to go on watching you. You have command of this project, but you can be replaced. Before this week is out, the U.S. army will set loose a killer plague on the citizens it is sworn to protect. Before it's all over, those citizens could turn into one big, ugly, rioting mob. The government could certainly fall, and we could have chaos—if people find out. Do you realize that, Vandiver? If they find out we started the plague, we won't even be able to tell them why, not without getting bombed by the Russians. If those test subjects had got to the other side of that fence, it might very well have ended things.

"So now I have to impress something on you. If you fuck up again, there will be no trial, no publicity, no General

Vandiver trying to explain his and General Stanhouse's actions at congressional hearings. You will be dead."

Vandiver felt a shock as the gun pushed harder against his nose. His heart began to hammer.

"I don't like you," Hagan said. "I think you'd sell your grandmother to get ahead. Okay, you're *getting* ahead. A better man than you'll ever be just put a brand-new star on your shoulder. That's the carrot. This thing I'm holding against your nose is the stick. Don't fuck up again."

Hagan holstered his automatic. Vandiver grabbed his arm as he started past. "Did General Stanhouse set you to watch me?"

Hagan looked down at the hand. Vandiver kept it firmly in place. "He didn't have to."

Vandiver smiled in relief. Stanhouse *hadn't* acted behind his back. Stanhouse *did* trust him. The rest of it he could deal with. He said: "Hagan, you're doing what you feel you have to do, without being told. Maybe we're more alike than you think."

Hagan jerked his arm free. The cabin door opened and closed and he was gone.

Chapter 22

2345 hours:

Morrissey hung on to the top of the fence and watched the young man on the sidewalk come closer. His heart was beating so hard he could feel his ribs pulse against the chainlink at his side. His fingers hurt where they curled over the top bar of the fence. The light drizzle had soaked him, and he was cold.

None of it mattered.

He gave his attention to the approaching man—barely more than a kid, really. Probably some kind of technician, judging from the white labcoat. Behind him Morrissey could see Detrick's main cluster of biolabs, tan monoliths gleaming wetly under rain-haloed lights. The kid had just come from the biggest lab. Was that where they were mass-producing L-6?

Think about that later.

The kid was walking with his head down, his hands jammed into the pockets of the labcoat.

Come on, Morrissey urged silently. Look up—look over here, damn you. He checked to make sure the strip he'd torn out of his shirt was still fixed to the barbed wire. A nice touch. Was it too obvious?

The guy was turning his head this way!

Morrissey launched himself out and down into the bushes at the base of the fence, waving his arms as he fell. He seemed to fall much too fast, not staying in sight nearly long enough to suit him. But the bushes snapped and cracked under him in satisfying fashion as he hit. He clutched the bushes and made as much commotion as he dared. *Careful—don't overdo it!*

He found a gap in the bushes and looked out. The kid had seen him! He was standing stock still on the sidewalk. Now he was coming across the grass toward the fence. Morrissey scowled in the darkness, trying to project animal combativeness. *Don't be a hero. Get help. Go call the frigging guards!*

The kid stopped and pretended to inspect something on the ground. Morrissey sighed with relief. Common sense was prevailing. There, he was going back to the sidewalk, heading toward the dormitories. He was inside. It shouldn't be long now.

Morrissey was suddenly doubtful. What if Alan and his human test subjects weren't *on* the back acres? What if nothing was on the other side of this fence but those rolling hills covered with woods you could see from the main base?

But how could that be? If there was nothing back there, then why that gate farther down the fence, behind the hospital? Why those three MPs trying to stay out of sight in the guardhouse beside it?

No, Morrissey thought resolutely, the phone call proves Alan's at Detrick somewhere. If he was anywhere on this side of the fence, I'd have seen him today. I got into every building. Morrissey patted his shirt pocket, grateful for his Army Labs pass, then remembered he'd hidden it under a stone with the rest of his I.D. before climbing up on the fence. It made him feel naked. He was a man without identity now.

Correction: He was one of Alan's test subjects.

Morrissey concentrated on sinking himself in his role. He was escaping from the secret installation beyond the fence.

No I.D., talking crazy, unable to answer questions. Desperate not to be taken back.

Which was exactly what the guards were duty-bound to do.

Morrissey leaned back against the fence. Pain sparked along the row of punctures he'd gouged into his stomach with the corkscrew of his jackknife. He could feel the blood drying, sticking his shirt to the wounds. It was the pièce de résistance. If the MPs believed he'd got those wounds on the barbed wire, climbing over the fence from the back acres, it would be worth it.

What was taking so long. Did that kid make the call or didn't he?

Morrissey shifted around, trying to relieve the strain on his knees. It was damned uncomfortable squatting in this bush. His shoes were pinching his toes. . .

His shoes! Would he take them off if he was going to climb a fence like this? Yes, it would be easier to climb barefoot. They'd expect him to take his shoes off and throw them over the fence before climbing out. He tore his shoes and socks off and threw them out of the bushes. He settled back again.

All right, he was ready.

He grinned savagely. *Come on, you bastards. Come and get me. Take me to your leader.*

17
DAYS

Saturday, October 25

Chapter 23

0130 hours:

I'll have the nightmare tonight, Vandiver thought.

He touched his temples and felt the veins throbbing. The back of his skull ached—the spot where his head had hit the wall at Froggie's. Unmistakable signs. That bastard, Hagan. Nothing for the last two years, and now the bald old ape had brought it all back with his gun.

Vandiver stared at the fireplace. Flames pirouetted over the oak logs and shimmered in reflection along the varnished pine ceiling. The cabin was rosy with warmth, but it seemed to sink no deeper than his skin no matter how close he pulled to the fire.

It was frustrating. He was tired. He needed sleep. But now he must wait. This wasn't home, where it was all right to wake up screaming. Here, if he let out a yell, they'd hear it in the MP cabins and at the guardposts and that would not do.

You will be dead, Hagan had said.

Vandiver rubbed the tip of his nose, failing to erase the lingering nerve imprint of Hagan's .45. Damn you, old man, he thought. Do you know what it is to be dead? I do.

Vandiver gave a cynical grunt. He was lapsing into melodrama now. Actually, he did not know what it was to be dead—not consciously. It was in the nightmare, but he had never remembered the nightmare.

And he didn't want to.

He got up and poked at the fire. When he put the poker down, he realized his hands were trembling. He glared at them, disgusted. Maybe he should take something from his medical bag to make him sleep. No, it would leave him dopey in the morning, and he couldn't afford that.

He sat again and tried to concentrate on the lulling sound of raindrops dripping from the pines and maples onto the roof.

Just that slight pressure against the nose, a scent of gun oil, and the bullet would plow up, smashing bone. There would be a searing white explosion in the brain, as the back of his skull shattered out. He would lie on the floor, eyes bulging from the hydrostatic pressure, the white patch of hair gone sticky and red, until they came and hauled him away in a trash bag.

Dead.

Vandiver rolled his head from side to side on the sofa back. He heard himself crooning: "It's all right, Alan. It's all right." He stopped and looked around sheepishly.

Screw it. He would not sit here cowering like this. If he screamed in his sleep, he screamed. He would sleep with his arm across his mouth. That used to help at home.

Unbuttoning his shirt, he paused. There was something nagging at the back of his mind: the bodies of the three test subjects. They were in the cooler, but they weren't locked away yet. He'd been going to do it, then Hagan had been waiting, and he'd forgotten. Better see to it now.

Vandiver opened the door and hesitated in surprise. A heavy mist had sprung up around the cabin. It was a cold, silvery color. And motionless. He'd never seen a mist hang so still in the air. He shivered. It had gone cold as an iceberg outside. No wonder he couldn't get warm in the cabin. This must be the aftermath of the rain—a front moving through, chilling the warmer ground.

Reluctant to leave the shelter of the cabin, he gazed into

the mist. It was so thick, he couldn't even make out the trees, let alone the walk-in cooler beyond. Wait: there were a couple of tree trunks—no three. Very faint, terminating just at a man's height. They seemed to be getting darker. Maybe the mist was clearing.

Vandiver's scalp prickled.

They weren't trees, they were men.

He stared, gripped in the illusion that they were inching toward him. It was no illusion! He could definitely see them better now.

"Who's there?" He was disgusted at the tremulous sound of his voice.

There was no answer.

"This is General Vandiver. Identify yourselves!" Damn! Now his voice was quavering out of control.

He heard a wet whispering sound, and realized it was feet moving through the damp leaves. The sound had a deadly, inexorable rhythm. That one in the lead—he could almost make him out now.

And then he knew who it was, even before the face lightened and coalesced.

Warlow!

A chill spread from the base of Vandiver's neck, up into his brain, down along his arms and legs. He couldn't move. Private Warlow, the dead L-6 subject. And the other two must be Privates Gilliam and Hufnagel. Yes, he could make them out now too: short Hufnagel, his fringe of hair smeared in points forward and up across his forehead like curving horns; Gilliam, thin and stiff as a stick-man, his kid's face now old and empty as a death mask.

I've gone insane, Vandiver thought.

The three men drifted forward, taking on solid form. Their eyes gleamed with a dead, silvery light, reflected from the mist.

Vandiver backed into the cabin. "Go away," he whispered.

Warlow's mouth opened. He gasped and then hissed.

Vandiver slammed the cabin door and sank to his knees against it. "Help," he said hoarsely. He could put no punch into his voice. Dimly, he was aware of the door rattling against him. No, it was his body, shaking.

The door bounced from a more powerful shock—once, twice. A fist, knocking. He heard the gasp again through the pine boards. "I-h-h-h-uuuh. I-h-h-h. I-h-h-h-nnn. *In!*"

"No," he whispered. "Help, someone help me."

The door burst open. He scuttled backward until his spine came up against the fireplace wall. *Coward!* he thought. *Stand up!* He couldn't make his legs work.

The three dead men were inside now. Warlow closed the door. His arm worked stiffly, like a marionette's. As he turned back, the firelight glittered in his eyes. He's not looking at me, Vandiver realized. He's staring at the wall. Could it be he doesn't see me?

Don't move, he thought.

Vandiver huddled against the wall, holding very still, moving his head just enough to keep the three corpses in view. He watched Warlow walk around the cabin, stiffly at first and then with greater ease. The other two aped him, stalking around and around the cabin, flexing and bending, raising their arms and letting them drop.

Vandiver began to hope. Maybe they *didn't* see him, or had forgotten him. Maybe they would go away.

His heart sank as he saw the three corpses converge on him and stop. "Go away," he pleaded. Warlow made a harsh, sucking noise. His chest swelled then deflated explosively. "Ah-g-g-g-h-h-h-h. Ah-h-h-h-k-k."

The skin of Vandiver's neck drew tight with goosebumps. He groped the wall, pushing himself up. He must get clear of the cabin. In the open, he could outrun them. He looked desperately for an opening between the three dead men. They set their feet apart and raised their hands to contain him.

Warlow's chest pumped like a bellows. "Wha-a-ay. Wait! Not hur-r-rt."

The breath of the words hit Vandiver in the face, cold, making him recoil. He swallowed hard and glanced at the bodies of Gilliam and Hufnagel, gelled into stillness on either side of Warlow. They looked unreal. If he hadn't seen them move into position, he would swear they were wax figures, the heads cleverly placed so that the black, button eyes were focused precisely on his.

Warlow tried again to talk. At first he produced only ghastly, disconnected sounds. Gradually his speech grew more intelligible. Vandiver began to get his nerve back. Just take it easy, he thought. Don't provoke them. Warlow said he wouldn't hurt you . . .

Listen to yourself!

Ashamed, he straightened, and forced himself to look Warlow in the eye. He felt an unpleasant crawl inside the back of his skull.

"What h-h-you . . . you do to us?" Warlow said.

Vandiver had to think a minute, his brain slow and muddled. What did he mean? The tests? Yes, the L-6 injections. It couldn't be anything else. But L-6 *preserved* life. Had L-6 somehow saved them from the fence? Vandiver's fear turned to astonishment.

"You're not dead!"

"Yes, dead. Are." Warlow raised an arm and dropped it woodenly. "Trapped."

Vandiver shuddered. Peter, what have you done?

Another thought struck him. *The project! What would happen to the project?*

Warlow said. "I-s-s-s . . . this-s part of experiment?"

"No, of course not. I . . ."

"Then accident."

"Yes, yes. Hell, yes, it's an accident. What kind of man do you think I am?"

"If accident, then you have no cure."

Vandiver hesitated. He had to be careful here, give Warlow the right answer. His life and the project might depend on it. Could he bring them back to life? Insane. This was all insane. He was talking with a dead man. *No, don't think about that.*

If he admitted he couldn't help them, there was no telling what they might do to him. But he couldn't say there *was* a cure either. They'd want it at once. *Stall them.*

"At this moment, there's no cure . . ."

Warlow stepped toward him.

"Keep away from me."

Warlow stopped. He stood still a minute then said, "General, listen. You know how L-6 works. You can figure out a way to undo it."

Vandiver was struck by the improvement in Warlow's voice. It was much clearer now, the breathing under adequate control, the vowels and consonants smooth and intelligible. But Warlow still did not sound normal. His voice was too flat—expressionless.

Vandiver realized the Warlow-thing was waiting for his answer. He must offer some hope. Maybe he *could* think of some way to help them. In any event, the important thing now was to buy time. "You'll have to be patient," he said. "Give me a chance to examine you. I give you my word, I'll try my best to get you out of this."

"Try?" Warlow said. He made a small hand signal.

Vandiver tried to dodge, but the other two grabbed him easily. Their fingers felt cold as steel digging into his arms, sending a shock of panic through him. He struggled, kicking their shins, biting at their hands. The flesh was cold and rubbery against his teeth. He jerked his head away, gagging. He struggled more fiercely, hauling the dead men around in a clumsy dance. They held on with iron patience. He caught a glimpse of the Warlow-thing, watching the struggle impassively as though he were a steer being dragged to slaughter. It brought up a fresh burst of panicky strength in him. He slammed a booted heel into the arch of one of the dead men's feet and heard bone crack. There was no cry of pain; the grip on his arms was tight as ever.

They're too strong, he thought. He sagged down between them, gasping for breath.

Warlow pulled a vial and a syringe from his pocket. Vandiver recognized the vial with a shock. L-6! Warlow must have broken into the lab stock before coming over. Warlow meant to inject him!

Vandiver tried to pull free again. The corpses held him more easily this time. He couldn't even throw them off balance. "What do you *want* from me?" he gasped.

"Want?" Warlow said. "We don't want anything."

Vandiver stared at him, struggling to understand. Was Warlow being sarcastic? There was no sign of it. The voice was as toneless as ever, but there was an awful sincerity in the words: *We don't want anything.*

"Then let me go," Vandiver said, looking at the syringe.

"You don't understand," Warlow said. "We must survive. There is no choice. Now, relax, Doctor. Just relax."

Vandiver strained uselessly against the grip, trying to twist his shoulder away. The needle sank in, a sharp prick of pain, and then a tingling as the L-6 spread into his muscle. He stopped struggling. All thought seemed to drain from his mind. The two dead soldiers steered him to the sofa and released him. He dropped and stared numbly up at the ceiling. Warlow came into his field of vision and he looked away into the fire, sickened.

"You did this to us," Warlow said. "Now you are in it too. Make us alive again. Or be like us."

Vandiver barely heard him. He stared into the fire, seized by a memory. Fire—fire all around, and smoke, but he felt no heat. *Froggie's.* This was the dream, the nightmare he'd had so many times and never remembered: He was lying on the floor, and Peter was bent over him, working frantically, doing something to his chest. External heart massage.

Vandiver realized he was seeing it all from above.

Somehow he was in the rafters looking down at his own body. But he wasn't quite free of the body. There was still a connection, thin as smoke, like a silver cord stretching down.

I'm dead, he thought.

He felt a sudden powerful revulsion for the corpse on the floor. He had to get away from it. If he could just pull free that last bit, he could soar away, far above the burning building. It would be over. He would be safe. But he couldn't do it. Peter wouldn't let him.

He screamed silently. *Let me die, Peter, let me go!*

But the cord drew tight. It pulled him back toward the corpse on the floor that had once been him. He was dropping down, down, back into his body and blackness.

Vandiver shuddered and closed his eyes. He must get hold of himself. He carried L-6 in his body now, but he was still a normal man, just as these three sickening creatures had been during the study before they ran into the high-voltage fence. Normal, except that he could now survive radiation without ill effects, as these test subjects had done while they were still alive.

So all he had to do was stay alive, *just stay alive.*

He opened his eyes to find Warlow's dead gaze on him. "Save us," Warlow said. "Save yourself."

Vandiver rubbed his shoulder where the L-6 still tingled and burned. "Yes," he said.

Chapter 24

0230 hours:

Morrissey gazed through the cabin doorway into Alan's stunned face. I did it! he thought exultantly.

Then he winced as the guard squeezed hard on his bicep. What had gotten into the man? Up to now, he'd been decent, almost apologetic. Morrissey looked at him and saw that he'd snapped to attention. The clench of fingers was an involuntary side effect. He's scared, Morrissey realized with surprise.

"S-sorry to disturb you, sir. We got another one here—but he's from before, sir."

Alan shook his head slowly, open-mouthed, never taking his eyes from Morrissey. "What the *hell* are you talking about, soldier?"

"The MPs on the main base caught him," the guard hurried in. "He'd just climbed out over their fence. He must've escaped over ours after the other three were . . . after they made the generator go down."

Alan stared at Morrissey. "Him? Trying to *escape*?"

"Yes sir." The man began to sound uncertain. "I didn't recall his face from your experiment guys, but he begged the base people not to bring him back here. He knew all about us. So I guess he must be."

Alan threw his head back and laughed.

This *is* funny, Morrissey thought. Despite himself, he smiled.

"Please don't take my stripe, sir."

"Never mind. Good work."

The man gave a relieved smile, and the squeezing fingers relaxed. "Thank you, sir. I'll just take him back to his barracks, then, and—"

"No. Leave him here and get back to your post."

"Uh . . ."

"Get going."

The guard took to his heels.

"Peter . . . Peter."

Morrissey tried to evade, but Alan got a bear hug on him and waltzed him inside. He stared over Alan's shoulder, mired in confusion. After going to such lengths to hide, why was Alan acting so glad to see him? And what was that on Alan's shoulder? Morrissey pulled back to focus on it. A star. They'd made Alan a general.

Because of L-6.

Morrissey pushed firmly away from Alan.

"You cagey old coon dog," Alan said, undeterred. "You don't know how glad I am to see you. And the way you did it: 'Don't t'row me in dat briar patch!' " Vandiver did a clumsy rabbit dance.

Morrissey smiled again, then caught himself. This was not how it was supposed to go. He concentrated on his anger. Damn it, he *needed* it if he was going to face Alan down.

He made his voice cold. "Let's drop the Uncle Remus act. If it'd been up to you, I'd still be chasing my tail back at the Labs."

"I won't deny that. I'm sorry, Peter. There were reasons. But forget that—everything's changed. I was about to go get you."

Morrissey stared at him. "Don't tell me that. I stabbed myself three times in the stomach to get in here." He jerked his shirt away from his belt, and then was irritated with himself. What was he trying to do, impress Alan? Play for sympathy? Only one thing mattered now—stopping L-6.

Vandiver grimaced at the puncture wounds. "You did that to yourself? Here, wait." He hurried to his medical bag. Morrissey slumped down on the couch in front of the fire, suddenly tired again. He'd made it, and reaction was setting in, threatening to dull his mind. The fire was deliciously warm, making him drowsy.

What was Alan doing up at 2:30 with a fire going?

Alan bent over him and swabbed the wounds. He seemed pathetically eager. Morrissey grunted at the cool sting of the pads. "That should do it." Alan's hand trembled as he put the bottle of alcohol back in his bag.

Morrissey said: "You're experimenting on humans with L-6."

"Yes."

"You've got to stop. There's a terrible—"

"I know."

Morrissey felt a chill at the nape of his neck. "You know?"

"I've got three dead test subjects."

Morrissey gaped at him, stunned. *Three dead L-6 humans? Three men like Monk?*

Morrissey listened with growing horror to the rest of it. The last part was the worst. He found himself standing beside Alan, a hand on his shoulder. "You're sure it was L-6 they shot into you?"

"I saw the bottle. They broke it out of the lab."

Morrissey tried to conceive of it. Dead men, holding Alan down, shooting L-6 into him. He shuddered.

Vandiver mustered a thin smile. "So, Dr. Frankenstein. Can we bring those poor bastards back to life?"

"I don't know."

"Then lie," Vandiver said with a rueful smile. " 'Sure Alan. We'll just stick a few plugs in their necks, take some stitches—' " His voice cracked.

Morrissey slumped down on the couch again. "If I hadn't

followed Janet,'' he said half to himself. ''If I'd told you about the dog . . .''

''The one L-6 saved from a lethal overdose?''

''L-6 didn't save it.'' Morrissey filled him in quickly on Monk. He told Alan about the necropsied rats, still alive with their abdominal cavities sliced open. He cut himself short as he saw Alan's face, pale and stricken. He tried to force reassurance into his voice: ''All right. The point now is to figure out what to do. We know that L-6 strengthens the electron bonds of atoms in a living animal or man. If that animal or man is killed, the bonds don't let go. All biological activity stops with death, but the cells don't start decaying. And the neuroelectric activity in the brain doesn't stop. That's what those men are, Alan: nerve and brain impulses operating a body that is dead but perfectly preserved.''

''Wait,'' Vandiver said. ''*Why* doesn't the brain activity stop?''

''I don't know. To answer that, we'd have to know what usually happens to the electrical part of us when we die.''

''Okay,'' Alan said. ''Let's assume that it leaves us, dissipates—whatever. Let's assume that the start of decay, triggered by death, releases the neuroelectric part of us—except in risens.''

Morrissey stared at him, chilled by the word. *Risens.* So now the walking dead men had a name, culled from his and Alan's shared childhood. A biblical name from Old Man Babcock's Sunday school class: Moses, the widow's son, the Centurion's daughter, Lazarus, and finally Christ himself, risen from the dead.

But the three L-6 test subjects had not risen from the dead, they had risen up dead.

''Even if the neuroelectric force *is* still inside the risens,'' Alan went on, ''it shouldn't be able to move the bodies. Okay, the nerves are preserved and able to carry electric signals, but what about the junctions *between* nerves, for Christ's sake? That's chemical, not electric. The upstream nerve has to release acetylcholine and all those other damned chemicals to the downstream nerve for the impulse to continue.''

"The neurotransmitters," Morrissey said. "Yeah. I've been thinking about that. All I can say is, the bodies *are* biologically dead. After seeing Monk, I'm sure of it. That means the enzymes that produce neurotransmitters are dried up. But remember, we're dealing with a monstrously magnified electric force in the bodies. Clearly it's powerful—and different—enough to jump the nerve junctions without chemical help . . ." Morrissey saw that Alan was no longer listening.

"They're trapped," Vandiver said. His eyes were wide with dread, fixed on some inner point. "That's what Warlow said. Just that one word: *trapped*. I didn't understand at the time. But now I do. Their cells won't decay. There is no release. They can't get out."

"Take it easy," Morrissey said.

Alan wandered around the room.

Morrissey tried to think. If only he wasn't so damned tired. He could feel something nagging just below consciousness. Something important about the risens. He recognized now that it had been drifting up toward the surface of his mind since last night—his dark ride through the city in Kellogg's truck. He had been too tired to think then. What had turned his mind to it now? Something Alan had just said?

They can't get out.

Did a risen *want* to get out? Risens could think and move and act. But what did it *feel* like to be a risen?

"Peter?"

Morrissey saw that Alan was standing by the fire holding a black notebook—the L-6 notes. "I wanted to ask you," Vandiver said. "This last page—so many names. Is that why you worked all those years to develop L-6?"

The list of the dead. Irritation flared in Morrissey. Then he realized that Alan did not mean to taunt him. The anger remained, turning against himself. He had worked so long, so hard, to beat death. And instead, he had given it arms and legs, a voice. A hand that could hold a needle and plunge it into the arm of his best friend.

"You wrote my name last," Vandiver mused. "And

you're right. I *was* dead that night. You saved me." He shut the notebook. "Can you do it again? Me and those three poor geeks?"

Morrissey held up a hand. Alan gripped it hard and he returned the pressure. But he felt no confidence. Bring a dead body back to life? Alan was asking him to be God. He felt a mocking bitterness toward himself. Isn't that what he'd been trying for all along?

No. God gave life. God or nature or evolution—he did not know which. He had only wanted to preserve it.

Morrissey watched Alan put the notebook back on his desk. "Where are the dead men now?" he asked.

"I put them in an unused cabin," Vandiver said.

"Will they stay put?"

"I don't know. When I left them there, they just stood against the wall. They didn't move, like they'd turned themselves off. I hung around watching them a minute, and then it got too damned weird."

With a chill Morrissey remembered the dog. Monk had been like that, too, standing there in the cellar all night without moving a muscle.

What did it feel like to be a risen?

"I think they'll stay put for now," Alan went on. "But they expect results fast. If it doesn't happen . . . well, you know what they threatened to do."

"We'll have to lock them away."

Vandiver jerked up a chair and sat on the edge of it. "Lock them away? How? Do we anesthetize them or maybe threaten to shoot them, like you shot the dog? They'll be watching for anything like that, Peter. They won't let it happen."

"Well, we can't just let them come after you."

"Maybe we could burn them, like you did the rats."

Morrissey stared at him, repulsed.

"For God's sake, Peter, they're already dead. Maybe we could trap them in the cabin and set it on fire. No, then they'd just jump out the windows. God *damn* it."

"Alan, don't. We've still got some time before they take action. We don't have to settle it this minute."

"You're right. The project has to be our first priority."

Morrissey felt a measure of relief. From the moment he'd shot Monk, he'd been pumping himself up for the effort of forcing Alan to shut down Parasol. At least he wouldn't have to do that now. "Who else do we have to see to get everything stopped?" he asked.

Alan raised his eyebrows in surprise. "No, no, Peter. We can't stop the project."

Morrissey was too stunned to speak.

"You don't know the whole story," Alan said. The Russians . . . No, damn it—I can't tell you. Not until I know you're with me. The point is the project *must* go on. There's no choice. And you've got to help me."

Morrissey struggled with a sense of unbelief. Alan could see the risen men, could have L-6 in him, and still think of going on? Impossible. Alan had had a bad shock. He wasn't thinking straight. Morrissey said: "I'll do everything I can for you personally. You know that. You and those three men. But I won't help you go on with your project. L-6 testing is finished."

Vandiver closed his eyes and held very still a second, as though restraining himself. "The Russians," he said quietly, "are going to launch a pre-emptive nuclear strike against this country in exactly seventeen days."

For a second Morrissey's mind went blank. He pushed up from the couch and had to catch the fireplace mantle to keep from falling down. He was dimly conscious of the heat of the fire against his legs. His mind spun. A nuclear strike? He must get Janet and the kids, get them on a plane out. Where? Australia? They'd said Australia would be a good place, in that movie—*On the Beach*. And Dad, he had to get Dad too. And Janet's folks. He couldn't leave them behind. . .

He heard himself cursing in a low monotone.

"One hundred and sixty-five million people will die," Alan said, "unless they have L-6 in their bodies."

My responsibility, Morrissey thought numbly. All of this—my fault. "You said in seventeen days?"

"The election. They hit us if Maxwell wins. Maxwell will win."

"You can't be sure of that."

"Would you bet your life against it?"

Morrissey tried to make his voice calm and reasoning. "L-6 only protects a person from radiation. It won't protect people from the blast . . ."

"Only a fourth of the casualties would be from blast."

Morrissey couldn't answer. His head swam with images of carnage. Leveled cities; smoking rubble stretching on for miles. A pall of smoke over everything. Heat, terrible lingering heat. People—risens—crawling from the wreckage with their bodies ripped open, arms blown off, skin burned and blackened. Their intestines dragging, like the L-6 rats. Inconceivable.

"Three times the number who die from the blast will survive," Alan went on. "They'll be as alive and normal as I am now. As for the others . . ." Vandiver frowned in distraction. His expression cleared. "Well, look, Peter; we've been making some assumptions here. It might not be so bad. Are those three men really dead? Or is it just their bodies? All right, it's true that it would be a shock to wake up and realize your heart isn't beating and your lungs aren't working—"

"A shock?"

"Just let me finish. Your body may be biologically dead, but your nerves and brain still work. You can still think and see and hear and move. That's worth something. Maybe a person could adjust to it."

"Could you adjust," Morrissey said, "to being trapped in a burned, mutilated body?"

"We'll help anyone like that, just like we're going to help my three subjects. If we can't, and they want out, we'll destroy them—incinerate them. A lot of the blast victims will be burned to ash anyway. We have to think of the others—millions of lives. For their sakes, we can't stop the project. We can't even delay it. We've got huge batches of L-6 coming along in the replication vats on the main base. It will barely be ready in time before the election. Even if we knew right now how to alter the L-6 gene so that it wouldn't hang on after death, it would be too late to start production of revised L-6. The best we can do in the time we have left is work on finding a way to neutralize L-6 in the bodies of survivors.''

Morrissey tried to gather his wits. He felt steamrollered by Alan's forceful voice. But Alan was wrong—horribly wrong. Morrissey said, ''We have no idea whether we can do a damned thing about L-6. And we don't know enough about risens—''

''And here's the clincher,'' Vandiver said as if he hadn't heard: ''If we get the present program finished in time, there'll be no attack. We'll let the Russians know we have L-6. We'll face the sons of bitches down with it!''

''There has to be another way out of this, Alan.''

Vandiver shook his head. ''No. And you've got to understand something else, too: I've told you about the preemptive strike. That means you can't leave this base now. You have to help me. You have no choice.''

Morrissey shook his head wearily. ''We're going to your C.O.,'' he said. ''Tonight—*now*. We're going to tell him about those dead men, make him understand that L-6 can't be used. If you won't, I'll do it alone.''

Vandiver looked anguished. ''Shit,'' he said.

Morrissey saw Alan's fist swinging up. *Duck!* he thought. There was a terrific jolt to his chin. He saw bright colors, and then he was falling, falling.

Chapter 25

0330 hours:

Vandiver pulled the needle from Morrissey's arm. He eased Peter's legs and feet onto the sofa and stood back.

"Christ bloody damn," he said.

He bent over and checked Peter's jaw again. Not much swelling. No breaks, thank God for that.

Had there been any other way? A drugged drink, perhaps?

No. He'd sneaked around and stolen and lied to Peter and felt like scum. At least he'd acted like a man this time.

Peter would probably prefer a straight left to more trickery.

Vandiver went to his desk and poured shots of Virginia Gentleman into two glasses. He drank one down, raised the other to Peter and drank it down. It burned smoothly all the way to his stomach.

He put his head down on the desk. The small muscles of his forearm twitched against his cheekbone. Christ, so much pressure. And this was only the start.

What should he do about Peter?

The shot of phenobarb would keep him out for a while—long enough to get him out of the camp. By now, word would have spread about a fourth escaped prisoner being brought back to camp. Hagan's quisling corporal would be calling him, and Hagan would come muscling in, wanting to know all about it.

Or maybe Hagan would just bring his gun.

Vandiver realized his fingers were clawing at the desktop. No, damn it, forget the gun.

He sat up and pushed at his forehead with the heels of his hands, and the idea began to formulate: The hospital on the main base had a psychiatric ward. A lot of the mistakes of Ft. Detrick were squirreled away there, along with burnt-out vets from the two Asian wars. The staff knew how to handle difficult cases without busting heads.

But they knew nothing about Project Parasol, and they could not possibly be told. The only way the hospital would work was if Peter was out of his head and unable to say damaging things. Was there a way to make that happen for a while without hurting him?

Vandiver was shocked at himself. What was he thinking? He couldn't do such a thing to Peter, even if there was a way.

What else could he do? What else that wasn't worse?

The phone rang. Vandiver jumped. *Hagan already?* His hands broke into an instant sweat. He rubbed them on his pants and made himself pick up the receiver. "Vandiver."

"Sorry to wake you, sir."

Vandiver almost smiled in relief. *Not Hagan. The Biop 4 switchboard.* "What is it?"

"We've got a woman calling, and you did clear her, day or night. Name of Morrissey. She used the correct password."

Janet. What could she want at this time of night?

"Sir?"

"Put her through."

The phone clicked. "Alan? Are you there?"

"Yes, Janet."

"Oh, thank God! Alan, I've got to talk to you."

CA-2! Alan thought. The perfect drug for Peter!

"Alan?"

"I'm here."

"I've looked everywhere for Peter. Have you seen him?"

Vandiver's attention was tugged from CA-2. Of course. Peter *would* have to be the reason she was calling. Didn't he have any luck? "Yes, he's here. Janet, are you sitting down?"

"What's wrong? Is he hurt?" Her voice rose to the edge of hysteria.

"Take it easy. He's fine . . . physically." Vandiver hesitated. Was there any CA-2 here on the base? There was a chance. This is where they'd developed the drug in the last stages of the Vietnam war. If it was anywhere in the world, it would be here.

"What do you mean, physically?"

"Where are you?"

"I'm at our summer place. What do you mean, physically?"

Vandiver closed his eyes. Good, the summer place. That was an hour away. But did he have to do this? Yes. If he tried to keep her in the dark, she'd stir up a fuss trying to find out what was going on. She might even have her rich banker father unleash the family's pet congressman!

But CA-2 could solve it all.

Shit, Vandiver thought. The sweat poured down his face.

"Switchboard? I've been cut off!" Her voice was panicky again.

"No, no," Vandiver said. "I'm here. Peter's . . . he's had a breakdown."

Janet said nothing. He heard her breathing.

"Now just listen," he said, "and try not to get too upset. They have a very fine psychiatric hospital here on the base. I've committed him there. I tried to call you at home, but there was no answer."

"How bad is it?"

He stared at the phone. She sounded almost accepting, as if she'd expected it. Was he going to be lucky after all? "It looks worse than it probably is," he said. "Right now he's very paranoid and delusional."

Yes, that was what CA-2 symptoms looked like. Just a temporary mental mix-up. No one had ever died from it.

"Alan, do you . . . do you know about the dog?"

Vandiver felt a shock of sympathy. She had seen the risen Doberman. "Yes."

"Is that why?"

"I'm sure that's part of it."

"I've been half out of my mind myself," Janet said, "just seeing that thing. It attacked me. For a while I was in shock. I wandered around the house. I've been driving everywhere, looking for Peter—" Her voice broke.

"It's all right," he said softly. "I'll take care of you."

"Alan, I'm coming out there. I want to see Peter, and then I want you to tell me everything you know about that dog."

"I can find a place for you to stay here. But Janet, it's very important that you understand this: You won't be able to leave for a while. Security—"

"It's all right. I want to be as near as I can to Peter. The girls are with his father now. He'll keep them as long as we need."

Vandiver closed his eyes. This was fate, the dark, tangled underside of why he had survived Froggie's. He must accept it and push on. "The base is closed this time of night," he said. "When you get here, wait for me at the front gate. I'll meet you there and escort you."

When they entered the ward, she reached for his arm. He gave her elbow a comforting squeeze. He wished he could protect her from this. Suddenly he was acutely aware of the harsh aura of the place. This time was even worse than an hour ago, when Sergeant Bruck had helped him carry Peter down this same corridor. The walls radiated misery—muffled echoes of a man screaming in another hall; a welter of reflected footsteps; the scents of urine and disinfectant. A hundred more coats of peach-colored paint couldn't hush those walls. Even the paintings, hung at precise intervals, were merciless—a mountaintop, a deer drinking from a woodland stream, a sweating farmer pitching hay. Cruel reminders of an impossibly remote world.

A steel door clanged and Vandiver cringed. The night orderly jangled his keys irritatingly behind them. In one of the rooms close by, a man started shouting: "Incoming! Incoming! Incoming!"

Janet stopped and leaned into Vandiver's grip.

His mouth went dry as the man went on screaming.

He hurried Janet across the commons area toward Morrissey's corridor. He saw the night nurse in her glassed-in nurses' station. She started to get up from her desk, struggling against the weight of her fat. He waved her back to her seat. He stopped at Peter's door and turned, hearing a soft footfall behind him. The orderly was still with them, the big black man with the shaved head, walking with catlike silence despite his size. The man's keys hadn't jangled since they'd entered the ward halls. He probably kept them muted so he could peek through the cell grilles without being detected. Or maybe it was out of pity for the men who would otherwise have to listen to his rounds, haunted by the knowledge that they were being watched.

"We won't be needing you," Vandiver said.

The man nodded and padded off.

"Doesn't he have to let us in?" Janet said.

Vandiver thought of the key in his pocket. Better keep that a secret for now. "I don't think that would be a good idea—not tonight. Peter's been violent. He may not even recognize us."

Janet gave a little cry and tried to rush the door. He held her back. "Wait. Janet, you have to prepare yourself. Try to keep control. Smile at him. Don't do anything that might agitate him."

She nodded. Her face was pale.

Vandiver dialed the speaking grille open and made way for her at the window. She looked through. Her eyes went shiny with tears. He looked down, clenching his hands until the nails dug into his palms.

"Peter? Honey, it's me, Janet."

"You? Mung."

He sounded sleepy. Vandiver eased his face in beside Janet's. Peter was huddled with his knees drawn up and his back against the padded wall.

God, Vandiver thought. What a miserable hellhole . . . He caught himself. It did no one any good to think of it that way. There wasn't a better psychiatric facility anywhere. There simply wasn't any way to make a room like this anything but a cage. Vandiver looked around the cell, trying to rationalize away its starkness, but each feature seared its way accusingly into his brain: an aluminum water fountain built into the wall; a bare toilet with no seat; blue padding covering all windows; a single ceiling bulb, protected by wire mesh, lighting the room with the dream glow of an opium den.

Except that this was a Thorazine den. *Tonight, a CA-2 den.*

Why wouldn't you see reason, Peter? Vandiver thought. Why wouldn't you help me? I'm sorry, I'm sorry.

Morrissey blinked dully at them. His mouth began to work. "Bit! Roug . . . Oug." He struggled to his feet and glared at the window. His fists clenched and rotated, as though twisting invisible doorknobs. Vandiver steeled himself. *Think about the project, about why you have to do this, why you have to succeed.*

He forced himself to look at Peter with clinical detachment. Peter was out of his head all right. The old batch of CA-2 was still good. Effective and fast. Just like with those Vietcong prisoners they'd brought to Detrick in '72.

Prisoners of war.

"Honey," Janet pleaded.

"Ah-h-h-h-h-h!" Peter rushed the window. She jerked back as he punched the glass. For a second, Vandiver could see Peter's knuckles grinding against the tempered pane. He found himself staring at the scar Peter had got from the broken bottle when they'd dived in the gravel pit that summer before college.

Vandiver pulled away from the window. "Janet, I think we should leave him be right now."

"Barth. Dard!" Morrissey pounded the glass. Vandiver

could feel his rage radiating through the door. He closed the speaking grille and led Janet a few steps away from the window, feeling relief but no pleasure. The acid test was over. There had been that small chance that Peter would be able to fight the drug enough to say something damaging. Janet would have seized on the smallest bit of meaning. But Peter had given her only gibberish.

Vandiver held Janet and patted her back as she sobbed on his shoulder. With a shock he focused on part of Peter's face beyond her, pressed against the foreshortened sliver of glass, one eye glaring balefully at him. He broke into a sweat and pulled Janet farther along, out of sight.

I let Peter see me holding her again, he thought. I should be horsewhipped.

Vandiver realized he was still holding on to Janet. He smelled the scent of her hair, felt the soft pressure of her breasts against his ribs. The crotch of his pants began to constrict him.

He stepped away from her at once, and walked ahead down the corridor so she couldn't see his face.

13
DAYS

Wednesday, October 29

Chapter 26

2000 hours:

Approaching the L-6 vats, Vandiver felt a chill. They looked oddly sentient, squatting there on their tripod legs like monster aliens. The ones looming up in the headlights gleamed while the rest of the row vanished into the darkness on either side of the cart. Vandiver glanced up, looking for some scale to put the vats into perspective. Through the clear plastic roof of the cart, he could barely make out the steel girders of the ceiling high above in the darkness.

This whole building was intimidating.

Vandiver began to be glad for the music coming from the driver's radio. Execrable stuff—rock and roll, or whatever they called it these days—but at least it provided a small point of contact with the world outside. He noticed beads of sweat rolling down the back of the driver's neck. He resisted the urge to pat his shoulder—the poor kid would probably jump out of his skin, and steering one of these top-heavy crates was hard enough as it was.

"Vat Number Five," Vandiver said.

"Yes sir."

Vat 5 towered over them as the technician jockeyed the box up to the spigot in its curving underbelly. The kid heaved a sigh and stepped back. Vandiver pushed his hands through the gloveholes in the front wall. He watched the limp, plastic paws outside the cart rise and take on life as he snugged his fingers into them.

Selecting a test tube from the exterior shelf under the gloves, he became aware of sweat rolling down his own face. They were cutting it very close. Only thirteen days to the election. But it should be all right. He would check the L-6, then give Stanhouse and Hagan the go-ahead.

They would start the plague.

Thinking of Stanhouse, Vandiver felt renewed respect. The old boy hasn't gone gutless after all, he thought. He's the top dog. He could have delegated it to me or Hagan. But he knows it's something you can't order another man to do. No matter how sick it makes him, before the night's over, Iron George will launch the plague. He'll force himself to kill thousands of his countrymen.

Vandiver steadied the test tube under the spigot and went over the remaining timetable for Project Parasol in his mind. There had to be time for the plague to spread and the panic to take hold. Then they had to allow a decent lag before they set up innoculation centers and distributed the L-6/antidote mix. If only they could have gotten the innoculation centers set up beforehand, while they waited for the plasmid DNA in the vats to replicate enough L-6. But that would have blown the whole thing. Let some inquiring reporter discover that the government was ready before the plague broke, and things would get very nasty very fast.

Never mind. They could just make it. The vials of plague innoculant were lined up on the huge conveyor belt in the dark behind the vats, waiting for the precise doses of L-6 to be mixed in. The army medical corp would be able to respond as soon as the plague hit the papers and Detrick announced it had the "cure." Medics would be rushed into place at public schools to receive the L-6. A fleet of huge CH-47 transport helicopters would be ready with only hours notice to descend like steel dragonflies on Ft. Detrick. Within thirty-six hours, the CH-47s would blanket America with vials of L-6.

Vandiver almost smiled, thinking of the irony, Detrick would be able to point to their "heroic" and "ready" response to justify all the years spent in germ-warfare research.

It all hinged on whether the L-6 was ready in those vats.

Vandiver watched the sample drip with agonizing slowness from the spigot into his test tube. His sweat became heavier. He wished he could wipe his face. The L-6 had better be ready.

If it wasn't, he'd still have to tell Stanhouse it was.

Then he would keep his fingers crossed. Another day or two *could* elapse before the innoculant/L-6 was ready. But Stanhouse must start the plague tonight.

Vandiver closed the spigot and replaced the full test tube in the rack below his hands. He nodded and the technician backed the box away from the vats. The cart crawled across the floor of the huge cavern, surrounded by its feeble circle of light. The rock music was over now, and a newscaster had come on. Vandiver found himself listening to the words:

". . . it appears that President Maddock's recent slight rally in the polls is slipping again as—"

"Shut that thing off," Vandiver snapped.

"Yes sir!"

The test station appeared in the headlights. Vandiver went back to work, punching in radio commands. The wheel-shaped table rotated until the slide station rolled beneath the cart's gloves. He prepared a slide, then rotated the electron microscope to him.

One look was enough. He closed his eyes in relief. He would not have to lie to Stanhouse. The L-6 was ready.

Dear God, how can I do this? Stanhouse wondered.

He stared through the windshield at Hagan's latest choice, a street of rowhouses. The grimy dwellings seemed to waver in the feverish orange glare of the anti-crime streetlights. They all looked the same: brick facade, front stoop, barred basement window, one after another. He gazed in sick fascination at the bars. The people who lived on this dingy street loved their lives as much as anyone. They'd done what they could to protect themselves, to keep out all the dark things they feared—burglars, murderers, rapists.

Stanhouse groaned softly. He was worse than all of those. And nothing could keep him out tonight.

He fingered the tops of the cola bottles in the two six-packs between his feet. He thought about what each bottle would do: *Rapidly rising fever. Then nausea and uncontrollable vomiting, diarrhea. Death within 24 hours for the weak, the old, the young, and those who got to the innoculation centers too late.*

Stanhouse pulled his hand back from the bottles and wiped it on his jacket. He was nauseous with dread. He must do this and get it over with, or he would be such a wreck he'd never do it.

He stared resentfully at the bottles. The fact was, he shouldn't *have* to do it.

Warren Maddock should.

After all, he thought, Maddock's the top man. The Commander-in-Chief, my superior officer. The people never elected me to anything. Most of them don't even know my name. But they *voted* for Maddock. They gave him the power of life and death over them. I should have told Maddock about the plague option.

I could still tell Maddock, he thought. He sat up straighter, turning the idea over and over, with desperate hope. I could have Hagan drive me straight to the White House, let Maddock decide. Let Maddock break the damned bottles.

He slumped again, disgusted. It was the same hopeless rationalization that had tormented him for days. Warren Maddock couldn't break the bottles. Maddock couldn't even allow it, much less order it. Maddock was a politician and a civilian. This was something only a soldier could do.

Or a psychopath.

Stanhouse pulled out a bottle, held it in his hand. It had a loathsome warmth of its own.

"Do you want me to do it?" Hagan said.

"No, damn it!"

"When you break it, get in fast. We don't want to take chances, even with a puny breeze like this."

Stanhouse looked at the bottle with abhorrence. If he broke this, he should stick his godforsaken face in the glass. He should lick the virus off the sidewalk. He should be the first to die. But he couldn't.

Not until he'd done the same to the other cities.

He flung the door open and stood on the sidewalk. The air was thick and suffocating. He could hardly breathe. He watched a cockroach hurry away from him across the sidewalk, as though it were aware of him and his errand. He looked up and down the street. It was deserted. The houses were dark, or lit softly behind the shades of upstairs bedroom windows. He heard a man and woman arguing, their sharp accusations muted behind the glass.

Elaine and he had argued from time to time. He could remember every fight now. Once he'd called her a silly old harridan. She'd been standing across the bed from him and her hair had been up in curlers. She hadn't cried, but her eyes had gone wet with hurt and anger. . .

Stanhouse groaned. The voices whined on and on inside the rowhouse. Don't, he thought urgently. Make up now. Hold each other.

He gritted his teeth and swung his arm back underhand. It froze there, refusing to come forward. Putting a leg out in a softball pitcher's stance, he sighted along the sidewalk. *Throw*, he thought. The arm would not come through. He tottered in the unfamiliar posture, sweat pouring down his face.

He tried to imagine missiles falling, 165 million people dying. His arm stayed frozen. He thought of Linda and little Todd being hacked to pieces by flying glass from the bow windows.

He threw the bottle.

The instant it left his fingers he cried out and fell to his knees. He heard the bottle hit with a thud. It did not break. *Can't see! Open your eyes, you old fool.* There—the bottle, lying ahead about ten feet on the apron of grass. Not broken, not broken!

He went half crazy with relief. Laughter tore at his throat. He clenched his teeth to keep it in.

I can't do it, he realized. My arm won't throw the bottle on the cement. No way.

He scrambled along the sidewalk on hands and knees, tearing a hole in his pants. The bottle was slippery with his sweat. He dried his hands on the grass, picked it up, and ran, stumbling, back to the car. Hagan had the door open. He slid in and put the bottle back in its case, and let his head fall back. He was exhausted, drained. At least he felt like himself. Not a cold-blooded murderer. A human being.

"That was it. I can't do it again. Do you understand? I'm not capable of it."

"I understand."

"Maddock might win. I'd have killed thousands of people for nothing."

"Even if Maddock wins," Hagan said, "we have to protect our people. If the Russians can decide to do this once, they can decide to do it any time. They might do it to us even if Maddock wins."

No, Stanhouse thought rebelliously. I won't listen. "We'll find some other way to get L-6 to the people."

"There is no other way."

"Hell, yes there is. We had that other plan. When the innoculation centers are set up, we blow the civil defense sirens. Do it during prime-time television. Go on TV and tell people to get to the centers. That's three or four in the morning in Moscow. We'll take the goddamned Russians by surprise. By the time they figure out what to do—"

"The Russians don't *need* to figure out what to do, General. We've been over that plan and over it. At *best*, there would be a hideous panic—massive traffic jams, a stampede of people trying to get to those schools. And all for nothing. The minute you go public, no matter what time it is in Moscow, they'll hit the buttons. By their reasoning they'll have no choice."

Stanhouse punched the dashboard in frustration. "Damn you, Hagan! Damn you!" He sagged forward, letting his head rest against the dash. "I'm sorry, old friend." He righted himself. His fist hurt. But he was calmer now—and resolute. Hagan knew the facts, but facts weren't everything. "By my reasoning *I* had no choice tonight," he said. "I *had* to break that bottle. But I didn't, and I'm not going to. So maybe they won't hit the buttons either. When it comes right down to it, maybe they won't. It's the best we can do. The best *I* can do. If you can't accept my decision, you can go over my head to the President."

Hagan stared out the window. "General," he said softly, "don't ever say anything like that to me again."

Stanhouse was filled with love and gratitude. He didn't trust his voice to speak. He squeezed Hagan's shoulder. Hagan gave his hand a pat.

"Fort Detrick, sir?"

Stanhouse nodded. "Let's get this stuff back in its cannister and buried again."

Hagan started the car and pulled out from the curb. He drove them between the ranks of ancient rowhouses into downtown Baltimore. The nightlife was in full swing. Stanhouse watched the people avidly. He felt close to them, like a father or grandfather. He'd saved them, protected them for tonight. They were still alive, able to go after their happiness, at least for a few more weeks. That counted for something, didn't it?

He watched a group in tuxedos and evening dresses hurry past glittering marquees and neon bar windows to a blank-fronted discotheque. They moved almost furtively, as though sensing that something might happen at any minute to spoil their good time. Stanhouse wondered if any of them had a friend like Hagan. No, they couldn't.

He felt a deep sorrow for them.

9 DAYS

Sunday, November 2

Chapter 27

0900 hours:

Morrissey smelled bacon frying. He lay with his eyes closed, savoring the smell and all the benefits it foretold. Sunday morning. Extra sack time. Deliverance from Dad's oatmeal. Instead there would be monster fried eggs from Frank Macomber's prize chickens.

And no school.

There would, however, be Sunday school. Trembly old Mr. Babcock asking them to recite this week's text. Giving them that sad beagle look when no one but Alan could do it. Could he con Mom out of Sunday school? Mom might fall for him playing sick, but then he'd get milktoast for breakfast instead of the bacon and eggs.

Morrissey slid an arm across the mattress. Strange—he could not find the edge of the bed. He pushed the arm full out, and still the mattress continued. There was no feel of sheets either. Cripes, his back wasn't even covered.

Morrissey opened his eyes and stared in confusion. Blue padding rolled away from his eye like the gym mats at school. About ten feet away it curved up, climbing the wall. Bud's bed was nowhere in sight. Morrissey looked for the dormer window, the crisp sunlight filtering through the branches of the elm. There was no window. Only that yellow glare from the ceiling.

Confusion gave way to fear. Where the hell was he?

He heard muted clinks and the squeak of wheels outside and down the hall. *The food cart*. He lay very still, afraid to disturb the delicate balance of his thoughts. He was in the hospital, yes, the psychiatric hospital. Alan had put him here.

He sat up slowly and stared at the blue padding. His throat ached with loss. He'd felt so warm and safe. Mom still at home and alive. Ruby already up and helping her with the bacon and eggs. Bud across in the other bed. A lost world. He longed to lie back down, drift away again, recapture it.

The sense of loss gave way to cold dread. Dear God, he had forgotten. It had been covered up in his mind.

But now he could think again!

The dread vanished in a flash of euphoria, unnatural and wrenching, but irresistible. He grinned. Yes, he remembered now. He'd hidden last night's capsule under his tongue. His mouth had been so dry that it had barely started to dissolve by the time they left. He'd been able to spit it out and flush it down the toilet. Clever Peter! Morrissey heard himself giggling and clapped a hand over his mouth, dismayed. He might be able to think again, but laughing for joy was insanely inappropriate. The Russians were planning a nuclear strike. To defend against the radiation, Alan was going to give L-6 to millions of people. Alan believed that ending up a risen was better than being dead.

But he's wrong, Morrissey thought.

How do I know?

He pressed a hand against his forehead. His mind was working again, but slowly. He remembered how L-6 worked—the strengthened electron bonds. What else did he know? Very little. From the moment he'd shot Monk, he'd been on the move, trying to catch up with Alan. He'd had no time to reason out the medical and psychological implications of L-6.

And yet he was desperate to stop Alan. Deep inside, he

must know why, but the reason was still buried in his unconscious.

Leave it alone for a minute, he told himself. Think about something else.

He let his mind range back to the period when he'd been totally under the drug. Everything was a blur—except for Alan and Janet. They had paid regular visits. He could remember that quite clearly—both of them always staying outside, looking in through the glass. He had screamed at them and pounded the window, frantic to tell Janet about Alan, the L-6, the risens. It had been terrible: fighting the thick glass and his own scrambled brain; trying and straining and shouting endless garbage.

Morrissey glared at the empty window. He felt his fists clench and realized he was growling. The sound startled him into a sweat; he swallowed hard and clamped his jaws shut. The growling stopped, but he felt shaken. First the giggling and now this. He was riding an emotional teeter-totter. It must be the drug Alan had given him. There were hundreds of biochemicals that could alter the emotions.

Never mind that. He must get out of here and stop Alan.

Or was he already too late?

Think: Janet and Alan had appeared at the window between brightenings and darkenings of the light over his head. That probably meant he had been here several days.

Shocked, he got up and staggered to the wall. Days! He had to get out at once. But how?

He heard the food cart again, much closer in the hall outside. The smell of bacon was strong now. Soon it would be his turn. He flexed his legs and arms. He was weak, the muscles flabby with disuse. He framed his waist with his hands. So skinny. He must have been skipping meals. He was ravenous now. He'd have to eat before he could do anything.

He heard the cart stop outside his door. He sprawled on his back and turned his head away from the window. The key snicked and a draft swept over him as the door swung in.

"Mawnin', Peter. Breakfast time."

Morrissey rolled over, pretending sluggishness. Damn

it, two of them! Yes, that was right, always two of them. Big and strong—especially the bald black guy. Morrissey blinked, keeping his face slack and stupid. The orderly with pasty white skin and gray eyes smiled down at him, filling him with a formless dislike. He'd had trouble with this man—the armlock when the thin nurse gave him the pill. Gray-eyes enjoyed hurting people.

Morrissey caught the black man studying him as the white orderly set his tray on the mat. "Nothing to say this morning, Mr. Morrissey?"

"Baggish," Morrissey said. He blushed. Where had that word come from? Gibberish. He could think, but he still couldn't talk. *Alan, what did you do to me?* He saw the orderlies glance at each other. The white one with the gray eyes smiled condescendingly. He realized that he was lucky he hadn't said anything sensible.

"That's fine, Pete," gray-eyes said. "Now y'all try and eat a little sump'n this mawnin' or we'll have to plug one of our yaller bottles into you."

And I'll plug my fingers into your eyes. Morrissey's heart pounded savagely. The drug, he thought. Take it easy.

He watched them set the tray on the floor and back out. As soon as they were gone, he pulled the tray to a corner away from the window. Besides the bacon, there were scrambled eggs, a jelly roll, and a glass of orange juice. He fell on the food, wolfing the first few mouthfuls. Then he forced himself to slow down. His stomach had shrunk. If he wasn't careful he'd lose it all again.

He picked away until he'd eaten everything. He felt the warmth of the food flowing into him, strengthening him, focusing his mind.

And then he understood why he must stop Alan.

Emotions.

Alan's three dead test subjects could think, but they could not feel.

Morrissey shuddered. Dear Christ Almighty. If he hadn't been so desperate, so harried, he'd have seen it earlier. He'd been halfway there. The dead test subjects could think and act—because the basis for thought was electric. Tiny currents still circled in the preserved tissues of muscle and brain. But the basis of emotion was not electric. It was chemical. Right now Alan's drug was screwing up his emotions by distorting the normal biochemical balance in his brain.

Everything that mattered in life depended on that balance.

Morrissey closed his eyes and groaned. *You opened the door and saw your wife in the arms of your best friend. First you saw it, then you understood, and then the brain sent a nerve pulse to open the floodgates of the adrenal glands. Adrenaline poured into your veins, rushed through your body, powering the muscles, breaking back over the brain as a wave of emotion: rage. The balance shifted some more, seratonin levels changed. The rage became sadness, devastation.*

At the hospital in Saigon you saw the tiny baby with its caramel skin and almond eyes, and your endorphin level rose, and you were overcome with love, and you named her Tsong after her dead mother.

Morrissey opened his eyes and found himself staring at the smear of egg on his plate. He pushed it away, sick to his stomach. Anger, love, excitement, desire—a thousand other biochemical shifts, and Alan's three risens would never feel any of them again. If Alan pushed Project Parasol through, a hundred million people might survive the fallout of a nuclear strike. But they would still die—by accident, or as victims of the savagery of a post-nuclear world. Perhaps a few would even die of old age. Every one of them would awaken trapped in his or her own corpse, stripped of the only thing that made life worth living.

Morrissey looked around him desperately. A weapon—he'd need a weapon. He inspected the tray. No knife. The plastic spoon and fork were flimsy and would snap under any significant force. The dishes were paper. Maybe he could split the fiberglass tray to make a shard. Yes, if he hammered it on the toilet or drinking fountain. That would make a hell of a noise, though. . .

He heard the key turn again. The two orderlies came in fast and warily. They saw him sitting in the corner. "There y'all are,'' said gray-eyes. ''Now, Pete, why'd y'all want to hide from us? And lookit that. He done cleaned his plate.''

Morrissey's heart sank. Two mistakes—hiding, and eating like a starved man. But he'd had to eat, even if it made them suspicious.

The black man stood back as the white approached and swept up his tray. Then they were gone, backing out again.

Morrissey slammed his fist into the padded wall. They were so watchful. How would he ever get an edge?

Alan, have you started injecting citizens yet?

Morrissey got up and began walking around the cramped enclosure of his cell, pushing himself faster and faster until he was dizzy from the abrupt turns. He could feel his legs waking up with the exercise and the calories from the breakfast.

He glanced at the door and stopped in alarm: gray-eyes, staring in at him!

The door swung in and gray-eyes led the way, followed by the black orderly and a nurse. She was about forty, wiry and short, with a mass of dark hair pinned up under her cap.

She was *the* nurse—the one who gave him his pills.

She had a loaded syringe in her hand!

He felt a surge of adrenaline. Yes, it had to be now.

The nurse stood between the two orderlies. ''Well, Mr. Morrissey, it seems we've been skipping our pills. That's really not good, because we'll just become more agitated.''

The orderlies started to step forward.

''So maybe we'd like a shot instead, until we can—''

The nurse, Morrissey thought. She's the weak link. He lunged between the men, shoving the inside shoulder of each. The nurse squawked and stumbled back. He grabbed her arm and swung her around so that she was between him and the orderlies. He jerked her back against him with a forearm across her neck. She dropped the syringe. The orderlies started for him and then stopped as he yanked his arm in against her throat.

''STAG!'' he shouted, then searched, horrified, for the word he'd wanted. ''St . . . stop. Stop. Stop.''

The black orderly raised his hands in a placating gesture.

"We're stopped, man. Now just take it easy. No one's going to hurt you."

"Stay away. Or I'll . . ." Morrissey hunted, hunted, his brain aching with the effort. *Christ, he could think. Why couldn't he speak?* "I'll snap her neck," he finished. "One jerk and he's dead—*she's* dead."

The black orderly nodded. "I know. I know. Take it easy, okay?"

"Not okay I'm leave. Leaving. Don't try and stop me."

"All right. Hang loose, man."

"Y'all best not hurt Nurse Avery," gray-eyes blustered, "or I'll . . ."

The black orderly cuffed his arm and he shut up.

Morrissey heard an odd noise: "Guh, guh, guh." *Got her neck too tight. Ease up, ease up.* He loosened his hold and backed into the hall, pulling the door shut behind him. As soon as the lock clicked shut, he let the nurse go, spun her around, and jerked at the key ring on her belt. It resisted. He pulled at it, dragging her along the corridor.

"Puh-please," she choked. She fumbled at her belt and he let her work at it until the key chain slipped free.

He ran from the corridor and found himself in a commons area with men in green-and-white striped bathrobes like his.

"He's there! Get him, get him!" It was the nurse, behind him. Who was she shouting at? Oh fuck, the orderlies. He'd forgotten to take *their* keys. They'd let themselves out and were after him.

Morrissey raced down the center of the commons area. He glimpsed startled faces peering at him, a group of patients sitting around a TV, young to middle-aged men, a couple of amputees.

"Which way out?" he shouted.

A man, thin as a skeleton, stood and pointed.

Morrissey sped by them, and past the glassed-in nurses' station. A young nurse stared at him. As he passed, he heard her slam the top of the station's dutch door shut. Behind him came the clatter of the orderlies' feet.

Come on, legs! he thought.

He hit the sides of a hall with his hands, slowing, turning, letting the walls channel him into a lobby. He saw a small room with outside windows, heavily screened over, and a large steel door. He slid to a stop against the door and fumbled with the nurse's keys.

Which was the right key? There must be half a dozen of them. He jammed the first one at the cylinder lock. It wouldn't go. He tried the next. No luck.

The footsteps—too close behind him!

He turned. The black orderly was in the lead, his face earnest. Morrissey dodged the grasping hand, but the man caught his robe with an extra lunge. It tore. The man clung to him. Morrissey doubled the keys in his hand and swung against the bald head. The keys cut into his fingers, searing his knuckles with pain. The orderly sank to his knees, eyes unfocused.

There, behind him—gray-eyes!

"You freaked-out sumbitch!"

As the man jumped on him, Morrissey raised a knee, catching him in the crotch. They fell back together, and the man's momentum slammed Morrissey hard against the knee. He rolled off, over and over, coming to rest doubled up and gasping.

Where were the keys? Dropped them! He looked around desperately. There! He reached for them, but the black man flipped them away. They slid across the tile into a corner.

Morrissey saw the other patients crowding down the short hall, wide-eyed.

"Help!" he shouted. "Help me."

The skinny man who'd told him which way to go pedaled into the lobby on the balls of his feet. He raised emaciated fists like a boxer. His eyes were focused far away.

Morrissey saw the black orderly reaching for him, ignoring the patient. Gray-eyes was rolling over toward him, too, his eyes pinched with pain and hate.

The windows! Morrissey leapt for them, tearing at the thick mesh of the screen. A weight slammed into him from behind, pinning him against the web of wire. He wriggled helplessly. From the corner of his eye he saw a black hand close firmly over his wrist, dark fingers locking into the screen. He felt his other hand being pinned too.

It was over.

He peered through the window. Outside were the buildings of Ft. Detrick, the high cyclone fence, the labs. So he was still on the base. . .

A fist slammed in from the side, unleashing terrible pain low in his back, spreading from his kidney. His vision went dark. He gasped, unable to move. Dimly he felt more blows raining in from the side.

". . . enough, Lester. Goddamnit, that's enough!"

The black man's voice, shouting close to his ear. The screen and window swam back into focus. It seemed to be tinted red now. The pain came surging back.

"Here, here. I've got him." He recognized the nurse's voice. A needle pricked his haunch. The black man loosened his grip a little. Morrissey gazed at the woods beyond the fence. That's where Alan's camp was. In the daylight the trees were beautiful, reds and golds mingled with the lush evergreens. The sky above the woods was a brilliant blue. It looked like a place of benign magic, an enchanted forest. Seeing it so close filled him with frustration.

He felt hands under his armpits, easing him back from the screen. He couldn't keep his head from lolling. He jerked it upright only to have it nod over again. He glimpsed the nurse standing well back, the spent syringe in her hand. Her throat had turned a mottled red. The pale orderly stood protectively beside her. He was glaring, bent slightly at the waist, his fists still doubled.

Beyond them stood the patients, very still, their faces sad.

"Help me." Morrissey's voice came out weak and slurred. "Vandiver's going to get everyone. L-6. Walking dead. The whole U.S."

Several of the patients nodded gravely. The nurse and orderly watched him with stony expressions.

He gathered himself desperately. "No. Not crazy. I'm serious. Undead . . . Risens."

The scene broke, slid into matching parts that overlapped. He was enveloped in a golden haze, warm and thick. He'd just close his eyes a second, rest, and then try again to make them understa. . .

5
DAYS

Thursday, November 6

Chapter 28

1500 hours:

"What the . . . uh, Sam Hill is going on?" Peter's father asked.

Janet slid her hand over the receiver and glanced through to the cabin's bedroom. Alan, holding the extension phone, gave her a look of pained apology and shook his head. She felt a spark of resentment. No, she thought. I mustn't be angry. Alan doesn't *want* to listen in. It's his duty.

But does he have to keep his finger poised above that button, ready to cut me off?

"Janet?"

"I'm sorry, Dad. I can't tell you any more than I have already. I accidentally got involved in some important secret work Peter's doing for the government, and now I have to stay under . . . a sort of quarantine. It's national security, Dad. Peter and I are all right."

"Any idea yet how much longer you got to be holed up?"

"Not long. If the girls are a problem . . ."

"My little angels?" His voice was suddenly light. One of the kids just walked in on him, Janet thought. A lump swelled in her throat. She envisioned June standing with Dad in the tiny living room. He'd be there in his rocker by the phone. June would be bouncing on the davenport, as Pa called it, or running at the round, threadbare rug, trying to slide on it. Janet ached with longing. I want to see you, baby, she thought. And Tsong. I want out of this place. I want to squeeze my little girls.

She swallowed and clutched the phone. She must get down to business. "Dad, you haven't let the girls talk you into going back to the house, have you?"

"Nope. Anyway, they're not keen to. Tsong seems glad to be outta there, like it was haunted or something. June wanted to get her insect collection, but I said no." Peter's father lowered his voice. "I'll be darned if I can give her a decent reason, though."

Janet thought of the dog's head, lying there on the floor, snapping at her. She shivered.

"Can I speak to the girls?"

"Tsong's out back. Here's Junie."

There was a pause. "Mommy?"

"Hi, honey." She bit her lip. "How's it going?"

"Fine. Grandpa's fixing us wild greens for supper. He grows 'em in the backyard. He says he used to find them in a holler. What's a holler?"

Janet heard Alan chuckle from across the cabin. She looked over. His hand was wrapped safely over the receiver. He was grinning, and yet he looked sad.

"A holler is a big valley, honey," she said. "The house Daddy and Grandpa grew up in had a holler behind it. So did Uncle Alan's."

"Is Uncle Alan there?"

Janet sucked in her breath, startled. "No. Why would he be here?"

"How come they don't just call it a valley? Is Daddy there?"

"He's . . . at work, honey."

"Why doesn't *he* call us?"

"He's been so busy . . ."

"Tell him we wish we could talk to him."

"I will.

"Okay. Bye, Mommy."

"June . . . ?" The line was dead. Janet lowered the receiver slowly to its cradle, feeling severed. She became aware of Alan's hand on her shoulder.

"They're fine," he said softly. "You did well."

She turned, and before she knew what was happening, his arms were around her. She readied herself to push him off, but he simply held her, nothing improper. She felt comfort flowing into her from his arms. She let herself relax a little. She could smell him suddenly, his clean scent of bay rum. She could sense every part of him. Though she was careful to hold her fingertips motionless, they still told her of slabs of muscle tapering down his back.

A slow wave of heat rose in her stomach. She slipped her hands between their bodies and eased herself back. Alan hugged his elbows, as though in pulling away she'd taken all his warmth.

She understood suddenly how much he wanted her.

For fourteen years he had wanted her. At this moment he was blind and drunk just with her nearness. She knew it absolutely, as though she were inside his mind.

It shocked her. She was an artist, reaching middle age, with wrinkles around her eyes, a slight droop beginning beneath the upper arms. But to this handsome man with the tall, powerful body of a god, she was the most desirable woman in the world.

She felt a giddy rush of blood to her head.

He took her hands and kissed her fingers one by one. Her breath hitched high in her chest. She was powerless to pull away.

Alan said: "I want to make love to you once before I die."

Her fingers clenched down on his hands. "You're not going to die."

"All right, once before I live forever." His voice was without wit or sarcasm, husky and mindless.

"Peter," was all she could say.

"You love Peter. You always will. And so will I." He drew a long, shuddering breath. "I was so young. I thought I had forever. The first time I saw you, I knew you were the one, but I wasn't ready. I wanted to play. I was a fool. You went to the right man. I couldn't love you and want you to have less than Peter. I'll make him well again, I swear it to you."

She felt tears coming. "Oh, Alan."

"I want you so much."

She closed her eyes, trying to contain the tears, but they squeezed out between her lashes. She felt his lips blotting them away. He began unbuttoning her blouse, not hurrying, giving her time. You have to decide, she thought. One way or the other. You can't just let it happen.

A burst of memory flared: college, before Peter. Walking with Alan along the tow path of the C&O canal one Sunday in late fall. One of their first few dates. Details stood out sharply. She had felt so short beside him. He was lean then—the way Peter still was—not filled out and muscular yet. He'd shed his sweater, tying the arms of it loosely around his neck, letting the rest hang down his back like a cape. Hair blew in a golden wave across his forehead.

There was no diamond of white in the back then.

He walked them off to themselves and spread a blanket. Bees droned in the high grass. The rich smell of wet leaves rose from the canal.

He took her hand.

Here it comes, she'd thought, cynical but a little turned on, too. Alan, the campus playboy.

He said, "Janet, be my friend."

What had she answered? She'd been taken aback, and amused—she remembered that—and then she'd hidden her smile as she realized how bleak his face was. . .

"Janet," Vandiver said.

She thought of the room in his house, the imaginary son. The day Alan had been so full of panic, afraid he might be a monster.

"Yes," she whispered.

He gave a hushed groan. She felt him lifting her, a brawny forearm under her knees, around her back. He carried her to his narrow cot and knelt on the floor beside her, leaning onto her with his centaur's upper body. She put one hand on his neck, thumb curled up and over the front of his ear. Her body went numb, all of her feeling going into the hand, caressing his hair with her fingers, tracing the earlobe with the tip of her thumb, soothing the straining cords of his neck as he stretched fully on top of her and came almost at once, pressing her into the thin mattress.

"AH-H-H-H-H-H!" he shouted at the end, his only sound.

He lay like a dead man on top of her for a long time, remaining buried hard inside her. She felt his tears on her face, mingling with her own. Please, she thought, don't try to make me come.

He pulled out of her with infinite gentleness and smiled down. "My life is complete," he said.

She forced her face into an answering smile. "Your son. . ." she said and then stopped, not knowing how to make it a joke, wondering what had possessed her to try.

But Alan smiled more broadly. "Yes," he said. "The first time conception ever came after birth."

On her way to her cabin she was sure the gawking soldiers working by the generator shed were seeing right through her. She stared back and they looked away, with sheepish expressions. It wasn't wrong, she thought defiantly. Forget it, *forget it*, please God.

She heard a loud, rapid thumping sound. It swelled quickly. She looked up through the pines in time to see a helicopter sweep low overhead. Huge—the biggest she had ever seen. And somehow sinister. For a second the noise was almost deafening; then it dropped away in the direction of the main compound.

She hurried into her cabin, turned and leaned against the door, her heart pounding. She felt menace all around her, crystallized in the inhuman sound of the helicopter. This was a dangerous place—sunshine, rustic cabins, and all.

Was she ever going to tell Peter what she had just done? Would the time ever come again when he'd be able to understand her if she did?

She gave her head a violent shake. Put it out of your mind, she thought. Never think of it again. It's done.

She closed her eyes and concentrated on the feel of the door against her forehead. She could smell pine in the wood, sluggish old sap warmed by the sun outside. Behind her, curtains ticked lightly at the open bedroom window. She was suddenly weary. It would be a few hours yet before Alan escorted her to see Peter again. Perhaps a nap would do her good while she waited for visiting hours. Yes, sleep . . . escape.

She walked, head down, into the bedroom. At the foot of her bed she froze. There was someone on the other side, crouching down, hiding!

She tried to scream. Only a squeak came out.

The man got awkwardly to his feet. "Don't yell, lady," he said urgently. "Please don't yell."

She clapped a hand over her mouth. She stared at him, and her fright eased back. He wasn't even a man. Barely more than a boy. Big, but so fat she could run away from him easily if he tried anything. Where had he come from? He looked disgusting. His shirt was filthy, from the collar down to where it came untucked from his belt. There was dirt on his face, too, and his hair was a mess of greasy cowlicks. And those scars crisscrossing the rolls of fat on his neck—horrible!

"Who are you?" she rasped.

"My name's Kellogg. I'm sorry I scared you. I had to get out of sight, and this cabin was close to the fence. The window was open . . ."

"Well, what are you doing?"

"I'm looking for someone. I didn't expect to see a lady here."

Janet pressed a hand against her chest, felt her heart begin to slow. That name—Kellogg. Familiar. Peter's lab assistant! He wouldn't do anything to hurt her. She sighed in relief. "You work for Peter."

He brightened. "That's right. Who're you . . . uhm, lady?"

"I'm Janet Morrissey."

Kellogg clapped a hand happily against his forehead. "Boy! This is great. Do you know where he is?"

"Of course. Why?"

"Mrs. Morrissey, I think he's in trouble."

Janet frowned. He sounded so sure. Did he know about Peter's breakdown? No, he couldn't. "Why do you say that?"

"He borrowed my truck to come out here and see Colonel Vandiver. That was a week ago. I rented a car and I've been hanging around the main base the past few days trying to figure out what happened to him. I know he's here somewhere—I found my truck parked in some bushes beside the road that runs around the base."

"But how did you get in *here*?"

"I sneaked in."

"There are soldiers," she said, "and guard dogs out there."

"I'm good with dogs," Kellogg said proudly. "I got 'em to come over and then I gave 'em some doped meat—not enough to hurt them, just make them sleep. I found places under the base fence and then that little fence around the camp where I could push my way under."

Suddenly she found herself liking Kellogg, admiring him. He might look sloppy and awkward, but he had nerve. And he must care for Peter very much. "I hate to tell you this, but that little fence you just pushed under is electrified."

Kellogg paled. "No sh—, no kidding?"

She smiled. "You can say shit. I think I can take it."

He blushed and then smiled back at her.

"You're lucky the current was off when you came under. They've been having trouble with the generator off and on."

"Where's Pete?"

She hesitated, not wanting to say it.

"I'm sorry to push you, Mrs. Morrissey, but I've got to *see* Pete. I'm not leaving this place until I do."

"Why?"

Kellogg looked confused. "Why? We're friends, and

he's in trouble. Please, Mrs. Morrissey, tell me where he is."

"Peter's in the psychiatric ward of the base hospital."

"No!"

"I'm afraid so. He's acting very irrational, paranoid. He's been that way for a week."

"You've seen him this way? Acting crazy?"

"For a whole week he hasn't said one word to me that I can understand."

"I don't believe it. Peter wouldn't go nuts."

She grabbed him by the shirt. "What do you know about it? You haven't been here for a week, you haven't had to watch him through a little piece of wired glass . . ." The flash of rage burned away. She focused on Kellogg. He was cringing away from her. She saw a fleck of her spit on his face. She became aware of the sweaty feel of his shirt and the soft mass of womanish breast beneath her doubled fists. *What was she doing?* She let go of him and backed away, astonished at herself. "I'm sorry. I've been under a strain."

Kellogg drew himself up. "Yes, you have. If you can believe that Pete's gone crazy, you've been under a real big strain."

"But Peter *is* psychotic. I've seen him every day, and every day it's the same. He rants and raves. His words don't make sense."

"Were you with him when it first happened?"

"No, but Alan—General Vandiver was. General Vandiver was the one who put him in the hospital." Why am I being so formal about Alan's name? she wondered. Am I embarrassed to let Kellogg know I'm friendly with the man who put Peter away? Friendly? Oh, yes—one might even say *intimate* . . . . She felt a spark of pain in her lip and realized she had bitten down on it.

Kellogg frowned. "General? Last I knew he was a colonel. Listen, Mrs. Morrissey. There are drugs that make you crazy. A doctor—especially a military doctor who's into research—would know about them."

Janet shook her head. "That's ridiculous. That's totally paranoid."

"Does Vandiver let you see Pete alone?"

"He can't. Security at the hospital . . ."

"What security? You're his wife, lady."

She stared at Kellogg. What did he mean? Was he implying that she should have done something else? Not listened to Alan? This wasn't her fault.

She felt a twinge of doubt. Why *hadn't* Alan let her see Peter alone—her own husband? Did he really think Peter might hurt her? Or was he trying to keep them as far apart as possible?

What would happen if she insisted on seeing Peter alone?

"Mrs. Morrissey? You asked me why I came. I guess maybe there's another reason. Pete plays it close to the chest sometimes. He thinks he has to protect you. Pete forgets that other people can do things and be strong. I want to show Pete that I'm strong too."

Suddenly she wanted to hug the kid. You're right, she thought. So right.

"Forget everything Dr. Vandiver's told you," Kellogg said, "and just answer me this: Ten days ago, would you have believed that Pete was about to go crazy and stay that way for a whole week, and not say one word to you that makes sense?"

"No. Not when you put it that way."

"Okay. Let's go."

"Where?"

"The psych hospital. We're going to bust him out of there. If he's really crazy, let's hear it from someone else—some expert with no ax to grind."

"We can't do that," Janet said. "Be reasonable. You're going off half-cocked . . ." She hesitated. Was he really? Maybe Kellogg was right and she should try to move Peter, just to be sure. She should be able to do that, or at least test whether she could. But what about the security requirements? Alan had explained why they had to stay here, and it made sense. The work on radiation, in case the Russians ever decided to attack. Very important work.

"No," she said. "We just can't."

"Okay. So long." Kellogg turned to the window.

"Wait . . ." She took a step after him, agonized.

Kellogg grinned. "Don't worry, Mrs. Morrissey. I'll be careful."

She watched him clamber out the window. She gnawed anxiously at a knuckle. I should stop him, she thought. Get Alan. For Kellogg's own good. He can't just go sneaking around here. If he tries to break into the hospital, he'll get into big trouble—

Janet heard a gunshot. She thought: Oh dear Lord—Kellogg!

She rushed to the back window, trying to see the fence. There were too many pine trees, screening it off. She rushed from the cabin and through the pines, dimly aware of needles slapping her face.

Kellogg was lying under the fence.

She doubled over him, breathless, as though someone had squeezed all the air from her chest. He was stuck halfway through, the bottom strands of fence raking his back, his cheek pressed into the dirt outside the fence. A red stain spread on his shirt between his shoulder blades.

She touched him frantically. She heard the shouts of approaching guards, the sound of their feet slashing through the grass and fallen leaves.

Kellogg raised his head an inch. He was trying to say something. She bent close. Blood bubbled out of his mouth, bright red. He swatted it away weakly.

"Tell Pete he was right," he grunted. "About the Tastykakes."

She nodded, not understanding. His head dropped back down. The leaves turned red around his mouth. His eye was wide and staring. There was a film on it, like dust.

"Oh no, oh no," she moaned. She bent over his legs, hugging them, clinging to their warmth.

Gradually she became aware of the guards clustering around her. She pushed back from the fence and watched, sickened. The men grabbed Kellogg's ankles and tried to drag him in from under the fence. One of them stood back, pale, gripping his rifle so hard his knuckles were white. A kid, just like Kellogg, and now a killer.

She heard a commotion behind her and turned. It was Alan, tearing through the trees behind her, blond hair flying. In his right hand was a pistol. When he saw her, he slowed, and his expression smoothed in relief. "Janet, thank God," he said.

She ran past him, flailing back at the slapping branches. She stumbled into her cabin, slammed the door and locked it, then ran to the window and locked it too. Sobs yanked at her throat. Alan had known nothing about Kellogg. He'd seen only that she was still inside the fence, and he'd been relieved.

Alan had made a bedroom for their imaginary son. Alan had just made love to her.

And now Alan had run after her with his gun out.

She looked around frantically. A weapon—she needed a weapon. A length of pipe, a tool, anything she could lay her hands on.

No, stop.

She made herself sit on the bed. She waited until the sobs died down. There was no more room for hysterics. She must plan carefully. She must be as clever as Alan had been.

And as brave as Kellogg.

"Hold on, Peter," she said softly. "I'm coming."

4
DAYS

Friday, November 7

Chapter 29

0800 hours:

And a mighty wind
rent the mountains around,
brake in pieces the rocks,
brake them before the Lord

Vandiver stopped shaving and stared at the stereo, shocked to stillness by the hidden second meaning of the words: a mighty wind, tearing mountains, smashing rock— *the shock-wave of a 50-megaton warhead.*

He laid his shaving brush across the mug and walked to the stereo, the hot water dripping from his face. He stared at the spinning record, feeling betrayed. The Elijah Oratorio was his favorite. Music was his last refuge.

And after the earthquake there came a fire. . .

Vandiver swatted the tone arm of the stereo aside, raking the needle across the record. It didn't matter. He would never listen to the damned thing again.

He turned the stereo off and returned to the mirror. He lathered his face and held the straight razor a few inches from his jaw until his hand stopped shaking. He began to shave, concentrating on making the movements calm and controlled. It was senseless to get so upset over a piece of music. The real betrayal was not the taunting double meaning of the Elijah, but General Stanhouse's cowardly turnabout. There was nothing to be done about that either. Stanhouse had vetoed the plague option and that was that. It was his duty to carry out Stanhouse's orders.

And let the 50-megaton warheads fall.

With forced precision, Vandiver dabbed more lather on his face and thought: It's Hagan's fault. Hagan had been there with the general, and Hagan wasn't sentimental. Hagan could have pushed Stanhouse into doing his duty. But Hagan had turned out to be gutless too.

Vandiver's jaw clenched with anger. If only Stanhouse had let *me* do it, he thought. I wouldn't like it any more than he did, but I would damn well do it. . .

He paused in midstroke, considering. Perhaps he could *still* do it. The timetable was drastically off now, with only four days left until the election. But the plague would start to kill within hours. Within two days, a large number of people would be dead—perhaps enough to start the panic. The innoculation centers were ready. The trailers were sitting there on school parking lots across the country, quietly waiting to immunize school kids against this winter's "expected" flu epidemic. There'd be no problem with the L-6 either. There had been no time to bottle it in anything but the waiting vials of anti-plague vaccine. As for the plague virus itself, Stanhouse and Hagan had simply reburied the cola bottles here on the back acreage of Detrick. He could dig them up again.

Yes! Vandiver thought. It could still be done.

He saw his excited face in the mirror and frowned. What was he thinking? Disobeying an order went against everything he believed in. He would be court-martialed.

And what about Hagan's spies? That toady corporal—Trickett—was surely watching him. There were no doubt others. Hagan had probably posted a guard around the burial site of the bottles. Hagan would stop him before he could do it. And the stopping would be done with a bullet.

Vandiver's shoulder tingled unpleasantly where he'd

been injected with L-6. A bullet, and then he'd be like those three poor devils in Cabin 3.

He held the razor away from his face a minute, then resumed shaving.

All this proved one thing: He'd been right not to tell Stanhouse or Hagan about the three risen soldiers. If they balked at starting the plague, think what they'd have done if he'd told them about the risens. They'd have called the project off entirely.

And it looked as if the risens were not so bad. They were leaving him strictly alone, staying in the empty cabin, causing no trouble. It was almost like they were turned off.

A fatalistic calm settled over Vandiver. There was nothing to do but make the best of Stanhouse's revised plan. Feeble and desperate as it was, it was still far better than nothing. The civil defense sirens would wail, people would go to their TVs and be told about the impending attack. They'd be ordered to hurry to the nearest high school for anti-radiation shots. From that moment it would be survival of the fittest. If the mad-dog Russians went through with it and struck, the survivors would be those Americans who had understood quickly, jumped into their cars, and raced to the innoculation centers. Russia would reel under an American counterstrike. Post-holocaust America would survive, populated with people who were not only radiation-resistant, but selected for toughness, quickness, and intelligence. You could almost approve that one part of it.

Vandiver rinsed his face, feeling the perfect smoothness of his skin, noting with satisfaction that he had not so much as nicked himself.

As he dressed, he heard the fence generator stutter, bang, and then die. Hadn't they got that fixed yet? He went to the window and looked out. A soldier walked from the power shed and glanced guiltily toward his cabin. Disgusted, Vandiver turned away and finished buttoning his shirt.

He sat on his bed and tugged his boots, turning his attention with relish to the coming hour. It was time to visit Janet. She'd been badly shaken up by the shooting of that fat kid. She needed reassurance and comfort.

And he wanted—no *needed*—to touch her. Perhaps they would make love again, like yesterday. That had been so good.

And tormenting. He was surprised to feel a knot in his throat again. Yesterday he had wept. Why?

Because he had made the biggest mistake of his life long ago. Because for fourteen years he had *not* had her. . .

Someone hammered rudely on the door. Vandiver scowled. He strode to the door and yanked it open.

It was Hagan.

Vandiver suppressed a groan. Just what he needed, another dance with old Bald Eagle.

"What is it, Colonel?"

"I want to talk to you."

"So talk."

"Inside."

Vandiver controlled his temper. He stood aside and let Hagan push past. The colonel turned, barely allowing him room to close the door. "Who is the man you put in the psych ward?" he demanded. "What's his connection to the project?"

Vandiver thought: I'm ready for you this time. "That," he said wearily, "is Dr. Peter Morrissey. He works at the Army Labs. He's my best friend."

"You've got a funny way of showing it."

"Do you want to talk or listen?"

"Do go on," Hagan said.

"Peter played an early part in L-6 development. I was concerned about the way the pressure and secrecy seemed to be affecting him. So, before moving things here, I put him on another project. He figured out where I was and finagled his way in here. He was agitated and paranoid—"

"You're a psychiatrist now?"

Don't let him bait you, Vandiver thought. "You prefer layman talk? All right, the poor bastard had slipped off the deep end. He knew just enough about L-6 to be dangerous. To avoid jeopardizing the study, I had him committed here."

Vandiver reviewed what he'd said. Did that cover it? No,

Hagan would know about Janet too. "I brought his wife out to forestall any fuss," he added. "She agreed to accept the tight security conditions in order to be near Peter."

Hagan nodded with cynical admiration. "Not a bad story, Vandiver. So now let's go see your . . . friend."

"He's in no condition to receive visitors."

"I'm not a visitor."

Vandiver glanced at his watch. 0840. Would they have given Peter his morning capsule by now? What if they had not? And what if Peter had managed to fool them again last night, faking his evening dose? Damn Hagan. For the sake of delay, he could make the colonel go through channels, but that would expand the importance of Peter, make him an issue.

Vandiver sighed. "You want to see him? We'll see him."

Peter was sitting in his usual spot against the wall opposite the door, hugging his knees. A wave of pity swept over Vandiver. Peter looked cold. How could he be cold? It was like an oven in here. It must be that awful thinness. I'll get him more blankets, Vandiver thought. As soon as we're out of here. *Be good today, Peter. Hang in a little longer, and I'll have you out of here. The minute it's too late for you to stop the project. I promise you.*

Vandiver opened the speaking grille with a clank. Morrissey gazed without interest at the window, then let his chin fall back to his knees. *Good*, Vandiver thought.

"Dr. Morrissey," Hagan said through the grille. More sharply he said, "Morrissey, can you hear me?"

Morrissey showed no sign of hearing.

"Open up," Hagan said. "Let's go inside."

"Out of the question. He gets violent without warning."

"I think two big strong men can handle him. I want to get up close, where I can talk to him properly."

Vandiver said, "I'm trying to play ball with you, Colonel, but this is getting out of hand. What are you so damned suspicious about?"

Hagan looked back through the glass. "If the General

will pardon me, I'll stop being suspicious when the General stops acting like he wants to hide something."

Vandiver sighed. What can it hurt? he thought. Peter's obviously out of it. He opened the door.

Morrissey looked up incuriously as they entered. Hagan squatted down on his haunches in front of him. Vandiver locked the door and leaned against it.

"Dr. Morrissey, I'm Colonel Hagan. I've come to see how you are."

"Grant," Morrissey said. His mouth kept working around the word. He let go of his knees and rolled awkwardly forward to a kneeling position. Vandiver watched, pained. Peter jabbed a finger at him over and over, as though once he'd started the motion, he couldn't stop it. Pitiful. Maybe the dose could be cut back.

"Minimal. Bro . . . broden."

"I can't understand you," Hagan said.

Morrissey pinched his eyes shut and waited. Then, forming and reforming his mouth, he said, "Alan . . . glands. Mosh . . . mosh . . . emotion."

Vandiver frowned. Peter was staring at him now instead of Hagan. His face looked pleading, urgent, as if he were trying to warn him. Glands? Emotion? Sweat prickled on Alan's face. Those were real words. Was Peter coming out of it?

"Yes?" Hagan prodded patiently.

Morrissey forced out a chain of gibberish. Hagan began to push. The more he pushed, the more incoherent Peter became. Vandiver relaxed. Finally he stepped forward. "That's enough, Colonel. As you can see, Peter's not a well man. It's time we let him be. Clearly we're upsetting him."

Hagan did not reply. He stared at Morrissey. Then, abruptly, he stood and turned to the door. Vandiver almost smiled in relief. *That's it, we made it, Peter ol' boy.*

Morrissey ground his hands savagely into his cheeks. "Wait!" he said.

Hagan turned back to him.

Damn! Vandiver thought.

"L-6 . . . bad. Dead gom, dad gum . . . No, *dead* . . . to line—like . . . *libe*. . .

He *is* coming out of it! Vandiver thought. I've got to stop him. He stood, rooted to the spot. What could he do? Rush over and clap his hand over Peter's mouth? No, of course not. *Think!*

Morrissey scowled and shook his head. He went on pressing his cheeks and lips, as though trying to make them shape the right word. "L-6—dead, dead."

"All right, Dr. Morrissey," Hagan said. "Take it easy. I'll be back." Hagan motioned and Vandiver unlocked the door with numb fingers, locked it again behind them. No, he thought, you'll *not* be back. I can't let you back here again. But how can I stop you?

Hagan said, "I want the charge nurse."

"What the hell for?"

"So you can tell her to suspend all medication for that man. He's to get nothing until further orders."

Vandiver went cold. "That's the last thing I'll do. He's a sick man. Without the medication, he'll become violent and possibly hurt himself. I won't be responsible for—"

Hagan unsnapped his holster. Vandiver looked down at the handle of the .45. His shoulder burned. The rest of him was frozen.

"You will do what I ask, General, and you will do it now."

Chapter 30

1100 hours:

Vandiver prepared to attack Hagan. He slid his rump forward to the edge of his bed. *Casual, now.* He leaned over and propped his forearms on his knees. He folded his hands. *That's it. Make Hagan see how relaxed you are.*

He heard the generator start up outside with a noisy clatter. Sergeant Bruck's men must still be trying to fix it. Good, the noise could provide cover.

Vandiver studied the way Hagan had positioned himself. The old geek wasn't dumb. He'd settled beside the desk at least five strides off. And he wasn't looking away, even for a second.

Vandiver began to doubt. Can I really take this man? he wondered. I should be able to. He's at least twenty-five years older than me, half a foot shorter, maybe forty pounds lighter. But he was once a combat soldier, a sergeant who moved up through the ranks. He's fought before—those scars. He's killed men in close. I was around action in 'Nam, but I haven't even used my fists since high school.

Vandiver began to be afraid again. He could smell Hagan's sweat, see each separate black hair on his forearms.

He looked again at the scar beside his mouth. Ugly—intimidating.

This was no good. He was only unnerving himself. And he couldn't afford that. When Peter came out from under CA-2, he'd sing like Pavarotti. He'd tell Hagan all about the reanimation effect of L-6. Let Hagan and Stanhouse get one look at the risen men and there would be no innoculation campaign. Hagan would bury the plan, make it like it had never been.

And hundreds of millions of people would die.

He *had* to take Hagan.

He shifted another inch on the bed. Damn this mushy mattress. When he tried to shove off, it would absorb a big part of his thrust. Had Hagan deliberately sat him here? Yes, probably. The thought sent tension spreading between Vandiver's shoulder blades, turning him rigid. No good. He had to be loose and fast. Just take it easy for a minute. Talk. Distract him. Wait for your moment.

"This is ridiculous, Hagan."

The generator banged again and then stopped.

Hagan stared impassively at him. "We've been all through it, General. There's nothing more to say. If I'm wrong, I'll apologize."

"Oh, that's all right, then," Vandiver said bitingly. "Meanwhile, I'm a prisoner in my own cabin." He glanced at Hagan's holster. The flap was unsnapped. That would make it a close thing—covering the five steps before Hagan could get the .45 out.

"I've got work to do. Peter isn't going to talk sense today, tonight, or next week. The hospital won't be calling any time soon. You can't expect me to just wait here until you understand that."

"It was your choice," Hagan said. "I'd just as soon have waited at the hospital."

"Don't be an ass. You know what I'm talking about. You're making a big mistake, and I'm not the only one paying for it. The longer you deprive Peter of his medicine, the crazier he'll talk and the crazier he'll act."

"Yes, his medicine," Hagan said thoughtfully. "Odd

thing about those symptoms—that crazy talk, as you put it. I've seen men act like that before. In 1972 they were experimenting right here at Detrick with a drug called CA-2. Detrick was trying to save DIA and CIA types from having to take a lethal capsule after capture to avoid spilling their guts to the enemy. CA-2 seemed like the answer. You could take short-term capsules. Or in concentrated form, a single capsule could stay in your system for a long time. 'Salting out in the fatty tissues' I think was how you medicine men put it. *C* stood for confusion and *A* for aphasia. If you got a chance just before capture, you could take CA-2 and stay incoherent, the way your *friend* Peter is now, for weeks. Long enough for rescue or for your sensitive knowledge to become obsolete."

Five steps, Vandiver thought. Five steps and that unlatched holster. He heard the faulty generator again. It was making noise regularly now—starting, then stopping while they tinkered, then starting again. If he could just get the gun, he could time it so the men outside would never hear the shot.

Vandiver realized with a shock what he was thinking. Was he going to kill Hagan? Yes, that's what he'd have to do. Otherwise, Hagan wouldn't rest until he found out what was in Peter's mind. It was too dangerous to try and confine such a man. Hagan was relentless. Hagan was after him, after the project. Hagan had to go.

Vandiver swallowed with distaste. He didn't like the old curmudgeon, but to actually *shoot* him?

"Trouble is," Hagan rambled on, "CA-2 sometimes worked too well." Vandiver noticed that the old man was staring at him now, never glancing away, never seeming to blink. "I saw one of the Vietcong P.O.W.s they tried it on here at Detrick. He'd been talking nothing but baby talk for a whole year. He was permanently fucked up. I wonder if you realized that might happen when you gave CA-2 to your good buddy Peter."

Blood rushed to Vandiver's face. It was too much. Hagan had plagued him from the start—spied on him, undercut him with Stanhouse, threatened him. And now, if he allowed it, the son of a bitch would ruin him, maybe even blow him away with that .45. It was unfair. What had he ever done to Hagan?

He said: "What is it with you, Hagan? Why do you hate me?"

"I don't hate you."

"Then why are you after me?"

Hagan looked almost sad. "You really don't know, do you?"

"I'm ambitious? Is that what irritates you?" Vandiver tapped Stanhouse's star. "The only thing this means to me, aside from the fact that it comes from a great man's shoulder, is that it gives me the power to do something for my country."

"Is that how you see yourself? Yeah, I suppose it would be. No, Vandiver. I've got nothing against ambition. I work for that great man you mentioned. He wouldn't be Chairman now if he hadn't been ambitious."

"Then what's your problem?"

"It's not my problem, it's yours. You're all alone, aren't you, Vandiver? There just isn't anyone else in your universe with you."

Vandiver stared at him. Amazing! Hagan, talking like a shrink? What was next?

"And if there's no one else, then you don't have to care, do you? It simplifies things. You need to get people in for their innoculations without the Russians catching on, you just start a plague, and kill off fifty thousand folks and scare the rest in. Simple. You want to be a general? Take charge of someone else's work and ride it to glory. If that someone gets in the way, shut them up. Your *friend* Morrissey *is* the one who thought up L-6, isn't he, Vandiver? And he knows something about it you don't want us to find out, doesn't he? That's why you put him away. No, I don't hate you; I pity you. You are absolutely ruthless."

Vandiver felt a strange, aching sadness for the man Hagan described. If it were truly him, he would deserve pity. But it wasn't him.

And there wasn't an ounce of pity in Hagan.

Such clever spite, such oily, self-righteous spite. And it was all garbage. Him, alone? He'd had friends around him all his life. He yearned to be sitting at the old chessboard with Peter, drinking Virginia Gentleman and bullshitting in a safe world. He yearned for other things, impossible things: to hold Janet in his arms, to have a son with her. Were those the desires of an uncaring man, a man alone? And steal L-6 from Peter? That was the unfairest barb of all. It was Peter who had tried to steal L-6 from Army Labs and from the country. As for the 50,000 people, he cared, hell yes, he cared. But it was the only sure way, and someone had to be strong enough to make the tough decisions.

Vandiver welcomed the anger boiling in him. It felt almost good, bracing him for what he had to do. He would take Hagan, finish him. But first Hagan would see how wrong he was. Hagan would take back what he'd said. "Have you ever killed a man, Colonel?"

Hagan gazed at him with the steadiness of a Sphinx. "I've killed a lot of men. You know that."

"But *you* were always sure it had to be done. You *never* doubted yourself afterward."

"I *always* doubted myself. You said once that we're not so different. *That's* the difference."

Vandiver laughed, and stopped at once, shocked by the brittle sound of it. "That's rich, Hagan," he said bitterly. "I've never killed a man in my life. I've saved maybe a hundred on the operating table, including General Stanhouse's son. You, on the other hand, have killed a lot of men. But I'm ruthless and you're not, because you wallow in your cleansing baths of self-doubt."

Hagan sighed. "Let's not talk anymore, General." He reached up and scratched his bald skull.

His gun hand. Energy surged into Vandiver's legs. Yes, this was it.

He sprang. *One step.* The mattress gave against his rump as he tried to push off. Shit, it was worse than he feared. Come on, *dig!*

Time slowed, congealing around him.

He struggled to get his body out front, where the legs could push it forward.

Two steps. He saw Hagan's hand starting to drop again.

Three steps. Vandiver felt his body gathering speed now, the force of a battering ram, but he saw that Hagan's hand was almost to his holster. He heard the generator start up outside.

Four steps. The gun was out now, and there was no sign of surprise on Hagan's face, no flinching of the shoulders, no disorganized bursts of movement from the startle reflex. He suckered me, Vandiver thought with horror. I'm dead.

Five steps. His arms reaching around Hagan's shoulders, his head down, he saw the hard, ugly barrel of the gun inches from his chest. He heard the muffled explosion and felt terrible pain, his chest crushing in, every nerve flaring and fading.

Numbness. He could not feel the floor under him. There was blackness overhead, even though he could tell that his eyes were open. He tried to scream. The nerve pulses cycled to a stop deep in his brain. *You bast.* . .

Vandiver stared at the ceiling. A couple of the loose boards above the rafters had been knocked apart, revealing a crawlspace large enough for a man to climb—or drop—through. The boards had not been like that before. What did it mean?

In an instant, Vandiver understood. At some point the risens had left their cabin and hidden above the loose boards in the ceiling so they could keep watch on him. They must have jumped down from there to try and protect him from Hagan.

But they'd been too late.

Hagan had shot him in the heart.

That was illogical. He should check for confirmation.

Vandiver groped his shirtfront. His arm felt numb, but it seemed to respond to commands. In that case, Hagan could not have. . .

He found the wet hole. It went through his shirt and into his body, just under the sternum. His finger met a smooth, slick surface. His heart. It wasn't beating. His lungs weren't moving either. He wasn't breathing.

He thought: I am dead. This time it's all the way. Peter can't pull me back.

Time to go.

He became aware of a buzzing inside his head. It swelled, spreading through his whole body, probing, rippling against the inside of his skin. There was no way out. But he *must* leave. Vandiver tried again. He felt his arms jerking, pounding the floor, his head flopping from side to side. His legs scissor-kicked the wooden boards as he surged up and down inside the body, trying to pull free.

"Stop," said a voice in a low monotone. "You can't get out."

Vandiver struggled to a sitting position and saw Warlow, looking down at him without expression. The other two risens stood together at the fireplace, as if wanting to give him privacy. Hagan was on the floor at their feet, sprawled on his back, one arm folded behind him. His neck was at a sharp angle. His eyes were half closed. Blood had clotted beneath his nose, turning the lower half of his face into a red mask.

Vandiver stared at Hagan. I hated him, he thought. I wanted him dead. I remember that clearly, but it's just words. Now I feel nothing. I'm dead. I'm inside a corpse and I can't leave. I should be afraid.

He closed his eyes and felt a faint tingling at two points in the small of his back. He knew what it was: nerve impulses firing into the ectodermal medullae of the adrenal glands. If he were alive, adrenaline would be pouring into him and he would be terrified. But the adrenals were shut down. The hormonal fluids had stopped, still as sludge at the gates of the capillaries.

He would not feel fear or anything else again.

It had been good to feel—even fear and pain. Now that feeling was gone, he could see it had been *everything* to feel.

It could be simply enough solved. He must get out of this corpse. So he need simply find a way to destroy his body.

Abruptly, Vandiver's vision jittered as a powerful sensation flared up from the rear of his skull. He thought: That was pain. Or it would have been, before. But now I can't react to it. It doesn't . . . *hurt*.

What did it mean?

He knew at once: I can't destroy myself, he thought. I must not harm the body. *It must survive.*

Vandiver saw Warlow looking down at him. Was Warlow a threat? No, not anymore. Then what did he want? Vandiver corrected himself: Warlow wanted nothing. None of us want anything, he thought. But we must survive.

And that will not be easy. When I was alive, Warlow made my skin crawl. I would have destroyed him if I could. Anyone alive who sees us will be desperate to destroy us.

Vandiver understood why Warlow and the others were here. Yes, he thought. It will take all of us working together. All of our brains to survive. I'm the best, the smartest. I'm used to command. They're waiting for me to take over and give them orders.

He thought a moment longer and knew what they had to do. He formed the question; his throat muscles tensed, but nothing came out.

"You've got to force air through," Warlow said. "Try. It will come back to you."

Vandiver drew a shuddering breath. It swelled like an icy balloon inside him. When he let it go, it blew out in a shriek. He pumped his lungs, trying to get control. "Th-h-sht shut. Ha-ahgan . . . hear?" He realized it was not good enough. He concentrated and tried again. "Th-h shot. Did ahnywhun . . . anywun hear it?"

"Very good," Warlow said. "You're getting it back faster than we did." He motioned to the other risens and they joined him, reaching hands down. Vandiver let them pull him up, walk him around the cabin. His legs were clumsy at first, dragging and lurching under him like stumps of deadwood. Then control seeped back and he was able to walk on his own. He stopped and faced Warlow.

He made a jerky motion at Hagan's body. "Did anyone h-hear the shot?" he repeated.

"No. The noise from the generator covered it."

"All right." Vandiver looked at Gilliam and Hufnagel. "You and you, put Hah-gan's—*Hagan's* body in the crawl-space and straighten the boards back out. Make sure no blood drips down."

"Where are you going?" Warlow asked.

"There's a man in the psych ward on base. He knows about you. If he's allowed to talk, we could be stopped before the people can be innoculated with L-6. Four walking dead men can be destroyed. But with a hundred million people innoculated, we will be safe. We will survive."

Warlow showed no surprise. Vandiver wondered if he had guessed the reason for the project, and then he reminded himself that Warlow would not show surprise whether he understood or not. There was no reason to show what you could not feel.

At least not in this room, with just the four of them.

"I have to go to the hospital now and kill Peter," Vandiver said.

"I'm coming with you," Warlow said.

Vandiver looked at him, considering. "You've never seen a risen as a living man. I have. We stand out. We don't move enough. Our expressions are wrong. It has a bad effect on a living person. We have to breathe, walk, and move like living people."

Warlow looked blankly at him, and then he smiled. "Is this all right?"

Vandiver studied the curving lips, the crinkles around Warlow's eyes. They aroused no reaction in him—*of course they didn't.* "I don't know," Vandiver said. "All right, you'd better come along. I might need you." He looked down at the bullet hole in his chest. The bottom of his shirt was caked with dry, rust-colored blood. Watching his chest, he practiced breathing, light, slow breaths that barely swelled the fabric.

Air used to have a taste, he thought. It tasted good. Now it's just gas.

"I'll change my shirt," he said.

Chapter 31

1200 hours:

Janet kept watch from her bedroom window. There—the perimeter guard, walking past again!

She checked her watch and wrote the interval on her pad: seventeen minutes. She counted the previous notations—eleven of them. This was the twelfth time the guard had passed since it had gotten light enough for her to see.

With dismay she realized what she was doing: she was stalling. Dear God, she was petrified. She had to get to Peter, but she'd let four hours go by just watching the dumb guard. By now she should have his pattern memorized. The only problem was, there was no pattern. She gnawed the eraser of her pencil and studied the pad. No two intervals were the same. The shortest between passes was five minutes, and the longest, half an hour.

Janet, Janet, she thought. If you can't tell when the guard is coming, how are you ever going to slip under the fence? And even if the coast is clear, how can you be sure that damned generator won't start up when you're halfway under?

You can't.

So first you leave the cabin.

She concentrated, gritting her teeth. *All right, go!*

And then she *was* moving, running through the bedroom, raising the window, slipping through. As she moved, her head cleared. Excitement gripped her. She was *doing* it!

She ran between the pines, making no effort to be quiet. When she got to the fence, she hurried along beside it until she found the place where they'd packed dirt into Kellogg's crawl hole. They'd bent the underside of the fence back into its proper shape. Still, this should be the easiest spot. The dirt would be loosest here, and the fence the most flexible.

She kicked off her shoes. What else? The flaps of her pockets—didn't want them catching on the fence going under. She smoothed her hands over her hips.

"Lose something, ma'am?"

She jerked around. The guard—back again already! Her heart hammered. She tried to think what to say. "You scared me!"

The guard looked concerned. "You're white as a sheet. Best let me take you back to your cabin." He came closer, his rifle still slung over his shoulder.

She calmed a little. He can't read my mind, she thought. He doesn't have a clue what I'm up to.

She looked at him more closely. He was young, no more than twenty, thick through the chest and shoulders. Bushy black eyebrows showed under the rim of his helmet, and one of his eyes didn't seem to track just right. There was a holstered handgun at his side.

She realized that he was looking at her hips with a quirky smile. That's right—she'd been trying to smooth her pockets down for the fence just as he saw her. She flushed. What did he think she was, some Fourteenth Street prostitute, preening for him?

Wait! Maybe she could make that work for her. What other choice did she have now that he'd caught her? She considered it as he gazed appreciatively at her. Oh hell, she thought.

She toyed with the top button of her blouse. "I was going to come out for a little sun," she said. "I didn't realize anyone might see me." She undid the button, watching his eyes. They were aimed with awakening concentration at her hand.

"Oh, yes ma'am. General's got us really watching this baby, especially when the power's down. You shouldn't get so close. Ever' time that generator goes on, it gets juice. Like to fry you if you even brushed it."

"It wasn't the fence that killed that poor kid yesterday."

The guard looked down, subdued. "I wasn't in on that."

Wrong turn, wrong turn. Keep it light, for God's sake. She glanced around pointedly, as if checking to see if they were alone. "Well, I wonder if anyone would mind," she said. That got him looking at her again. She undid another button.

"I sure wouldn't," he said with a nervous smile.

"I bet you wouldn't. Neither would I." She stepped closer to him, looking demurely down at the ground. There, that rock. It was about the right size. She looked up coquettishly, letting a veil of hair fall forward across her eyes. God, how stupid and obvious. But it was working. He moved a step toward her. "I don't know what General Vandiver's said about me . . ." She let the sentence hang.

"Nothing," the guard said. "Generals don't have to explain." He smiled meaningfully.

"So you've had working girls in camp before?"

The soldier's smile faded, replaced by calculation. He unslung his rifle and leaned it against a tree behind him. "Working girls? No. You're the only, uh, girl he's had here. We thought you were his . . . girl friend."

Janet laughed and undid another button. She felt the breeze fan bare skin below her bra. She shivered. She was running out of buttons—she was almost to her waist. She saw the guard glance over his shoulder in the direction of Alan's cabin.

The generator started up again.

It filled her with desperation. For this to work, the fence had to be off. Otherwise, she was in deep, deep trouble. But there was nothing to do now except go ahead and hope they hadn't got it fixed this time. She finished unbuttoning her blouse, down to her belt. The soldier's attention was on her totally now. His eyes were pinched, as though he was afraid to have her see him looking at her. *No, don't go shy on me now.* She said, "You've been here quite a while, with no women."

The guard swallowed. "I don't know. General Van—"

"Why should he have all the fun?"

"He's paying all the bills."

Janet hooked her thumbs into the belt of her jeans, tipping the fabric an inch from her waist. She felt her face flushing a bright red. Her stomach rolled sickly inside her. "I think the general's had all he can handle," she said. "But I'm still a little . . . you know, horny." *God, God, God.*

The man licked his lips. "How much do you want?"

Oh no. What should she say? What did prostitutes make for a trick? If she was too low, he'd get suspicious. "Let's do it," she said desperately, "and then you pay me what you think it's worth."

"You're pretty confident, aren't you?"

Oh, yes. Confident. That's me. "I know I can please you," she said. She got down on her back on the carpet of pine needles, drawing her knees up slowly. She let her hand stray out until her knuckles brushed the rock.

He looked both ways again. "I don't think we can do much with you dressed like that," he said hoarsely.

"Why don't you do something about it?" *Oh, God, Peter. You owe me for this.*

The guard looked at the sky and groaned as if in appeal. He hurried to her, dropping down between her knees. Her breath caught in revulsion as his fingers grappled with her belt buckle. One hand snaked inside her blouse, pinching her breast. The fingers were callused. She gripped his wrist, and he glanced up at her with surprise and quick resentment.

"Your helmet. I'd like to see you." Her voice came out breathy with fear.

"S'pposed to keep it on."

"Come on. Let me look at you. You're so handsome—better looking than the general." Outrageous flattery. Surely now he'd know she was maneuvering him. But no, he smiled smugly and reached up, removing his helmet. His hair stuck up in a crow's tail like a little boy's. She felt a second's pity for him. He got her buckle open and zipped her jeans down, and her pity vanished.

Where was the rock? Grabbing his wrist she'd lost contact with it, and now she couldn't find it again. She groped for it, trying not to be too obvious, as he jerked her jeans down. *Oh, Lord, he was going to do it, right here, too fast! Where was the damned rock?*

She tried to make it more difficult for him by bending her knees, but he tugged the pants over them easily.

Panic welled up in her. Forget caution. She raised her head, searching frantically for the rock. There it was! She grabbed it and looked up. His head was down, his eyes on his next goal, her panties. She swung the rock up against his head. He said, "Oh," and flopped down on her. His forehead banged hers hard, striking sparks of pain that boomed into sunspots before her eyes.

She gritted her teeth and clung to awareness. The spots broke apart slowly and she could see again. God, he'd split her skull with his thick head. He was crushing her. She tried to push him off, but her arms felt as heavy and slack as sandbags. She grunted and pushed, and groaned with each stabbing pain in her head.

The generator stopped. This was her chance! She kicked and pushed in a frenzy until he rolled off her.

She got to her hands and knees, then stood and pulled her jeans back up. She staggered drunkenly to the fence, leaned against it. I'm knocked silly, she thought. What else is there? *The gun!*

She hurried back to the fallen man and pulled his .45 loose from its holster. She realized that her blouse was still unbuttoned. It was too loose. It would surely catch on the fence. *Hurry, before they turn the generator back on.* She fumbled with the buttons, her fingers thick and uncoordinated. Finally the blouse was snugly fastened again.

She sat down in front of the fence, and froze. What if they turned it on again just as she. . .

No, do it!

She pushed her feet against the bottom. It bent outward. She slid the automatic under, then got her legs farther under by pushing off with her arms behind her. When she was through to the top of her thighs, she lay back and squirmed wildly from side to side. The dirt they'd shoveled into Kellogg's crawlspace gave beneath her, compressing enough to provide the clearance she needed. She was moving so slowly, only inches forward for every twist of her body. *They're getting ready to start it up again,* she thought. It gave her a powerful surge of fear. She grabbed the fence, yanking it back toward her face and sliding under to her throat. She flipped over and pulled her head through. The fence flopped back into place.

The generator started up.

She heard a faint buzzing in her ears. A scream pushed up in her throat. She clapped a hand over her mouth and stared at the fence. Another second and it would have killed her. It didn't look any different. She had an almost overpowering urge to touch it and see.

Run!

She scooped up the automatic and ran across the space they'd cleared outside the fence. When she reached the cover of the woods, she dropped down to her knees and laughed. "I made it! I made it, oh, dear Jesus, thank you."

She began to tremble in reaction. She grabbed the branch of a pine tree, trying to stabilize herself. The sharp needles felt feathery in her hand. Nothing could hurt her!

"Hey," she said. "Hey!" She felt wonderful—more alive than she ever had been.

What was that? Dogs, barking in the distance!

Her euphoria vanished. The guard dogs! They knew she was here! She heard them barking to her right, perhaps a half-mile away, a faint sound, but drawing closer. She wasn't safe yet, not by a long shot. That bump on her head must have scrambled her brains.

She sprang up and ran, away from the sound of the dogs. She fingered the knot on her head. It had swollen to the size of a grape. She grimaced. The guard wanted to bang you, she thought, and he did.

She stumbled and almost fell before she got her footing

again. The woods, so kind a minute ago, had turned treacherous to her running feet—uneven, and covered with roots.

The dogs were louder, homing in on her. She thought of Monk. No, not dogs, not dogs, *please!*

She had to run faster. Careful—don't fall. Where was she? Which way was out? She corrected her path, heading away from the camp and toward the main base. It brought her to right angles with the approaching dogs. Spurts of fear drove her legs. This was her only hope, to make a beeline for the base and pray the dogs wouldn't get to her first.

If they did, she'd have to shoot them. She couldn't go up against a dog again, never again—even a normal one.

She looked frantically ahead. There was a road along here somewhere—that jeep path the soldier had used taking her and Alan back and forth to see Peter. Where was it?

The dogs, closing in, only a hundred yards back by the sound of their barking.

The woods opened up and she stumbled through onto the jeep path. Good, now she could run faster.

And so could the dogs.

She pushed herself, all out. Her hips felt like spears jabbing up through her lungs, all the way to her shoulders. The dogs were close. She could hear them crashing through the brush now.

She wasn't going to make it. No chance.

She heard the drone of a jeep, muffled by the trees that filled in the curvature of the road. It was headed toward her. Oh no—men from the base. They must have discovered the man she'd knocked out. Now they were after her too. In a second they'd come around the curve and spot her.

She had to get out of sight.

She staggered off the road into the woods and dropped behind some bushes. She had to hold still, be quiet, but she couldn't, she was gasping too hard. Oh God, here came the dogs, clearing the woods on the other side of the road. She was almost paralyzed with panic. She watched them come, low, legs churning, sunlight on buff chests. German shepherds. Two of them.

The pistol, quick! Shoot them!

She aimed the pistol. Sweat poured into her eyes. The dogs arrowed for her, impossible jerking targets. She squeezed the trigger. Nothing happened. Jammed—the gun was jammed. She sobbed in fright, jerking at the trigger. The lead dog brushed her.

It wheeled and charged back to the road, baying. She stared after it, numb with confusion. The other dog had already turned. She saw the jeep and huddled down behind the bush. Brakes squealed, and the baying and yapping became frenzied. There was fear in the dogs' sounds, harsh and unmistakable.

Janet edged around until she found a small gap in the brush. She looked out. The jeep was directly across from her, stopped on the road. Alan and another man were standing up in the front seat close together as the dogs leapt up against the low doors on either side, trying to get at them. They seemed almost frozen, both of them. They stared down at the dogs with expressionless faces. The dogs were making a sound she had never heard before, a high whining snarl.

Alan and the other man weren't behaving normally either. Normal men would be swearing, flinching away.

Get down, she thought. You mustn't let them see you. She stayed on hands and knees, unable to take her eyes off Alan.

He looked at his driver, then drew his automatic. The soldier pulled his out, too, and they did something to the guns with their free hands, almost in unison. Safety catch, she thought numbly. That's why mine wouldn't fire.

The guns exploded in a volley of shots. The dogs leapt away from the jeep, thrashed briefly, and were still. She closed her eyes, appalled. When she opened them again she saw two more men running from the woods beyond the jeep. They must be the trainers. They stopped and stared down at the dead animals. Alan slipped his gun back into its holster and nudged his driver. The man copied him. They sat at the same time.

Janet stared at them. Goosebumps prickled the length of her spine. One of the guards knelt between the dogs. The other glared at Alan. His face was flushed and his eyes were red. "What did you do that for?"

"Watch your tone, Corporal." Vandiver sounded very calm.

"You shot my dogs. You killed them."

"They are not your dogs. They are U.S. army dogs, and they were attacking us."

The guard took a threatening step toward the jeep. "You son of a—"

Vandiver stood and pointed a finger at the guard. Janet cringed down in the bushes. A simple gesture, but there was something terrible about it. She saw the man stop and falter a step back.

Vandiver let his hand drop. "Get these dogs out of here and bring some more in," he said.

"Yes sir." The man seemed cowed now, unable even to meet Alan's eyes.

Alan looked on while the guards dragged the dogs out of the jeep's path. When they had finished, the men scurried back into the woods, almost running from Alan.

Janet held her breath. Don't move, she thought. Don't even blink. She could not stop trembling.

Vandiver said, "Drive."

"Wait," said the other man. He stood. Oh God, he was looking over toward her. *Duck!* she thought. *No don't.* She held herself still as the man's eyes quartered every inch of the bush, never blinking. They centered on her, and she was filled with horror. It was not a man. It was something . . . sickening—dreadful. *Like the Doberman.* She held her eyes wide. They were drying out. She had to blink, to look away, but she mustn't. *Please, God. . .*

The man's eyes moved on past her.

She held herself stiff, fighting the limpness of relief. He never saw me, she thought. Those eyes. So fixed. Maybe he'd needed her to move before he could pick her out—the way a hunting cat saw.

She heard the jeep idle up and pull away.

She sagged down onto her hands and knees. She was dizzy. Her heart pounded furiously. If she could just sit here a minute. No, she mustn't stop now. The dogs were dead. She had to get moving, before others were brought in.

She walked down the road in the direction the jeep had gone. She avoided the bloody corpses of the dogs, keeping to the side of the road until she was well past. Pitiful. At least, with them dead, she could walk, conserve her strength. That way there'd be no danger she'd catch up with Alan. He must be well down the road by now, anyway. He'd been in a great hurry.

She frowned. Why? Where was he going? In the past week, the only reason he'd left camp was to—

Janet stopped still on the path. *To see Peter.*

She pulled the .45 from her jeans, found the safety catch and flicked it off. Then she began to run.

Chapter 32

1315 hours:

No more medicine, Morrissey thought with glee. That's the command that old colonel had given Alan out in the hall.

Morrissey raised a hand and watched his fingers tremble. Still pretty shaky. He shrugged. He couldn't expect full recovery so quickly. Fortunately, the colonel and Alan had come before he'd got today's pill. And last night, he'd conned the staff again, acting dull and meek, swallowing the pill without protest. They'd checked his mouth thoroughly. The second they were gone, he'd stuck his finger down his throat.

That meant he hadn't had a dose in well over twenty-four hours.

Handy, having a toilet right in your room.

He smiled. He was going to be free—able to walk beyond ten feet in a straight line, able to see trees, feel solid ground under his feet. Able to go to his workshop and finish the birdhouse for Mrs. Steiner. He grinned in delight and threw his arms into the air.

Watch it! he thought. The damned drug. Still enough left to stir his moods like a swizzle stick. If he let his feelings swing too high, he might lose his grip on reality. He must be sane and solemn when that colonel came back.

Sane and solemn, sane and solemn, sane asylum.

Stop it!

Maybe he should practice his talking again. "My name is Peter Morrissey." Good. "I made L-6." Good, good. "It's very . . . very . . . *dangerous.*"

His pleasure evaporated. Yes, dangerous. There would be nothing to grin about when he got out. A consciousness operating a dead body, a consciousness stripped of human emotion. A hundred million of them.

And that was not the worst of it.

Thinking about it made him nauseous. He rocked forward on his knees, head down, arms crossed tightly on his chest, waiting for it to pass. Not the worst, oh no. Because a consciousness that could not feel should want nothing, fear nothing, need nothing. It should lie forever in repose, threatening no one. But the three risen test subjects had threatened Alan, tried to control him. And there could be only one reason: instinct. The biological part of them was stopped, the biochemical faucets of emotion turned off forever. But their preserved brains were still "wired" as in life—the same neural pathways of perception, thought, memory; *instinct.*

And the most powerful instinct of all was survival.

Survival was neuroelectric, not chemical. It was "hardwired" into the brain from before birth. The internal command to survive dominated all others. It could drive men to steal, kill, even to eat each other. It could make a man hold his breath in the gas chamber. It could force the body to fight on after the rest of the brain was in coma.

In all human history, only one thing had proved stronger than the survival instinct.

Emotion.

Out of love for her child, a mother might brave a burning building. To save his buddies, a soldier might throw himself on a grenade. In the grip of deep depression, a man might put a gun to his head and blow out his brains.

A risen would not do any of those things.

A risen would do anything in its power to survive.

Morrissey groaned. If he could just have found the right key in time, gotten out that door before the orderlies caught him. Now he'd lost more time—to drugged blackness, to drooling stupors and nightmares, phased to the slow pulse of that light above his head. How much further had the project gone?

He got up and walked around the cell. His joints pained him. His body seemed pulled out thin, his head drifting too high above his feet. Unreal. All of this. Nothing would be real again until he was out of here.

Sweat began to pour down Morrissey's face. He skimmed it away with his hands. He put his back to the padding and slid down to his rump. His legs poked out like scarecrow limbs lost in the baggy folds of the pajamas. He looked at his hands again. The shaking had spread to his forearms.

All right, just pull yourself together.

He heard the key turning in the door. At last! He felt a sudden sharp embarrassment. Sitting there in a heap on his ass! He must get up, meet his deliverer standing. He pulled himself back up the wall.

Alan came in first. Morrissey looked impatiently past him to the second man. Dismay filled him. It was not the colonel! This man was much younger. The colonel had had a hard look. This man had no look at all. His face was vacant as a mask on a wall.

The skin on Morrissey's neck crawled. A risen, he thought. One of Alan's dead L-6 subjects.

"Hello, Peter," Alan said.

Morrissey focused on Vandiver's face. Alan was smiling. There was nothing in his eyes. His lips pulled back evenly like a man about to pick his teeth. *Alan too—a risen!*

Dimly, Morrissey felt his fingers pulling and twisting behind him at the buttons of the matting. He thought: *Not Alan. Alan can't be dead.* He stared at the corpse, horrified. Dear God in heaven, why? It isn't fair. Alan didn't know what it was about.

I killed him.

"It should have been me," he said.

"I'm afraid it *is* your turn now," the Vandiver-risen said evenly.

Morrissey stared at him, stunned and breathless, as though he'd been punched in the stomach.

Alan's face drew suddenly into a mask of pain. "No. We've been friends for so long. I can't do it."

Morrissey felt hope. "Alan?"

Vandiver's face relaxed at once. "Did I fool you, Peter? Please tell me. It's important."

Morrissey shook his head, trying to throw off the powerful illusion of a living man. Somehow he had to deal with this thing standing in front of him. And it wasn't Alan, *not Alan.* "I know what's happened to you," he said. "I'm not going to hurt you. I'll see that you survive, no matter what."

"That's not logical, Peter." After Alan said it, his face took on a sorrowful look. The timing was wrong, but he was doing better. It looked almost convincing.

"You have to destroy us if you can," the Vandiver thing went on. "I know that."

Morrissey reached a hand out. *Grab him*, he thought. *Push him aside, run out!* But he couldn't move. He felt pain in his lip. He realized he was biting it, drawing blood. He was filled with a galling bitterness. This was his fault. He had fought death for twelve years like it was his own personal enemy. It didn't even know he existed, but he had fought it with everything he had, and it had beaten him. No, it had used him and *then* beaten him. Death had been nothing, a mere condition. The running down and stopping of ruined cells. But he had made it more. He had freed it from the grave. It walked the earth because of him.

And it had barely started.

The Alan-risen had come here to kill him. He was the only man alive who knew about L-6. He would die, and the project would go on. The Alan thing would have a hundred million allies instead of just three.

Then no one would ever destroy them.

Morrissey held himself rigid, clutching the mat. I've got to stop it, he thought.

Alan's body set his briefcase on the floor. The case made

a clanking sound. The Alan-risen drew a soft-drink bottle from the case. It looked at the bottle, then slid it back inside, withdrawing a small vial instead. It drew a syringe from the case and fit a needle to it.

"Don't do it," Morrissey said. "I never lied to you in all our life together. I tell you, I'll see that you survive."

"You're lying now, Peter. The first time."

Morrissey knew that the thing was right.

The Alan-risen pulled clear fluid from the vial into the syringe. "We're going to have a plague," it said in the maddening, matter-of-fact voice. "You'll be first."

Morrissey lunged at Vandiver's body. The other risen blurred into motion, grabbing him. Morrissey punched the thing's throat and felt cartilage give. The risen absorbed the blow without making a sound and pinned his arms. He went on struggling, jerking. It was no use. The hospital, the drug, had weakened him. And the brain of a risen could use its preserved muscles without mercy, feeling no pain, holding nothing back. The risen's fingers tightened like cold vises around his arms, cutting off the circulation. His hands began to go numb. He sagged, exhausted.

Alan's body jerked toward him, suddenly stiff and uncoordinated.

Morrissey watched in dread fascination. It was almost as though an internal struggle was going on. Was there something left of Alan's feelings? No, there couldn't be. Then what?

The thing pressed the needle against his shoulder.

"Alan," Morrissey whispered.

The Vandiver risen moaned. It stared at the syringe as if seeing it for the first time. "No! I will not!"

Hope surged in Morrissey. "Throw it away, Alan!"

Vandiver raised his arm as though to hurl the syringe away. His hand stayed frozen in place, trembling.

"Throw it!" Morrissey shouted.

Vandiver brought the syringe down slowly. His dead face turned smooth and empty. "I *did* fool you, Peter."

The Vandiver-risen plunged the needle into Morrissey's shoulder.

Chapter 33

1500 hours:

At the top of the fence, Janet stalled.

Go, she thought. Just keep going. She looked at the barbs on the three top wires. They floated along the strands, sharp and wicked. Beyond them was a blurred mass of buildings and walks. She felt horribly exposed. Those smudges—people moving along the walks. Where had they all come from so suddenly? When she'd started up the fence, the walks had looked empty. She was afraid to focus on them, for fear it would somehow make them see her too.

If just one person saw her, it was all over.

Using the hard bulge of the gun in her waistband as a shield, she shifted her stomach onto the wire. She eased her legs up along the strands. Thank goodness the barbed wire slanted away from her or she'd never get over.

The gun gouged into the skin of her stomach. Had she put the safety catch back on? She couldn't remember. If her squirming around made the gun fire, it would blow her leg away. They would find her dangling up here, bleeding to death.

No, she mustn't think of that. There really was nothing to this. Just like a Richard Simmons morning exercise. She shifted her hips up very gingerly, and reversed her grip. She tried to imagine Simmons's perky baby-talk as she hung over the wire, feeling the pressure of the barbs against the crotch of her jeans.

Drop the legs, swing the toes into the fence, change grip from the top wire to the mesh, and then climb down.

Nothing to it.

Here we go, one-two-three, sang Simmons's voice in her mind. She scrambled to the bottom of the fence and walked away. Her heart beat fast and high in her chest like a bird's. I did it, she thought exultantly. That was it. Now I can get Peter.

She made sure the gun was hidden by her blouse and started for the hospital. Her sense of triumph faded. It was going to work now, yes. That fence had been the last hurdle. She could go right up to the psych-ward door and force her way in. But suddenly this seemed so impulsive. She'd gone off half-cocked, spurred by all the suspicions Kellogg had planted and then the terrible shock of the poor boy being shot. What would she do if Kellogg had been wrong, and there was an explanation for everything, and Peter *was* sick? What if she forced her way in with the gun and then Peter raged and foamed at her the way he had before? How could she hope to get him out in that condition?

Depression settled over her. She couldn't stand it if she did all this for Peter and he still seemed to . . . to *hate* her.

Never mind. She could not stop now. She would just have to carry this out to its end, and then she would see.

She took the stairs to the fourth floor, keeping her head down as she passed an orderly in white, and someone from the kitchen carrying a tray. She went down the short hall to the door and pushed the button, her mouth dry. The sound of the buzzer filtered faintly back to her through the steel door. She touched the butt of the .45 under her blouse. The fence *wasn't* the last hurdle. In seconds she'd have to take this ugly gun out and point it at someone. She might have to shoot it. Could she really do that? The very thought made her sick. She *hated* guns.

No, think of Peter—Peter in his right mind, being drugged

into craziness, waiting, hoping you'll come to help him. Think of that horrible man Alan had with him in the jeep—the man who seemed like a hunting cat. Think of the dead Doberman.

The window plate in the door slid back, and the eyes of the black orderly gazed through at her. Good. It wasn't that mean-looking one with the bad skin.

"Yes?"

"I've come to see my husband."

"Oh—Mrs. Morrissey." His eyes disappeared from the window. With surprise Janet heard his key turn in the lock. Was he going to just let her in? The door opened all the way and the orderly stood back, admitting her.

Alan had said hospital rules required her to be escorted by an authorized officer—him. She'd been such a wimp, such a fool. Alan had lied, and she'd never dreamed of challenging him.

She had another thought and felt better: If Alan had lied about that, it probably meant he'd lied about Peter being crazy too.

She hurried after the orderly down the familiar peach-colored hall. "I was surprised you didn't come in with General Vandiver today," he said.

She tensed. "You mean he's here?"

"Just left. You couldn't have missed him by more than a minute."

She blew out a pent-up breath. What if she'd run smack into Alan? What could she have done? In the strain of getting over the fence, she'd all but forgotten about him. But she'd been afraid he might be headed here, and he had.

What had he wanted with Peter?

She followed the orderly around the hall corner and past the commons area. A few patients far up in the commons looked incuriously at her, lost in their Thorazine fog. Where was the nurse? The station looked deserted. And the other orderly was nowhere in sight either. She put her hand anxiously on the gun butt.

The orderly unlocked Peter's door and turned. "Since the general's not with you, I'd better stick around, ma'am, just in—" He saw the gun in her hand and blinked. "Aw, now. . ."

"You first," she said. Her throat was so dry that it came out in a loud whisper. Come on, she thought. You've got the gun. You have to *scare* these people. The orderly didn't look scared. But he nodded and walked through in front of her. She pushed through eagerly behind him. There was Peter, but the nurse and the other orderly were with him. What were they doing? The nurse was holding something out toward Peter's face—a capsule. In her other hand was a paper cup of water. The white orderly was holding Peter's arms behind him. Peter was bent forward and his face was screwed up in pain. That bastard was hurting him with an armlock.

"Let him go!" She felt the anger swelling up inside her, bracing her.

Peter looked up and his eyes widened in surprise. "Look out!" he said.

She saw the black orderly start to move. She jerked the gun toward him and he stepped back and raised his hands. She felt sweat pouring out on her palm and fingers, making the gun slippery. God, if she wasn't careful, she'd drop it. . .

Peter could talk! Peter wasn't crazy!

She was filled with elation. No, she mustn't let her guard down for a second. She could look at Peter, talk to Peter later.

"Get over there," she said.

The black orderly joined the other two.

She gestured at the white orderly. "I said let him go."

The orderly jacked Peter's arm higher. "Drop the gun," he said, "or I'll bust his arm."

Janet extended the .45 until it rested against the nurse's forehead. The woman's fingers opened and the capsule and water fell to the matting. "Let him go, or nursie here will make modern art all over the walls." *Jesus, was that her talking?*

"Do what she says, you honkie moron," snapped the black orderly. The man released Peter and stepped back sullenly. Peter stumbled to Janet, rubbing his shoulder. She motioned with the gun, herding the nurse and two orderlies together. She jabbed the gun toward the white orderly's face and he flinched back. "Pick up that capsule."

"Janet, let's go," Peter said.

"In a minute. Pick it up. Now."

The man bent over and retrieved the capsule.

"Eat it."

He hesitated, then slipped it into his mouth, making a whining noise.

"Swallow. Swallow it, God damn you." Janet watched until his Adam's apple convulsed. It gave her a savage satisfaction. She wanted to start shooting—just shoot these people's faces in for what they'd done to Peter. *Yes, and she could save one shell for herself, because she'd let it happen.*

"Too bad there's none for the rest of you," she said. "All right. Throw your keys on the floor. All of you." They worked silently at their belts, pulling the key chains free and dropping them. The orderly's face slowly blanched to a mottled whiteness, like cottage cheese. She bent, keeping her eyes raised, and picked up the keys. "Where are my husband's clothes?"

"They're in one of those lockers at the end of this hall," the black orderly said. "Same number as the room. That little key there is a master for all the lockers."

"All right. I'm going to lock you in. It'll take Peter a few minutes to dress, and we'll be right down the hall for that time. If I hear a peep from here before I leave, there will be some shooting, and I don't mean with needles, either." By God, she was almost beginning to enjoy this!

She locked the three of them up in Peter's cell. Outside he said, "Boy, am I glad to see you."

"I'm a girl. You haven't forgotten, have you?"

He gave her a pained smile.

"I'll help you dress," she said. "We'll talk later."

Just looking at him made her feel fantastic and wretched all at once. There was a feverish flush, high on his cheeks. He had trouble standing on one leg to pull his pants on. She steadied him gently. He seemed so fragile. She wanted to ask him how he felt, smother him with kisses, touch him all over. But there would be time for that in a few minutes. First, they had to get out of here.

Every movement he made seemed to require concentration. Hurry, she thought, *hurry*, but she couldn't bear to say it. He looked as if the slightest pressure might topple him. She put an arm around his waist as they left the hospital. So skinny! She could feel his ribs. Tears began to come, and she choked them back. They weren't out of here yet. When they were, then she could cry.

She walked slowly with him leaning on her, down the main walkway of the base to the parking lot. She searched anxiously through the rows of cars. It had been over a week since she'd driven here. What if they'd moved her car, impounded it, maybe?

No, there it was.

A soldier, coming straight at them! She tensed, ready to reach for the gun. He nodded at her indifferently as he passed. She clamped her teeth to keep from heaving an incriminating sigh of relief.

She thought of another worry. That guard back at the camp. How long had it been since she'd knocked him out? Forty-five minutes, maybe more. They must know she was missing by now. Would they radio orders to stop her if she tried to leave by the main gate? Probably.

She touched Peter's arm as they reached the car. "Do you think you can drive a short ways?"

"Yup." His voice was hoarse.

"Okay." she said. "I'm going to lie in the trunk until you get us past the gate. No one knows you've escaped yet. But they'll be looking for me by now."

"I don't know if you can squeeze those into an M.G. trunk."

She saw he was looking at her hips. There was a twinkle in his eye. She felt like crying again. After all he'd been through, he could joke. "Just drive, buster."

The trunk *was* a tight fit. She had to draw her knees up tightly and cramp her head over. When at last she felt the car bump over gravel and stop, she was soaked with sweat and her neck felt as if it would break. He let her out. She faced him on the shoulder of the road and took his hands. He pulled her to him and hugged her, his arms tightening with surprising strength. She felt his ear pressing against hers. It gave her a strange, powerful feeling of intimacy.

All right, she thought. *Now.*

She started to cry. She didn't sob, but let the tears run safely down her cheeks where he couldn't see them.

"You are really something," he said in his hoarse voice. "You are really something." He hugged her and patted her back with both hands and leaned on her.

She helped him to the passenger side of the car.

She got in, feeling as if a weight had been rolled off her. She had done well. She had saved them both. It would be all right now. They could go away somewhere safe and work on healing him and healing themselves.

She glanced across at Peter and caught him giving her a stark, measuring look. *What is it?* she thought with alarm. *Oh God, we're not out of it yet. There's something else.* "Tell me," she said.

"I wish I didn't have to."

"Don't say that. Don't say it ever again."

He sat in silence a minute, then said, "Did Alan tell you about the . . . the reanimation effect of L-6?"

"I found the dog, Peter."

He groaned.

"It's all right."

He looked at her again, with respect. "We're going to have to do one last thing," he said. "I can't do it alone. I need your help."

She straightened and gripped the wheel, feeling warm with pleasure. "You've got it."

"I can only wait five minutes, lady," the cab driver said.

"That should be enough."

Janet got out of the cab and hurried up the front steps of the brownstone. She fumbled the key into the lock, pushed the door open, barely aware of what she was doing. If she could just be sure Peter was all right. He'd sworn over and over that he was, but he looked so awful. She longed to get him to the hospital—a regular one with no locks.

But he was right. They must stop Alan first.

Alan, going out to start a plague. How could such an awful situation have developed?

She hurried up to Peter's bedroom closet. She realized her nerves were screaming. Her own house repelled her! It was so deathly quiet. Nothing looked the same. All these things—the pictures on the wall, the bedroom rug and curtains they'd lavished so much thought and care over—didn't seem like hers anymore. That awful thing in the basement had contaminated the place. It had seeped up like poisonous fumes while they were gone and deadened the house, room by room.

She pulled open the closet door. Dust motes floated under the closet light. There was Peter's fishing net, right where he'd said it would be, behind the extra leaf to the dining-room table. She took it and hurried to her own closet and removed the largest overnight case. She ran back downstairs, rushing headlong so that she wouldn't think of stopping.

The kitchen seemed unnaturally dark as she hurried through to the basement door. She paused and glanced out the window over the sink. The sky was full of heavy storm clouds. She heard the first big drops of rain rattling the window.

Damn, she had stopped, lost her momentum.

Downstairs, she commanded herself. Your cab is waiting. You don't want to run the meter up. She laughed shakily and hurried down into the cool dark of the basement.

As soon as she cleared the overhang, she located the dog's head. There it lay, that dark blur just outside the square of pewter light from the back door. It was exactly where she had left it. She heard a rumble of thunder. The light from the back door dimmed to the color of lead.

What if it's really dead now? she wondered. Just plain dead? No, please don't be. We need you.

She pulled the light-string, and the dark mass of the dog's head was lit in detail by the swinging bulb. The brown-black eyes centered on her and the muzzle peeled back from the teeth. She shuddered. *Still conscious.* She stood a moment, staring at it. I can't believe I came back here, she thought. Let's hear it for Wonder Woman.

A jumpy-bug leapt across in front of her. Amazing! She didn't even blink! She laughed. The dog's muzzle relaxed. It went on staring at her.

Good, she thought defiantly. Stare away. If you don't convince people about L-6, nothing will.

She took a step toward it and stopped. Oh crud, why couldn't Peter have done this part, and let her drive on ahead to the Pentagon? No, that's right—Peter was the only one with an Army Labs Pentagon pass. Besides, what did she know from generals?

She crept toward the dog head, holding out the net. The air of the basement seemed to thicken around her. She thought: That is just a *thing* over there. A weird toy. Go ahead, scoop it up, put it in the case, get going. She forced herself to take another step. The hairs bristled along her arms. She heard something behind her, a whisper of fabric.

She was not alone!

She whirled around in fright. There—someone stepping out of the shadow by the cellar door. She saw his boots, his pantlegs, and screamed as the light of the swinging bulb circled the golden helmet of his hair.

"Hello, Janet," said the Vandiver-risen.

Chapter 34

1700 hours:

I'm going to die, Morrissey thought.

But not before I stop the project.

While he waited for Major Cathcart to come back, he reviewed what he would say to General Stanhouse. The Alan-risen would start the plague in Washington, of course, because it was here now. Then it would get transportation—probably military flights—to other cities. How many cities? Enough to spread the panic across the country. Then, when everyone swarmed in to get innoculated against the plague, they would get L-6 mixed into the same injection.

Yes, that had to be the plan.

Morrissey stared at the notices tacked up on the major's walls. They began to blend into the beige plaster, and he moved his eyes, focusing with an effort on the picture the major kept on his desk: a good-looking woman with a pixie face and a sprinkling of white hairs among the curly black ones; a kid with a miniature of the major's choirboy face. Morrissey felt a painful contact with the two faces. Would they be dead by this time tomorrow? Did they live near where Alan was going to start the plague?

He thought: Hurry, Major.

The chair pressed hard against his aching bones and joints. He was burning up. Couldn't happen to a more deserving fellow, he thought, refusing to pity himself. L-6 was his. He had sworn to control it, to let it hurt no one, and he had failed.

But it wasn't over yet.

Ah! Cathcart, coming back through the door at last.

"Well? Did you talk to the Chairman?"

Cathcart sighed and sat down across the desk. "As I told you, Doctor, I have to go through chain of command. The colonel's not back yet, but he's due any time. As soon as he—"

"Colonel Hagan?"

"That's right."

Morrissey slapped the arms of the chair in frustration. "God damn it, Major, Hagan may be dead. I told you that."

"Yes sir, you did. And it's a very serious suggestion to make. Colonel Hagan, dead, killed by General Vandiver."

Morrissey saw the major's gaze flicking discreetly up and down him. I look like shit to this man, he realized. Never mind my security clearance and Labs I.D.—he probably thinks I'm not the same man on the card. My hair needs washing, or I should have at least combed it.

Morrissey brushed the greasy strands away from his forehead. "Look, Major, if you don't get me through to the Chairman, the United States Army is going to kill off tens of thousands of American citizens . . ."

Cathcart cleared his throat uncomfortably. "Yes, you said that. Tens of thousands. Dr. Morrissey, I *did* call Army Labs. The second-in-command over there says you've not reported for duty in over a week. He says you assaulted a military policeman there. As a matter of fact, he'd like us to have the police hold you for him."

Morrissey tried to stand, but his hands slipped off the arms of the chair, dumping him back in place. *Hold him? No, they mustn't. He'd die if they put him in another cell. And millions of other people would die too. Die and rise up dead.*

"What are you going to do?" he said.

"Frankly, I'm not sure what to do. This lab break-in thing isn't our problem, so I'm inclined to let you go. But you keep trying to make it our problem, so maybe I should oblige the Labs and have you held until their people get here."

Morrissey stared at the major. No subtlety, a direct warning: Go away and stop bothering me. "Look, Cathcart, I'm not leaving, and you'd better make sure I don't get arrested."

"Dr. Morrissey, I've tried to be patient with you . . ."

"You've verified I'm who I say I am," Morrissey said desperately. "I can prove everything I've told you, and there's a lot more that I can only tell General Stanhouse. My wife is on the way here with the proof. I'll be meeting her at the concourse in a few minutes." Morrissey stopped, feeling a sharp pain in his throat, followed by a pulsing soreness. The virus was getting worse—worse every minute. There was so little time. He had to get through to the Chairman of the Joint Chiefs, and he couldn't even get this earnest young major to listen to him.

"Your *wife* is coming with proof."

"That's exactly right, Major."

"Well, when she gets here, bring the proof around, and we'll take it from there. Meantime, you'll have to excuse me. I've got a lot of work. Just a word of warning: Army Labs *is* sending one of their MPs over to identify you for the police so they can run you in."

Morrissey got up and had to brace himself on the desk. Hot, so hot.

"Do you need help?" Cathcart asked. "You don't look well."

"No," Morrissey said. "No . . . no." He shook his head in confusion. The major was right. Not well, not well at all. I've got to go somewhere cool, he thought. Put my head under a fountain. Can't think like this.

He shuffled out of the aide's office into the hall. Overhead lights smeared in the tiles ahead of his feet, leading him on and on down the corridor. I need help, he thought. A hospital. No, a hospital won't have medicine for what I've got. A plague—that's what Alan had called it. They'd use something made right at Ft. Detrick before the ban on biological warfare, something Detrick already had the antidote for.

Morrissey stopped and raised his head to the lights, using the bleary glare to help goad his brain into alertness. That's right: a plague, an antidote mixed with L-6—*and innoculation centers.* For this plan to work, there must be *places* for people to get their anti-plague—and L-6—shots. Lots of places. With the election so close, they must be set up by now. Where would they be? If he could get to one. . .

He shook his head and continued down the hall. There wasn't time. The Alan-risen was out there now, perhaps spreading the plague this minute. He had to get to General Stanhouse before he did anything else.

The hall emptied Morrissey past the security checkpoint and into the concourse. He scanned the entrance to Woodward and Lothrop. He couldn't see Janet. He walked over to make sure. No, she wasn't here yet.

He leaned against the wall beside the entrance, resting his forehead against the chill surface. Something was wrong. Janet had had more than enough time. Traffic jam? No, even slow traffic would have gotten her here by now. Some problem with the dog's head? But what? She just needed to scoop it up, put it in the case, and—

Morrissey straightened from the wall, struck by a terrible thought. If he wanted the dog's head for proof, Alan might want to destroy it for the same reason.

What if Alan had gone straight from the psych ward to the brownstone? Dear Christ! He—it—would have been there when Janet arrived!

The strength of panic poured into Morrissey. Janet, with Alan's corpse. That corpse had tried to kill him. Janet's presence at the brownstone would prove that she was a threat too. What would it do to her?

Morrissey took a few hurried steps and stopped. Where the hell had he left her car? Below, outside the old tunnel cab stand.

He turned toward the nearest concourse exit and saw the

MP and the policeman striding through the crowds across from him. Corporal Carrera!

Run!

No, they would surely see him if he ran. He pushed into the department store, through the shoppers, and out the other entrance. He looked across the mall. The two men were almost out of sight up the concourse.

Watch out, Carrera was turning to look back!

Morrissey ran. He ducked through other stores. Sweat poured from his face. His knees barely held and he was getting sharp warnings from the old fracture. He had to stop. He looked over his shoulder. There was no sign of the two men. Carrera hadn't seen him.

He took the stairs down and ran out the tunnel. He'd parked the car right here at the cement security barriers that sealed off the old tunnel traffic entrance. Where was it? Gone! They'd towed it away already.

He cursed and hurried up the inclined pavement and around a massive, underflexed corner of the Pentagon. He ran to the nearest District cab, a banged-up yellow-and-black Pontiac. A tattooed arm lolled out the window. Morrissey pulled open the back door and slid in.

"Twenty-one twenty-one Emerson Street, above Rock Creek Park. Hurry!"

The cabbie looked over his shoulder. "You don't look too good, mister. I don't need no germs."

"Thirty dollars," Morrissey said.

The cabbie shrugged. "If you put it that way."

Morrissey pressed his face against the window. The glass felt cool, everything he touched now seemed cool. He gripped the seat to keep his balance as the cab accelerated and pulled away from the Pentagon. Why was it so dark? He looked across Arlington cemetery to a sky black with rain clouds. It had already rained—the pavement was dark and shiny.

Janet, be there; be all right. Please, God.

Morrissey leaned forward, urging the cab on as they crossed the Potomac on Memorial Bridge, passed the Kennedy Center, and swung into the park at last. The cabbie kept checking the rearview mirror. "You're sweating like a junkie," he said suddenly. "What you got, anyway? You ain't got T.B. or something, have you?"

"No, no. Of course not. Just . . ." Quick, what was some "nothing" sickness—something benign enough not to make the guy more scared? Can't think.

The cab turned up the Connecticut Avenue exit and one of the wheels dropped into a rut, jarring him. Morrissey doubled over with a jag of coughing, unable to stop himself.

The cab screeched to a stop, throwing him against the front seat. "That's it," the cabbie said. "Out."

"Please . . ."

"Get outa' here, mister. Forget the fare. Move it."

Morrissey groaned. If only he had Janet's gun.

He got out of the cab and began to walk. There were about fifty feet of hill left. He looked up and almost fell over backward in a wave of dizzyness. Fifty feet. For a healthy man, not enough to raise a sweat. He struggled to move each foot ahead. There was a searing pain in his leg. He fell forward against the incline and rolled over cursing. He massaged the calf. His hands were weak, the palms scraped raw from breaking his fall. He got up and tried again. By the time he got to street level, he was staggering. The sweat poured into his eyes, stinging, almost blinding him.

Not sweat—it was cool: rain. He turned his face up gratefully, letting the sprinkle cool him. Thunder rumbled, tearing along his nerves.

He squinted ahead through the light rain. Just over a block left. Come on, *come on!*

He made it to the first brownstone on his block and stopped, leaning against a lamppost. Just a little farther. He walked on, weaving across the sidewalk, onto the curbside grass and back.

As he got closer to his house, his stomach knotted inside him. Goosebumps rose on his neck and arms. It was like the dog, when he'd sensed it outside his window. Alan *was* there, in there with Janet. He thought: Don't hurt her, please. If there's any piece of you left, Alan. . .

Morrissey heard a car pull even with him and slow. He

leaned forward against the steps of his front walk. The concrete was gritty against his hands and wet with rain. The steps seemed to elongate and loom over him. He forced his head up and stared along the sidewalk to the door. It seemed to recede as he looked, small and high up and impossibly far away, as though he was peering the wrong way through a telescope. The house swung around and around. He swallowed against a wave of nausea.

A hand gripped his shoulder, pulling him around. Blue, a blue uniform. The police. Thank God!

He tried to tell them about Janet. He heard his voice buzzing and mumbling in the bones of his head.

"Okay, buddy," the cop said. "You're way outa your neighborhood. And you're definitely in the bag. Let's go downtown and sober up."

Morrissey tried to fight. It had no effect. The policeman pulled him along easily, away from the house, away from Janet, toward the squad car.

Chapter 35

1800 hours:

She's beautiful, Vandiver thought. Even terrified, she is beautiful. I can still see it, but I can't feel it.

He became aware of a sharp tingle in his hands, the back of his head, his groin. Nerve impulses battering away at dead cells.

"Don't scream, Janet," he said. "Please. It's me—Alan."

He saw that she knew better. It was there in her face—horror and repugnance. Dry pains stabbed Vandiver's throat. His eyes prickled so that he could barely see her. How could he clear his vision of the distracting pinpricks of nerve? It was important to see her clearly. She was a danger to him and he must be wary.

She's not looking at you anyway, he told himself. She's looking at a corpse. Something monstrous and evil. If you could just let her destroy it. But you can't.

"I won't hurt you," he said.

She began to look confused. "Alan? Is it really you?"

"Yes," he said. "Something terrible was wrong with me, but now I'm all right. Peter must have told you . . . ?"

Don't answer, Vandiver thought. *I don't care. I don't*

want to know what Peter's doing. If I know, I'll be able to stop him. He considered saying it, but he could not find the will even to move his lips. He must accept the inevitable: The command to survive was below reason—beyond reason. If he could *feel*, he could overwhelm survival.

But he could not feel.

Very well. Before he killed Janet, he must get any information she had. He considered: How did she know he was a risen? She could only know from talking to Peter. Clearly, she'd broken out of camp, and somehow got Peter out of the hospital, and Peter had told her everything.

The full implications began to hit him. He thought: Peter's after me. His brain is better than mine. Maybe no matter what I do, he'll be able to destroy me. . .

A huge tremor struck forward from the back of Vandiver's skull. He waited for it to pass. It was of no consequence—only an empty sensation. If he were alive, it would have triggered chemical sprays of panic in his brain. Instead, it was just a paroxysm of nerve.

He realized Janet was talking.

"If you're really Alan, what are you doing here?"

"The same as you," he said smoothly. "As Peter must have told you, that dog head is evidence. I want to take it to my superiors, prove to them that they can't go on with the L-6 plan."

Janet frowned.

She's still suspicious, Vandiver thought.

"Why didn't you let Peter out?" she said.

"This is more important. I planned to go back for him as soon as I got the project stopped."

Vandiver saw her frown fade. He was winning her over. He thought: She hasn't said a thing about Peter being injected with the plague virus. Peter must not have told her that part of it because he knows she'd insist on getting him to a hospital at once, and there isn't time for that. Gutty decision. But if he doesn't get treatment soon, he'll die. It all depends on the dog's head. If he shows it to Stanhouse, he can probably get Project Parasol stopped. Without the dog's head Stanhouse will think he's crazy. He'll die before he can get anyone important to listen to him.

And I have the dog's head.

Vandiver took a step toward Janet, and the bottles in his briefcase clinked together.

"What was that?" she asked.

"Don't worry about it. We need to—"

"Bottles. It's L-6, isn't it? It couldn't be anything else."

"Relax. I took it from the lab to make sure no one can use it."

She let out a long breath. "Alan . . . if only I could be sure you're . . . yourself."

"I love you." It's true, Vandiver thought. I love her in my mind. But I can't feel it.

"I always have and I always will," he said.

"Oh Alan." Her eyes filled with tears. "I'm so scared. Peter said you—"

"Janet, we haven't any time to waste. Where's Peter now?"

"He's at the Pentagon trying to work his way through the aides to some general. The top one. The Chairman, I think he said. He thought we had to stop you. I was supposed to take the dog's head over to him for proof."

That was it. Full confirmation. Vandiver realized that a man would nod. He moved his head through the gesture, practicing. Then he said, "I have to kill you."

Janet stepped back, looking shocked. Then she flushed. She reached into her blouse and pulled out a .45. "Put the briefcase on the floor," she said tightly.

Very good, Vandiver thought. He felt another dull pulse in the back of his brain. He ignored it, thinking: She's doing only one thing wrong. She should aim at my head. But amateur gunmen never do—too difficult a target.

"Put it down, *now!*

"All right," he said agreeably. "I was about to do that anyway." He set the briefcase down. "You should know that won't do you any good." Vandiver realized his fingers were unbuttoning his shirt. Yes, he thought. If she's going to shoot, I'd better save the shirt. Otherwise I'll have to take time to get another. A living man wouldn't walk around with a bullet hole in his shirt.

"What are you doing?" Janet said. "Stop that."

"You might as well put that thing down." Vandiver rolled the shirt off his shoulders, letting it slide from his arms. He saw that she was staring at the bullet hole Hagan had made.

His legs carried him toward her. What was he going to do? He must stop himself.

"Get back." She held the gun out in a double-handed grip.

"You can't shoot me, Janet. You love me."

Vandiver unzipped the fly of his uniform. If I could just feel, he thought, I wouldn't kill her. Maybe there's something left, some trace of juice that hasn't dried away. If I could hold her in my arms.

"I'm warning you." Her voice was shaky.

"You don't want to hurt me," he said. "You don't want to spoil this body. You want it against you. In you, again, like we did before. Don't you, Janet? Don't you still?" Vandiver reached out toward the gun. It wavered. His hand closed around the .45, pulling it from her fingers. "That's good, Janet. You never wanted to hurt me. Just relax now." Vandiver was aware of a loud buzz in his mind. He was confused. He could not settle his thoughts. His arms seemed to act on their own, pulling her close, holding her to him. He felt her quaking at his touch, her lungs expanding against his arms as she tried to draw breath.

There was a tingle in his groin. It increased, became a flame.

Keeping one arm locked around her, he reached down and pulled himself through the fly. His penis was shriveled and limp. The nerve was there. But there was no blood to rush in and fill and swell the cavities and make him rigid and potent and *alive*. . .

"Stuh-stop!" Janet gasped. "Get *away* from me." She shuddered and pushed, trying to shove him away.

He felt numb pains around his heart. "Hold me, please," he said. "One last time. Just hold me." He saw that her eyes were screwed shut. The cords stood out on her neck. Her body was rigid and rejecting against him.

He tightened his grip, pushing his lips against her, pursuing her mouth as her head whipped back and forth. He was aware of the mass of his biceps bulging. He heard her grunt as he squeezed her against his chest. He saw her mouth sucking for air. Her face began to discolor, from white to pink, to a bluish tint.

He thought: I'm crushing her.

But it's necessary.

His arms went on tightening.

Distantly he heard thunder roll outside. Rain began to splash against the door to the back yard. If I could black myself out, he thought. But I can't. I don't need air. What else? Is there any other way?

Janet went limp in his arms. He let her go, watched her drop to the floor.

He tried to tear his eyes from her. Distantly he was aware of his body kneeling beside her, bending over her. He saw his hand close over her mouth, blocking her nostrils.

He shouted at the top of his lungs: "PETER-R-R-R!"

Chapter 36

1815 hours:

"C'mon buddy," the cop said. "Let's go dry you out." He looked up into the pounding rain with disgust. "Let's go dry us *both* out."

Morrissey dug his heels into the grass and leaned back against the pull of the cop's hand on his shirt. He tried to speak. His throat was dry and sore, grinding the words into a whisper. "Not drunk," he said desperately. "This is my house. I need help." Beyond the cop, through the open door of the squad car, Morrissey could see another cop gazing with a bored expression out the front windshield.

The cop looked skeptical. "Your house, huh? Maybe you'd care to show me your license."

"My wife is in there with . . . a killer."

The policeman leaned close and sniffed his breath, then twirled him around and patted his pockets, withdrawing his wallet. Morrissey suppressed the urge to snatch it back. Why wouldn't the dumb bastard listen?

The cop pulled a business card from the wallet and frowned. "What're you doing with this?"

Morrissey squinted at the card. Thunder cracked. Rain poured down over his ears and off his chin, soaking the small white square: Ambrose Cummings, Detective Sergeant, Washington, D.C., Police Department. Phone 555-1000. *The cop who had come to the hospital to see Kellogg.*

"Cummings," Morrissey said. "Get him over here. Have your partner call him on your radio. You and I have got to go in right now."

The cop pulled his license from the wallet and looked at the address, and Morrissey lurched away. "God damn it. Fuck you. I'm going in." He labored up the front steps.

Behind him, he heard the cop tell his partner to call Cummings. He tried the knob of the front door. Locked. He rummaged in his pocket, found the key ring. The rain was a drenching downpour now. He heard someone bounding up behind him. It was the cop, crowding in against the door, muttering curses as he tried to get out of the rain.

Morrissey got the door open and grabbed the cop's wrist. "Forget how I look and listen to me," he said. "The man in here is very dangerous. He may have hurt or killed my wife. He's a soldier." Morrissey tried to think. Was there anything else? Yes—a bullet couldn't kill the Alan-risen, but it could disfigure the flesh, make it harder for the thing to pass itself off as human. "He's wearing a bulletproof vest," Morrissey temporized. "So aim for his face—his head."

The cop gave him a hard look, then motioned to his partner in the squad car. He took out his .38. The other cop ran up the front walk, freeing his own gun. "This better not be your idea of a joke."

Morrissey led the way through the foyer and kitchen to the basement door. He grabbed the handle and leaned against it as the room swung around him. The edges of his vision went gray. *Hang on.* He jerked the door open.

The Vandiver thing was at the bottom of the steps.

Janet was there, too, sprawled on her back. Morrissey could see no mark on her. She looked only unconscious. *God, let it be true!* Vandiver's corpse was down on its haunches, dancing around her like a chimp, its rump nearly brushing the floor. Its tongue was out, hanging far out, swinging as it scurried around and around her.

Morrissey stared at it horrified, unable to move. Dimly,

he realized what he was seeing. Alan's corpse was totally in the grip of the hindbrain now. It was a patterned dance, as emotionless as the ritual curling movements a dog made before bedding down. At this moment, the remains of Alan Vandiver—surgeon, musician, wit—was a mute, primitive proto-man from three million years ago, signaling to itself that it had felled an enemy.

Morrissey felt the cop's knees bump against his back.

The Vandiver thing abruptly stopped its dance and laid a hand across Janet's mouth, so that the heel of the palm closed off her nostrils too. It was smothering her! Morrissey watched it press its head against her chest and listen. He gave an agonized groan. He must move, spring down on it, but there was no strength in his body. His heart labored in his chest. He could see nothing but the horrible face. It was turned directly toward him, but it seemed not to see him. With its tongue out, its blank goatlike leer, it looked nothing like Alan.

It saw him!

Morrissey shrank back against the cop's legs as the Alan-risen leapt up from Janet's body. It growled at him. The sound was low and even. It numbed him to his bones.

"Jesus," he whispered. "Jesus, Jesus."

He tried again to move and failed.

The cop shoved him aside and ran down the steps as the thing disappeared in the direction of the cellar. The second cop pushed by, and then Morrissey shoved off with his arms and legs, sliding down behind them.

"Janet!"

Her face was blue. She did not move. Her stillness filled him with aching dread. He knelt beside her and groped her wrist. It felt cold, shocking his fingers. He groaned and searched for a pulse.

There was none.

Almost blind with rage, he glared around the basement. Where was the Alan-risen? He would knock it down, kick the brain in. There! Over by the cellar! But it looked like Alan again, standing straight and tall. The face seemed normal. In Alan's hand was a cola bottle. Morrissey struggled to get up. He couldn't coordinate his legs.

One of the cops held his gun out, two-handed, in the classic shooting stance.

Yes, Morrissey thought savagely, the face, the face!

"Don't shoot or I'll drop this," Alan's voice said.

Why was he holding that bottle out? *Plague virus!*

"Drop your guns," Vandiver said.

"Don't do it," Morrissey gasped. "But don't shoot—not unless he drops the bottle. It's loaded with plague virus. If he drops it . . ."

"Ten thousand people in this city will die," Vandiver finished.

"Look, uh, General . . . ?" said the cop.

"That's right. General Alan Vandiver, United States Army, director of the Army Labs."

"Okay, why don't you put that bottle down, General, and we'll talk this over."

"I don't know what lies this man has told you," the Alan-risen said, "but I'm on urgent military business. I have no intention of dropping this bottle, but if you shoot me or interfere with me in any way, it may fall, and you will be responsible. This man was my friend. But he's killed his wife, and now it appears he's trying to pin it on me."

"Don't listen," Morrissey said.

"Look, we can go down to the station and get this all straightened out . . ."

"I know you're just trying to do your duty," Vandiver said, "but I can't be delayed. I'm trying to head off a national security crisis. As I'm sure you know, a national emergency takes precedence over civilian authority. I've given you my name and position, and you'll have no trouble finding me later. Now I'm going to leave. Get out of my way." Alan stepped toward the dog head.

Morrissey said: "If he takes another step, shoot him in the head."

Vandiver's body stopped. The eyes looked at him. "If you do that, the bottle will fall. You'll all die."

"If you get away, we'll all die anyway," Morrissey said.

"And you can't afford to have your face disfigured, can you? It looks like you have the most to lose."

The patrolman looked down at Alan's feet and saw the dog's head. It faced them from the floor, its eyes moving from man to man, its muzzle wrinkling in silent snarls. The cop's face went white. "Holy shit," he said.

Morrissey stared at Vandiver's dead face. *My life is over,* he thought. *Without Janet, I'm finished. But I'm going to stop you. I'll stop you and die.*

"You're bluffing," the risen said.

"I'm not. With a bullet hole in your face, you won't dare be seen. You can't oversee the campaign, you can't show your face to Stanhouse. Nothing."

The risen stood very still, as if considering.

"Get out of here," Morrissey said.

Vandiver's body whirled and rushed out through the back door, heading for the park. A gust of wind blew in, sprinkling the floor with rain. Thunder rolled, on and on.

Morrissey realized what the rain meant. He felt a mirthless grin twisting his face. It can't break that bottle yet! he thought. If it breaks the bottle now, the rain will wash the plague straight into the sewers. I still have a chance. . .

He became aware of Janet's cold wrist still in his hand. He doubled over her and burst into tears.

One of the cops knelt beside him, and gently took Janet's wrist from his hand.

"This woman isn't dead," the cop said.

Morrissey's heart leapt. He grabbed her wrist back. Yes, there *was* a pulse! He'd had his fingers wrong. And the coldness he felt must have been in contrast to his own fever. She was alive! He could feel her life under his fingertips, light and racing, growing slower and stronger as he held it. He looked at her face in an ecstacy of relief. She was coming around. The bluish tint was fading, replaced by a pink flush.

"Man, I don't know about this . . ."

Morrissey glimpsed the second cop backing toward the steps. He was still looking at the severed dog head. He looked sick. The other cop circled behind Janet and grabbed his partner's arm, half supporting him.

Morrissey heard a siren, faint but growing louder. It reached a crescendo and died in front of the house. Janet moaned and he gathered her up in his arms. She opened her eyes. For a second her face was vacant, and then she cringed in panic and tried to push away from him.

"No, please!" she whimpered. "Don't—"

He caught her wrists, and held them until her eyes focused on him.

"Peter! Thank God!"

He hugged her. "You're all right. You're all right."

He heard more feet clattering down the steps. It was Cummings. The detective stared at the severed dog head. "*Bora mlani shetani.*" His voice was hushed, almost reverent. "So that is Monk."

Janet pushed up from the floor. Morrissey tried to get up and fell back. Janet and Cummings each took an arm and lifted him up between them.

Everything was spinning around. Couldn't even keep his head up. How was he going to go after the risen?

It was time to find an innoculation center. He couldn't put it off any longer. If they were set up and he could get to one in time, it might keep him going long enough to get to the Chairman and stop the innoculation plan. If he tried to do it without the plague antidote, he'd never make it.

At least the rain, the blessed, blessed rain, was on his side. As long as it rained, the Vandiver-risen wouldn't break the bottles.

There was just the one ugly catch: L-6. It would be mixed with the plague antidote. He'd have to take both together.

If it would help him go on, so be it.

"Cummings," he said. "Has the police department been informed of any plan by the army to set up innoculation centers in the city?"

The detective stared at him. "How the hell did you know that?"

"Where's the nearest one, do you remember?"

"That whole scam is top secret. If I talk about that, they won't just bust me back to blue—they'll throw my rump in jail."

''If I don't get to one of those centers in the next few minutes,'' Morrissey said, ''they'll throw my rump in a coffin.''

Janet gasped.

''Well, shit,'' Cummings said. ''That tops me.''

Morrissey sat close to Janet in the backseat of the patrol car. He struggled to keep upright as Cummings wheeled the car sharply around a corner. Janet reached across his chest, holding him up. I shouldn't let her touch me, he thought. I shouldn't even let her near me. He closed his eyes. A fever glow pursued him beneath the lids.

There was nothing else he could have done. He had to have their help. The disease was raging through him this fast because he had been directly injected with a massive dose of virus. None of them had. If they caught the virus from him, it would take time to breed up in their bodies to the point where the symptoms could bring them down. Hours, maybe as much as a day. If he stopped the thing in Vandiver, there would be time to get them antidote without L-6 in it.

If he didn't, it wouldn't matter.

The cop sitting next to Cummings looked unhappily down at the overnight case on his lap. He opened his mouth.

''Just hold on to it, Stoudt,'' Cummings said before he could speak. ''It's not going to bite you through the case—I don't think.'' Stoudt looked miserably out the window.

''How did you know its name was Monk?'' Morrissey asked Cummings.

''Remember when your buddy Kellogg was writing answers on a pad that day at the hospital?''

Morrissey felt Janet's hand squeeze his arm convulsively, but when he looked at her, she gave him a bright, glassy smile.

''I slipped the pad out with me,'' Cummings went on. ''A sheet had already been torn off, but Kellogg had pressed down pretty hard. The pencil impression went down six more sheets. One word: *Monk.* I've been puzzling and puzzling over that name, Doctor. Mornings, and when I was falling asleep at night. One of those things, those little mysteries that bug you. I never expected to solve this one. I'm not sure I'm glad I did."

Cummings wheeled the car around a corner. Morrissey saw that they were about five blocks away from the school now. North Park Junior High. The police radio jabbered. The loud voice and bursts of static flamed along his nerves. "Are you all right?" he murmured to Janet.

The fear came back into her eyes. "He . . . it squeezed me until I blacked out," she said. "I saw it dancing around me. Then it put its hand on my mouth—"

"Okay, shh-h-h. You're all right now. It's okay."

"Peter, is it . . . is it the devil?"

The police radio stopped. Morrissey saw Cummings's eyes focus on him in the rearview mirror. The patrolman beside him started to hum tunelessly, then stopped, swallowed hard.

"No," Morrissey said. "It's a mistake. A terrible one. Mine."

Cummings slowed and pulled into the parking lot of the junior high school. Morrissey strained to see. The lot was mostly empty. A woman who looked like a teacher scurried across the pavement to her car, hunched and holding the neck of her coat closed against the rain. Morrissey felt an odd, pained nostalgia. Teachers, tests, recess. Just another school day drawing to a close. Maybe one of the last ones ever.

He looked around the lot. There was the trailer in a corner, away from the playground. It was plain white. As the car pulled closer, he could make out a more vivid patch beside the door where something, probably a sign, had shielded the paint from the sun. In a few more days, the sign would go up again, a caduceus, or perhaps a red cross, but for now the trailer looked plain and anonymous. The curtains were drawn at the windows, but as the car stopped, Morrissey saw one draw back an inch.

"Remember," he said. "These guys won't want to admit to anything but their cover story. They're military, and almost certainly armed."

He felt a pressure against his forehead. Noises buzzed in

his ears, louder and softer, in irritating cycles, and then he felt things shaping up around him again. He hung on, chewing his lower lip, concentrating on the pain.

"Peter? Peter . . ."

He let Janet tug him upright. His forehead felt sticky pulling away from the back of Cummings's seat. He was worse off than he'd thought. He tried to remember what he'd been saying. "Military . . . armed," he mumbled.

"Yeah, you said that. Come on, Stoudt."

Suddenly Cummings was outside the car, on the top step of the trailer, with the patrolman behind him. Morrissey blinked. How had he done that? The fever. Heating up. Frying his brain now. Snipping little gaps out of his consciousness.

He struggled to get out the back door of the squad car. Janet clung to his arm, holding him back easily. "No, Peter. Let them handle it."

"Please. They don't know what to ask for."

She got out her side, came around and pulled him out of the car, slung his arm over her shoulder. Dimly he heard voices. He forced his head up. Cummings was talking to someone now—a large, raw-boned man in an ill-fitting suit. The man stood in the trailer's open doorway, blocking Cummings's way inside.

"What is this, Officer?"

"We've got a man here, needs what you've got."

"There must be some mistake. We're just here setting up for a flu innoculation pro—"

"Don't jive me, man. There isn't time. You've seen my badge, now let's get it done."

"I've seen your badge," the big man agreed, "and you've seen a certain memo. You're to stay clear unless we ask for help."

"Help doing what? Holding little kids for their flu shots?"

"It's not your place to worry about that."

Morrissey saw the man's head jerk back. Cummings had the .38 out. When had he drawn it? Morrissey leaned against Janet, fighting to keep his eyes open.

"I *know* my place, turkey," Cummings said softly. "Shall we go inside?"

"You'll regret this."

"Oh, I hope not, I sincerely do hope not."

Morrissey leaned on Janet and struggled up the steep fold-down steps. God, his feet were heavy. Each one of them weighed a ton. The inside of the trailer was an oven. Why did they keep it so dim? He could barely see. He heard rain drumming against the roof, loud enough to deafen. Nice rain. Keep it up, rain.

Morrissey let them ease him onto the bench of a fold-down table in the trailer's kitchenette. He put an arm out on the table to steady himself and knocked over a Styrofoam cup of coffee. The liquid felt tepid against his arm, even though he could see steam rising from it. He got his head up far enough to see two kids with short, military-style haircuts looking at him with round, scared eyes. They don't know what this is all about, he thought. Only the big guy might know that it's not flu, and he wouldn't know anything more than that. They think they're really here to vaccinate some school kids. He peered through the dimness, saw Cummings taking a standard issue .45 from a holster on the big man's belt.

"I've already got the plague," Morrissey said. "So give me the strongest dose you can."

"I don't know what you're talking about," the big man said.

"Sure, sure," Cummings said. "Just shoot up my man, here. We can all call it flu and everybody will be happy."

The man in the suit nodded to one of the corpsmen. "The type B," he said.

Morrissey closed his eyes. Here it comes, he thought. He felt nothing. He opened his eyes and saw them pulling the needle out. "Did they do it?" he asked.

Cummings gave him a thumbs-up. "They zapped you, babe."

Morrissey nodded. How long would it take L-6 to set up in his cells? Not long. A few hours.

He felt a sick, crawling sensation through his whole body. L-6 was home to roost.

Chapter 37

2100 hours:

"I can't show Major Cathcart the dog," Morrissey said.

Cummings stared at him. "What are you talking about, man? You've got to show him. How else you gonna get through to the general?"

"You're going to force Cathcart to put us through."

Cummings sighed. He shut his eyes and pressed a thumb and forefinger against the lids. "Oh man."

Morrissey leaned back into the soft embrace of the waiting-room chair. It felt good to sit. It felt even better to sweat. His shirt and pants were slimy with it. He must look like he'd just climbed out of the pool at a wild party. He didn't care. The fever was broken. His bones had stopped aching. The chair was soft as a cradle.

And his brain had started working right, thank God.

He'd come damned close to disaster. He might have already come *too* close. He suppressed a shudder. Cummings knew too much. So did the two patrolmen. And how much had he told Major Cathcart the last time he was here?

Janet came back from the fountain with a cup of water and he sipped gratefully.

"Run this by me again, Doc," Cummings said.

Morrissey looked across the waiting room at the duty officer. The duty desk was twenty feet away. The man seemed engrossed in some papers, but appearances could be deceiving.

Morrissey spoke in a low voice. "Listen, Sergeant. You've seen the dog. You've also seen what looks like a general of the United States Army running around with cola bottles full of plague virus. And you've seen a United States Army medical corps trailer already set up on a school parking lot, even though there's no plague yet. What do you think it means?"

Cummings nodded. "Uh-huh, uh-huh. My feeble brain has been piecing it together and it ain't pretty. The U.S. Army's going into the germ-warfare business—on its own people."

"Quiet!" Morrissey said in alarm. "For God's sake, Cummings." He glanced at the duty officer. The man's head was still down. "It's not the whole U.S. Army. It's a few people at the top. I know this is hard to believe, but they thought they had good reason. The point is, we've got to stop it without letting a hint slip that it almost happened."

Cummings frowned. "Bullshit, man. The people have a right to—"

"Bullshit yourself, Cummings," Morrissey snapped. He saw the duty officer look up. *Easy does it.* "Do you want to be the one who tries to control the riots?" he said. "Have you got a plan for putting American society back together again if this gets out?"

Cummings said nothing.

"And there's more. This doesn't even have to leak to our good trusting citizens for this country to be destroyed. There are people around this city, people in this building right now, who are listening for tremors. They work for Uncle Ivan, not Uncle Sam. Major Cathcart, or someone Major Cathcart gossips with, could be one of them. If just one of those people hears what we know, or even what the major might piece together, there will be no riots, no crisis in government, nothing, because this country won't be here tomorrow."

"You're talking heavy shit, man."

"I'm talking the end of the world."

Janet put a hand on his shoulder. He felt the heat of Cummings's stare. Strange, how little he felt the words themselves: *the end of the world.* It was true. In the next few hours he had to be very careful because of it. It should make the hairs stand up all over him. But it was nothing. A damned inconvenience. The only thing he wanted was to stop what he had started.

"Why is it I believe you, Morrissey?" Cummings said.

Morrissey gave a grim smile. "Good. Now, when Cathcart shows up, he's going to be steamed at us for hauling him back here after hours. He may be stubborn. You'll have to lean on him. He's got to tell us where we can find Stanhouse, and he can't know why. The general's the only one who's going to see inside that case."

Cummings grunted sourly. "Right. Anything else I can do for you. Help you across the street, maybe?"

Come on, Cummings, Morrissey thought. *Faster.*

A huge billboard with the face of candidate Maxwell Howard loomed and was gone, lingering on his eyes. It gave him a quick, sharp feeling of doom. A shopping center flashed by on his left, a blur of neon and glistening brick against the suffocating blackness of the sky. He could barely hear the siren dopplering away behind them. He leaned forward and checked the speedometer: 85 mph. It would have to do. If they crashed, it was all over.

He sipped from the bottle of grape soda Janet held for him. A nerve throbbed in his stomach. *Are you there yet, Alan? You were his good friend. You know where he lives. You have a head start.*

Janet wiped Morrissey's face with the paper towels from the Pentagon bathroom and he felt a surge of affection. She was so strong. So good. He wanted to hug her, tell her, but Cummings might see them in the rearview mirror.

And he had to concentrate, to plan.

The Alan-risen would know they must warn Stanhouse. If the Chairman found out the truth about L-6 he would abort the innoculation campaign, and destroy the ugly evidence of what they had almost done. Four risen men could not stand against the resources of the U.S. army.

So the Alan-risen must try to stop them now.

What would Alan—an Alan empty of human feeling—do to stop them? He could take a chance on intercepting them before they got to Stanhouse. But he wouldn't know how much force they might bring along. No, Alan would prefer to go straight to the Chairman and wait for them. Then, when they arrived, he would use his friendship and influence with Stanhouse to discredit them.

Morrissey frowned. How could Alan hope to discredit us? he wondered. I could just take Cummings's gun and pump a few rounds into Alan. Unmask him on the spot. We wouldn't even need the dog's head.

Christ, no!

Sweat popped out cold on Morrissey's face. He couldn't dare do that. The Alan-risen needed Stanhouse alive and on its side. If they unmasked it in front of Stanhouse, it might kill them all, before the general had a chance to order the project stopped.

So what do we do? Morrissey wondered. How do we stop a thing that bullets can't kill, a thing with no human feelings to hold it back, a powerful body and brain ruled only by instincts?

Morrissey sat up straighter. *Instincts—plural!* Personal survival wasn't the only human instinct. There was also survival of the *species*. Project Parasol would create many more risens, a hideous threat to humanity. Shouldn't that cause a conflict in the risens? Yes, it would have to! Alan was born a human. Even though he was now something very different, *human* was still his ingrained identity, still the basis for the instincts wired into his brain from before birth.

Morrissey closed his eyes and felt an immediate queasiness from the motion of the car. He opened them again and stared at the dark floor between his knees, struggling to concentrate. Would it be possible to influence a person, manipulate his instincts, playing them off, one against another? Yes. Even though instincts were "hard-wired" into the brain, they were like every other motive for behavior: whether they operated or lay dormant depended on what a person *perceived*. The survival instinct wouldn't stop a man from drinking coffee handed to him by a friend—unless he thought the coffee was poisoned. Then, the instinct would spring into play, even if the man was wrong and the coffee *wasn't* poisoned.

Even instinct depended on what you saw and what you thought, right or wrong, real or unreal.

There had to be some way to take advantage of that fact—some way to propel survival of the species to the forefront of Alan's dead brain.

Morrissey jumped, startled, as Janet pressed a towel against his face again. He put his arm around her. *To hell with the rearview mirror.* "I love you," he said.

He saw Cummings's gaze flick to the mirror, then back to the road. The cop's head nodded almost imperceptibly.

The car turned down the dirt road that Major Cathcart had shown them on the map. Morrissey stared out the window in near panic. No, he thought. I'm not ready yet.

His mind raced futilely as they pulled up in front of a private drive. At the end of it, a hundred yards back from the road, a huge Victorian house loomed in the rain, windows glowing like the embrasures of a castle.

Morrissey forced himself to calm. This was it, ready or not.

A sentry met them, checked Cummings's I.D., and crowded in beside patrolman Stoudt. Morrissey edged against the door, staring at the back of the soldier's head. *Alan's risens had been soldiers.*

The windshield began to fog in front of the man's face as they pulled up the drive. Relieved, Morrissey let his hand drop from the door handle. The window wouldn't fog unless the man had exhaled air warmed by living lungs.

Cummings parked the cruiser. The sentry led them across the wide porch and into the house. He stopped at a pair of white doors and knocked softly. There was a long pause.

"Come in," rasped a heavy, tired voice.

The soldier released Cummings's arm and opened the

doors. General Stanhouse was standing behind a desk at the far end of the room, surrounded like a country squire by walls of books and mounted trophy fish. The general's aristocratic features were drawn down in a mask of weariness. The silver hair was mussed and his eyes were red. Morrissey heard soothing music—Mozart—coming from hidden speakers.

Then he heard Janet gasp. He turned and there was the Alan-risen, standing against the back wall of the room. In its hand was the briefcase. Morrissey's skin crawled. Alan looked so alive. Was anything left of what he had been? Morrissey thought: *I'm going to set you free. I swear it.*

"These are the people I've been telling you about, sir," Alan said. His voice sounded utterly human. He looked in every way like the man he had been.

Morrissey said: "General, we must talk with you in private."

"General Vandiver has told me about you, Dr. Morrissey. I'm going to give you five minutes. Anything you have to say, you'll say to both of us."

Dear God, Morrissey thought. *Five minutes.* He said: "General, you can't use L-6 to immunize this country against radiation."

Stanhouse gave no visible reaction. He took a cigar from his desk, holding it gently, lighting it almost reverently, as though it were the only pleasure left to him in life. He blew out a cloud of smoke. "I haven't the faintest idea what you're talking about."

"Please," Morrissey said. How could he say this without sounding crazy? "I don't know what . . . what Alan's been telling you about us. But I developed L-6. I know what it does—*everything* it does. It does provide radiation immunity to people—*living* people. But if a person with L-6 in his cells dies, the body does not decay. The human consciousness is trapped inside."

Stanhouse sighed wearily. "What are you a doctor of, Morrissey? You're talking like a witch doctor."

"Three of Alan's test subjects are that way right now."

Vandiver's body lounged against a bookcase. His face smiled with pained tolerance.

Stanhouse pushed a button on the corner of his desk. The piped-in music was arrested and there was a crackle of static. An intercom, Morrissey thought in near panic. He's going to call the guard. "Wait! Please! I have something to show you."

Reluctantly, Stanhouse slid his finger from the button and the music resumed.

Morrissey motioned to Stoudt. The patrolman took Janet's case to the general, opened it gingerly, keeping his fingers away from the edges. Stanhouse glanced into the case. His face paled, but there was no sign of surprise. "Is this your idea of a joke, Morrissey?"

"Look at it, General."

"I don't need to look. Alan already told me about your grisly experiments. I would have to agree with him. Only a disturbed man would do something like this."

Morrissey almost groaned in frustration. "That is an L-6 animal, General. It is clinically dead. It was dead even before its head was cut off. If people are given L-6, they will be like this dog."

Stanhouse grunted. "I don't know how you managed that . . . that grotesque *thing* in your box, Morrissey. Alan explained it, but I'm afraid I'm not much of a scientist. I do know that I have a lot on my mind right now, and I am neither impressed nor amused."

Morrissey began to feel numb. This was his proof. But the general refused to accept it. For Stanhouse, it came down to taking the word of a friend—and scientist—he trusted or the wild story of a scarecrow man he'd never seen before.

But I've got nothing else, Morrissey thought.

He tried to recover himself, revise his plan. Perhaps the dog's head could still be proof. He'd get the general to call in other biologists. After it had been microscopically examined by experts . . . No, even that wouldn't work. There would be no sign of L-6. The cells would look normal. He'd seen the very faint pink band only that one time. Even if the experts saw it, it wouldn't prove a thing about L-6.

Morrissey stared at Alan's dead, composed face, feeling helpless.

Then something clicked in his mind. Even the *cells* of the dog would look normal. Morrissey stared through Alan, distracted. That might be a way out—out of everything. The Russians wouldn't be able to tell the cells of a normal man from those of a living L-6 subject. That fact could be used. L-6 might do what Alan—the *living* Alan—had hoped for after all. If he could just—

Janet's nails dug into his arm, jerking him back to the present.

"Is there anything else, *Doctor* Morrissey?" Stanhouse said.

The Vandiver thing stepped away from the bookcase and nodded with distaste at the dog's head. "You see what I mean about Peter's psychosis, sir? As I told you, he genuinely thinks he invented L-6. Actually, he was just one of the people working on it. He played a rather minor part."

"He's lying," Morrissey said.

Vandiver's face was a picture of patient misery, a man forgiving the insults of his raving friend. "It's all right, Peter. Let me take you back to the hospital."

Cummings cleared his throat. "General, I've been on the D.C. police force for seventeen years. I'm now a detective sergeant. I can swear to you that Dr. Morrissey is a senior project director at Army Labs. Not a witch doctor. Not the sort of man to be helping out on someone else's project. And he is definitely not insane."

Stanhouse frowned. He looked toward Vandiver and Morrissey saw the first shadow of doubt on his face.

"No offense, Detective Cummings," Alan said easily, "but are you also a psychiatrist?"

Janet said, "General, listen. This isn't Alan. Can't you see it?"

"Not Alan, young woman?" the Chairman said gently.

"Alan was my husband's best friend," Janet said, "and mine. A few hours ago, he—what is left of him—tried to kill me. Alan Vandiver *is* dead. I can prove it. Order him to take off his shirt.''

No! Morrissey thought. But he wavered, trapped in indecision. She wanted to unmask Alan. It was horribly dangerous. But what else was left? To kill them, the Alan-risen would have to believe that it could cover up the murders and take over Stanhouse's role as top command of the project. If it decided it could not, it might do nothing and they would have won.

''My dear child,'' Stanhouse said to Janet. ''I know you must feel badly for your husband. But what you're suggesting is quite—''

''Even if Peter is crazy,'' she said, ''what are the odds that I'm crazy too?''

Stanhouse hesitated. His eyes edged down to the head of the dog.

''There's a bullet hole in the middle of Alan's chest,'' Janet said. ''A wound no man could survive. Just order him to show you. Make him prove I'm lying.''

Stanhouse closed the lid on the case gently. He sank into the chair behind his desk and laid his cigar in an ashtray. In the silence Morrissey became aware of the music still playing, a sane, orderly sound, and through it a grandfather clock clacking somewhere in the room. How many ticks left?

''I guess you'd better do it, Alan,'' Stanhouse said.

''Sir, I object. You can make a simple phone call to the psychiatric facility at Fort Detrick and they'll confirm that Peter is an escaped psychotic. His wife, quite naturally, has been taken in by him. I don't think—''

''No,'' Stanhouse cut in. ''I can't make a simple phone call. My phone lines are down. The storm.''

An alarm went off in Morrissey's head. *The lines down.* The storm? Or the other risens?

''Dr. Morrissey may be crazy,'' Stanhouse said, ''but we've got to do something to satisfy this poor young woman here. It's simple enough for you to show us your chest if that's what she wants.''

Alan's face looked hurt. "I'd like to feel that you trust me, sir."

"Don't talk rot, Alan. I trust you. But let's get this settled right now. Just go ahead and take your shirt off."

"Is that an order?"

"Yes, damn it, yes."

"All right, sir. But that has to be the end of it."

"Of course."

Morrissey tensed as Vandiver set his briefcase on the floor and began to unbutton his shirt. Where was Cummings? On the other side of Janet. Patrolman Stoudt was closer, about two feet. His holster was unsnapped.

Morrissey swallowed. The nerves of his hand rehearsed the movements: tug the gun free, aim, fire.

And then what? A bullet couldn't hurt a corpse.

The risen had the shirt open to the waist. It lifted the hem of the undershirt. Morrissey stared, frozen. Alan's chest was smooth and unmarked. There was no bullet hole.

Chapter 38

2300 hours:

Morrissey stared at the unwounded skin over Alan's heart. He heard Janet groan. It can't be, he thought. Unless. . .

"You see, General?" the risen said triumphantly.

Morrissey thought: It's won. The Chairman won't let us near him again.

He pushed Janet down and jerked Stoudt's gun free. He squeezed the trigger again and again. Two holes opened in Vandiver's stomach, dark and bloodless.

The Alan-risen stood very still, gazing at him with cold, blank eyes.

Morrissey straightened. His ears rang. He saw Cummings and Stoudt gaping at Vandiver. Janet crouched over, hands on her ears.

"Alan was a surgeon," Morrissey said. "He must have cut a plug of skin from somewhere else on his body to hide the bullet hole in his chest."

Stanhouse looked faint. He leaned forward on his desk, his head hanging drunkenly.

The Alan-risen bent and removed a cola bottle from its briefcase. No! Morrissey thought. It hurled the bottle against the ceiling. The bottle smashed, spraying brown liquid and glass over the floor and Stanhouse's desk. Morrissey felt a twinge in his cheek—a piece of glass stuck in the skin. He flicked it away.

He thought: Plague. Everyone alive in this room, except me, will die.

Janet.

The gun slipped from his fingers. He heard it thump on the carpet.

The risen drew Vandiver's service revolver. "You will all sit. You—policeman: put your gun on the floor."

Morrissey shivered at the cold remnant of Alan's voice. The need to fake human expressiveness was now gone.

Cummings did as he was told.

"We'll wait," the risen said. "The bottle is very concentrated. In a few hours, you'll join those who are now dying in DuPont Circle and Tyson's Corner."

Morrissey stared at the risen. "You wouldn't have—not while it's raining. The rain would wash it away."

"Did you think I just carried these bottles around all that time before the rain, waiting for it to stop me? There was a good wind before the storm."

Morrissey fought a wave of horror. It *had* broken the bottles. It had doomed thousands of people to prolonged, painful deaths and it didn't care, one way or the other—just as it had no feeling for the millions it meant to destroy next.

"What are you going to do now?" Morrissey's voice came out a near whisper. "You need General Stanhouse."

"No. I'd have preferred him to continue, but you spoiled that. You will die of plague tonight. The project committee will understand. You were part of the project, and you got too close to the virus."

"You can't get away with this," Stanhouse said weakly. "Hagan will stop you."

"Hagan is dead."

Stanhouse sagged into his chair. He pulled out a handkerchief and wiped his eyes. "Alan, Alan . . ."

The risen gave Morrissey an impassive look. "You see? Even when he knows, he still thinks I am a man. General Stanhouse—"

The Chairman looked up slowly.

"Turn off the music."

Stanhouse pushed a button on the intercom and the Mozart cut off. "You *aren't* Alan. Alan always loved that tape."

Vandiver's eyes bored into the old general's. "It's only sound. I love nothing now."

He turned back to Morrissey. "I'll go to the project committee tomorrow. Explain your unfortunate, accidental deaths. They'll have no choice but to turn to me. By tomorrow night, I'll be in charge."

He's right, Morrissey thought. He felt Janet's face press into his shoulder. The lights, he thought. *If* Cummings can get to the lights. He tried to catch Cummings's eye. The cop was staring at the risen as if mesmerized. *Look at me*, Morrissey thought.

Janet turned from his shoulder. "Alan. I know you're still there. You don't want to do this!"

Alan's head moved around toward her. "Alan is *not* still here," the risen said. "The brain thinks, the instincts command, but that is all."

Morrissey stared at the risen, thinking again of what had occurred to him on the way here. He said: "What about the species?"

Alan's head swiveled away from Janet toward him. "What?"

"Survival of the species," Morrissey said. "No matter what you may have become, you were still born human. If you go through with Project Parasol, it may be the end of your race." As he said it, Morrissey realized it was no good—too vague. At best, he was only appealing to Alan's reason. He was talking about an ideal now, not an instinct. If ideals were enough, the Alan-risen would already have destroyed itself.

Morrissey saw that the risen was gazing at Janet again.

And then he knew what he had to say. He felt a wave of revulsion.

He said: "Janet is your . . . mate. In your mind, she's always been your mate. That's true, isn't it, Alan? Ever since college, when you were dating her and then she and I . . ." He stopped. "Your *mate*. You *can't* destroy her."

Morrissey saw that Janet was staring at him.

"I can have no children," the risen said woodenly.

Morrissey said: "You haven't been dead very long. There must still be live sperm in your body. You could do the surgery on yourself . . ." He was unable to go on.

The risen's dead eyes bored into his. "That's a good idea. But you're trying to confuse me and *that* is useless."

Morrissey's teeth clenched in frustration. He was close, but being close counted for nothing with this creature. Instinct was a thin wire, either tripped or missed completely. He was trying to play on the Alan-risen's old love for Janet, when the risen could love nothing anymore. If it did have a slim chance left at impregnating a woman, any woman would do.

It still had no reason to spare Janet, and if it didn't spare her, it would kill them all.

"Alan . . ." Janet began.

"Be quiet." Vandiver's head cocked in an attitude of listening. He strode to the front exposure of the study and looked out the venetian blinds.

Sirens, Morrissey thought. Louder! They're coming here! He looked past Vandiver's body and saw two station wagons speeding up the long driveway. They were painted a dark, army green. Major Cathcart must have decided to check things out for himself. Red sparks flickered in the bushes along the drive. There was a loud chatter—machine guns. The cars had run straight into an ambush. The other risens *were* out there.

Morrissey's heart sank. Now Vandiver would have to shoot them.

Morrissey rammed his shoulder into Vandiver's body and shouted, "Cummings!" He grabbed Vandiver's waist and felt the body lurch back against him. There was a second impact and he saw Stoudt's arm pin Vandiver's wrist and thigh together. He heard Cummings grunting out curses in a foreign language. He grappled for a hold on the body. It was cold under his fingers. He saw Cummings's hand jerking at Vandiver's ankles. They all toppled over together.

Morrissey squirmed to the side, still grasping for a hold. Cummings's face was pressed against his, so close he couldn't focus.

"Get going!" Cummings gasped.

"No."

"We're greased anyway, man. If you stay, it'll kill you too. Get the general to a center."

Morrissey saw Vandiver's hand grab the detective's ear. Then there was a raw spot on the side of Cummings's head, spouting blood. Morrissey's gorge rose.

"Blow!" Cummings gasped.

"No, damn it!"

Hands closed around Morrissey's shoulders, pulling him off the pile. Twisting, he saw it was Stanhouse. He tried to jerk free, but the general held him. "He's right, son. Whoever stays here is dead. We've got to get loose and stop that thing, or it gets everyone."

Fuck! Morrissey thought. He let the general and Janet pull him toward the door. The last second he looked back. The risen was twisting Cummings's head around. The cop's chin was past his shoulder and his face was a mask of blood.

Forgive me, Cummings.

The general led them down a hall and through a sitting room and kitchen. As they ran out the back door, Morrissey heard a ripping stream of gunfire and then answering shots, all from the front of the house.

Stanhouse pointed across the backyard. "There's a trail behind that shed. It goes to a back road. I've got a jeep there."

Morrissey nodded

They were almost to the shed when something dark reared up in front of them. *A risen!* Janet screamed. Morrissey stared at the thing, revolted. It no longer looked human. It's uniform shirt and trousers were shredded by bullets. Skin hung from its face and arms, and one leg was bent under it at a sickening angle. One eye was gone. Most of its muscle had been shot away.

Cathcart's men must have shot it, and it had crawled away.

Morrissey saw that it was reaching for something on the grass in front of it. A gun! He kicked the weapon away. The risen grabbed his leg and pulled. His other foot slipped on the wet grass, and he went down hard. Its hands pulled at him, dragging him to it. He screamed. He got a dizzy glimpse of Janet and Stanhouse overhead, kicking it, punching it. He pried at the fingers and felt bare, slippery bone.

Dear Jesus God!

His leg pulled free and he crawled madly across the lawn away from it. Hands grabbed his arms, pulling him upright, and then he was running, around the shed and into a dark tunnel of brush. His stomach heaved as he ran. No, he must not throw up. He would strangle. He had to run—run his legs off, get away from the horrible thing.

He heard Janet sobbing behind him and got himself back under control. He slowed, and let her and Stanhouse by him on the path. He ran behind them, drawing on the aftershock of panic. It drained away quickly and the strength went out of his legs. The ground squelched and slid under his feet. The air turned heavy with the stink of rotted leaves and fungus, so thick he could barely suck it into his lungs.

The fever, he thought. It drained me. I can't make it.

Pain exploded in the old fracture site. He fell, biting back a cry of agony. He heard the others running on ahead. He tried to shout and couldn't. *Get up, damn you!* His hands pushed impotently beside his shoulders. He couldn't even lift his head.

He felt Janet and Stanhouse pulling at his armpits. The general said, "Just a little farther, Doctor."

Morrissey stumbled along with them. Fire raged in his lungs, his side, his leg. He squinted ahead, looking for the jeep. The path widened into a clearing cloaked in ground mist. A gust of wind thinned the mist and Morrissey saw the jeep.

"Damn!" Stanhouse said.

The jeep was settled too low to the ground. Its tires had

been slashed to ribbons. "The phone lines," Stanhouse said. "And the jeep, too. He didn't miss anything."

Morrissey heard the machine-gun fire, very faint, rattling from the direction of the house. If enough guns fired, the bodies of Alan's test subjects would be chewed away until they could do no more harm.

But Vandiver's corpse would come on. By now it would have killed Cummings and Stoudt and started after them. The risen by the shed would have told it where they'd gone.

The skin crawled on Morrissey's neck as he sensed Vandiver on the trail behind them, bearing down relentlessly. He stared at the ruined tires. The back of the jeep slumped mournfully, heavy with gas.

Gas!

He realized he was grinning like a maniac. *No more running. Come on, Alan. I'll set you free.*

Janet tugged on his arm. "Peter, we have to run."

"General, is there a gas can on that jeep?"

Stanhouse frowned. "Yes . . ."

"Do you have a lighter?"

"Yes, but . . ."

"Listen to me. Do exactly what I say. Get that can and bring it to me."

"Peter," Janet urged. "We can still get away."

"No," he said. "There's no getting away. We get it or it gets us. General, do it."

Stanhouse hurried back to the jeep. Morrissey looked around the clearing, back toward the path. That maple tree—it had a low, leafy branch overhanging the point where the risen must pass. Perfect!

Stanhouse came back with the can. Morrissey hurried to the tree and struggled up as they shoved and boosted him. He reached down and took the can from Stanhouse. He heard footsteps on the path. A smooth, even stride, drawing closer.

"General, get as close as you can. Throw your lighter as soon as I've poured the gas." *Yes, burn it, like the rats!*

He realized he was panting with exertion and a fierce excitement. He opened his mouth wide to dampen the noise.

What was Janet doing? She was steering the general away toward the jeep. The general was shaking his head. She was pulling the cigarette lighter from his hand!

Morrissey motioned frantically. *No! Not you. Let him do it.*

She would not look at him. He stifled a groan. She was right. The Alan-risen might shoot Stanhouse at once, but there was a chance he would hesitate with her.

Morrissey wedged the heavy gas can onto his lap, steadied his legs in the cold, damp cover of the leaves. Don't shoot her, he prayed. Please, God.

Vandiver's body ran into the clearing.

Morrissey caught his breath. Too soon—the gas can was still shut.

The risen stopped directly below him. It seemed frozen by the sight of Janet standing alone in the clearing.

Morrissey looked down on Alan's blond hair. He saw blood gleaming on Vandiver's hands. Cummings, he thought, sickened. Cummings and Stoudt.

The risen pointed Alan's .45 at Janet. "Where's Peter?"

Morrissey thought: Dear Christ, it's going to shoot her! It's not even going to wait for an answer.

He twisted the cap of the can. It sheared, hideously loud. Alan's head cocked, and Morrissey froze, holding his breath.

The risen looked at Janet again. "I said, where's Peter?"

"Oh, Alan."

It looked beyond her. "General, get away from that jeep. Move over here where I can see you."

Stanhouse crawled out from behind the jeep.

Morrissey started to tip the can, and jerked it upright again as Janet moved close to Alan. She was too close! The gas would fall on her too. Horrified, he watched her draw even nearer to the risen, looking up into Alan's face only inches away. Now she was talking to it. Morrissey strained to hear, but her voice was too low. . .

Janet was weak with terror. But her mind was clear. She had to do this horrible thing, for her and Peter, and most of all, for Alan. "Do you hear me?" she said softly to the risen.

"I've got to kill you now," it said.

"You can't. I'm pregnant, Alan. Your child."

The risen's arm jerked downward so that the gun was pointing at the ground. "You couldn't know that," it said. "There hasn't been time . . ."

"I do know it, whether it could be proven medically yet, or not," Janet said. "I knew the day June was conceived, and I know it this time too: I'm going to have your child, Alan." *Dear Lord,* she thought. *Don't let Peter hear.*

God in heaven, Morrissey thought. *Make her move back!* The smell of gas spiked up through his nose. In seconds, the risen must smell it too. *Move back,* Morrissey urged silently, straining to get the command through to her, to push her back with the force of his mind. He saw the tears streaming down her face. Her right hand was clenched around the lighter.

Vandiver bent over. He jerked straight again. The arm with the gun snapped out to the side. He's fighting himself! Morrissey thought wildly. The rest of Alan's body began to shake. He clawed the air in front of his face with the other hand. Janet flinched but did not step back. Vandiver stopped shaking and became perfectly still.

With horror Morrissey saw the risen's head turn toward him. Alan's eyes stared at him hot and vacant. The hackles rose on Morrissey's neck.

"Hurry, Peter," the Alan-risen said.

He knows I'm up here, Morrissey thought, astonished. He *wants* me to burn him!

The risen shoved Janet. She stumbled back safely out of reach of the gas.

Morrissey upended the can. The silvery column of gas poured down on Alan's face. The risen raised the gun, aimed it at him. Morrissey stared down with horrified comprehension. At the last second, the risen's own survival was winning out.

He saw Janet crawling back up behind it, flicking the lighter, throwing it, her face contorted with grief.

A ball of flame exploded up from Vandiver's feet, reaching almost into the tree. Morrissey tried to look away, but he could not. Within the ball of flame, the dead eyes stayed fixed on him. He saw the gun center on his forehead.

"Alan!" Morrissey shouted.

The flames engulfed Vandiver's body. His finger pulled slowly out of the trigger guard and straightened along the barrel of the .45.

A terrible growl blasted from his throat, like a dozen bass organ pedals mashed down at once.

"NOOOOOOOOOOOOO!"

Morrissey saw the darkening skin of Alan's lips move silently, shaping a word: *Good—good!*

The whole burning mass toppled over into the leaves.

Morrissey looked up and saw the moon shining down like a great silver eye in the fog. He clung to the branch and sobbed.

Chapter 39

2355 hours:

Morrissey let Janet and Stanhouse help him down from the tree.

He could not seem to stop weeping. Alan was free. Alan was gone.

And there was no time to cry for him.

He must pull himself together, but he couldn't, not so quickly. He saw that Janet and the general were crying too. In some strange way it helped. He put his arms around them both and walked them behind the jeep, where they could not see Alan's body. His throat began to relax and the sobs stopped. The tears continued to pour down his cheeks.

He listened toward the house. The gunfire had stopped. Men were shouting to each other.

Janet clenched his arm. He held her. Stanhouse straightened and turned away from them, clearing his throat over and over. "Alan," he muttered. "Hagan . . . Hagan."

"We've got to go," Morrissey said. "Back to the house. We'll get one of the cars and drive to Fort Detrick. They should have some plague antidote without L-6."

"That won't be necessary," Stanhouse said. "The bottle

Alan . . . the bottle that *thing* broke, had nothing in it but cola."

Morrissey stared at him. "I don't understand."

"When we reburied the plague virus," Stanhouse said, "Hagan thought Alan might try to dig the bottles up and break them himself, against my orders. I told Hagan . . . I told him he was full of shit. But he insisted on burying ordinary soft drinks. He had the real stuff put back in cannisters and cased in cement."

"But Alan injected me. I got sick. I was dying."

"Are you sure it was from a cola bottle?"

Morrissey tried to remember. The risen had pulled a bottle up from Alan's briefcase . . . *then eased it down again!* It had taken plague virus, not from one of the bottles, but from a small vial. It must not have wanted to open one of the large bottles just to infect one man. Yes, it would need all the harmless-looking sealed bottles to carry out its plan. Cola bottles wouldn't raise suspicion, even though each was a city-killer.

Morrissey felt a surge of joy. Janet would not get sick! And there would be no plague in Washington! He wanted to give Stanhouse a bear hug and then he thought of Cummings. "You knew this, and you let me leave Cummings back there."

"Think, son. Even after I knew it was dead, I called that thing Alan. No one would know it wasn't him. He's already in charge at Detrick. There's plenty more virus back there, sitting around in vials. As soon as that thing realized no plague was spreading in the city, it could go get more. And if you had stayed with Cummings, you would surely be dead."

"Spoken like a general," Morrissey said, and was immediately sorry.

Stanhouse looked down. "You're right," he said bitterly. "I was always the grand strategist. And it doesn't matter. We're all finished, anyway. L-6 can't be used to protect against radiation. Now we have nothing to save us from the Russians."

Morrissey thought about the dog's head—the cells that would look so normal. "There might still be a way," he said.

LAST DAY

Monday, November 10

Chapter 40

0700 hours:

Ambassador Anatoly Dobrynin looked around his office and searched himself for regret. Surely there must be some sad feeling at leaving the wonderfully decadent impressionist paintings, the lush furniture, the red velvet curtains standing like liveried retainers around the chamber.

No. There was only fear. He was too afraid to feel any other emotion.

I escape now, he thought, this last day of America, but where in the world is safe?

He shook his head in disbelief at himself. He was lingering, losing time. *Go! Go you fool, before the plane leaves without you.*

He snatched up his briefcase and hurried to the double doors. When he opened them, he found himself facing Vostoc, from the receiving room downstairs. Behind him were two men in gray suits—Americans, by their tailoring.

What the devil was this? Why hadn't Vostoc simply used the intercom?

Dobrynin recognized one of the men and felt suddenly cold. Oliver something-or-other. *A Secret Service agent!*

Dobrynin tried to keep his face impassive. He raised an eyebrow in query.

"Excuse me, Mr. Ambassador," Vostoc said, "but these men have an urgent message from President Maddock. They told me that they must be taken to you immediately. I tried to explain. . ."

"Never mind. Thank you. You may go." Dobrynin stood still, letting the two men in gray stare stonily past his shoulders until Vostoc was gone. He tried to breathe evenly, to soothe the pounding of his heart. *The Americans had found out. And now they had come for him. How many times in the past weeks had he dreamt of something like this?*

He could not permit it, of course.

"Gentlemen, why this highly irregular visit?"

The man named Oliver nodded deferentially. "Mr. Ambassador, please come with us. President Maddock wants to discuss a crisis between our two countries."

Dobrynin winced inside, mortified despite his fear. He was an ambassador. The decorum of that position had been his whole life. Such a summons might not be honorably refused, and yet he must try.

If he was to live, he must succeed.

"I'm sorry," he said, "but I've just received a similar call from my own government. As you see, I was on my way out. I must catch the special plane immediately. Please convey my apologies and regrets to President Maddock."

Oliver glanced at his companion. "Yes sir, we thought you might be about to leave. I'm glad we caught you."

"But, as I said, my orders are to return immediately to my country." Dobrynin's forehead prickled with sweat. He resisted the impulse to snatch his handkerchief from his coat pocket. Damnation. He shouldn't have made that excuse, a *similar* call, but what other would have any hope of success?

"You're refusing to go with us?"

He smiled broadly in helpless apology. "I must."

Oliver opened his coat and revealed his gun, tucked handle-down into a spring shoulder holster. "Then I will have to shoot you now," he said.

Dobrynin faltered back a step. "You're mad. You'd

never dare do such a thing. Surely President Maddock did not tell you to *shoot* me?''

''Yes sir, he did. He said to tell you you're the only man who can stop it. He said you'd understand.''

''I don't know what you're talking about.''

''Are you coming, sir, or do I shoot?''

The Ambassador closed his eyes, and wiped the sweat from his forehead. He started to protest again, then stopped. What was it that Oliver had just said? *You're the only man who can stop it.* He was suddenly torn. He must get on the plane—*Stop it, stop it, you can stop it.*

By the cursed Czars!

''Very well,'' he said.

Dobrynin looked around him nervously. The lab was stark and ugly. There was a powerful smell, like ammonia, and something else, very pungent. It made him think of the dancing bears at the Moscow Circus. Not altogether disagreeable. But why weren't there any windows? The place was suffocating. That blue paint, ceiling-to-floor, made the walls seem heavy, pressing in with smothering weight.

He saw a large cage. Ah, that must be the source of the smell. The barred side was at a sharp angle, and he couldn't see inside. A whip-lean man with dark hair was leaning on the cage, gazing down at the floor.

Some people came through another door. Dobrynin drew himself up. President Maddock! And that second man was the famous Dr. Vassily Fodorenko of the Leningrad Physics Institute, red-faced and white-bearded like the Americans' Santa Claus. Who was that with Fodorenko? Harkavy, the immunologist with the visiting delegation.

Dobrynin frowned in alarm. What were Fodorenko and Harkavy still doing in the United States? These men, these innocent men, should be long gone by now. Or did the Kremlin intend to sacrifice them just to keep up the appearance of normalcy? This was an outrage. . .

But never mind that. Why were they meeting in this strange place? Why weren't they sitting down in the Oval Office, or some underground bunker?

Durak! Your manners! You should be attending the President, not asking yourself useless questions.

"Mr. President," he said, giving a courtly nod.

Warren Maddock neither smiled nor held out his hand. "Mr. Ambassador, thank you for coming. There is something I must show you. We don't have much time, so I'll introduce you to the man who'll be doing most of the talking. Please give your close attention to him. He is Dr. Peter Morrissey. Dr. Morrissey is a molecular biologist for the Army Labs here."

Dobrynin's attention was seized again by the thin man who had been leaning on the cage. The man straightened and looked at him. His face was pale. His eyes were fierce and intense, like coals on the point of igniting. So much pain in that face. Dobrynin realized that Morrissey had nodded and was now giving him a slight smile. With the smile, twenty years seemed to drop from his age. He's only forty, Dobrynin thought with surprise. He could not stop himself from smiling and nodding in return. Then he was irritated. Who was this nonentity to have such an effect on him? Some strange American version of Rasputin?

Dobrynin turned back to Maddock. "Mr. President, I—"

"Please, Mr. Dobrynin. Just watch and listen. Then we'll talk."

"Mr. Ambassador," Morrissey said, "your two countrymen are here to verify scientifically what I am about to show you. Dr. Harkavy has already examined me and the chimpanzee in that cage. He can confirm that the chimp is healthy and normal and that I am a normal man, though, alas, not quite so healthy." Morrissey gave a pained smile. "I'm just getting over the Asian flu."

The smile vanished. Dobrynin watched Morrissey pick up a full glass from a lab table. "Mr. Ambassador, this is ordinary water from a faucet. I had Dr. Fodorenko bring it with him from his hotel. Dr. Fodorenko has also watched me add another substance to it. This substance will protect me totally against nuclear radiation."

Fodorenko laughed. "Impossible—absolutely impossible!"

Dobrynin stared at Morrissey. Yes, it sounded impossible; the man must be lying. But how could he hope to get away with a lie so outrageous? Dobrynin was suddenly dizzy. *Total immunity to nuclear radiation.*

"The immunizer is very quickly absorbed," Morrissey said. "Two minutes for it to reach the stomach, three minutes for almost total absorption by the stomach walls. As Dr. Harkavy can tell you, the average blood cell makes a complete circuit of the body in about ninety seconds. Those figures added together make a total of six and one half minutes. Do you understand?"

Dobrynin could not trust himself to speak. He nodded. He pressed a hand to his chest, feeling his pounding heart.

"As you may know," Morrissey said, "this is a radiation lab. I'm going into the chamber now. Doctors Harkavy and Fodorenko, radiation suits have been provided for you. There is also a four-inch panel of lead positioned to protect each of you. Will you come into the radiation chamber with me?"

The two scientists looked at each other. "How much radiation?" Fodorenko asked.

"Five thousand roentgens," Morrissey said.

Fodorenko gasped and Dobrynin saw Harkavy's face go white in an instant.

"Come now," Morrissey said. "I'm going in with nothing."

Fodorenko gave a jerky nod.

"No," Harkavy said.

"It's all right, Alex," Fodorenko said. "With the lead shield you will be safe."

"Never mind," Morrissey said. "One of you is enough. Dr. Fodorenko, you brought your dosimeter?"

Fodorenko nodded. Dobrynin watched the chubby nuclear physicist struggle awkwardly into the bulky, air-cooled suit. He looked like an astronaut—or that cartoon character in the American commercials—the Pillsbury doughboy. Dobrynin suppressed the insane urge to giggle.

"Mr. Dobrynin, Dr. Harkavy, please watch the outside monitor." Morrissey led the chimp into the radiation chamber. Fodorenko followed, feet dragging. Like a common serf, the President of the United States helped out, pushing the heavy door shut and pointing to a monitor. On the monitor Dobrynin saw Morrissey seat himself at a table. He held the chimp on his lap. It put its arms around him and nuzzled his face. Fodorenko leaned close to the lead shield over his chair, prodding and inspecting it thoroughly before sitting down. He put his dosimeter on the table in front of Morrissey, where he could see it too. That Fodorenko has the courage of Krushchev, Dobrynin thought proudly.

Morrissey smiled into the monitor. "Dr. Harkavy, would you be so kind as to throw the switch."

The immunologist closed a switch on the wall of the chamber. "The American is crazy," he whispered. Five thousand roentgens. He'll die!" Dobrynin saw that Harkavy was awash in sweat. He felt a repulsive rush of sweat under his own armpits. If Morrissey could survive this, he was truly a Rasputin.

The Ambassador watched the monitor. The chimp—it was hunching over, beginning to stagger. With revulsion Dobrynin saw ropes of saliva dangling from the chimp's mouth. It slumped, shivering. He closed his eyes as its bowels emptied on the floor of the chamber.

The man—what about the man? He must watch. He forced his eyes open. He saw Morrissey pick up the dying chimp and cradle it on his lap. He saw tears flowing down the man's cheeks and knew they were genuine—as genuine as the rain of death in the chamber. Fodorenko sat very still, staring at his dosimeter. He kept his hands and arms carefully bunched against his body, under the lead shield. His voice came scratchily through the suit speaker and the pick-up in the chamber. "Five thousand. It's true. Impossible!"

Time blurred. No one spoke. Dobrynin was mesmerized by the scene on the monitor. *Total immunity to radiation.*

"One half hour," Harkavy mumbled finally.

Dobrynin blinked and focused on Morrissey. He was still sitting with calm, almost mantric detachment.

"The chimp is dead," Harkavy said in a hushed voice.

Dobrynin saw that he was watching a smaller, green scope. All the lines on the scope were flat.

The chimp was dead, but Dr. Morrissey was alive. Alive and healthy.

"Well, Mr. Ambassador?" the President said.

Dobrynin tried to collect his wits. He needed to sit down. *No, think. Concentrate!* "You are prepared to drop this . . . this substance into your water supplies?"

"That's right, Mr. Dobrynin."

"Your substance seems to work very fast, but it wouldn't be fast enough in many cases, would it? How long does it take water to get from a waterworks pump station to a house in the suburbs? After all—"

"We are not using the city waterworks, Mr. Ambassador. We've buried pumps and tanks of our substance at strategic points along the water lines. No citizen will have to wait more than ten minutes for treated water to come from his faucet."

Dobrynin was staggered. The Americans must have been at this for some time—long before they could have learned of the strike plan. Years, perhaps.

If they had done it at all.

"An immense undertaking," he said skeptically.

"Actually, it was quite a bit cheaper and easier than building the minuteman silos," Maddock said in an ironic tone.

"But something like this would take years."

"Fortunately, one of my predecessors in office foresaw this moment quite some time ago."

"And you would let us verify this equipment and the locations?"

"Certainly not," Maddock said.

Dobrynin almost smiled. Of course you would not, he thought. You wouldn't show us your missile silos either.

He looked at Fodorenko on the monitor. The physicist was staring fixedly through his faceplate at the dosimeter.

Dobrynin felt awe setting in. Holy Mother Russia. If this was really true, the Americans were in the driver's seat. At the first sign of attack, they could flush their substance into the water supply. They'd run the sirens and go on television and tell people simply to take a drink from their faucets. Judging by the speed with which Morrissey had gotten into the chamber after drinking, this substance would be in the stomachs and then the bodies of millions of Americans well before the missiles could complete their trip.

We've lost our civil-defense edge, Dobrynin thought. And now they have a much greater edge. Even after a preemptive strike, they could strike back and destroy Russia without being destroyed themselves.

The strike must be called off!

Dobrynin felt joy and panic together. He must get through to Secretary Charnov at once! He must—

Wait. There was an obvious hole in this. Dobrynin looked at Maddock, fearing. *Please*, he thought, *give me a good answer.* "Mr. President, if you are really ready to protect your citizens, why haven't you done it already? Why take the time, trouble, and expense of digging to install cannisters of this substance along the water pipelines?"

"Because, Mr. Ambassador, for some reason, we don't trust you. Once a person has been changed, he can be studied. We think we can keep an adequate watch on Dr. Morrissey, here, but we don't want the rest of our people to live under the threat of being snatched and dissected in some Russian laboratory."

Dobrynin heard Harkavy grunt. Yes, it was an insult. It could not be allowed to pass. He drew himself up rigidly. "Forgive me, Mr. President, but what you are really saying is that you intend to hoard your secret from the world."

Maddock gave him a dry smile and said nothing.

Dobrynin looked at the monitor. Incredible. It seemed airtight, and yet could it somehow be a fake? Some kind of colossal—what was the American slang word—*sting*?

If so, it had fooled Harkavy and Fodorenko, two of the top scientists in the Soviet Union. They had all seen it with their own eyes. The chimpanzee had been on Morrissey's lap. It had died and he had lived.

Whether or not *everything* Maddock had said was true,

one thing was clear: Morrissey had been made impervious to lethal radiation.

Dobrynin gazed at Maddock. Suppose he could see into the American President's mind and learn that this *was* all some fantastic bluff . . . ? *What should he do then?*

"Mr. Ambassador," Maddock said, "perhaps we should go to the White House now, or to your embassy, whichever would be most effective. I think there's a phone call that you want to make."

Joy and relief—incredible relief—flooded Dobrynin. *Careful—your dignity! Harkavy is watching!*

"My office, if you don't mind, Mr. President," he said gravely. "I would like to go back to my office."

December 12

Epilogue

Morrissey listened through the crackle of the fireplace log to the sounds from the girls' bedroom: faint laughter, the thump of a headboard against the wall. Their giggles reached a crescendo and then stopped, as though they realized he was eavesdropping.

He smiled. Wonderful sounds. He felt almost . . . *content*. All the family together. The kids roughhousing around, giddy over being at the summer place in autumn.

What would they say when he told them it was not just a vacation, that they would never go back to the brownstone? And what reason was he going to give them?

He thought of the brownstone, the way his hackles had risen just for that short time he'd gone in to show the movers around last week.

Lie like hell, he thought. The girls will let you.

He heard Janet's slippers scuffing from kitchen tile to the hardwood of the living room. She handed him a snifter of brandy and sat down beside him. He clinked glasses with her. She turned her knees toward him on the couch and rested a hand on his arm. Her fingers felt warm. "It's over," she said.

He looked at her, knowing it was partly a question. *Lie like hell.* No. She'd broken him out of the hospital. She'd destroyed the risen. The last thing she needed was his protection. "It isn't over."

He felt her fingers digging into his arm.

"I have to go on with my research. L-7."

"How could you? After all of this . . ."

"Because we die," he said.

She stared into the fire. "Yes," she said. "Besides, you . . . you . . ."

"I've got L-6 in me," Morrissey finished for her. He'd thought he could say it without feeling chills. *Wrong.* The brandy began to hit his veins at last, flushing heat into his capillaries. *Hello, old friend,* he thought gratefully. *Help me say it.* "Maybe I can find a way to neutralize the reanimation effect," he said. "If I can't, when I die, I want you to burn me, right away. Gasoline. Just like we . . . like we did Alan. Promise me you'll do that."

"Silly man," she said. "Of course I'll burn you."

He looked at her, and they both burst out laughing. He laughed until the knot in his throat went away. "It's not a bit funny," he said.

"No. It's very sweet. We'll both be old and wrinkled, and there I'll be, waiting for you to die. I'll have a lighter in my hand, and a canteen of gas . . ."

"All right, all right."

The log in the fireplace crumbled with a shower of sparks and the room sank into a violet twilight. "I wonder about Alan," Janet said. "His body was dead. He had to get out. But . . . is he free, or is he just gone."

Morrissey did not look at her. "As far as we're concerned, he's gone."

"But as long as we remember him . . ."

"Yes," he said shortly. He felt a pain deep inside him. I want to talk to you, Alan, he thought. I want you to talk to me. I want to play chess. I want to trade jokes.

And I want to go to the lab tomorrow and see Kellogg, that goofy, half-assed grin, a rat cradled in each hand.

He realized it was quite dark now, a low, cozy light.

"Are you going to put another log on?" Janet said.

He turned toward her on the couch and buried his face in the angle of her neck. Her skin felt smooth and warm, alive. He felt her arms around his shoulders, hugging him. "The fire can wait," he said.

"Yes," she said. "Peter . . . I have something to tell you."

He pulled back gently from her arms and looked at her. Her face was calm, but her eyes were luminous with unshed tears. He felt a strange hollowness in the pit of his stomach. "Yes?" he said.

"I'm pregnant."

Morrissey remembered Alan's words—the ones he'd overheard the Vandiver-risen say to Janet just before he'd poured the gasoline down on it: *You couldn't know that. There hasn't been time.*

He took Janet's hands. Tears began to flow down his cheeks. He felt his heart opening up, filling with joy. He said: "That's the most wonderful thing I've ever heard."

Steven Spruill has a B.A. in Biology and a Ph.D. in Clinical Psychology. He's a full-time novelist. His previous novels include: KEEPERS OF THE GATE, THE JANUS EQUATION, THE PSYCHOPATH PLAGUE, THE IMPERATOR PLOT, and HELLSTONE. He lives in Virginia with his wife, Nancy, who is a Senior Defense Analyst at the Pentagon, and their two geriatric cats, Id and Ego.